HEART OF A LION

BOOKS BY GILBERT MORRIS

Through a Glass Darkly

THE HOUSE OF WINSLOW SERIES

1. *The Honorable Imposter*
2. *The Captive Bride*
3. *The Indentured Heart*
4. *The Gentle Rebel*
5. *The Saintly Buccaneer*
6. *The Holy Warrior*
7. *The Reluctant Bridegroom*
8. *The Last Confederate*
9. *The Dixie Widow*
10. *The Wounded Yankee*
11. *The Union Belle*
12. *The Final Adversary*
13. *The Crossed Sabres*
14. *The Valiant Gunman*
15. *The Gallant Outlaw*
16. *The Jeweled Spur*
17. *The Yukon Queen*
18. *The Rough Rider*
19. *The Iron Lady*
20. *The Silver Star*
21. *The Shadow Portrait*
22. *The White Hunter*
23. *The Flying Cavalier*
24. *The Glorious Prodigal*
25. *The Amazon Quest*
26. *The Golden Angel*
27. *The Heavenly Fugitive*
28. *The Fiery Ring*

THE LIBERTY BELL

1. *Sound the Trumpet*
2. *Song in a Strange Land*
3. *Tread Upon the Lion*
4. *Arrow of the Almighty*
5. *Wind From the Wilderness*
6. *The Right Hand of God*
7. *Command the Sun*

CHENEY DUVALL, M.D.[1]

1. *The Stars for a Light*
2. *Shadow of the Mountains*
3. *A City Not Forsaken*
4. *Toward the Sunrising*
5. *Secret Place of Thunder*
6. *In the Twilight, in the Evening*
7. *Island of the Innocent*
8. *Driven With the Wind*

CHENEY AND SHILOH: THE INHERITANCE[1]

1. *Where Two Seas Met*

THE SPIRIT OF APPALACHIA[2]

1. *Over the Misty Mountains*
2. *Beyond the Quiet Hills*
3. *Among the King's Soldiers*
4. *Beneath the Mockingbird's Wings*
5. *Around the River's Bend*

LIONS OF JUDAH

1. *Heart of a Lion*

[1]with Lynn Morris [2]with Aaron McCarver

02C

GILBERT MORRIS

LIONS OF JUDAH

HEART OF A LION

BETHANY HOUSE
MINNEAPOLIS, MINNESOTA

Heart of a Lion
Copyright © 2002
Gilbert Morris

Cover design by Lookout Design Group, Inc.

Published by Bethany House Publishers
A Ministry of Bethany Fellowship International
11400 Hampshire Avenue South
Bloomington, Minnesota 55438
www.bethanyhouse.com

Printed in the United States of America by
Bethany Press International, Bloomington, Minnesota 55438

Library of Congress Cataloging-in-Publication Data

Morris, Gilbert.
Heart of a lion / by Gilbert Morris.
p. cm. — (Lions of Judah ; 1)
ISBN 0-7642-2681-9
1. Noah (Biblical figure)—Fiction. 2. Bible. O.T.—History of Biblical events—Fiction. 3. Noah's ark—Fiction. 4. Deluge—Fiction. I. Title.
PS3563.O8742 H427 2002
813'.54—dc21 2002010226

To Dr. Daniel Grant

There are many scholars in this old world of ours, and there are many spiritual men—but only rarely do scholarship and warm spirituality exist in the same individual. When I think of the handful of believers who manifest a marriage of heart and brain, the name Dan Grant is at the top of my list.

Thank you, Dr. Grant, for being what you are—and for being a friend to me when I sorely needed one!

GILBERT MORRIS spent ten years as a pastor before becoming Professor of English at Ouachita Baptist University in Arkansas and earning a Ph.D. at the University of Arkansas. During the summers of 1984 and 1985, he did postgraduate work at the University of London. A prolific writer, he has had over 25 scholarly articles and 200 poems published in various periodicals, and over the past years has had more than 175 books published. His family includes three grown children, and he and his wife live in Alabama.

PROLOGUE

The sun's white disc still burned brightly in the sky as it settled toward the western horizon. A solitary figure knelt on a promontory of yellow sandstone that jutted out over the valley, his hands lifted reverently toward the heavens. The heavy silence that had cloaked the landscape was pierced by his trumpetlike voice. At the disturbance, a flock of ibis rose like a cloud from the valley floor, melded into a single image above the river, spiraled upward on invisible thermals, then disappeared into the dusky air.

"O Ancient One, maker of all things, I offer thanks for your might and your power. By your hand is the river filled so that the land will bear fruit. By your voice the seeds burst into life. The sun and the moon, yes, and all the starry lights are the work of your mighty hand. . . ."

The voice of Zorah, the seer, flowed over the valley below, rising and falling in its musical cadence and echoing off the canyon walls before falling silent. The wise one held his arms aloft, as still as a candle in a crypt, as immovable as the hills at his back. He stayed in this position while the sun's white brilliance faded to a bloodred glow, sinking lower and lower until a mere crescent of crimson fire balanced on the lacy branches of distant trees.

When ebony darkness had swallowed the earth, Zorah lifted his voice again . . . this time in a hoarse whisper of desperation. "O Ancient One, I cannot hear your voice! Be not silent to me, I beg! Speak in my heart as you have in times of old!"

The seer's plea died on the silent air. His thin frame began to sway like a sapling in a strong wind. With eyes squeezed shut, his mouth gaped open, gulping in the life-giving air like a fish gasping for breath on dry land.

Then he heard it. His ears perked up in the darkness, his heart listening in rapt recognition to a voice . . . a still, small voice that had first addressed him when he was but a stripling.

Hear my word, faithful one. Remember how I once said to you, "Go to the clan of Lamech," and you obeyed my voice. You watched as the male child was born, and you cut the cord yourself. You spoke the words I gave you for Lamech and his wife: "This man-child shall comfort you concerning your work and the toil of your hands."

The voice ceased and Zorah cried, "O Ancient One, I did obey, and I have kept watch over the child. But what would you have me do now?"

I have chosen Noah to be my servant, even as I chose you. You have been faithful, and now I will show you what is to come. Tell no one, but keep the young man Noah from harm.

The voice ceased and Zorah heard a rushing wind. His frail body trembled first at the noise, then at the frightful vision that rose before him, illuminating the darkness with images more terrible than he could have imagined. He knew he could tell no man of it, yet neither would he ever forget the sight being unveiled before him.

Falling forward on the ground, he screamed in anguish, covering his head with his hands to shut out the vision. But it was a scene perceived by the spirit, not the eye. There was no escaping its clutches. He cried out in terror, "I see, O Holy One—but what is it? What does it mean? It frightens me so! Help me to understand. . . ." He stumbled to his feet, trying to flee the terrors in his mind, but he could not bear the weight of it. Falling like a dead man, he knew no more.

Sleep lay heavily on Zorah, the seer, as he rested from the terrors of the night. When he awoke, the morning light was spilling gently into the valley, shimmering on the river, over which hovered a gossamer cloud, its foggy softness caressing the water with comforting stillness. He sat up and soaked in the calm peace, quieting his soul from the fearful visions.

He waited for the Ancient One to speak to him again, to tell him what he was to do. He listened intently, in an attitude of humility, but only a heavy silence enveloped him. Struggling to his feet, he bowed his head and whispered, "Holy One, I was there the day Noah was but a helpless infant. I watched over him when he knew it not. The vision you have given me is terrible, and I understand only that Noah must face great evil. Keep him clasped in your hands, O Strong One, for he stands at a crossroads. Who knows what evil may do to a young man? Let him not go in the way of Cain, but in the way of his ancestors Seth and Enoch, who walked with you!"

The wind quietly stirred, whispering in Zorah's ears and caressing his cheeks. The hand of the Ancient and Mighty One had touched him. He lifted his tortured face to the sky, knowing that the unborn days ahead would bring unspeakable horrors to the peoples of the earth. . . .

PART ONE

CHAPTER

I

The pale crimson rays of the rising sun drove away the early dawn grayness and illuminated the village that occupied the flat ground in a clearing. The huts were scattered about like stones a man would toss from his hand, letting them fall where they would. Tendrils of gray smoke rose from the humble dwellings, twisting into serpentine shapes on the morning breeze.

Two hundred yards from the village, in a sea of waving grass, a solitary figure stood motionless, watching the glowing sun arc into the morning sky. Wonder touched his features as the light vanquished the darkness of night.

He was young, his face bearing the first silky promise of a beard. His light brown hair glinted with reddish tinges as the sunlight touched it. He had a broad forehead, high cheekbones, and a prominent nose over a wide mouth. His deep-set eyes were a warm brown, much lighter than those of the other members of his clan, and his eyebrows were the same color as his hair. The sun had bronzed his face and exposed body to a reddish tint. His youthful features were smooth, not yet marked by the struggle for life or the passage of hard years. He was not handsome—rather homely, in fact—but his appearance hinted at an imaginative spirit and an inner strength.

As the sun freed itself from the horizon and swelled into a yellow disk, the young man remained motionless, the butt of the long spear in his hand resting on the earth. The morning breeze ruffled his hair, which was silky, unlike the stiff locks of most of his family. He was tall and slender, his future strength suggested by the roundness of his arms and the wide span of his shoulders. He wore a simple garment of animal skin that hung to his knees and was fastened over one shoulder by a bone clasp. He wore nothing to protect his feet. The coltish awkwardness of the very young marked his movements.

The young man lifted his spear and examined it eagerly, an anxious light in his eyes. The worn shaft, made of acacia wood, was about eight feet long. Holding it out straight from his face and peering down its length, he was pleased to see that it was true, with no sign of warping. He inspected the head of the spear, its metal tip glinting in the sunlight. The head was bound to the shaft with rawhide that had been soaked and dried to the hardness of iron. Grasping the shaft in his right hand and the spearhead in his left, the young man twisted and pulled, noting no movement of the spearhead. It was as if the metal had grown into the wood.

The spearhead had belonged to his grandfather, Methuselah, who had received it from his own father, Enoch. Metal of any kind was precious, so the spearhead was worth more than any number of possessions. He held the spear tightly, pondering the value of it, then grasped the shaft at the balance point. Spreading his feet apart, he scowled and lunged, bringing the spear forward with all of his might. It penetrated a ball of dried grass, and he grunted with satisfaction, then ran to retrieve his spear.

"Did you kill it?"

Caught off guard, the youth whirled and found himself facing a young woman he had never seen before. He scowled and held the spear tightly, for any strangers were suspect in his world. He felt his face grow hot as she smiled at him, one hand resting on her hip, the other balancing a basket of fresh-picked wild berries on her head. He was easily embarrassed and hated anyone making fun of him, which, by her coquettish grin and stance, he assumed she was.

"Who are you?" he demanded. His still-changing voice broke into a humiliating squeal.

"My name is Lomeen."

The young woman approached him with laughing eyes, her supple curves clearly outlined by the simple cloth garment she wore. Her almond-shaped eyes were dark, her mouth wide and perfectly formed. Her golden skin was darker than his own, her face smooth and attractive.. The youth surmised she was several years older than he.

"What's *your* name?" she went on when he said nothing.

The young man cleared his throat to be sure there was no more squeal. "I'm Noah. This is my father's clan."

"Your father's name is Lamech?"

"Yes." Noah found it hard to meet the young woman's eyes. For reasons he could not fathom, she made him very nervous. The way she moved, the way she smiled at him in a knowing fashion, confused him. He found his voice enough to ask, "Where did you come from?"

"I'm from the clan of Jaalam. I've come to see my friend Keziah."

"Oh, you know Keziah?"

"Yes. We met at one of our festivals." The young woman moved closer until she stood directly in front of Noah. "You're a tall one, aren't you?" She smiled up at him, her eyes dancing in the early light.

He stepped back a pace. "I guess so," he mumbled. "Did you come by yourself?"

"Yes, but I had company part of the way."

"How far away is your clan?"

"Oh, it's a good day's journey."

Noah stood absolutely still. He was accustomed to the young women of his own tribe, but the presence of this beautiful stranger disturbed him greatly. He tried to speak again but found his throat too tight to make a sound.

She laughed outright. "Haven't you ever seen a woman before?"

"A w-woman?" Noah stuttered. "Why, of course I've seen a woman—*lots* of them!"

"I'll bet you have." Lomeen smiled. "A good-looking man like you. I'll bet you've had a lot of women." Her smile grew broader, and she reached up and laid her hand on his chest. "The women of your clan must fight over you, Noah."

Totally confused, Noah could not answer. He felt like a fool, and the touch of her hand on his chest caused such an inner tumult he could only mumble, "Well, not really."

Lomeen left her hand on his chest, challenging him to respond to her. He knew he should remove it, tell her to go her way, but he could not bring himself to do so. Rather, he felt an inexplicable urge to put both of his hands on her.

A sudden voice broke the silence. "Noah, it's time to go."

Noah swiveled his head and saw his brother Jodak, who had come from the village. He stood ten feet away, a spear in his hand and a bag around his shoulder. Displeasure marred his usually cheerful features, and

Noah felt a twinge of guilt as he stepped back away from the young woman.

"Oh, all right, Jodak." Noah hesitated, then said, "This is Lomeen. She's a friend of Keziah."

Jodak gave her a curt nod, then turned to Noah. "Let's go," he said gruffly.

As Noah followed his brother, Lomeen called out to him, "I'll be staying with Keziah for a few days. Maybe I'll see you later, Noah."

"All right," he said, twisting around as he walked to see her waving at him, then hastening to catch up with Jodak, who was moving rapidly away.

Noah tried to shake off his feelings of guilt and shame over the incident. After all, what had he done wrong? he reasoned. Yet his stomach tightened as he heard Lomeen's musical voice once again floating to him. "I'll be looking for you, Noah. . . ."

Noah now kept his eyes on his brother, who was marching along the river trail directly in front of him. Jodak was shorter than Noah and much older. Already past his hundredth year by four years, Jodak had been almost solely responsible for raising his youngest brother. He had the stiff black hair of their father, Lamech, and was slighter in build than most men of the clan. He was usually good humored, but now his voice was brusque as he snapped, "Leave women like that alone, boy!"

"You know her?" Noah managed to speak without his voice breaking.

"I've known some like her. She's nothing but trouble. Stay away from her."

Noah did not argue. As they moved along the worn path toward the river, he somehow felt that his brother's advice was wise. Still, he could almost feel the pressure of Lomeen's hand on his chest, the pleasure he'd felt when she touched him. . . .

The broad river wound through the flat valley in a lazy serpentine pattern. As Noah and Jodak approached the water, the smell of rich, loamy earth and decaying matter hung in the air. Jodak paused and fixed his eyes on his younger brother. "You're too inexperienced to hunt the river beast."

"No I'm not!" Noah protested. "And you promised!"

"You don't remember when our brother was killed on just such a hunt as this. Maz was in his prime—only a hundred and twenty-three years old. I saw it happen and couldn't do a thing about it. He fell out of the boat into the river, and . . . and the monster just bit him in two!" The bitter memory twisted Jodak's mouth into an ugly curve, and he shook his head as if to rid himself of the thought.

Noah had been through this before, begging Jodak to take him on a hunt for the dangerous leviathan that prowled the river. Jodak had finally given his permission, but he was clearly having second thoughts. Now Jodak stared at Noah, considering his brother's plea.

Noah's heart sank as he saw refusal building up in his brother's eyes. "Please let me go, Jodak!" he begged. "I'll be careful. I'll do everything you say."

Jodak shook his head and started to speak, but a movement caught his eye. He swirled to his left and stiffened as an old man came toward them. "It's the seer," Jodak muttered. "What's he doing here?"

The man who approached was shorter than most men, and his body was lean, almost emaciated. Many years of blistering sunshine had tanned his skin to the texture of old leather. He leaned on a staff as he came steadily toward the two. His piercing eyes were an odd yellowish color, almost like gold, and when he was angry—as he appeared to be now—they would burn like twin flames. A rough mane of silvery hair hung down over his shoulders, and his beard matched it. His name was Zorah, but he was called the seer, for he saw visions. It was whispered that he had even seen the Ancient One with his own eyes! Some called him the *sayer* because of his habit of appearing before the clan and proclaiming a startling message he said was directly from the Ancient One.

Noah had always been a little afraid of Zorah, and he involuntarily took a step backward. The old man with the golden eyes seemed to have selected Noah for special attention. More than once the seer had stopped and stared at him, and a few times had questioned him sharply. Noah had never noticed him doing that with any other youth, and he could not imagine why the frightening old man had singled him out. The seer now stood before him and his brother. As Noah felt the pressure of the seer's penetrating eyes, he swallowed hard, attempting to show no fear.

Zorah turned his gaze from Noah to his brother. "Jodak, come with me. I would have a word with you."

Jodak nodded and walked away with the seer. Noah stood nervously watching the two men talk, their voices inaudible. From time to time one of them would turn and examine Noah. *They're talking about me! What have I done now?* He saw Zorah put his finger before Jodak's face, and although

Noah could not make out his words, he knew they were harsh. Zorah gave Noah one final look, then turned and walked away. Jodak returned, a strange expression on his face. He said nothing, keeping his eyes fixed on Noah.

"Well, what did he want, Jodak?"

"He's worried about you. He warned me not to let anything happen to you."

"Why does he care?"

"I don't know, but it's not the first time. He's always had a special interest in you, Noah. Another reason for me to keep you from going on the hunt."

"Did he say I couldn't go?"

"No, he didn't say that, but—"

"Then I want to go, and you *promised*."

Jodak gave up, throwing his hands in the air. "All right, but you do *exactly* what I say. Understand? You'll take no chances."

"Anything you say," Noah responded quickly, relieved and pleased that he would not be sent away.

The two hurried along the riverbank so thickly lined with tall reeds that at times they could not even see the river itself. But Noah was always conscious of its soft, swishing melody, and through the reeds he could spot the rippling backs of crocodiles in the shallows. Noah was more aware of the world about him than most, and his eyes moved constantly, missing nothing.

"There they are," Jodak said. "We're late."

The two approached an open area on the bank where three reed boats were pulled ashore. Noah ran his eyes over the hunters who were waiting for them. Nophat, the best hunter of the clan, was a huge man with only one eye but great strength. Next to him stood Ruea, not much of a hunter but a fine singer. He might not be able to kill a river beast, but he would surely make a fine song about the adventure! Close to him was Boz, only two years older than Noah. He was a cheerful fellow, always getting into mischief, and he winked at Noah as the two arrived. Kul, a husky young man with a wild mop of kinky hair, and Senzi, an older man with a sour look, completed the hunting party.

Senzi spoke up with irritation. "We've been waiting for ages. Where have you two been?"

Jodak hurried to one of the boats and glanced at Senzi. "Sorry to be late." Turning to Nophat, he said, "We're ready now."

Nophat scratched his wild beard and grunted. "Are you sure you want to take that tadpole with you?" He stared at Noah, seeming to find him wanting.

"Oh, let him come along, Nophat," Boz urged. "We can use him for bait!" He laughed at his own joke, his teeth white in the morning light.

"All right," Nophat grumbled. "Get in the boat, little one. But don't get in our way when we go for the kill."

"Wait a minute," Jodak said. "Let's ask the Strong One to give us strength and keep us safe."

Nophat did not believe in anything but the strength of his own arm. Impatiently he muttered, "Go ahead and ask—for all the good it will do."

Ignoring Nophat's indifference to the power of the Strong One, the others all looked to Jodak, who lifted his hands and closed his eyes. "O Ancient One, keeper of those who trust in you, we ask you to keep us safe. Make our eyes quick and our hands strong."

A silence followed the simple request. Then Nophat snapped, "All right, let's go."

As they climbed into their boat, Jodak whispered to Noah, "I offered a dove to the Ancient One before we left home, so we'll be all right."

The three lightweight reed boats moved swiftly into the muddy river, one man at the back of each boat poling along with the current. Noah found no difficulty keeping his balance as he poled. His eyes were bright, and he laughed as Ruea lifted up his voice in a song:

"There's a woman waiting for me.
She waits with her arms open.
Her lips are red
And her eyes are dark as the night.
She loves me because I am the great hunter.
I will come to you, my love.
Wait until I bring you the trophy."

"The only trophy you're going to get," Kul yelled, "is one of your legs bitten off by the river beast. I'll take care of Suni."

Kul and Ruea had been competing fiercely for Suni, the most attractive girl in the clan. Now as they poled their boats downriver, they bantered back and forth about who would win her heart, until Senzi shushed them loudly. "Shut your mouths! We're getting close."

The hunters fell silent at his warning. The water rippled in the morning quiet as the pointed prows sliced through the river. Noah spotted several crocodiles lying just below the calm surface of the water. Brilliant white birds flew up from the banks as the boats skimmed past. The vegetation in the river began to thicken, a sign that they were approaching the favorite haunt of the river beast.

Without warning a scene flashed into Noah's mind, causing him to miss a stroke and drawing a sharp admonition from Jodak. The scene was from a dream he'd had a week ago. It came back now, sharp and clear, and he realized it was a dream of this very hunt, in which he had been on the water and was very frightened. He saw the open red mouth of a mighty river beast and then heard the terrified cries of his own voice.

"There's the beast!" Nophat whispered hoarsely, the gleam of battle blazing in his single eye. "Ruea and I will go first. Boz, you bring your boat on the end to help. Noah, you and Jodak stay back."

Noah's sharp eyes were quick to pick out the rounded hump of the river beast, its body mounded like a small hill, its eyes and nostrils punctuating the surface. Although it appeared awkward, the river beast could move with terrible speed, and its powerful jaws could bite a crocodile in two, or snap a reed boat if it so chose!

Noah felt light-headed as he watched Nophat stand in the front of his boat, holding his spear ready and staring at the river beast. Behind him Ruea continued poling slowly but was ready to grab his spear at the right moment. Boz guided his boat around, and Senzi and Kul stood with their spears poised. The boats converged on the beast, which continued chomping on river vegetation, ignoring their approach.

With a mighty yell, Nophat lifted his spear high and plunged it down into the flesh of the startled river beast. Noah's shouts rose while the other hunters moved their crafts closer to the animal, which was now thrashing in the bloody froth.

Without warning, the boat containing the three men rose high into the air, and with wild cries, Boz, Kul, and Senzi were catapulted into the water. Terrified for their lives, Noah screamed, "What can we do, Jodak?"

"Come on! We must help them!"

Noah poled the boat forward with all his strength while Jodak held his spear high. The screams of the hunters rent the air as they clambered to get to safety. Nophat had lost his spear and was scrambling wildly in the boat to get an extra one. Noah's pounding heart seemed to burst out of his breast when his boat was struck a tremendous blow. Whirling around, he saw the back of a second river beast under the hull. The boat shot upward and to the side, hurling him into the water too. The water closing over his head strangled his cry. Feeling the rough hide of the river beast scraping against his leg, he panicked at the nearness of death. Fear shot through him as he realized this was the dream! He had seen it all before.

He broke the surface, his arms and legs pumping wildly. Looking back over his shoulder, he saw that the river beast had spotted him and was heading his way. Noah knew he was a dead man, for no one could outswim one of these monsters!

He struggled toward the boat as the beast's cavernous mouth gaped open, and its eyes appeared to be flaming. For some inexplicable reason, the fear left him at that moment. He was conscious only of a great regret that his life would be cut so short.

When the monster was but a few feet away, it stopped and whirled sideways. Noah gasped, seeing that a spear had penetrated the animal's left eye. The raging creature writhed in pain, and Jodak screamed, "Noah, get in the boat!"

The reed boat moved closer, and Noah reached up and grabbed the side. He felt Jodak's hands pulling at him, and then he sprawled in the bottom of the boat, gasping for breath. He scrambled to his feet and the two pulled away, watching the river beast flounder, repeatedly breaking the surface and trying to shake the spear loose. Nophat and Ruea had moved in closer and were now stabbing the beast, the other hunters, who had also reached the safety of their boat, soon joining in.

When the mad screams of the hunters and the thrashing water finally stilled, Nophat let out a tremendous shout. "We have killed two river beasts!"

Noah stared at the hulking forms of the dead creatures floating on the surface of the water. His throat was too constricted to utter a word at first. Then turning, he reached out and grabbed his brother. "If it hadn't been for you, Jodak, I would have died. The river beast would have killed me for sure."

Jodak put his arms around his little brother and said in a husky voice, "Then what would I have told Zorah? And what would I have told our mother and father if I had let that beast get you?" He hugged his brother tightly, and the two clung to each other. "I couldn't let you die, Noah—" His voice broke as he added, "You're the best of us!"

CHAPTER 2

Not even the most optimistic of the hunters had expected to slay *two* of the mighty river beasts! It had never happened before, and the hunters rejoiced noisily and with great gusto. The celebration included slicing thick chunks of the fat meat from one of the beasts and sampling it raw. Noah carved out two handfuls with his bronze knife and wolfed down the raw flesh, the first fresh meat he'd tasted in several weeks.

Nophat quickly supervised the building of two reed rafts to transport the meat back to the village. By late afternoon the hunters were towing the rafts, each laden with a great mound of meat. Going back upstream with such a load was difficult, but no one complained.

Noah made the return trip in a boat with Boz instead of Jodak and had forgotten what a prankster the man was. Noah was paddling as rapidly as possible when something wet and wiggling fell inside the back of his garment. He yelled as sharp claws dug into his skin, and he began frantically clawing at his back. In his wild attempt to free himself of the wiggling creature, he fell over backward in the boat. He looked up to see Boz laughing so hard that tears were running down his cheeks.

"You scoundrel!" Noah screamed. "What did you put down my back?"

Boz leaned forward and rammed his hand down the inside of Noah's garment, yanking out a baby crocodile no more than five inches long. "You are Noah, the slayer of mighty crocodiles!"

"I ought to throw *you* to the crocodiles, Boz!" Noah shouted. He hit Boz on the chest and was about to strike him again when Nophat's voice boomed over the water. "Stop that foolishness, you two! We've got to get this meat home!"

Noah glared at Boz, then snatched up his paddle. For the rest of the trip, Noah was referred to as the "crocodile killer," and Ruea, Boz, and Kul delighted in making up ribald songs about his prowess in killing crocodiles.

Noah could not stay angry with Boz. It was like the prankster to put a tiny crocodile down his back. *I'm only glad it wasn't a scorpion—or worse!* He turned around and grinned at Boz, who was poling the boat. "You just wait, Boz! I'll get you for that!"

"No you won't. You're too nice a fellow to do anything mean. Leave the tricks to evil people like me and Senzi back there. If he put anything down your back, it'd be a poisonous serpent."

Noah laughed aloud, for he was feeling good about his performance at the hunt. At least he had not run away. He glanced over at the boat where his brother was poling, and the thought passed through his mind, *Jodak risked his life to save me. What a wonderful thing to have a brother like him!*

Tirzah, the wife of Jodak, was an attractive young woman, barely over thirty. When Jodak had taken her for his bride, she had been the most beautiful girl in her clan, rivaling any of the young women in Jodak's clan. With each year she seemed to grow even more beautiful. Her dark hair spilled down her back in a wealth of waves, and her sculpted eyes were a rich dark blue that at times turned almost black. She was small but shapely, and her cheerful spirit matched her pleasing appearance. Jodak's parents, Lamech and Dezia, were very fond of their daughter-in-law.

Dezia looked up from the hide she was tanning and noted that Tirzah kept glancing anxiously toward the river. "Are you worried about Jodak, my daughter?" she asked.

"Oh no. He'll be fine." Tirzah smiled pleasantly, her milk white teeth contrasting with her olive complexion. She was grinding wild wheat in a hollowed-out stone, using a smaller rounded stone to crush the grains. Despite herself, she glanced again toward the west. "I know you're worried about Noah, Mother."

"Yes . . . he's so young! I wish Jodak hadn't agreed to take him."

"But he wanted to go so badly, and Jodak promised he wouldn't let him get into any danger."

"Who can say about danger? When they hunt the river beast, no one can tell what will happen."

Tirzah cast a quick glance at her mother-in-law. She understood well that she was thinking of her son Maz, who had been killed by just such a beast. Dezia spoke often of her lost son, as if he had been slain only a few months ago instead of years back.

Still working at their tanning and grinding, the women both looked up to see Lamech strolling toward them. He was a short, heavy man with muscular arms and legs, dark hair, and a broad, blunt face. His speech was as rough as his manner. Being the head of the clan, he felt he needed to be harsh, keeping most of the clanspeople in awe and fear of him, some in absolute terror. His wife and his daughter-in-law knew, however, that much of his severity was simply assumed.

"Well, are you two ever going to let Noah be a man? I know what you've been talking about." He grinned, baring his yellowed teeth, and laughed deep in his chest. "You're worried about your infant being out on the river hunting the river beast, aren't you, Dezia?"

Dezia shook her head. "I wish you hadn't let him go."

"He's sixteen years old, wife! That's plenty old enough. I went when I was much younger."

"But you're much stronger than Noah."

Lamech shrugged. "He's growing stronger every day. He's got to learn to be a man."

While they talked, the women continued their work and Lamech glanced around at the village, which was humming with activity. The babble of voices and the smell of the sharp, acrid smoke from cooking fires filled his senses with pleasure. The sights and sounds of his little village always pleased Lamech, and he sat down contentedly watching his daughter-in-law grind the wheat. "When are you going to give me a grandchild?" he demanded. "It seems to me I've waited long enough."

"I'm as anxious as you are, Father. It just hasn't happened yet." Tirzah smiled tentatively. It was a great source of shame to her that she had not yet borne a child, and Lamech was constantly reminding her of her womanly duty to bear children.

"I'll have to have a talk with that son of mine. He needs to try harder." Lamech laughed at the expression on Tirzah's face. Reaching over, he slapped her with what he thought was a light tap, but it rocked her back, and she shook her head but was not displeased.

"It will happen soon," she said. "The Ancient One must have His reasons for withholding this blessing from me. You must be patient, Father."

Lamech snorted and turned to touch the hide Dezia was working on.

He found it pleasantly soft and nodded. "That's good work, wife." Then he chortled as he thought of his youngest son. "The next thing you know, that whelp of ours will be out looking for a woman."

"Oh, don't be foolish, Lamech! Noah's too young," Dezia protested.

"Too young? I was looking at women long before I was as old as him!"

"Please, don't tell us any more stories about when you were young."

Lamech blinked with surprise, then scowled. "You used to like my stories."

"I still do, but—"

"I know." Lamech nodded. "You're worried about your cub."

"I am a little. They should have been back by now."

"They'll be all right." Lamech was actually worried himself, though he would never admit it to the two women. *I should have gone with them,* he thought. *Nophat's a good man, but three of those hunters are no more than babies. I wouldn't want anything to happen to my sons.*

Even as these thoughts ran through Lamech's mind, a sudden shout caught his attention. A village boy, no more than twelve, was running so fast he stumbled. He was shouting and waving his arms, and Lamech got to his feet, his face wreathed in a smile. "I think he's trying to tell us the hunters are back."

Instantly everyone in the village left their work. Women picked up their babies and shifted them to their hips. Everyone scurried down the path that led to the river. Tirzah lingered so she could walk with Dezia, who was still worried despite Lamech's awkward attempts to reassure her. "Come along," she said, taking the older woman's arm. "I'll bet Noah and Jodak are there now."

The two joined the scramble down toward the river, and before they arrived they heard the happy shouts from the hunters and the rest of the clan.

"It's good news," Tirzah said, her voice rising with excitement. "No one's singing the song of the dead. They're all right."

Dezia sighed and smiled at her daughter-in-law. "The Strong One kept them safe." As she hurried on toward the river, she breathed out a prayer of thanksgiving.

When Tirzah and Dezia reached the riverbank, Jodak met them with a grin. Noah stood beside him, proud and excited, his light brown eyes glowing with pleasure.

"We killed two river beasts!" Jodak cried out. He grabbed Tirzah with both arms and swung her around. She laughed with delight, hugging him and patting his cheek.

Dezia put out her arms and hugged Noah with all her strength. He laughed and squeezed her in return. "Why, Mother, you weren't worried about me, were you?"

Dezia held on to him, her head against his chest. She was a tall woman, but Noah had surpassed her. She reached up and grabbed two handfuls of his reddish hair. Both mother and son shared the unusual red tint, which no other members of the clan had. "Do you think I'd worry about a big lout like you?" she scolded.

Noah knew his mother well. "There was no real danger, Mother," he said to comfort her. "We hunters look after each other, you know."

"We got enough meat to feed the whole clan for a long time," Jodak said proudly to his father.

Lamech looked over at the mountains of flesh piled on the two rafts and turned to his son. "You did well, boy! Was that whelp of a brother any help?"

"Oh yes. He was a great help."

Noah had been afraid that Jodak would speak of his fall from the boat, but Jodak winked at him, keeping the wink carefully hidden from their father. "He did very well."

"Well, that's good, then," Lamech said gruffly. "Now let's get this meat back to the village."

Immediately they all began grabbing as much meat as they could. There were enough members of the clan to carry it all in one trip, and they made a triumphant procession back toward the village. Noah felt proud as he walked among the other hunters, and soon Ruea began to make up a victory song as they strode along.

"We are the great beast slayers!
The leviathan opened his mouth to swallow us,
But our spears pierced him to the heart!
Sing for the victory of Nophat,
The slayer of the mighty beast of the river!"

Tirzah clung to her husband and whispered, "Did Noah do all right?"

"Don't tell Mother and Father, but he had a close call." Jodak related the incident of Noah's fall and how only a spear in the eye of the river beast had saved him.

She stopped walking and turned to Jodak. "Did *you* put that spear in the beast's eye?"

"Well . . . yes I did."

"That was good, husband! You are a good man!"

Noah had eaten so much his stomach was as tight as a melon. He sat now with his back against a small tree as he watched the celebration. The whole village was there, and they had all gorged themselves on the roasted river beast.

It's either feast or famine, never just enough, Noah thought, and indeed this was true. At times the most diligent hunt would produce nothing, or the wild grain could not be found. Sometimes even the fish in the river refused to cooperate, so that the cries of hungry babies and women rose in the village. But at other times when the hunters were successful, or the fish traps were full, or the wild grain put forth bearded heads, there was more than enough for everyone to eat.

With the smell of roasted meat permeating the air, the villagers rested against the trees or rocks, relaxing or dozing contentedly, waiting for the celebration to start. As always after a successful hunt, everyone ate like starved dogs, then celebrated in festive abandonment. Once or twice a quarrel had broken out, but Lamech had shut it off with a curt threat.

Noah shifted his gaze to where Zorah was standing, the old man's yellowish eyes taking in the scene. There was an unearthly wildness about the seer that Noah feared. He noted that Zorah had eaten sparingly, refusing the best parts of the beast that Lamech had offered him. Lamech himself, Noah realized, was cautious of Zorah—and Lamech was the bravest man in the clan!

Even as these thoughts ran through Noah's mind, his eyes met Zorah's. The old man's stringy gray hair partially covered his face, but his eyes gleamed like live coals. They held Noah transfixed, and he was unable to move or turn away. Noah was relieved when the old seer himself slowly turned away and moved over into the fringes of the crowd.

Darkness fell, and the fires threw their flickering shadows among the people. Soon the dancing began, and several young girls batted their eyes at Noah, but he ignored them. He noticed only Lomeen, who twisted her lithe body and swayed in a sensuous rhythm to the pounding of the drums and the warbling of reed flutes. Noah saw with some consternation that she was also being watched closely by most of the young men.

Boz came up and threw himself down on the ground beside Noah, nudging him with his elbow and winking. "How'd you like to have *that* one, eh?"

Noah was disturbed by the question and the way Boz had asked it. He had never known a woman, and he was fairly sure Boz had not either—but a young man would never confess to such a thing. "She is pretty," Noah admitted cautiously.

"Pretty?" Boz scoffed. "Look at her! Every man here is staring at her, wondering what it would be like to be with her—even those who already have mates."

Noah took his eyes off of the young woman long enough to scan the crowd of watching men. Boz's observation was clearly evident in the expressions on their faces. He saw Nophat staring at the girl as she gracefully gyrated and slapped her feet on the bare ground in time to the drums. Noah also saw Nophat's wife, Nenai, glaring at the girl and casting her jealous eyes at her husband.

Boz grinned at Noah. "Nenai had better watch out—Nophat might be taking a second bride."

As the dancing went on into the night, Ruea's voice rose clearly into the air, along with showers of sparks from the fires, to mingle with the stars overhead. Ruea's song came as naturally as that of a bird:

"Oh, the clan of Lamech went to the river,
The river that flows and waters the earth
And gives life to all things.
The clan of Lamech, armed with spears and courage,
Went forth to war against the mighty river beast. . . ."

On and on the song went, recounting the hunt and even including, Noah was alarmed to hear, the incident when he fell into the water and was nearly killed. Ruea then sang of how Jodak had saved his brother and how the mighty Nophat had struck the blows that killed both beasts.

At the end Ruea sang about Noah, the mighty crocodile hunter, and how he had slain the crocodile that had been put down his back. It was a fitting end to a song, but Noah bowed his head in embarrassment, unable to look up as laughter filled the air.

Tirzah came over and sat down beside him. "Did that really happen?" she demanded.

"Yes it did. That fool put a little croc down my back!"

"I don't mean *that*—I mean, did you nearly get killed?"

"Well, yes I did, but Jodak saved my life."

"It is well he did, or I would never have let him touch me again." Tirzah had practically raised Noah. Dezia had been pregnant with Noah when Tirzah came to the village as a young bride. Her new mother-in-law had become very ill after Noah's birth, so Tirzah had helped care for the infant. Even after Dezia regained her health, Tirzah had continued to raise Noah almost as her own son. He helped fill the void she had felt over the years at not yet bearing any children of her own. Now she reached over and got a handful of his hair. "Next time I will not let you go."

"I have to go, Tirzah! I'm a man."

Tirzah said no more, for Methuselah, Noah's grandfather, had stood up to speak and everyone fell silent.

Methuselah had once been a tall man but was now stooped with age. His face was marked with deep wrinkles, and his hair was as white as the clouds on a sunny day. His dark eyes were the liveliest part of his expression. He was sought out by all who cared to hear about the history of the clan, for he could trace his lineage back hundreds of years. It was whispered among the people that his father, Enoch, had talked with those who knew Adam, the first man created by the Ancient One.

Methuselah stood in the flickering shadows of the fires and began to tell a tale—he always had a tale—and everyone listened. There was no other way to know the past except through this man, and even his own son Lamech was in awe of him.

Noah listened avidly as the ancient man spoke of the heroes of the past. He had always been close to Methuselah, for his grandfather had made a pet out of him, often taking him on his long walks. The two had fished together in the river, and Noah had learned to cook the fish and other game just the way Methuselah liked it. He had done so tonight, preparing the river beast with special wild herbs Methuselah had shown him where to gather. As they ate the succulent meat, Methuselah had looked at his grandson with fond approval.

"There was a time, a good time, before the Nephilim appeared. My father, Enoch, spoke often to me of those times. It was a time of good fellowship, when men and women served the Ancient One—the Strong One. Everyone, it seemed, wanted to serve his fellow man, and there was almost no killing, no violence among men. . . ."

On and on the tale went, and the word *Nephilim* was repeated often. No one actually knew the origin of the Nephilim, but everyone knew of their reputation. The men were brutal giants, and the women were no less fierce. They took what they wanted and had no mercy on man, woman, or child.

"Before the Nephilim came," Methuselah continued, "men and women walked together in harmony, but the Nephilim brought much killing and pain."

The old man fell silent, his head bowed over. He appeared to be finished, but then he abruptly lifted his head and everyone leaned forward as he said, "It is the Ancient One we must serve! My father, Enoch, served him faithfully, and the Ancient One took him so that he never passed through death."

Noah sat bolt upright, listening. He loved to hear the stories about Enoch and the good men in the old days, but when he even heard the word *Nephilim,* it frightened him. It was terrifying to think that men who were like savage beasts still roamed the earth.

Everyone's attention suddenly turned to a figure that had stepped out of the shadows. Zorah stood outlined by the light of the fires, and the flickering flames caused the shadows to deepen the lines of his face. He lifted his voice and cried out, "The sons of the Holy One have taken the daughters of men, and blood will follow! The Ancient One will have vengeance on those who follow the ways of the Nephilim. Beware, you young men, lest you be enticed by the daughters of earth! Follow the ways of the Ancient One, for He is good. He is righteous and would have mercy on all. But He is also just, and those who turn from Him to follow after the flesh will pay—will pay—will pay!"

Noah sat beside the fire, staring into the flames that had burned down low. The red coals exuded a warmth that caused the young man's face to glow as he leaned forward with half-closed eyes. Most of the clan had gone to their huts now, except for a few women who were putting up the meat for future use.

He felt a movement by his side and turned to see Tirzah. "You'd better go to sleep, mighty hunter," she said fondly.

Noah reached out and caught her hand. He loved his sister-in-law greatly, for she was actually more like a mother to him. "You had better go yourself." He smiled and squeezed her hand. "I heard my father say that he wants you to give him a grandson."

"I will—when the Ancient One wills it."

"That would be good. You would be a fine mother—as you always were to me. I remember when I got hurt, I'd come to you, and you would take me in your lap and hold me until the hurt went away."

Tirzah was pleased by his mention of those times. She put her hand on his head and stroked it. "You have hair like your mother and the same gentle spirit."

"Tirzah, I didn't understand what Zorah was talking about, but it scared me. I mean what the seer said about the children of earth, the daughters of men. What did he mean?"

"I'm not sure," Tirzah said slowly. "But be very careful, Noah. The Ancient One wants you to follow Him, but there are many who would seek your destruction. You will be greatly tempted to turn from Him, I fear, and follow your feelings, but you mustn't. You must stay strong."

Noah nodded solemnly at her warning; then she rose and left him, bidding him a good night. Finally he rose too and started toward the reed hut where his bed awaited him. He stopped abruptly, however, when a figure stepped out of the shadows. "Who's that?" he demanded.

"Why, it's only me, Noah—Lomeen."

For an instant Noah was tempted to run, but Lomeen stood before him, holding him with her eyes. She reached up and put her hand on his hair, stroking it gently. "You have nice hair," she said. "It's so soft . . . and almost red sometimes."

"I . . . I got that from my mother," Noah stammered.

Lomeen did not remove her hand immediately but let it drop down to his cheek. "You're so tall. You're going to be a fine man when you come to full strength."

For the life of him, Noah could not answer. He felt slightly sick—or perhaps it wasn't that. He remembered waterfowl on the river he had heard many times that would dive underwater and make strange moaning cries. If he had to describe how he felt at this moment, that sound would be a good comparison. In the darkness the starlight shone down, touching the girl's face with silver. Her garment hung softly about her, and Noah wasn't sure if he wanted to stare at her or run away. In confusion he brought his eyes up to look full in her face and saw that she was smiling at him.

"Why don't you ever come to our village to one of our festivals?" she whispered.

"I don't know." In truth, Noah had heard of the clan of Jaalam, and the young men grew excited when they talked about it. One had even gone and come back whispering of strange goings-on that both tempted and repelled Noah.

"You're a man now." She leaned against him, and the touch of her against his body burned like fire. "You're a *man* now, Noah," she repeated. "We can show you some things you haven't seen." Her voice lowered to a whisper. "Will you come?"

Noah cleared his throat. "Maybe I will."

Lomeen ran her hand down his chest and then laughed, amused by his shyness. "I'll see you there, Noah."

Noah stood still and watched Lomeen as she left, then walked slowly toward his hut. He had been stirred by her touch in a way that disturbed him. Jodak was standing at the door, and Noah knew his brother had seen the two of them together.

"She's a bad woman, Noah. She's pretty on the outside, but inside she's bad."

"She doesn't seem so bad to me, Jodak."

"We mustn't judge by appearances, Noah. You're a follower of the Ancient One. You heard what the seer said. Have nothing to do with these daughters of the earth!"

Noah could not answer, and Jodak's eyes grew sharp. "Did she ask you to come to one of those festivals at her village?"

"Well . . . yes, she did."

"Stay away from them, Noah! It will bring you nothing but trouble."

Not wishing to argue with his brother, Noah said nothing, but inwardly he began to wonder what Jodak was so worried about. How could Lomeen be so bad that he should have nothing to do with her and her family? Maybe the only way for him to find out was to accept her invitation and see for himself.

After getting himself ready to sleep, he crawled onto his straw mattress, pulled the thick pelt covering over himself, then closed his eyes. The night was already long gone, and dawn would arrive shortly. He relived, for a moment, the triumphs of the hunt. Then the village dance . . . and Lomeen twirling in the firelight. Before drifting off to sleep her beautiful face filled his mind, her enormous eyes gazing into his, her sweet scent touching his senses, and her softness inviting him to come to her as she leaned against him. . . .

CHAPTER 3

The spectral image before Noah was faceless and terrifying as it rushed toward him with an enormous club lifted high to strike. A jagged black flint jutted out cruelly from the end of the club—one strike would split him open like a melon.

A mere glimmer of luminescence surrounded the monstrous form in the engulfing darkness. Noah tried to scream, but his throat felt as if it were being crushed by a massive boa constrictor, and he could only cry silently. He began to shake, desperately longing to flee, to be anywhere except in the shadow of the dreadful figure. And then he saw the face! Fear drained him completely at the sight of the evil, glaring eyes, the cruel mouth twisted in a horrible sneer, and the yellowed, jagged, flesh-tearing teeth.

Swifter than thought the monster hurtled toward him, screaming vile curses, the club lifted high overhead. Noah saw the muscles bunch in the giant's arms and shoulders as the club descended. It would surely kill him, blot him out of existence like a bug squashed underfoot. Throwing up his hands, he forced out a strangled cry—"No! Please don't kill me!"

Suddenly Noah found himself sitting straight up in his bed, sweating profusely, panting, clinging to the pelts that covered him, his body racked by hoarse cries.

As he gradually got his bearings, he smelled the rank fur of the covers under his nose . . . heard the far-off call of a night bird. . . . He was alive! Uttering a sobbing sigh of relief, he lay down and buried his face in the thick fur.

He lay there until the body tremors subsided, wishing for the dawn to come, but the stark fear of the night terrors lingered. Like a little boy, he wanted to run to his mother or Tirzah, cling to them as he had in his childhood—but he fought off the impulse, ashamed of his cowardice.

He had always been a dreamer, as far back as he could remember. Sometimes the dreams were pleasant, but some, like the one he had just had, were so frightful, so hideous, they made him long to bury himself in a deep hole and hide. The vivid dreams were occurring more often of late. He had once told his father about one of his dreams, but Lamech had laughed at him roughly. *"We don't need dreamers, boy! We need men who can fight and work and bring forth male children into the world!"*

His father's careless words had discouraged Noah from sharing this part of himself with others. He knew his mother and Tirzah were aware of his bad dreams, but unable to confide such things to them as he grew older, he had learned to endure them alone. He often wondered if others had such savage dreams, but if they did, no one spoke of them. Many times his dreams occurred in a flash, but they always remained to torment him even after he awoke.

Now as he lay on his narrow mat, Noah knew with a dark despair that for days and weeks, perhaps forever, he would relive the terror of this nightmare over and over, even during the daylight hours. He would see the terrible giant leering at him, screaming curses, and lifting the deadly club with the razor-sharp flint embedded in the end. The dream, like a severe fever, would fade away until almost forgotten but then would sweep back with an even more potent force.

Finally the tremors passed away, and Noah lay still, drained of all strength. He watched through the small window across the room as the thick darkness outside began to break into a pale milky light. As always after a bad dream, he welcomed the dawn. He lay quietly until he heard the muted voices of early risers floating gently to him. He buried himself under the pelts, knowing he should get up but having no willpower to do so.

What did the dream *mean*? he wondered. He heard others talk about what their dreams signified, but rarely did he understand his own. Only one thing was certain—the dream was evil, and he prayed desperately to the Strong One that he would never meet such a terrifying creature in the real world!

Finally he threw the covers back and rose, making a firm resolution to himself: *I'll go work in the vineyard so hard I won't even think of the dream!*

Methuselah shuffled along the dusty path, barely lifting his feet enough to slide them forward. His head was bent, his back stooped as he leaned on his staff. His hearing had gotten bad over the past hundred years. He had always had the keenest hearing of any man in the clan, even as he grew older with the centuries. He could remember his father laughing at him when he was young, pulling his ears and saying playfully, *"I do believe you have better hearing than a hare, though your ears are not as long!"*

The ancient memory warmed the old man, and he picked up his pace slightly. Once he had been so swift of foot he could outrun any man. That time was long gone, however, and he contented himself now with moving slowly along the path that led to the small field just outside of the village. Glancing over his shoulder, he saw spirals of gray smoke rising from cooking fires, then he looked up and watched a falcon diving steeply toward the earth at breakneck speed. Observing the world about him had always been one of Methuselah's greatest pleasures, and many of his fondest memories centered on birds and animals. He watched the falcon disappear behind a clump of bushes, then, even with his muted hearing, he noted the high-pitched squeal of a rabbit as it was snatched by the sharp talons of the hunter.

Methuselah was well accustomed to death. He could not even remember the time when he first understood that all living things died. The creatures of the wild preyed upon each other, and in these later centuries, some men had become red in tooth and claw as well, more vicious than any beast that roamed the earth.

Finally the old man turned off the winding path and made his way to a low stone wall, which he recalled helping to build when his son Lamech was but a stripling. That was in the dim past. Time had moved on for him and for everyone he knew. The older he grew, the more conscious he became of the passage of time, and it never ceased to mystify him. When he was young he had paid no attention to the passing of days and weeks and months. Night after night the stars had continued drifting slowly overhead, doing their great cosmic dance in the heavens. The sun would always rise in the morning and set in the evening. As a youth he had accepted these daily events without question but had not stopped to consider how they marked the passing of time itself. Now that he was approaching the end of his long life, however, he carefully measured every day. Each moment was like a precious jewel—to be cherished and enjoyed even when life grew hard.

The warm sun soothed Methuselah's stiff shoulders as he made his way down the path next to the stone wall. Finally he found what he was seeking. A few steps away a young man was moving along a grape arbor made of stakes joined together by horizontal saplings, which were lashed together with strips of rawhide. The old man smiled to see the young man so engrossed in digging a hole at the foot of each of the stakes that he was unaware of Methuselah's presence.

"Hello, Noah. Still at it, I see."

Noah jerked up his head, startled by his grandfather's voice. He had been trying to put the nightmare out of his mind, but now he smiled and leaped to his feet. "Hello, Grandfather. What are you doing out so early?"

"I came to watch you work." Methuselah glanced around and spotted a flat section on top of the wall. He moved toward it, sat down stiffly, and sighed with pleasure. "That sun feels good!" He studied the rawboned youth before him, then looked down at the hole the boy had been digging. "You like to do that sort of thing, don't you?"

Noah nodded and glanced at the hole he had dug out with a sharpened stick, which he'd hardened by fire. "I do, Grandfather." He peered down the line of stakes, noting the tiny vines that had already begun to creep upward, reaching for the sun, and he smiled with pride. "It's fun to make things grow. I like it more than hunting or anything else."

Methuselah squinted his eyes against the sun's bright rays as he studied the young man's thin face and scrawny frame. *One day soon,* he thought, *solid flesh will give strength to that lanky body.* He kept his eyes fixed on Noah and murmured, "You remind me sometimes of my father."

Noah stood up, fully attentive to his grandfather. He loved his tales of olden times and asked eagerly, "Of Enoch? Do I look like him?"

"Yes, you do look a great deal like him. Of course, I never saw him when he was your age." Methuselah smiled. "When you're a hundred years or so older, you'll look exactly like him." He looked down at the hole and nodded. "My father always used a flint hoe."

"Flint? Did he know how to make spearheads?"

"I don't think he did. We had a man in our clan who was very good at that, so he made them all. My father was a fine hunter, but he loved to dig in the earth just as you do—always planting something, as I remember it. The rest of us went out and gathered grain or berries—things that grew wild—but he would plant things, water them, and build fences around them to keep the animals away." He sighed and shook his head. "I haven't thought of that in many years."

Noah piped up eagerly, "Did you have bronze in those days?"

"Oh yes. I can remember the first piece I ever saw—a dagger that one of my uncles had traded for. It was the pride of the whole clan."

"Who was it that first learned how to make bronze?"

"My father told me it was a man called Tubal-Cain. He was a descendant of one of the first men named Cain."

"Tell me more about your father."

"You're interested in him, aren't you, son? Come sit next to me and I'll tell you."

Noah sat down on the wall and eagerly waited for his grandfather to tell him more.

"Well, Noah," Methuselah said, "my father was the best man I ever knew. He walked all his life with the Strong One. I can remember sitting at his feet listening to him talk and talk about the Strong One—not even aware that the sun was making its way clear across the sky as he talked. He would sometimes call him the Holy One or the One Who Knows. I was always amazed at how much he loved the Strong One and talked about Him as if they were the best of friends!"

"I don't understand about the Strong One, Grandfather."

"Why, of course you don't, boy. Nobody does! If you could *understand* Him, he wouldn't be a god. He would just be a man. The Strong One isn't someone you can figure out."

Noah digested this, then thought suddenly of his bad dream. It flashed before his eyes with such startling realism he could almost smell the raw scent of the giant figure. "Why are some men so evil, Grandfather?"

Methuselah shook his head sadly. "The descendants of Cain—they're a bad lot. My father called Cain's descendants 'the sons and daughters of men.' "

"But aren't we *all* the sons and daughters of men?"

"It's a little bit more complicated than that." Methuselah gathered his thoughts. He hunched his shoulders and fingered the staff that lay crossways across his bony knees, keeping silent for what seemed like a long time to Noah. Finally he sighed deeply. "I think it amounts to this, my son—everyone you see comes from one of two bloodlines. Some come from Cain, such as Tubal-Cain, and others are descended from Seth."

Noah hesitated, then asked, "What about the Nephilim? Where do they come from?"

"The Nephilim? Sometimes I think they are not men at all."

"Not men? What are they, then?"

"They are the most terrible creatures one can imagine, Noah! I hope you never see one—but I hear they are moving in closer from the east. Lamech has heard rumors, and I know he is worried."

"But what *are* they?"

"They are totally evil—more like beasts than men. They show no mercy and kill with pleasure. Some say they are fallen gods, Noah."

I'll bet the thing I saw in my dream was one of the Nephilim, Noah thought, then said with a worried frown, "But *we're* not like them, are we, Grandfather?"

"Certainly not! We come from the line of Seth, who was a good man."

"So we are the sons of Seth?"

"Yes. And you must always remember that, Noah. The Ancient One has it in His mind to bless the world through our family. How that will be, I cannot say."

"What happened to your father? I have never understood your stories about him."

A light suddenly flared in Methuselah's faded eyes. He squinted at his grandson, then said in a warm voice, "He went out one day and never came back. At first we thought he'd been killed, but later we realized he hadn't been. He was always talking about the Ancient One. The rest of us couldn't understand how close he was to God. This was in the days when the Nephilim were beginning to come into the land, and the descendants of Cain were growing more numerous."

"But . . . what exactly happened to your father? Did he say good-bye, or did he just leave?"

"He grew very quiet during his last days," Methuselah whispered. "He talked about going *home,* and none of us knew what he meant by that. We thought *home* was the village where we lived—or that it was the clan. But it always meant something different to my father. Finally one day he came to me and put his arms around me and held me tightly. He told me he was going on a long journey, and I asked if I could go with him. I remember that moment so well! He smiled, but his smile was sad. I became frightened."

"Did he say anything?"

"He just said, 'Be a good man, Methuselah, my son. You will see me again one day.' "

Methuselah fell silent, and Noah sat transfixed. He whispered, "Did you ever see him again?"

"No, but the Strong One spoke to me and told me that He had taken my father to *His* home."

"The Ancient One took him home? But . . . where is that? Why have we never seen it?"

"You're as curious as a woman, boy! All I know is that the Ancient One said that He took my father to His home."

"But *where* is that?" Noah demanded.

"I don't know," Methuselah admitted. "But I know one thing, Noah, my father is wherever the Ancient One lives—and I think all who have died loving the Holy One are there too." Then, in a voice so gentle the boy had to lean forward to catch the words, he whispered, "Just think, Noah, the Ancient One is there! He who made the earth, the moon, the sun, and all the stars. How I long to see Him!"

Noah bombarded his grandfather with many more questions and listened avidly as the old man answered as best he could. Noah's few years seemed so insignificant when his grandfather spoke of the centuries he had lived and of all the things he had seen. Abruptly the thought came to Noah that one day soon Methuselah would die too. And Noah himself would die one day. A burning desire to know more about the Ancient One was birthed in him at that moment. He wanted to be with his family forever, and the only hope he had of that was for the Ancient One to take him and all his family to live in His home.

Finally Methuselah rose and smiled at the young man. "No more questions, boy. My old bones are tired."

Noah rose quickly and spoke up again before his grandfather could leave. "That girl, Lomeen . . . she wants me to come to the village where she lives."

"The clan of Jaalam?"

"Yes. Her father is the chief there. She's asked me twice to come and visit. They're having a religious festival soon."

Methuselah's face grew stern. "Zorah says that Jaalam's clan is not to be trusted. He tells me they worship the moon and the sun—and even snakes." With an intensity that startled Noah, the old man lifted his voice. "That woman is one of the daughters of men! Do not go with her, son."

"You don't want me to go?"

"No, I do not. The sons of the Ancient One should have nothing to do with the daughters of men. I have watched for years, and all that fall under the sway of these women do not fare well. There's a darkness in them that pulls men down—makes them lose control and robs them of their honor and dignity. Sooner or later all who get mixed up with such women will die on the inside."

Noah was startled. "How can that be? I know of many young men of our clan who have visited there. They have told me it is fun. There is lots of dancing and games and feasting. What is the harm in having a little fun?"

"These young men you speak of—I know who they are. I have watched them go to these festivals and return changed on the inside. Oh, they go about their business—working, eating, sleeping—but all that was once good and holy inside of them has shriveled up. They've turned away from the Ancient One, and now they worship abominable things." Methuselah stood and put his hands firmly on Noah's shoulder. There was a fierce strength in his grip as he whispered, "Do not be enticed by this woman! I know she is young and beautiful, and she will offer you many things, even her body! But the sons of Seth are strictly commanded to stay away from the daughters of men. She will destroy you, Noah!"

Noah sat absolutely still, feeling the power of his grandfather's hands on his shoulders. He was shocked by the fire that burned in the old man's spirit.

When Methuselah turned and walked away, Noah suddenly felt weak. He slid off the wall and slumped down beside the hole he had been digging, but he could not continue his work. His grandfather's rebuke was frightening, and he knew that very soon he would have to decide what kind of man he himself was.

"I'm a son of Seth," he whispered fiercely—but even as he spoke, he had a swift impression of Lomeen and her dark beauty. Despite his grandfather's warnings, he could not deny how much he wanted her at that moment.

CHAPTER

4

Lamech tore the red meat from the bone with his strong yellow teeth and bolted it down like one of the wild dogs of the desert. He drank deeply from the carved wooden cup, savoring the taste of the goat's milk, and then, leaning back, belched explosively. The sound reverberated off the mud walls of the small dwelling, and he smiled, satisfied. He turned to face his son and grunted, "So you want to go running off to visit Jaalam's clan, do you?"

Noah had struggled for days now with the desire to see Lomeen again. He had tried unsuccessfully to heed his grandfather's stern warnings and put all thoughts of her aside. But at night he had tossed restlessly, plagued with a fierce and powerful aching for her. He was deeply ashamed of the longing that so consumed him, but he could find no relief from it. He well knew this was part of growing up, for he had heard the other young men's rough, crude jests about women. He had ignored such talk before, but now he could not get such thoughts out of his head. He kept this turmoil of feelings hidden, however, and when he had asked his father for permission to visit Jaalam's clan, he'd said nothing about Lomeen.

"Why do you want to go over there?" Lamech demanded. He was in a good mood, being full of food.

"I never get to go anywhere," Noah complained. "You've traveled a lot, Father. Now that I'm getting older, I need to see more of what other people are like."

Lamech's eyes narrowed, and he studied his youngest son carefully, considering his request. Lamech was eager for Noah to grow up, to learn to fend for himself and become a man. He worried that the boy was too tied to his mother and sister-in-law for his own good. But he had misgivings about letting him go off to Jaalam's clan. He had heard many tales of how powerful that clan was growing, and such rumors alarmed him. When a clan grew strong, there was always the possibility of trouble. Suddenly he made his decision. "I don't see that any harm can come of it. And listen, boy, while you're there, keep your eyes open."

Noah blinked with surprise. "Open for what, sir?"

"For whatever you see! How many warriors do they have? Are they strong? Do they ever talk about us? If you're going to be a man, you've got to learn to think like a man. You think I've kept this clan together by sitting around daydreaming?" Here Lamech frowned, for he was annoyed at Noah's penchant for letting his imagination run away with him. "One day you may be the chief of this clan. You need to learn how to read men—so watch what goes on, then come back and tell me about it."

While Noah gathered his things together for the trip, Lamech told the family about his decision to allow his son to visit Jaalam's clan. Jodak instantly opposed his father, and Dezia begged her husband to think more about it. Lamech just laughed at them. "The boy's got to see some of the world. It'll do him no harm, and besides, I'd like to know more about that clan."

Dezia was a strong woman and far more insightful than her husband, but women had little say in such matters. She was often able to change her husband's rasher decisions through subtle hints, which usually worked better than direct confrontation. Now, however, she felt compelled to protest more strongly. Her face was twisted with worry as she said, "I have a bad feeling about this, husband. I think it would be better if he didn't go."

But Lamech's mind was made up that Noah should go and bring back a report to the clan about the strength of Jaalam's fighting men. Noah, for his part, was happy to have an excuse to make the trip, and he had almost convinced himself that his real reason for wanting to go was indeed to help out his father.

Tirzah said nothing throughout the discussion, but she slipped out afterward and waited for her opportunity to intercept Noah as he left.

"Noah, wait!" she called out as he was about to depart.

Surprised, he turned to see her running toward him. She stepped in front of him, blocking his path.

"What is it, Tirzah? Did I forget something?"

Tirzah could not think of how to best say what was in her heart, but she decided she must be direct. As she smiled up at him, there was a pleading tone in her voice. "I think it's a mistake for you to go, Noah."

Noah had already seen the displeasure in the eyes of both Tirzah and Jodak. He hated to disappoint them, but he was also excited about this opportunity. This was an adventure for him, and like all young men, he had grown tired of the monotony of life in his little village. Besides, his thoughts of Lomeen had become steadily more powerful. Of course, he would admit that to no one. Instead he said, "Why, Tirzah, you mustn't worry so. I'll be back in a few days."

"You're going to see that woman, aren't you?"

A flush appeared on Noah's cheeks. He hated himself for revealing the feelings he thought he had concealed so well. "I suppose I'll see her," he said stiffly. "What's wrong with that?"

"You don't know anything about women, Noah."

"Well, then, I'll learn!"

Tirzah knew she was handling this situation badly. Noah's defenses were up now, and she forced herself to speak quietly. "I don't mean to try to run your life, Noah, but I worry about you. Things here are different from the world outside. I've had a chance to see some of that world, and I've learned that some women aren't to be trusted."

Noah listened as Tirzah pleaded with him. His grandfather's stern warning echoed in his mind as she spoke, but then he became angry. It seemed that his family was trying to run his life. "I'll be careful," he muttered. "It's just for a few days."

Tirzah knew now there was nothing she could say to change his mind. She put her hand on Noah's cheek. "Be *very* careful, my little brother. I've talked with those who know about that clan. They do terrible things."

Noah swallowed hard. "What kind of terrible things?"

"Drunkenness, for one, and the men are cruel—especially to the women—and they worship a terrible god called Ur-Baal."

"Ur-Baal? I've never heard of him."

"Well, I have, and he's bad!" Tirzah lamented, hope rising in her again that she was having some influence on Noah. "I've even heard they sacrifice their children to him!"

"Oh, that's just gossip," Noah protested. "You don't really know that, Tirzah. I'll go see for myself what all these rumors are about!" And with that, he shouldered his pack and picked up his spear, making it clear that his mind was made up.

Tirzah wanted to cry out, to forbid him to go, but she was only a woman, while Noah was a man—or at least on the way to becoming one. Instead she shook her head sadly and whispered, "Good-bye, Noah. Be very careful." Then she turned and walked away.

As Noah watched her leave he called out, "I'll be all right. Don't worry about me." But she did not even look back, and he knew she was grieved. It made him feel sad to disappoint her, but then he thought, *She's just like Mother—always worrying about me.* He headed toward the path out of the village, putting Tirzah's pleadings out of his mind.

He had not gone far, however, when he heard another voice calling, and he turned to see his good friend Kul. "What are you doing here, Kul?"

Kul was probably the best looking of all the young men of the clan. A few years older than Noah, he was filled with self-confidence. "I'm going with you, Noah, to Jaalam's clan."

Noah stared at him. "When did this come about?"

"Oh, I'm bored with everything around here. The same old thing day after day."

"Did your family say you could go?"

"I didn't ask them." Kul shrugged carelessly. "You're only going to be gone a few days, aren't you?"

"That's right."

"They don't have to know everything. Come on. Let's get started."

Actually, Noah was glad to have a companion. He had always liked Kul. He was a cheerful soul, a good singer, and a very popular young man. "All right," Noah said. "I'll race you to the river."

The two broke into a run, and as Noah strained to beat his friend, he was glad to be going on a new adventure. But most of all, his thoughts leaped forward to the moment when he would once again see Lomeen.

"I think we ought to stay here for the night, Kul," Noah said, setting his pack and spear down by a shady tree. He was not all that tired, for the journey had not been hard so far. But darkness was beginning to fall, and Noah had no desire to travel after dark.

"Suits me," Kul said casually.

The two had brought some food in their leather packs, and Kul suggested, "Why don't you get a fire started. I'll help you gather up the wood."

A short time later they were seated in front of a fire that crackled cheerfully, shedding its amber beams into the darkness. It made a warm spot in the night, and Noah leaned forward from time to time to poke it and watch the sparks fly upward. They had eaten their fill and now stayed awake, talking about what they would see in the strange village. Finally Kul yawned. "I'm sleepy," he said. "Think I'll turn in." He moved back from the fire, laid his head on his pack, and went to sleep as quickly as a house cat relaxing by a cozy hearth.

Noah envied Kul's ability to fall asleep like that. *I'll bet he never has bad dreams—or any other kind, for that matter,* he thought. He was so excited about being away from home on his own, he feared he would not be able to sleep at all. He sat gazing dreamily into the fire, listening to the sounds of the night, enjoying the smells of the open country. They were camped by a small stream, which made a pleasant, sibilant gurgling, and from time to time a frog would belch forth a booming croak.

Eventually Noah began to nod off, but soon jerked awake with a start. He started to lie down, when a sudden movement in the darkness caught his eye. Fear washed through him, for there were wild dogs in this country—even lions from time to time. He whirled about, reaching for his spear. He froze as still as a stone when he saw a man standing there. Jumping up and pointing his spear toward the dim figure, he demanded, "Who are you? What do you want?"

As the man moved forward out of the shadows, Noah saw that it was no robber, but Zorah. Relief washed over him, and he said roughly, "You ought not to sneak up on people like that. It could be dangerous. You could get a spear in your belly."

Zorah came forward without invitation and sat down in front of the fire. "Do you have anything to eat?"

Noah was upset by the way the old man seemed to assume it was his right to demand food and a share of the fire. Nevertheless, he nodded and said, "Yes, sir. We brought some meat with us."

Zorah waited as Noah fished in the bag and spitted some meat on the stick that he himself had used. Zorah took it and held it over the fire, then watched as the fat began to drip in sizzling globs into the flames. He said nothing, just sat contentedly, watching the meat cook. When it was done, he pulled a flint knife out from under his garment and began to slice off small chunks. "I don't have enough teeth to eat as I should.

Mmm, this is good," he mumbled. The grease ran out of the meat and down his beard, falling in great greasy splotches onto his rough leather jerkin. His wild hair looked as if it had been hacked off in the back with the same flint he had used to slice the meat.

Noah shifted his position, ill at ease, wondering what Zorah wanted. He glanced over at Kul, hoping his friend would wake up, but he had not budged.

That's funny, Noah thought. *You'd think he'd wake up when a stranger came into camp.*

"He will sleep for a while," Zorah said.

The old man's words startled Noah. Did he even know what he was thinking?

Noah stared suspiciously at the old man, not knowing what to make of all this. But then, he never knew what to make of Zorah. His presence frightened and fascinated him at the same time. Noah was enthralled by Zorah's tales of the Ancient One. This man probably knew more about Him than any human on the face of the earth. Still, there was something fearful about this frail character too. Noah knew he had the strength in his arms to defeat the old man if he had to, yet just the thought of opposing Zorah frightened him further.

Noah waited until Zorah had finished eating and had drunk from the brook. When he came back and settled himself again by the fire, Noah asked him, "Where are you going, sir?"

Zorah looked at Noah, and once again the unusual tint of his eyes unnerved the boy. The fire made them appear even fiercer, like golden coals glowing in his deep eye sockets. They seemed to see right through him. "I heard about your journey to the clan of Jaalam."

Noah shook his head. "Nobody has any secrets in the clan, do they? I guess everybody in the village knows now where I'm going."

"Probably. Why are you going there, boy?"

The impulse to tell the truth came over Noah. He almost said, *I'm going to see a woman who's driving me crazy!* but somehow that seemed weak and wrong. "My father wants me to look the clan over," he said instead, glad that he could answer at least a partial truth.

The eyes glowed more fiercely than ever. "That is *not* why you are going, Noah. You used to be a young man full of truth."

Noah exploded with anger inside at the old man's admonishment. He struggled to control his tongue, but the anger got the better of him. "You're always watching me. Why don't you leave me alone?"

"Yes, you're right. I've always watched you." Zorah nodded in agreement. "But it's not my doing."

"What's that supposed to mean?" Noah snapped.

"The Strong One has commanded me to watch over you. He told me before you were even born that I would have to be careful of you. It was I, not the women, who cut the cord when you were born. Even when you were a baby, I watched you."

Noah suddenly felt afraid. "Why would the Strong One tell you to watch *me*?"

"I do not know His mind. I only obey His voice."

Noah swallowed hard, then leaned forward. "Did you ever *see* the Ancient One?"

"No, not I."

"But He talks to you."

"Not like you might think," Zorah said quietly. His voice was raspy with long use, and now he leaned forward and clasped his gnarled hands together. "He speaks inside my head or inside my heart. It is with the spirit I hear Him, not with my ears."

"How do you know it's Him?"

"Sometimes I don't." Zorah shrugged his thin shoulders.

"Then how do you know you were right about me?"

"Because the Ancient One has spoken to me about you not once but many times." His eyes examined Noah with a steadiness that nearly caused Noah to retreat. "Some may actually *see* the Ancient One," Zorah went on. "I think your ancestor Enoch did." He hesitated, as if he did not want the words on his tongue to be born, but finally he exhaled a sigh and said, "You may see him yourself one day."

Noah was shocked. "Me? *I'll* see Him?"

"Not with your eyes, perhaps. The Ancient One is not a man. If He were, I would not serve and worship Him. But He can do as He pleases. If He chooses to take a form, He can do so."

Noah could not make much of Zorah's words, and after a few moments of silence he said, "Why did you come here?"

"I came to stop you from going to Jaalam's village. I know those people. They are evil."

"Why is everyone trying to stop me?"

"Doesn't that tell you *something*, you foolish boy?"

Noah recoiled from the fierce gaze of the seer.

"Everyone's telling you not to go because it's dangerous! Even a pup like you should know enough to realize that."

"I don't see why," Noah said defensively.

Zorah shook his head at the boy's obstinacy. "Well, in any case, Noah, I came to stop you—then the Ancient One told me not to forbid you to go."

Noah was relieved to hear that, feeling justified in going after all. "I'm glad of that," he said. "It'll be all right, then."

"Perhaps it'll do you good to see what other people are like," the old man said. He shifted stiffly, moving his legs to a more comfortable position, and continued to speak. "When men and women are tempted, they either embrace sin or they hate it. It's about time you found out which path you're going to take." He looked searchingly at Noah. "The Ancient One is always seeking men and women who will serve Him. I think you are under His eye."

"But I'm only a boy," Noah protested. "You said so yourself."

"Yes, but you are old enough to make a man's decisions."

"What do you mean? I can't do anything well. I'm not a great hunter. I don't think I can take my father's place as chief. Why would the Ancient One choose somebody like me to serve Him?"

This remark brought a smile to Zorah's lips. "The Ancient One makes strange choices. He may choose a beggar instead of a chief for His purpose. I was the only son of the poorest family in my clan. When the Strong One first spoke to me, I couldn't believe He wanted me to serve Him. He had to speak loudly, for sure!"

For the first time, Noah felt at least partially comfortable in the presence of the seer, after hearing this confession of the seer's own weaknesses. "Tell me more about the Ancient One, Zorah."

"I'm glad to see you have sense enough to be curious. All right, we will talk about Him. He is strong and can do whatever He pleases. . . ."

Zorah spoke for a long time, so long that the fire almost went out, and Noah grew very sleepy. He glanced over at Kul, who had not moved during the whole time Zorah had been talking. "I don't think I can stay awake anymore."

"Go to sleep then, son. You have a long road to travel. I cannot see the end of your journey, but I can tell you this. It will not be easy or pleasant."

Noah was so drowsy he hardly heard these last words. He rolled over and went to sleep more quickly than he ever had in his life.

CHAPTER 5

"Hey, Noah—are you going to sleep all day?"

Noah sat up and looked around wildly. He had been having one of his dreams. He vaguely recalled a huge golden lion with blazing eyes but could not remember any details. Shaking his head to clear it, he saw Kul staring at him curiously.

"What were you shouting about?" Kul asked. "You woke me up."

Noah stretched and yawned, then scrambled to his feet. "Just a dream," he muttered. He looked at Kul and said, "Didn't you hear anything last night?" Surely he must have heard *something* of his conversation with Zorah!

"I don't know what you're talking about. I only heard you thrashing around and yelling just now," Kul said, shouldering his leather bag and spear. "Come on, I'm anxious to get to the village." He winked knowingly. "Maybe we'll see that young woman who came to our village. What was her name?—oh yes, Lomeen."

Ignoring Kul, Noah said, "I'm starving. Let's have some breakfast first."

Sighing loudly, Kul laid his belongings back on the ground and opened his bag. Pulling out goat cheese and a chunk of bread, he settled back against the tree and ate his fill while he watched his friend. Noah chewed on his own piece of wild-grain bread in silence. The young men drank from the stream before continuing on their journey.

As they walked along the rocky pathway, keeping a close watch out for wild animals, Noah tried to recall the details of his dream. He had seen a tall, rawboned figure standing before a great lion. He wasn't sure why the dream had frightened him so, but even now, recalling the scene in his mind, he found himself trembling.

Shaking off his thoughts, he picked up his pace until Kul protested breathlessly, "Slow down! What's your hurry?"

Noah did not answer his friend, and the two continued in silence, encountering no one. Noah's thoughts raced ahead to the village. Tirzah's warnings hammered in his mind, but he pushed them aside and inwardly admonished himself to grow up. *I'll be careful. What does she think I am—just a baby? I'm a man now!*

They did not stop to rest, and the sun was high in the sky when the landscape began to change into steeper, rockier hills. There was no path to guide them, but one of the older men of the village had given Noah clear directions. Old Shuzi had done so reluctantly, however, with another severe warning to Noah that it would be best for him to stay home "with your own kind."

In his mind he ticked off the various landmarks as they passed them—the red-rock outcrop with a single acacia tree clinging to a ledge, the giant stump that looked like an enemy warrior brandishing a spear, the field of towering termite mounds. Finally he pointed ahead. "You see that cone-shaped hill over there, Kul? From what Shuzi told me, the village is right at the foot of it. Come on. I'll race you to those two big trees over there."

The two young men threw themselves into a hard run, and Kul reached the twin trees only three steps before Noah. He laughed and said, "You're nothing but a turtle! A woman could run faster than you!"

Noah was about to make a surly retort when he froze. Four rough-looking men had stepped out from behind a stand of trees and were approaching Noah and Kul with menacing expressions.

Noah held up his hands. "We come in peace." The four large men wore leather aprons around their waists and armbands of a burnished metal. They were muscular and strong with clubs over their shoulders and knives in their belts. They were darkly tanned and much hairier than the men of Noah's tribe. Swallowing hard, he said, "My name is Noah. This is Kul."

The leader, a huge man with suspicious brown eyes, advanced, holding his club ready. "What are you doing here?" he growled. "We don't like strangers."

"I am the son of Lamech," Noah explained. "We have come in peace—simply to visit."

"You're from Lamech's clan, eh?" He looked the young men up and down and laughed hoarsely. "Well, if you two are a good sample, we don't have anything to fear from your people." A rude laugh went up, and the four men circled the two younger ones. One of them reached out and poked Noah in the ribs with his thumb. "Not enough meat on him to feed one of the dogs," he uttered in a guttural tone. "Visitors, huh? They're probably spies."

"No, no, we're not spies," Noah said anxiously. "We came at Lomeen's invitation."

"You know Lomeen?" The leader raised an eyebrow.

"Yes. She's been to our village."

"That's right," Kul put in, pulling himself to his full height. "You men are too suspicious. Haven't you ever had visitors before?"

The leader grinned and winked at his companions. "Some come—and sometimes this is as far as they get." Then he added, "Lomeen is my sister. I don't like strangers claiming they know her."

Noah wished at that moment he had stayed home where he belonged. Nonetheless, he was stubborn enough to continue. "We mean no harm. We just came for a visit."

"All right," the biggest man said. "I'm Comir, son of Chief Jaalam. We'll take you to him, but he's in a foul mood today. You'll be lucky if you're not skinned alive and dried over a fire."

Noah tried to show no concern at this possibility. He exchanged a quick glance with Kul, and the two moved forward, prodded by the clubs of their grinning captors.

"Not a very friendly bunch, are they?" Kul whispered.

"It'll be all right," Noah assured his friend with far more confidence than he felt. "We're a bit suspicious of strangers ourselves. Remember?"

Noah and Kul became increasingly uneasy as their captors made sport of them. With their rough, profane talk, they were obviously trying to frighten the two young visitors. Noah was determined not to give in to his fear, and he stood his ground as well as he could.

They crested a small ridge, and Noah peered down into a lush green valley watered by a stream that snaked its way around a motley collection of reed huts. The dwellings were similar to those in Noah's village but were not as carefully constructed. As they descended the hill, villagers tending their smoky cooking fires all turned their heads to see what the hunters had brought. By the time they reached the center of the village, Noah and Kul had been poked and shouted at by most of Jaalam's people.

Stopping in front of one of the larger huts, Comir called out, "Chief, we have guests! Spies, I should say!"

The tall man who stepped out of the hut was even larger than his son. He wore a necklace of bronze plates that reflected the midday sunlight. His eyes were small but glittered with a strange intensity. His brow beetled over his eyes, as if he were peering out of a dark cave into the brightness of day. "Who are these boys, Comir?" he demanded roughly.

"Spies, Father," the warrior responded. "Probably scouting out our land so they'll know how to attack us."

"No we're not!" Noah insisted. "I'm the son of Lamech. We've simply come for a visit."

Jaalam snorted. "A likely story. Well, we know how to treat spies around here. Tie them up!"

Noah and Kul were seized, and one of the captors cracked Noah in the temple with his fist. Stars floated by the millions across Noah's field of vision, but he did not cry out.

"Wait! These men are not spies!"

Shaking his head to clear it, Noah saw Lomeen stepping out of the chief's house. She stood beside the two captors and gave Noah a quick smile. "He is who he says he is, Father. The son of Lamech. His name is Noah. I do not know his friend, however."

"This is Kul," Noah said, relieved when the young woman gave them both a smile.

Jaalam stared at the two, then suddenly threw his head back and roared. "So you've done it again, daughter!" He winked at his son Comir and said, "You know your sister. She draws men like honey draws flies! Turn them loose."

Relief washed through Noah as the two men who had been holding him stepped back. "Hello, Lomeen," he said weakly. "I've come to visit, as you asked."

"So you did. You've come at a good time. We have a festival tonight." She smiled at her father. "I will see to them, Father."

Jaalam grunted, turned, and reentered his hut as Lomeen said to her brother, "Comir, go about your business."

Comir stared at his sister, then laughed roughly. "Come on," he ordered his companions. "We may still have time to make a kill."

Kul drew a hand across his face, shaken by the experience. "You give your visitors a rough welcome, Lomeen."

"We have to be careful, for we have many enemies. Come along. I'll show you around."

The three young people were soon joined by several others about their age. Lomeen introduced them to her visitors and then asked, "Is everything ready for the celebration tonight?"

A tall girl named Benei stepped closer to Kul. "Yes it is." She looked at him with her dark eyes, a strange smile on her broad lips. "You've never been to a festival of Ur-Baal?"

"No," Kul said.

Benei moved even closer. She reached out and put her hand on his chest, and her eyes almost closed as she studied him. "You will enjoy it, I think."

Noah glanced at Lomeen and saw that a small smile played around her lips as Benei made her overtures to Kul.

"I'm glad to see you again, Lomeen," Noah said.

"I didn't think you'd come. I'd venture your sister-in-law warned you against coming to our village."

Noah was startled. How could she have known about Tirzah's warning? But then, women seemed to know more about such things than men. He tactfully avoided her question and said instead, "I'd like to see the village."

"Come along. I'll show you," Lomeen said, taking his arm. Her touch reminded him suddenly of how he had felt when he first met her. He wondered why she affected him this way, for no woman ever had before. "I'm looking forward to the festival, Lomeen. Who is Ur-Baal? Is that your god?"

"Yes. You have not heard of him?"

"No. What's he like?"

"Not like the one you serve."

"Oh?" Noah said, curious. "How are they different?"

Lomeen merely shook her head. Her lustrous black hair, hanging down almost to her waist, glistened in the sun. She did not answer, but her smile gave promise of the night ahead. "Come," she said. "I will show you our village."

A warm darkness lay over the land like a dusky cloak. A handful of stars were scattered across the heavens, and the full moon cast a silvery glow over the village. Noah glanced at Lomeen beside him. The moonlight brightened her eyes, which glowed like old silver; her skin was seemingly coated with the same substance. As they walked toward a circle of fires in the center of the village, Noah asked, "Is that where the festival is?"

"Yes, we're early, but it will start soon."

Glancing over his shoulder, Noah saw that Kul was accompanied by Benei, who clung to him possessively. He did not seem to mind, Noah noted. While couples of all ages were making their way toward the fires, Noah glanced around, feeling an inexplicable sense of alarm. It was not cold, yet something in the air troubled him—like the heaviness one feels before the onset of a terrible storm.

When they were just a few feet from the fires, Noah turned and squinted into the darkness. A shock ran through him as he saw a woman sitting on the ground, tied to a stake and holding an infant. She looked up at Noah, and as she did so, he flinched. He had never seen such fear in the eyes of anyone!

"Who is that woman, Lomeen? Why is she tied to that stake with her baby?"

Lomeen pulled Noah closer. "Oh, they just play a part in the ceremony. Don't worry about it."

The tinge of amusement in Lomeen's voice troubled Noah greatly. But he asked no more questions as they took their place outside the ring of fires. He had never known a woman like this and felt uncomfortable yet excited by the way she looked at him with her enigmatic smile.

Inside the ring of fires burned a larger fire, where an ox roasted on a spit. Noah's stomach growled at the pungent smell of the roasting meat, and he looked forward to the celebratory meal. He watched a short, husky man strip the beast of flesh and pile steaming hunks of it on bark platters.

After the chief and his council of warlords had been given their portion, the meat was passed around to the waiting crowd. Noah ate ravenously, for he had not had any food since his meager breakfast of goat cheese and bread early that morning. While he chewed on the succulent oxen meat, Lomeen kept up a steady, soft conversation, telling him about various members of the tribe. She never spoke of Ur-Baal, however—which was what Noah really wanted to hear about. Then unexpectedly she stood up to leave, whispering in his ear, "You wait here."

Noah did as he was told, staying seated and looking around at the other couples in the firelight. Kul and Benei were still sitting very close together. He could sense an air of expectancy as the talk and laughter grew louder with each moment.

Lomeen returned with a clay jar. "Here," she said. "You will like this."

Noah took the large vessel, surprised at the weight of it. "What is it?" he asked.

"It will make you feel good." Lomeen smiled, then leaned forward and touched her forehead to his. "You're not afraid, are you, Noah? You don't think I'd poison you, do you?"

"Of course not, Lomeen," Noah said with more courage than he felt.

"Here. I'll drink first to show you it's safe." Lomeen took the vessel, lifted it and swallowed, then laughed and handed it back. "Now you."

More confident now that the substance would not hurt him, Noah did likewise, tipping the vessel and swallowing. It burned like fire as he lowered the jar, coughing and spluttering at the sensation.

"What *is* this stuff, Lomeen? Maybe you *are* trying to kill me!"

Lomeen laughed delightedly at Noah's inexperience. "That's only one swallow. Drink deeply," she urged, holding the jar back up to his mouth and tipping.

Noah gagged down several swallows, then handed it back to her. Even as he did so, he felt a strangeness invade him. The once-heavy jar seemed to float in midair as he passed it back to her . . . her laughter was like the distant mating calls of the river fowl . . . her hair sparkled in the flickering light and flowed down around her feet like black liquid fire. He watched Lomeen pass the vessel along to Benei . . . moving slowly, as if in a dream. Benei drank, then made Kul drink deeply.

All rational thought left Noah as he observed his surroundings with new insight. His vision grew sharp. He stared at Lomeen's head, seeing every hair as an individual. Her throat pulsed . . . her temple throbbed. He thought he had never seen anything more lovely. Turning his head slowly, he looked about at faces enlarged to twice their size, eyes reflecting the silver of the moon.

The sounds about him were different too. He could hear voices with crystal clarity, yet at the same time they seemed to be a long way off, and every voice had a sinister echo.

"Here, drink more."

"I . . . I th-think I've had enough." Noah could barely move his lips to speak.

Lomeen reached out and grabbed his hair. "Don't be like that," she whispered fiercely. The smell and touch of her warm breath, the softness of her body against his, her enticing voice in his ear were all magnified beyond words and filled him with so much desire that he felt as if he were falling. At the same time a thin thread of fear found its way along his nerves. Noah was a young man who liked to be in control of himself, whose mind was always alert and watchful. Now it seemed as though something or someone else was occupying his head . . . a force so evil and sinister he felt powerless to resist it. Lomeen urged him on, and with each swallow of the liquid fire, his self-control and reason slipped further into oblivion, stolen by some unnamed monstrous force.

From out of the laughter and talk, a strange song emerged and floated on the night air. Noah felt himself being pulled to his feet, feet that no longer felt the ground—he seemed to float just above it. Others about him were standing too, hovering just above the ground as he was. He was trying to make sense of the haunting melody and words when dancers materialized from out of the smoke of the fires.

A line of young women led by Lomeen swirled about in the center of the ring, blending in Noah's sight with the fires that leaped high with yellow-and-red tongues. The dancers moved around the circle, bending, reaching out with their arms to embrace the watchers. Noah stood stunned by the sensuous beauty of the dance. The dances he was used to were nothing at all like this! As the dance went on, men began to break from the circle one by one and seize a dancer, dragging her away. The women left willingly, smiling and clinging to their captors.

Then, out of the haze of Noah's mind, Lomeen's face appeared before him. She slipped her arms around his neck, her silky skin soft on his, and whispered, "Do you love me, Noah?"

Noah's mind whirled as something deep inside cried out in agony—a warning to stop—but with her arms around him and her lips on his, he knew only that he wanted her. . . .

"Come, Noah. The ceremony is about to begin."

Noah tried to rise, but he found himself so dizzy he could hardly stand. He heard Lomeen's soft laughter but could not answer. His mind felt a little clearer now, enough so that he was painfully aware of the encounter he had just had with Lomeen. He felt deeply shaken . . . confused and ashamed . . . but he had no time to think, for she was pulling him back to the fires. He heard wild chanting from old and young alike—"Ur-Baal! Ur-Baal! Ur-Baal!"

"Who is that tall man?" he whispered groggily. His attention had focused on a sinewy man standing beside the large central fire. Huge logs had been piled on the fire, and the hungry flames reached higher into the night sky, absorbing the light of the smaller fires. The man had a face like stone, and his black eyes glittered. He wore a cape made of bird feathers, and as he moved, the iridescent feathers fluttered, as if the birds had come alive again. He held up his hand and the chanting stopped.

"That's Magor, the high priest of Ur-Baal," Lomeen whispered. "Never cross him. He has great powers."

Magor began speaking in a powerful, dark voice. It reached out into the darkness and up to the very stars, Noah thought. The high priest called out to Ur-Baal, and the people around Noah began to moan.

"What's happening, Lomeen?"

"It's time for the offering."

"The offering? What's that?" Noah whispered. A cold fear clamped about his heart like a fist. He could not explain it, but he knew something terrible was happening.

A movement caught his eyes, and he saw three men dragging the woman who had been tied to the stake. She was screaming for mercy but was powerless in the mighty hands of her captors. Two of them held her tight, and another held the child in his massive hands. The infant was wailing too, but the faces of those who held the woman and her baby showed no emotion.

Magor lifted his hands and began to cry aloud. "Ur-Baal, we worship you! You are the god who gives strength and power!" He went on, his voice gaining intensity with every word. The moaning of the people increased until it became such an unearthly and frightful wailing that Noah put his hands over his ears to shut it out.

"What's happening, Lomeen? What offering is this?"

She did not have to answer him, for at that moment, Magor moved forward. He thrust out his hands, and the guard laid the infant in them. Noah stared in terror as the priest raised the frightened baby high above his head.

Magor shouted, "We make our offering to you, O mighty Ur-Baal!"

And then Noah saw the high priest cast the infant into the heart of the fire. Sickened, he turned away as quickly as he could but not before getting a terrible glimpse of the child falling into the flames and hearing his pitiful cry of agony above the terrified wailing of his mother.

Noah ripped his arm free from Lomeen and stumbled blindly away.

He knew he would remember this scene as long as he lived! The chanting continued, and he heard Lomeen call his name, but he fled, stumbling, his hands clamped tightly over his ears. He heard another scream of agony—and knew that the mother had just been offered to Ur-Baal too.

He fell flat, got up, and ran as hard as he could, seeking the darkness to cover the memory of what he had seen and heard. He fled until he could no longer hear the voices of the worshipers. When he could run no farther, he fell on his face and wept. He cried till the darkness overcame him and he sank into a deep, black pit of unconsciousness.

"Who is it?" Kul opened his eyes, frightened, and then saw the face of the one who was bending over him. "Oh, Noah, it's you."

Noah had awakened at dawn to find his face pressed against the rocky ground and crept back to the village to rescue his friend. He had searched quietly until he found Kul lying close to one of the dying fires. "We've got to get out of here, Kul," he whispered.

Kul sat up and looked around, then winced. "Ah, my head's killing me."

Noah did not answer. He simply grabbed Kul and dragged him away, avoiding the villagers who were scattered on the ground, sleeping, spent from the night's revels. "Let's get out of this place," he whispered.

The two stumbled away, and when they were clear of the village, Noah put his head down and said through clenched teeth, "I wish we had never come to this place, Kul."

Kul did not answer for a time, but when he did, his words surprised Noah. "I may come back."

Noah whirled and stared at Kul. "After what you saw, you'd come back to this terrible place?"

Kul shook his head and shrugged. "Yes . . . I'd come back. We're sure never going to have women like that back home, Noah." Kul looked at his friend, puzzled. "Didn't you like Lomeen?"

Noah could not answer. A fiery wave of shame rose in him and caught at his gut until he thought he might retch. Yes, he had liked Lomeen—the ecstasy of her touch, her urgent whispers in his ears. He wanted to remember the pleasure of that moment, but he also knew with sickening awareness how wrong it all was—and how he could never undo the effects of this night. Nor would he ever forget what had happened inside the ring of fire.

CHAPTER 6

For many days after Noah and Kul had returned from their visit to Jaalam's clan, Noah knew no peace. Whether awake or asleep, his experiences in the village seared his mind. Night after night in frightening dreams he would see the huge fire and the high priest of Ur-Baal raising the helpless infant over the flames. Although he would squeeze his eyes tightly and clamp his hands over his ears, nothing could shut out the sight of the child's face or the agony of its screams as his tiny body was cast into the blazing inferno. The dream returned again and again, and Noah woke up shaking and weeping every time.

During these days his mother was painfully aware that her son was troubled. Busy with governing the tribe, Lamech was too distracted to notice, but Dezia was a sensitive woman of great insight. She watched her tall son walking around as if in a trance, and finally asked him, "What in the world happened in that place, Noah? You haven't been the same since you returned."

Noah longed to share his burden with someone, but he could not bring himself to tell his mother, or anyone else, about the human sacrifice. It so disgusted him that just the memory of it made him sick to his stomach. And he *certainly* could never tell his mother about his experience with Lomeen!

At Dezia's question, he merely muttered that he wasn't feeling well. But he knew in his heart and by the expression on her face that she did not believe him. The sadness in her eyes as she turned away from him only heightened his guilt over all the terrible things he had done and witnessed, especially after she had begged him not to go.

Noah so wished that his brother Jodak was still around. He and his wife, Tirzah, had gone on an extended visit to her family's clan, a day's journey away. They had already left when Noah returned from Jaalam's village. Noah had begged his father for permission to go see them, but his pleas had been denied. "I need your help here, Noah. I can't have you off running around all creation," Lamech had growled.

And so Noah endured the days alone with his thoughts. His only comfort was in working the fields or the vineyard, encouraging the immature vines to sink deep roots into the earth and climb the trellis he had built out of saplings. He also tended the cattle, sheep, and goats and went hunting a couple of times, but nothing brought peace to his troubled spirit.

One night he stayed up long past his usual bedtime. His parents had settled down, and the village was quiet. He sat outside their reed hut going over and over in his mind his visit to Lomeen's village. Despite his guilt over what had happened with Lomeen, he could not shake his feelings for her. Her beauty haunted him day and night, so much so that he felt he must surely be in love with her. Yet he could not reconcile his desire for her with the awful things he had seen in that circle of fire.

"How can she endure such terrible cruelty?" he moaned. "How can such a beautiful woman take part in so awful a sacrifice?"

Unable to contain his feelings, he rose and, heedless of the nighttime dangers, made his way down the dark trail to the river. The soft gurgling of the water soothed him, and he lay down flat on his back, staring up at the sky. The stars were out, and as he often did when he looked at the glittering points of light across the velvety black vault, he wondered what they were and what they meant. What were these magnificent wonders beyond his own world? When he gazed at the moon surrounded by the glittering flakes of light, he grew silent. He knew there was a power outside of himself—a power outside of the clan—for surely these things could not have made themselves. He thought about the many times he had dressed animals, noticing the intricate workings of their bodies—all so complicated and speaking of some grand design.

As he lay on the muddy riverbank, wearying himself with endless thoughts about the meaning of life, he wished he could turn his mind off and think nothing at all. He almost envied the beasts, who had no worries aside from filling their bellies from day to day. They could not look backward and remember, nor could they look forward and dread the days to come.

He finally drifted off into a deep slumber. Tiny animals came upon the still, sleeping young man and sniffed him curiously. A crocodile of monstrous length crawled up on the shore, but Noah was so still the beast barely paused, merely glancing at the still form, then crawling awkwardly along the bank and sliding into the water again with scarcely a splash.

As Noah slept, his dream came to him again—the one in which he knew he was dreaming. He was in it but was also standing outside of it, and his mind rebelled against such a contradiction. In his dream stupor he was running, pursued by a terrible beast. He ran until his lungs burned. Fear swallowed him, making him impotent. Unable to run any farther, he turned to face his pursuer, prepared for anything—a monstrous river beast, a towering cobra with dripping fangs and glittering eyes, a giant vulture ready to peck his eyes out! What he saw, however, was a lion—huge and rough—with a black mane and a tawny hide. Its eyes were strange, like golden fire, reminding him of Zorah's eyes. They fastened themselves onto the young man, and he felt himself being pulled forward toward the huge beast and certain death, powerless to stop himself.

Noah was close enough to see the mighty claws and massive teeth, glistening like ivory daggers. But it was the eyes in particular that brought fear and trembling upon him. He stood staring into the glowing orbs until he felt himself swallowed up—no longer Noah, but now part of the lion....

And then he awoke, his body stiff as a rod, stretched out on the riverbank. He was clutching at the ground as if he were falling upward into the sky and crying out with all of his might for help.

He forced his eyes open and gasped with relief. "It was a dream—nothing but a dream!" He staggered to his feet, scarcely able to stand. The breeze turned the sweat on his body cold, and he turned and fled into the night. As he ran, he wanted desperately to see Tirzah and Jodak—to tell them everything.

"I must go see them. They'll understand. Tirzah has always understood me...."

After three days Noah finally won Lamech's grudging permission to visit his brother. Lamech had come to rely on Noah's work. Not sure how he would manage without him, he was reluctant to let him go again so soon—even for a few days. But Noah had so persisted that Lamech had finally thrown up his hands and sighed. "All right, Noah. You can go—but you must be back in five days."

Having obtained his father's permission, Noah was anxious to prepare to leave the following day, but he first set out to finish up his work in the field. Kul joined him, and the two worked silently together, breaking up the earth with their hoes—sharp flints attached to tough sapling handles.

"I hate this infernal work," Kul said sullenly. He threw down the hoe and shook his wild mop of kinky hair. "I'm going home."

Noah looked up in surprise. "Why do you hate it?" he asked. "I've always loved it."

"Grubbing in the ground! What's fun about that?"

"I don't know," Noah replied. He leaned on his hoe, and his eyes grew thoughtful. He made a striking figure in the bright sunlight, the red tint of his hair glinting, the muscles of his tanned body rippling along his strong young arms and legs. The sun directly overhead shadowed his cheekbones, and his prominent nose shaded his lips. He smiled at Kul and shrugged. "I just like it. That's all."

Kul shook his head with disgust. "Men are supposed to be hunters. Whoever thought of doing things like this? It was better in the old days."

"No, it wasn't," Noah said. "You ought to listen to my grandfather talk about it. Before we learned how to plant the grain so we could harvest it and keep the animals out of it, people nearly starved to death. And since then we've learned how to keep cattle and sheep. Now when we get hungry we don't have to depend on the luck of the hunt."

Kul moved restlessly as Noah spoke. They had had this conversation many times before. Finally Kul gave Noah a peculiar glance. "Have you thought about going back to Jaalam's village?"

"No, I haven't," Noah answered curtly.

Kul did not seem to believe his friend and examined him curiously. He narrowed his eyes, and a smile touched his lips. "*I'd* like to go back there."

"Whatever for?" Noah spat, heaving his hoe into the ground and forcefully turning over another clod of earth. "It was awful."

"Well, that sacrifice was pretty raw, I'll admit, but we wouldn't have to go for that," Kul said, a twinkle in his eye. "I'll tell you what. Instead of visiting your brother, come with me and we'll go back there. I'm dying to see Benei again."

Noah did not answer, turning his head away. He'd had the same thought himself about Lomeen but did not want Kul to know it.

"What's the matter?" Kul asked. "I know you want to go back. Those women will be glad to see us again." A playful smile touched his lips as he winked and urged, "Come on, Noah. Don't be such a stick-in-the-mud. I know you liked Lomeen—you can't tell me you didn't!" Kul started to dance around, imitating the young women's brazen behavior that night. He laid his hand delicately on Noah's chest, cooing in a taunting falsetto, "Oh, Noah—you're so strong and hand—"

"No, Kul!" Noah shoved his friend away and threw the hoe down, narrowly missing Kul's bare feet. "I don't *ever* want to go back to that place again! It wouldn't be right."

Kul's eyes flashed with anger. "All right, then," he said. "You do as you please, but *I'm* going."

"No, Kul—it would be better if you didn't."

"Don't be giving me orders, Chief Know-It-All! Remember I'm older than you are—and smarter too by the looks of it."

Noah wanted to say *More foolish, you mean,* but he valued Kul's friendship. He watched sadly as the young man stalked away, his back stiff with anger, and shook his head. *He'll just get into trouble there.*

He picked up his hoe and began working again, taking comfort in watching the rich soil turn over as he moved steadily along the row of plants. He could do this all day long, every day, and still find pleasure in it. He could not explain it. It was a power the earth had over him, always drawing him. He began to hum a nameless tune as he continued his work.

The afternoon brought cooler breezes, and Noah turned toward home, his hoe over his shoulder. As he approached the village he saw Zorah standing in the path, apparently waiting for him. His heart gave a quick lurch as it always did at the sight of the strange old man. If he'd been able, he would have turned and gone another way to avoid being seen, but it was too late, for Zorah was staring straight at him. Noah held his head up. *There's nothing to be afraid of. He's just an old man.* He stopped in front of the seer and greeted him pleasantly. "Hello, Zorah."

"Hello, Noah."

"I've been out working in the field."

"Yes, I know."

How does he know so much? Does he spend all his time watching me?

He would have moved on, but Zorah said, "Sit down awhile."

"Well, actually I'm—"

Zorah ignored Noah's protest. Taking the young man's arm, he guided him to the shade of a tree. Many vultures were circling in the sky, and Zorah watched them carefully. He appeared to have forgotten that he had asked Noah to sit down, and the longer Noah sat there, the more uncomfortable he became. Once again the terrible scenes at Jaalam's village flooded his mind, and without meaning to, he began to speak of his experiences to the old man. At first he just spoke generally of the clan, but then he could not still the words that rose up, and he found himself telling Zorah about the human sacrifice. "It was awful," he said. "How could anybody do a thing like that to a little baby or to a helpless woman?"

"There are evil men in our world, Noah." Zorah's voice was strangely quiet, and his eyes were fixed on the earth, watching a line of ants trundling a burden along. Picking up a twig, Zorah put it in front of them and seemed to take some pleasure in watching them go around it. Finally he looked up and said, "What else happened?"

"What do you mean?" Noah kept his head down, not able to meet the old man's eyes.

"There's something else, isn't there?"

And then Noah knew he had to confess. He had kept his encounter with Lomeen to himself, but it was like trying to hide something dead. Sooner or later, the stench of it would get out. Now he swallowed hard, still unable to meet the old man's eyes. "There was this woman named Lomeen. . . ."

"Yes, I know her," Zorah said, nodding.

"Well, she seemed to like me. . . ." Miserably Noah struggled on until he finally cried out, "I couldn't help it. There was something in that jug she gave me to drink. I wasn't myself."

Zorah's golden eyes were fixed on Noah's face. Although the young man did not know it, the old prophet had a special affection for Noah. He had no children of his own, but somehow this tall young man with a sensitive spirit and a vivid imagination was like the son that he had never had. He sighed deeply and shook his head in a troubled fashion. "Don't blame your actions on the potion she gave you, Noah."

"But it was—"

"I know the power it has over men—it weakened your will. But you did not have to drink it. I hope you never let yourself be led away like that again—especially in *that* place. Now you have to face up to what you've done."

"But . . . but it was *her* fault!"

"It *wasn't* her fault. It was *your* fault! When we do something wrong, it's always our fault." Zorah seemed to be caught by a pain, for his face grew cloudy and his lips contorted. "Do you think I haven't been through such temptation? I wasn't always old, Noah. I was sixteen once just like you are. There were women then who were willing enough—women like Lomeen—but I was never forced to go to any of them."

Noah fell silent, not wanting to face the seer. He waited for Zorah to speak again, and when the old man did not, Noah said, "I'm sorry. I wish I could do it over again. It would be different."

For the first time Noah could remember, the old man seemed touched, a gentle light in his eyes. Noah was shocked when Zorah reached over and put his hand on his knee. It was the first physical sign of affection Noah had ever seen Zorah show to anyone. He looked up into the old man's eyes and was stunned to see tears glimmering there.

"What is it, Zorah?" he asked, troubled by the old man's pain.

"I hate to see you hurt, Noah."

Noah was profoundly moved by Zorah's simple words. He could not think what to say, however, so he simply sat there, conscious of the old man's tortured features and of his gnarled hand on his knee.

"The earth has been divided, my son," Zorah said almost in a whisper. "There should be only good men here—I cannot help but think that is the will of the Ancient One. He loves goodness, and He himself is good. Whenever we see evil, we know it must come not from Him but from someone else."

"Who could it come from, Zorah?"

"I don't know. It's beyond me, but I know that there is a dark power that the Ancient One is at war with. The Strong One has His servants, but the servants of the evil one—whoever he is—are growing every day."

"What do you mean—the earth has been divided?"

"I mean that the earth is divided into those who love the Ancient One and those who do not."

Noah sat quietly pondering these thoughts, for Zorah had never spoken of these things before. It reminded him of his conversation with his grandfather Methuselah when he had spoken about the sons of Seth and the sons of Cain. Was this what Zorah meant? It was hard for Noah to understand, since he had so little knowledge of life outside his own small village. His visit to Lomeen's clan, however, had awakened him to a world that was not as peaceful as the home he had always known.

It was obvious to him that Zorah loved the Ancient One in a way he could not comprehend. Breaking the silence, Noah asked, "How can you love someone you can't see?"

"It is difficult, Noah . . . but possible. If we could see the Ancient One, He would be no more than we are. But He is not a man. He does not have our weaknesses. No, He is the one who helps us in our weaknesses."

Noah struggled with these concepts, and finally he saw a troubled light in the old man's eyes. "What is it? Is something wrong, Zorah?"

"I think so . . . and it concerns you."

Fear grabbed at Noah's insides. "What is it?" he demanded. "Tell me."

"I do not know. Sometimes I can see things clearly that have not yet happened, and then when they do happen, I realize that the Ancient One showed them to me."

"Do you see something about me?"

"I see only darkness in your way, a hard and difficult path ahead—but I do not know what this darkness is."

Noah hesitated, then whispered, "Does it have anything to do with a lion?"

"A lion? I have not seen any lion." Zorah's eyes fastened on the young man. "Why do you ask?"

"I dream about a lion over and over again, Zorah."

"You dream of a wild animal? Does he attack you?"

"No. He just looks at me, and I look back at him. But he could destroy me. He is bigger than any lion you ever saw, and his eyes seem to devour me!"

Zorah sighed. "I do not know the meaning of that. But you must think about it. It must mean something—so be very careful. There are powers that would destroy you. I know somehow, my son, that the Ancient One has a work for you, but I cannot see what it is."

"I'm going to visit my brother tomorrow," Noah said. "I must go home and get ready."

As the two arose, Noah realized he felt differently about Zorah than he ever had before. For the first time he had seen a gentleness in the old man, though Zorah had tried not to let it show. "Thanks for talking to me," Noah said awkwardly.

Zorah nodded, then turned and moved away without another word. Noah watched him go, then headed toward his hut. He was troubled by the meeting and by the old man's last words. *What could he mean about a darkness ahead? I don't need anything like that.* He tried to shake the thoughts out of his head, but he knew they would persist, for Zorah's words had a way of staying with him.

It was close to sunset the following day when Noah picked up his pace along the way to the village of Tirzah's clan. He had made the journey in good time and now was close to where Jodak and Tirzah were staying. A warm sense of pleasure grew in him at the thought of seeing the couple again. He had managed to put Zorah's words out of his mind as much as possible, and now, as he came within sight of the village, he broke into a trot.

He had not gone far, however, when he heard the sound of wailing and crying, and looking up, he saw people running. He recognized one old man from a previous visit he had made to the village with Jodak and Tirzah when he was a boy. The man's name was Ahiza. Noah remembered that he was a skilled flint maker, and he had enjoyed talking to him.

Now Noah cried out, "Ahiza, what's wrong? Where's everybody going?"

Bent with age and quite feeble, Ahiza was moving with all the force he could muster. Noah was shocked to see agonizing fear etched on the old man's face.

"What's wrong?" Noah repeated. "What is it?"

"Run, boy!" Ahiza hollered as he passed Noah. "It's the Nephilim—the giants!"

"The Nephilim? Where?" Noah cried.

"There—back in the village! They're killing our people! Get away while you can!"

Noah was almost knocked to the ground by the fleeing villagers. Old men like Ahiza made their way painfully, while young men bounded past. Women carried babies and tried to help the older ones who could barely walk.

Noah almost turned and ran away himself, but then he thought of his sister-in-law and cried out her name as he bolted forward. "Tirzah—Tirzah!"

Swiftly he ran toward the village, and as he reached the collection of simple dwellings, he saw a terrible sight. Villagers were sprawled on the ground, scarlet blood lacing their bodies. Scattered among the dead were five or six men, bigger than any Noah had ever seen. They were truly giants, and Noah felt the icy hand of fear. He had his spear in his hand, but he knew it would be useless against such powerful men. He turned to flee, but as he did so, he caught a sight that stopped him dead in his tracks.

There in front of a small reed hut stood his brother Jodak. He had a staff in his hand, but it looked like a straw against the huge club being brandished by the giant who stood laughing down at him. The Nephilim was grasping Tirzah by the arm. She cried and struggled to get free, but she was like a child in the giant's embrace.

Noah saw Jodak start forward, but he heard the giant say, "Get away, little man! I'll take your woman, and I'll kill you if you try to stop me!"

Noah knew his brother would try to rescue his wife no matter what. Sure enough, Jodak raised his staff and struck the giant, but the big man took the blow on his shoulder as if he'd been struck by a feather. Then the Nephilim raised his own massive club, and as Noah ran forward, he saw an enormous blade of black flint embedded in it. And then he remembered his dream. It was exact in every detail—the huge, hairy man with the leather garment raising a club, an evil, leering expression on his face!

"Jodak!" Noah screamed and dashed onward, holding his spear, but the giant's club was already coming down. Jodak tried to dodge, but it caught him squarely on the head. Noah knew he would never forget the sickening sound as the club crushed Jodak's skull.

"Jodak!" Noah screamed again. He lunged toward the giant, crying out in rage.

The Nephilim turned to him, his eyes narrowed. The ragged scar on his cheek twitched as he bellowed, "Stay away, boy!"

"I'll kill you!" Noah raged, tears of anger and grief flooding his eyes. Grasping his spear, he ran straight at the giant. He ignored Tirzah's frantic cries for him to run away. Instead he drew back his spear and drove it straight toward the giant's chest.

With the ease of a practiced warrior, the giant simply parried the thrust with his club, then raised his weapon again and laughed. "Get away, you little gnat! I am Mak! I have the woman, and I will keep her!"

Noah grabbed his spear and aimed it again. "Let her go!" he cried. "Let her go!"

And then he clearly saw Tirzah's face twisted with grief and pain, the giant's fingers digging into her arm. He focused on the cruel visage of the giant as he lunged forward again. This time Mak simply turned to one side, lifted his club, and brought it down on Noah.

The world exploded in a fireball of yellow light, and all sound ceased.

CHAPTER 7

Methuselah sat outside Lamech's hut, leaning against the reed wall. The warm sunshine fell full upon his face, heightening the crisscross network of wrinkles. His frail hands lay folded in his lap, his eyes closed. He had been sitting all morning without changing position, carrying on a private conversation with the Ancient One. From time to time he became aware of the voices of the children who were playing with a kid in a small field, the bleating cries of the baby animal mingling with the children's laughter. The singing of the women as they worked added to the harmony of the day, and once again the old man's lips moved faintly as he spoke to the Ancient One.

Lamech appeared from around the corner of the hut, attempting to lead a wild donkey that insisted on bracing its feet on the rocky ground and refused to budge. The stubborn beast was only persuaded to continue by a sharp rap on his nose with Lamech's fist. The donkey uttered a series of short shrill brays, then plodded on for another twenty paces before repeating the procedure.

Stopping in front of the hut, Lamech held the rawhide strap that was tied around the recalcitrant animal's neck and grunted to one of the young boys nearby, "Here, Javen, take this fool beast—and make sure he doesn't run away again." He did not wait to see the boy slip onto the back of the donkey but stepped right over to his father. He stood there staring down, amazed, as always, at how many years the old man had lived on the earth. His father's memory reached back to those dim times that were recorded only in songs and legends passed down from father to son. Watching Methuselah, Lamech felt uneasy, wondering how much longer his father's days could continue.

Squatting down beside the old man, he wrapped his arms under his knees and sat patiently waiting. Time meant little to Lamech, as it meant little to most people. If a thing was not done today, it would be done tomorrow. If not tomorrow, some other time. Time was a river that one drifted upon, and now as the sun moved across the slate blue heavens, Lamech sat resting his weary muscles.

A movement from Methuselah drew the younger man's eyes, and he watched as the old eyes opened and turned slowly to fix themselves on him. Waiting until his father recovered and came fully awake, Lamech said quietly, "I don't understand why Zorah has been hanging around Noah so much. What do you make of it, Father?"

Methuselah scratched his stomach and turned his head away. He gazed at a group of sparrows tumbling in the dust, fighting over a few morsels of food. After a moment he said, "I never understand much that Zorah does."

"Well, I don't like it."

"What don't you like about it, son?"

"You know how those seers are. They're just not like everybody else."

"No, they're not, but we need them all the same."

Lamech made a sour expression and slapped at a fly that lit on his cheek. He examined the results with satisfaction, then wiped his hand on his leather garment. "Ever since Noah got his head caved in by that Nephilim, Zorah's been hanging around here."

Methuselah cleared his throat, hocked, and spat in the dirt. "It's a good thing he did. Noah would have died if it hadn't been for Zorah's care."

Lamech could not reply, for the truth of his father's statement was evident. When Noah had not returned to their village in five days as he had promised, Lamech had sent two of his servants to find out why. They had come back to Lamech with the terrible news about Jadok and Tirzah, and carrying the stricken young man, who had been more dead than alive. An old woman of the village had kept him from death—but just barely. The servants had tended to Noah's wounds, but his head had been split wide open, and he was so drained of blood, no one thought he would live. The old seer had stayed constantly by his side. He had fed him as one would feed a bird, a mere morsel at a time, and put water down his throat by squeezing drops of it from a rag.

"I'm grateful for Zorah's care of Noah," Lamech said finally, "but the boy's well enough now, and the old man's still hanging around."

"What are you afraid of, son?" Methuselah asked.

"I don't know. I think he's put a curse on Noah. Have you noticed how different the boy is?"

"I think anybody that gets as close to death as Noah did would be different. It changes a man to come to that invisible line separating life from death—to step over it and then pull your foot back! I've never been convinced that Noah wasn't actually dead for a time."

Lamech stared at his father in disbelief. "Are you saying that Zorah can bring people back to life?"

"No, I don't think *he* can, but the Ancient One can—any time He chooses."

This sort of talk always bothered Lamech. He believed in the Ancient One—more or less—but not with the absolute, rock-solid faith of his father, Methuselah. It was enough for Lamech to take care of his family and see that his people survived. He had done this for many years now, and at times he had been prone to express a cynical spirit toward the Ancient One. He did not do so in his father's presence, however, for he still remembered the one time he had permitted himself this freedom, and Methuselah had almost peeled his hide from his bones.

"Yes, Noah has changed," Methuselah went on. "But it wasn't Zorah that changed him. Losing his brother and his sister-in-law was a worse blow than the one he got on the head."

Lamech's face clouded with anger at the memory of his tragic loss. "I wish I'd been there. I would have given those Nephilim something to think about!"

Methuselah turned his head and studied his son. He knew him well enough to understand that Lamech often overestimated his capabilities. He said mildly, "I don't think you would have made much headway against them."

Insulted, Lamech jumped to his feet. "Well, I don't like it! Noah was always a dreamer, but now he moons around like a sick calf. He's got to come to his senses!"

Methuselah did not answer, and when Lamech stalked away, he shook his head. *You'll never understand Noah, my son, because there's something in him that isn't in other men.* Having settled this, he got to his feet painfully, arched his aching back, and hobbled off to see if the fig tree had any juicy figs within reach.

At the very moment that Methuselah and Lamech were talking,

Noah had gone back to his grape arbor to work, but he was taking little pleasure in it. For a long time he trimmed and watered, and yet the joy he'd once known was no longer there.

Perhaps it was because Zorah was watching him, seated quietly on a rock and saying nothing. When the old man had come and sat down, Noah had expected him to begin a conversation. But Zorah had said nothing, and Noah determined he would not be the one to break the silence. He had trimmed and watered three rows without a word being spoken, and finally he could stand it no longer. He turned and stalked over, stiff-legged, lines of anger creasing his craggy features, until he stood over the seer. His voice was sharp and rough with the rage that had resided in him ever since Jodak had been killed and Tirzah carried off by the Nephilim. Angrily he kicked at a stone, hurting his toe, which made him even more sullen.

"Why do you watch me this way?" he demanded. "Don't you have anything else to do with yourself?"

Zorah did not address his question but said mildly, "You are angry, my son."

"Well, it doesn't take a seer to know that!"

"No, it doesn't. You've been angry for weeks now. I've been waiting for you to get over it, but I'm not sure you ever will."

"I don't *want* to get over it," Noah said, sticking out his lower lip in a petulant attitude. It was a holdover from his childhood, an expression he still used whenever he was irritated or annoyed. The rage within him was like the anger of a hurt child. Angrily he snapped, "Why didn't the Strong One help me when I was fighting Mak? You've always said He is good! There is nothing good about the Nephilim. They killed my brother, and they—they stole Tirzah!"

Even as he forced himself to speak this truth, Noah felt a weakness creeping over him. After the blow to his head, he had remained unconscious for days, and when he had come to and gotten well enough to understand, the first question he asked concerned Tirzah. He was told merely that Mak, the Nephilim, had taken her away. No one knew any more than that.

"Better Tirzah had been killed than to be a slave to that monster!" he cried bitterly. "Where was the Ancient One when all this was happening? Was He taking a nap? Couldn't be bothered to be disturbed? Why do we pray to Him—thank Him for everything and ask for His help—

if when we need Him the most, He simply disappears? Can you answer me that, Zorah?"

Zorah sat quietly listening, enduring the outburst. It was clearly Noah's pain and anger that were speaking, not the tender, sensitive young man he knew so well. He waited until Noah had exhausted himself, finally crying out in his agony, "I hate him—I hate the Ancient One!"

"No you don't," Zorah said calmly. "No one knows why the Ancient One does things—or why He doesn't do them. If He were a man, perhaps we could find out why He does this or doesn't do something else. But He is not a man, and we are. He is the Ancient One."

Noah glared at the seer. "I don't think He even exists."

Zorah shook his head, a look of pity in his old eyes. "Yes you do. But you're going to be different from other people, Noah."

The young man momentarily forgot his anger. He leaned closer and stared into Zorah's face. "What do you mean I'm going to 'be different'?"

"You're going to be like your great-grandfather Enoch."

All his life Noah had heard about Enoch, what a great and good man he was, and how he walked with the Ancient One. He had been so good that he did not die as other men do but was simply taken out of this life directly into the home of the Ancient One.

Noah was utterly shocked that Zorah would dare compare him to Enoch, and he could not answer for a moment. Finally he shook his head. "I'm not like him."

"Ah, you're thinking about your trip to Jaalam's village and the things you did there that were wrong."

"Well, I did them, and that proves I'm not a good man like Enoch."

"It proves nothing of the sort. You think he was never sixteen years old? Do you think he never did anything wrong?"

"Well, nobody talks about that. Even you have never told me anything bad he did."

"It's not my place to say things like that. He was the favorite of the Ancient One, Noah, and that's all I need to know."

Noah bowed his head, a rebellious curve in his neck and a sullenness around his mouth. "I don't want to be different! I just want to *see* Him. If He's really God, then let Him appear to me!"

"That's the remark of a very young man—of a child, really."

"Well, don't you want to see Him, Zorah?"

"No, I don't. Because if I could see Him, I wouldn't serve Him."

This puzzled Noah greatly. He shook his head and demanded,

"What do you mean if you could see Him, you wouldn't serve Him? If you could see Him, you would know He was there!"

"But, Noah, I *do* know He's there. Not because I can see Him with my eyes, but because He speaks to my spirit."

"That could be your imagination."

"It could be, but it isn't." Zorah knew that as long as Noah was in this mood, there was little use in talking to him, so he said no more.

Finally it was Noah who spoke again. "Well, have you had any more visions about me—or that darkness I'm supposed to be going through? Or was that it—getting my head split open by Mak and losing my brother and sister-in-law?"

"That wasn't what I saw, Noah. There is more that you must face. The fact that you're still alive is proof that the Ancient One isn't finished with you yet."

"What's that supposed to mean?"

"How did you survive? The giant hit you in the head with his club with that huge flint in it, but he hit you with the flat of it. Why didn't he turn the sharp edge down? Your head would have been split in two like a melon."

Noah had wondered the same thing himself. Now he shook his head stubbornly. "I don't know anything about that. I just know that I want to be left alone." He turned and stalked away, half hoping that Zorah would call him back. But there was no answering voice, and the young man, filled with his own miseries and sense of tragic loss, marched away from the one person on earth who really understood him.

Noah did not dream again of the lion, but in one sense he did not need to. The dreams he'd had in the past were so clear he relived them many times—especially the last one. Often during a bright, sunshiny day, the whole scene would flash before him. At other times he would awaken at night and the lion would appear, staring at him with those strange golden eyes.

As the days went by, Noah struggled to stifle these memories. He was engaged in something more earthly than dreams. As his strength gradually returned, he discovered two things. First, he was beginning to grow a beard. He received an inordinate amount of teasing from Kul and Boz and the others, but that did not bother him. The beard was a sign that the boy was being left behind and a man was emerging.

The other thing that happened in his life was that a deep-seated hatred of Mak had grown in him until it filled every part of his body and mind. Day and night he would think of the giant killing his brother and would remember Tirzah's face as she fought against the strength of the giant's hand.

As soon as he was able, he went to Nophat and said, "I want to be the best hunter in the tribe."

"You mean next to me," Nophat said, grinning.

"No, I mean the best."

Nophat was astonished at the young man's intensity. He stared at him carefully, then said slowly, "I can guess why you want this. You want to kill Mak."

Noah locked eyes with Nophat and said, "Never mind my reasons. Will you teach me how to fight?"

Nophat felt nervous. "Why do you not ask your father?"

"Because you're the best fighter we have, not him. He's the chief, but you have killed men, haven't you?"

"Yes, but I'm not proud of it," Nophat said quietly. "It's not something to brag about."

"Will you teach me?"

"If your father says it is good, then I will teach you."

Lamech was quick to grant Noah's request. His mother begged her husband to withhold his permission, but Lamech simply said, "A man has to be able to fight, Dezia. That's the kind of world we live in."

And so the lessons started, and Noah proved an apt pupil. As time passed, his beard grew out with a rich reddish tinge just like his hair, his shoulders broadened, and the muscles grew in his arms, legs, and abdomen. He spent all of his days under the tutelage of Nophat, and soon the entire clan was aware that the youthful son of Lamech had it in his heart to hunt down and kill Mak, the Nephilim.

Senzi, always pessimistic, spoke of this to Kul. "That friend of yours is going to get himself killed trying to fight a Nephilim."

"I'm not so sure about that," Kul said. "Maybe he's got it in him to succeed." Kul had gone back to Jaalam's village for an extended stay, and on his return he had been shocked at how much Noah had filled out. "He's a strong fellow now," Kul told his friend.

"Strength is not enough," Senzi insisted. "The Nephilim are not even human. They're beasts. No mere man has ever defeated one."

"How do you know that, Senzi? Perhaps men have killed a hundred of them. How would we know?"

"Have you ever heard of it?"

"Well, no, but—"

"Then it hasn't happened. I've told Lamech he'd better advise his son to stay away from giants. They're bad for a man's health."

Methuselah and Zorah walked slowly along the dusty path. They were on their way to the river, where the two had formed a habit of spending the long, cool afternoons fishing. Neither man spoke for a time, but Zorah saw that Methuselah was discouraged. "Is something wrong, my friend?"

"I'm worried about Noah."

"So am I, but things must happen. That is the way of life. You know that, having seen so much more of life than any of us."

"Yes, I have seen many years. How many suns have I seen come up and go down again?" Methuselah muttered. "How many babies have I seen born with great hopes placed in them and who are now dead? Life is hard. But about Noah . . . I'm worried."

Zorah did not speak until they had gone another ten paces, then said, "The Ancient One has told me that He has a task for Noah."

"I thought as much. Noah reminds me so much of my father, Enoch. I told him that. But he's changing."

"Yes, he has changed—and not for the better, I fear. You must talk to him, Methuselah. He won't listen to me, but he loves you. You must change what he is about to become."

"I know," Methuselah said softly. He held on to his staff, took three more steps, then stopped. "He wants to kill Mak."

"Yes, I know. And if he does, the Strong One will not be able to use him. He will fall into the trap that ensnares most men. He will become a man of blood. That must not happen."

In Methuselah's heart he sensed a cry that came from far off. It was not a human cry, nor that of an animal, yet he had heard it before many times in his long life—always just before trouble struck. Now he said to Zorah, "You are the seer, my friend, but I feel something terrible will happen to Noah."

"That is why you must talk to him."

"I will try," Methuselah agreed with a sigh. "But I do not think he will listen."

Noah returned from practicing with his spear. He had learned all he could from Nophat, for he had surpassed his master. He could throw the spear farther than any man in the clan and sink it so deep into the target that it required a strong man to pull it loose. His mind was filled with thoughts of killing Mak as he walked along the path, and he would have passed right by his grandfather had Methuselah not called out, "Noah, come and talk with me."

Noah turned at once from the path and went to sit beside his grandfather, who was resting under the shade of a large tree. Noah sank down to the ground but held on to his spear, as had become his custom lately. "What is it, Grandfather?"

Methuselah studied the bronzed young man beside him. *He's so big and is going to get bigger,* Methuselah thought. Even though his grandson was not handsome, there was some force that made him attractive both to men and women. The determined chin, the prominent nose, the wide mouth, all seemed to be made for facing trials. They were the features of a strong man, a leader. The warm brown eyes appeared to have grown darker of late and now were half hooded in an almost secretive manner.

Methuselah took a breath and said without emotion, "Noah, you must not kill Mak."

Astonishment swept over Noah's face. "Why not?" he demanded. "He killed my brother and carried away my sister-in-law."

"I cannot tell you why."

"But he is evil! Isn't it right, Grandfather, to resist evil?"

Methuselah was trapped. If he said no, that would be to deny everything he had spoken about to this young man. But if he said yes, Noah would say, "Then that is what I'm going to do." Methuselah sat there silently and finally heaved a sigh. "I believe that the Strong One himself will bring judgment." He saw the resistance on Noah's face. "I remember my father, Enoch, used to tell me that one day the Strong One will come to this earth and will right all wrong. He will rid the earth of all evil, and only that which is good and just will remain."

"Did he say when He planned to do this?" Noah asked.

"No, and that was hundreds of years ago. But my father was an honorable man. He walked with the Strong One. He did not lie, Noah. Even in those days the Nephilim were in the land, and there were battles. But my father always said that to shed blood was not the mark of a man.

The true mark of a man is to *keep* from shedding blood."

Noah sat quietly. He had been pulled in so many directions that he was exhausted in his spirit. "Tell me more about Enoch, Grandfather. I want to know."

Methuselah examined his grandson. For the first time he had a ray of hope that Noah could be redirected down a nobler path. He knew that deep down this young man was not a killer. Noah was understandably bitter over his tragic loss, which had very nearly destroyed him. Losing the two he loved so deeply had been far worse for him than the blow on the head from Mak.

Methuselah spoke, carefully weighing his words. "It is always hard to do the right thing, Noah, and it is always easy to do the wrong thing. Sometimes we cannot even tell the difference, but the Strong One always knows."

"But how am I to know?" Noah asked. "Almost everyone says it's good to kill your enemies."

"I know. Over the years I have learned one thing—when men kill, they become killers. I believe that somehow, if we will believe in the Strong One, He will keep our hearts pure. Even though evil surrounds us, we can walk through it, and our hearts will not be touched. For it is the heart, grandson, that is important." He leaned over and put his hand on Noah's chest, and Noah looked down and saw how frail the ancient hand was. Yet there was a strength in this man he could not explain! Noah had always seen it, and now he felt it flowing through him. Even as he sat there, he understood the truth of what his grandfather was saying.

"We will talk of this more, Grandfather," Noah said, a new gentleness in his voice.

"Yes we will, Noah. Zorah knows the Strong One like no other man on earth, and he has told you, has he not, that the Ancient One has a special purpose for you?"

"He has said so, but I do not see how that can be."

"None of us understands the ways of the Ancient One, but if you will wait patiently, you will find the way."

Noah felt very peculiar at that moment. A strong emotion he could not identify ran through him, and for one instant he saw in his mind the lion staring at him again. In that brief vision something inside Noah seemed to turn over. He knew that the revenge he had been preparing for could not be his way. Zorah and Methuselah had convinced him otherwise, and as he saw the image of the lion, he whispered to the Ancient One, "I do not know what you want with me, but whatever it is, I will do it."

PART TWO

CHAPTER 8

The bronze chisel hissed as the tall man ran it across the edge of the wooden beam. A wisp of wood curled up, then drifted to a small mound of shavings on the ground. The woodworker moved with an easy regularity, the long, ropy muscles in his back prominent, the veins in his biceps standing out like small cords. Again and again he chiseled shavings so fine that they lifted on the breeze and twisted lazily to the earth. The pungent acacia wood tickled his nostrils, and his wide mouth curled upward in a satisfied smile. He straightened, ran his palm over the smooth timber, and nodded.

As Noah turned and hung the chisel on a peg on the back wall of his lean-to workshop, the sun freed itself from behind a cloud, spilling sunshine over a portion of his work area. Noah squinted at the sudden bright light, which highlighted the reddish glints in his brown hair and deepened the creases on either side of his mouth.

The mature man at his workbench bore little resemblance to the stripling who had been nearly killed by the giant Mak. Noah was several inches taller now, with broader shoulders and heavy thighs. He wore only a loincloth, and sweat ran down his bronzed chest. His stomach muscles knotted into sinewy squares as hard as the beam he was forming. His countenance was partially hidden by a heavy beard, but his nose still protruded prominently, and he still bore the same warm brown eyes. Small wrinkles at the corner of each eye hinted at the many years that had transpired since his encounter with Mak.

Brushing wood shavings from his chest, Noah stepped off the platform, crowded with both finished pieces and rough timbers ready to be molded by his skillful hands. He glanced at the workshop where he spent most of his waking hours, his mind busy with the projects that lay before him. Stooping down, he lifted a heavy timber, ten cubits long, as easily as if it were made of bundled reeds. His years as a carpenter had given him phenomenal strength. He did not hunt or farm much anymore, for he could easily trade the products of his craft for food.

The breeze picked up, ruffling his hair, and he absently brushed the locks away from his high forehead. He thought back on why he had become a carpenter. After Jodak's death and Tirzah's kidnapping by the Nephilim, he had nearly gone crazy and had found hard work the only consolation for his grief. An old woodworker named Phelim had taken him in hand, teaching Noah everything he knew. The young man had thrown himself into learning how to handle and shape wood. At first it worked like strong drink, numbing his mind so that he thought of nothing else but the next job. It helped him bury his grief and move on with his life. As Noah surpassed his teacher in the art of carpentry and established a thriving business of his own, members of his clan as well as many from distant towns sought out his skills as a builder.

Noah's thoughts were interrupted by a cheerful voice calling out his name. He turned to see Boz and smiled broadly at the man who had been a good friend from his youth. Boz too had become prosperous, but unlike Noah, he now spent the fruit of his labor on sumptuous living. He was as big around as some of the trees Noah felled with his ax, his ample body draped with a maroon garment streaked with bright blue. Noah shook his head at his friend's extravagance. *Why, it used to be a rawhide apron was good enough for Boz,* Noah thought. *Now he has to wear the finest cloth.* The development of weaving had changed the apparel habits of all the clan. Instead of deerskins and rough hides, the wealthier people now wore soft garments spun from cotton or flax. Noah himself cared little for fancy dress and was as likely to wear an old leather girdle around his waist as anything else.

"Do you work all the time, Noah?" Boz quipped, punching his friend in the arm.

Noah grinned. "Do you work *any* of the time, Boz?"

Boz laughed, and the action shook his huge belly and multiple chins. Noah silently wondered how the once strong, vibrant Boz had disappeared inside that heap of flesh. Aloud, he asked, "What are you up to, Boz?"

"I've got a job for you."

"I don't need any more jobs."

"Ah," Boz said, nodding and glancing around at the numerous projects in progress. "But this one is for a *very* rich man, a friend of mine named Yaphet who lives upriver. We've done business together, and he's been asking me about you. Set your price as high as you please. He can afford it."

Noah shrugged. "And what would I do with the money?"

"Spend it on yourself, man! Look at that old rag of a loincloth you're wearing. Why, the lowliest beggar in the clan dresses better than you do!"

Accustomed to Boz's jabs, Noah ignored the comment. "How's your wife, Boz?"

"Which one?" Boz smirked.

"Any of them. How many do you have now?"

"Enough to drive me crazy. Who bothers to count? You know, Noah, sometimes I envy you." Boz grew serious and gnawed on his lower lip. "Those women make my life miserable! They're all so jealous and fight over me like dogs over a scrap of meat."

Noah shook his head. "Well, they were your choice. Nobody made you marry all those women."

"I know. I was a fool." Envy crept across Boz's round face. "You live alone with that crazy old seer and one old servant woman. You do what you please. I wish I could live like that."

"No you don't!" Noah laughed. "You're too soft to live like me. You couldn't stand to work anymore."

Boz sighed. "You're probably right, my friend." Then his eyes lit up, and he said, "Do you remember the old days, Noah? I think of them a lot. I remember the day we went out on your first hunt. How many years ago was that?"

"Too many to count," Noah said with sadness in his eyes.

Boz caught the look and asked, "Are you still grieving over your brother Jodak?"

"I guess I always will."

"How can you say that, after so long? He's gone, Noah, and nothing can bring him back. There's no point hanging on to such things."

Noah said nothing.

At his friend's silence, Boz continued, "Did you ever hear what happened to his wife, Tirzah?"

"No."

"You almost went crazy there for a while. I remember you were going to become a great warrior and kill Mak and find your sister-in-law."

"Those days are over, Boz."

"I hear rumors about Mak once in a while. He's still around, I understand—raiding and pillaging every chance he gets. Just as mean as ever."

Noah turned to leave. "I've got to get on home, Boz."

Not dissuaded, Boz followed Noah and asked, "How's the old man?"

"Zorah's doing very well," Noah said as they walked down the road toward his home. "He's surprised to still be around on this earth, though. He never expected to live this long."

"Why don't you get rid of that ugly old servant woman and get yourself a plump young thing?" Boz dug his elbow into Noah's muscular side and winked. "She'd be good for things besides cooking, eh?"

Noah shrugged. "We get along very well with Ofra."

"But she's so ugly . . . and old! I've never understood why you took her in."

Indeed, few people understood Noah. Being the son of a chief, he could have done anything he pleased. Over the years dozens of women with marriageable daughters had tried to maneuver Noah into matrimony, but he was not easily impressed and had ignored them all. The old woman Ofra had been widowed and left to face her husband's debtors alone. They were about to sell her into slavery when Noah had intervened, paid the slave price, and taken her into his home. No one would have been shocked if the muscular carpenter had acquired an attractive young woman as a servant, but Ofra? Why, she could never have been pretty, even when young, and now she was homely indeed. Noah had never felt the need to explain his reasoning to anyone; he had simply felt sorry for the old woman and out of compassion had made a place for her in his home. In gratitude for rescuing her, she gladly cooked for Noah, while old Zorah kept the house clean.

Noah only half listened as Boz explained how he would make a great deal of money from Yaphet. His mind was on other matters. Suddenly he heard Boz asking an unrelated question. "Why haven't you ever taken a mate, Noah?"

"Huh?" Noah's mind snapped back to their conversation. "Oh, I don't know, Boz. Who can say about such things?"

Boz's memory was as sharp as a thorn, and he asked, "Have you ever thought about Lomeen?"

The name jarred on Noah's ears, and he half missed a step. He turned to stare down at Boz and shook his head without answering. Even after the passing of so many years, he had not forgotten the woman of his youthful desires.

Boz was a shrewd man, full of earthy wisdom, and he did not miss the look of pain in his friend's eyes. "Yes, Lomeen—she's the woman you've always wanted, isn't she? Is that why you never wanted to marry?"

Noah quickened his steps, and his long legs set a pace that Boz could not keep up with. The heavyset man stood and watched Noah go his way, almost breaking into a run as he disappeared into the crowded marketplace. Boz shook his head. *I always thought Noah had sense when he was young, but now he's as crazy as that old prophet he lives with. Imagine hanging on to a first love like that! The silly man's never gotten over her, and I don't think he ever will. . . .*

Noah made his way through the dirt streets of his hometown, thinking back on his growing-up years. The simple village of reed huts where he had been born had since grown into a thriving settlement, well-known as a center for trade and commerce. Noah looked around at the merchants vending their goods from stalls, women haggling over prices in high-pitched voices, children running everywhere, screaming and laughing.

As the population of his town had increased, so had his own family grown. After the death of Jodak, Dezia's womb had opened again, so Noah's father, Lamech, now had many children and grandchildren and great-grandchildren. Some had remained here in their hometown, and others had scattered, marrying into distant clans. Noah felt a pang of regret, for he missed the small village he had grown up in, where he had once known everyone and all had known him. Now he did not even recognize all of his own brothers and sisters, nieces and nephews. The town hummed like a beehive, full of activity, and as he often did, he felt a growing urge to leave, to flee to the hills and live once more off the land.

He reached the site of his boyhood home, though no one but Noah would have remembered the little reed hut that used to leak like a sieve whenever it rained. In its place stood a fine house of stout timber, built by Noah himself. It had been his first big job, and he remembered with a smile how everyone had thought he was crazy. *Building houses of wood! Imagine that!* Despite their comments, he had long ago demonstrated how comfortable a wooden house could be, and since then, the idea had caught on until most of the townspeople lived in wooden houses.

Entering the large house Noah had built for his parents, he heard children's voices, and before he knew it, he was engulfed by a noisy tribe of youngsters. He bent over and picked up two of them, one in each arm, a black-eyed girl and a brown-eyed boy. He could never remember all their names, but he smiled at them and listened as they prated and pulled at his beard and hair.

"You leave your uncle alone," said Noah's mother as she walked into the room, wearing a light blue woven dress. She walked over to Noah and put her hand on his cheek. "Where have you been hiding?"

"Lots of work to do, Mother."

"You work too hard. Come sit down. I know you're tired."

Noah meekly obeyed, and as he crossed the large room that served as both a living area and dining room, he saw a young woman waiting to one side. "Hello, Nomi," he greeted her.

"Hello, Noah." Nomi smiled at him brightly. She was a tall, shapely girl, considered to be a great catch in the clan. Her father was a wealthy man, having acquired his riches through his metalwork business. Nomi had had many offers of marriage but had refused them all. "I'll get you something to drink," she said.

"Thank you. That would be good." Noah sat down, and his mother shooed the children off, sitting down herself.

"How do you ever tell them apart?" Noah asked her. "How many children do you have now, Mother—and great-grandchildren and great-great-grandchildren?"

Dezia laughed at his question. She did indeed have many children. She could barely keep track of them herself! Being a strong woman, she had continued to bear children over the years, welcoming grandchildren and great-grandchildren into the world along with her own babies. She looked at Noah with her rich brown eyes, exactly the same color as his. Her high cheekbones gave her a touch of the beauty she'd had as a young woman. Despite her gray hair and aging body, she was still healthy and alert.

Dezia eyed the servant girl as she brought them drinks, and after Nomi had left, Dezia turned to her son. "Don't you think Nomi is attractive?"

"Yes, she is," Noah said absently.

"She likes you, I think."

Noah lifted his head and laughed loudly. He reached over and grabbed his mother's hands in one of his. "You never stop trying, do you, Mother? Why don't you give up?"

"You're getting to be an old man, Noah. Don't you ever intend to marry?"

"Not until I find someone as smart and pretty as you are, Mother."

"Don't be a fool!" she said sharply, though her eyes laughed at him. She grew more serious then and freed her hand. She stroked his arm, always pleased at the hard muscles. Knowing that he was her son and the strongest man in the entire clan was a matter of pride to her. "You must get lonely, Noah, without a woman."

"I've got Ofra."

"Oh, that old woman! I'm talking about a *young* woman. One to warm your bed and give you sons and me grandsons."

"You've got an army of grandchildren now. What would a few more mean?"

Dezia shook her head. "But they would be *your* sons, and oh, how I've longed for your sons to come. I don't know why that is, Noah. I love my grandchildren—but yours would be very special to me. Can't you even think of taking a wife? Nomi would make a fine one."

Noah knew better than to argue with his mother, so he remained silent and listened to her admonitions. When Nomi came back in, he had to admit that his mother was right about her. She was a very attractive young woman—and to his surprise, she seemed to be interested in him. What she saw in an old man like him, he could not imagine. There was a sensuous air about her, and as she served him, he was aware that more than once she let her hand touch him in a way that was apparently not accidental. Now his eyes met hers, and something in her expression—was it an invitation?—made him nervous. Rising quickly, he made an excuse to leave, then followed his mother to the door and outside.

"Must you go so soon, Noah? Why don't you stay and eat with us tonight?" Dezia pleaded.

"Some other night, Mother."

Dezia watched her tall son as he made his way down the street, noting the curious looks people gave him as he passed. With a pang she realized that he was the odd man in the clan, the one who had never married and always kept to himself, living with two very old people. Her heart went out to him, and she whispered softly, "Oh, Noah, will it always be like this? Won't you *ever* have anyone?"

As Noah approached his own house, he felt a sense of satisfaction. It was not a large place, but he had put much care into building it. Whenever he arrived home after a day's work, he felt like a weary traveler reaching his destination.

"Ho, get down, boy!"

A monstrous silver-blue dog had come to greet him, rearing up on his hind legs and licking Noah in the face. The mongrel had one brown eye and one light blue one, which gave him an odd, comic expression.

"Get down, Blue!" Noah yelled at him. "You're as big as a horse!" He caressed the animal roughly, then shoved him out of the way and entered his house.

"It's about time you got home!" Ofra called out.

No one knew exactly how old Ofra was. In all likelihood she herself did not know. She was like an ancient tree with gnarled limbs. Her face was lined with a hundred wrinkles, but her eyes were as black as night and still as sharp as when she was a young girl. Noah had saved her from a life of slavery, and not once had she ever spoken her thanks. Rather, she had *shown* her gratitude in a life of constant and loving service. She was better than a dozen servants to Noah. She did not weary him with talk, but despite her lack of spoken communication, he knew she cared for him, for her eyes followed him wherever he went.

"I'm sorry I'm late, Ofra."

"You go sit down. Everything's getting cold."

Noah sat down at a smooth wooden table with benches. He ran his hand over the table, admiring the grain of the wood, and nodded to the old man who sat on the bench opposite him, watching Noah silently.

"Hello, Zorah. How's your day been?"

The old man shrugged. "Like every other day."

Noah laughed and said, "Aren't you going to ask me now how my day's gone?"

"Well, how has it gone?"

"Like every other day."

The two men smiled at each other. There was a startling contrast in the two. One tall, strong, muscular, and exuding life, the other small, withered, and marked by many, many years of exposure to weather and hardship. Zorah's mind was as sharp as ever, but physically he was failing. Noah never mentioned this and pretended not to notice his old friend's feebleness.

"How's that crazy invention of yours coming, Noah?"

"You mean the boat? It's almost finished."

"Fool idea! Whoever heard of a boat made out of wood?" Zorah snorted. "If a reed boat was good enough for your father and your grandfather, it ought to be good enough for you!"

"Well then, maybe we ought to go out and live in a cave, and you can sleep on rocks. If that was good enough for your grandfather, it ought to be good enough for you."

Zorah's eyes twinkled. He enjoyed these little clashes with Noah. The two had become like the right and left hands of a man. After so many years together, they knew each other's ways. The two had that special sort of relationship that made silence as comforting as conversation. They often went on long walks together down to the river, where they would sit for hours and say nothing, simply watching the graceful ibis tending their nests and the scaly crocodiles silently cruising up and down looking for prey. Often they would spend the whole day together, saying no more than half a dozen sentences.

On the other hand, there were times when the old man would overflow with conversation, talking for hours on end about the old days, about the days when those who served the Ancient One were numerous and the Nephilim were not powerful. Noah drank in all these tales, hungry for knowledge of the mysterious and wonderful God they worshiped. Today seemed to be one of the silent days when Noah simply waited for Zorah to speak.

Ofra brought in the food on a large wooden tray—delicious wild-rice cakes baked in the oven Noah had designed, fish cooked with the spices and herbs Noah loved, and grape juice from the vines he had planted. Noah ate noisily, listening to Ofra as she dispensed the latest news of the townspeople—the one topic that Ofra never tired of talking about. It never ceased to amaze Noah that one small head could contain so much knowledge about her neighbors, and he listened until the meal was over.

"That was good, Ofra," Noah grunted.

"You always say that no matter what it is," Ofra scolded. "Now, get out of here and let me clean up."

"Come along, Zorah. Let's go sit outside."

The two men stepped out onto the front stoop. The shadows were deepening now, and the earth was turning cool after the blistering hot day. Noah carefully sat down beside the old man, and as the sun settled behind the horizon, the two simply watched the townspeople going about their business.

Finally Zorah turned to face Noah. "Have you heard about your father's latest idiocy?"

"What is it now?"

"He's going to let our clanspeople have a choice."

"What do you mean? A choice of what?"

"A choice between following the Ancient One or Ur-Baal."

Noah's head snapped around, and his eyes flew open. "You don't mean that!"

"Don't I? Ask him." Zorah's anger caused his yellowish eyes to glow, and his lips twisted with disgust. "Your father is a weak man. It's your mother who's strong. You get all your strength from her. Now, *her* father—he was a man!"

"I don't believe it," Noah said. "Father wouldn't do such a thing."

"You ask him. He's not making any secret about it."

"I'll have to talk to him," Noah said. "We can't have that." Noah, troubled by Zorah's disclosure, did not speak for a long time. He knew that Zorah was right, that his father was a weak man—not physically, but in matters of judgment. There was a goodness in Lamech, but he seemed to lack the ability to see things as they were. Many years of guiding his people had made him an astute leader, but he had lost some of his integrity along the way and was now willing to make compromises.

The silence ran on between the two men as darkness continued to fall. Without warning, Zorah stood up and said, "I'm tired. I think I'll go to bed."

"Just a minute." Noah grasped the old man's thin arm. "I want to ask you something."

Zorah leaned back against the house and waited. When Noah did not speak right away, Zorah turned and stared at his friend. "What is it, Noah? You're troubled."

"How long have we lived together?"

"Too many years to count."

"All the years I've listened to you talk about the Ancient One, I've also been waiting for Him to speak to me as He does to you—but He never has." A tortured expression twisted Noah's face. "I need Him to make himself known to me, Zorah. I've waited long enough."

Zorah was silent for a time, and then he shook his head. "You cannot force the Strong One to do anything. He will accomplish His will when He is ready. Meanwhile, you must wait."

"I've waited long enough, Zorah. It seems like forever!"

"Then wait some more."

"I'm not sure I can do that."

"It's always hard to follow the Ancient One. He doesn't offer an easy path. I think He tests us."

"What do you mean by that?"

"I mean anyone would follow a god who is always good to him, who is always there. But the Ancient One wants men and women who will serve Him when they feel as dry as dust in their hearts, when they've cried out, yet the heavens are silent. Those who feel as alone as is possible for a human being to feel, but after all of that, still love God—they are the followers the Ancient One seeks."

The words depressed Noah. "Must I wait forever, then?"

"Perhaps." The old seer turned and put his hand on Noah's muscular shoulder. "Do you still have dreams as you had as a young man?"

"Sometimes they come. But I want to *walk* with Him as Enoch did."

"I'm not sure any man will ever walk that close to the Strong One again. There was something in Enoch that's not in most of us."

Noah shifted restlessly. "You remember when I was young? When Ur-Baal was worshiped by some of the clans, but not many? Now it seems *everyone* is running to his altars! Can't they see how evil he is?"

"Perhaps they can, but he offers them something visible. They can see him—or what they think is him anyway. People want to see the god they worship."

Noah sat listening as the old man spoke of the old days. Then, like a father to a son, Zorah urged Noah to be faithful and confront Lamech about his compromises.

Noah bowed his head. "I'll speak to Lamech, but I doubt if it'll do any good."

"You must try. All we can do is try."

Noah was tired and went to bed as soon as he went inside. He fell asleep at once, and the dream returned to him almost instantly, or so it seemed. He saw the lion again, as he had many times before, with its golden eyes, rough black mane, and powerful muscles. Noah stood in his dream, looking into those unearthly eyes, and cried out, "Why don't you speak? What do you want of me?"

And then the lion *did* speak . . . but when Noah awoke he could not remember what it said. In desperation he cried out, "Why do you torment me? What does this dream mean, O Ancient One?"

But there was no answer, and Noah lay back on his bed, threw his forearm over his eyes, and wept in frustration.

CHAPTER 9

Noah stared at his father, disgusted with the brute stubbornness of the old man. Lamech was just as disgusted with the argument Noah had brought to him, and now the two stared at each other like bitter enemies.

"You're not going to tell *me* what to do! I'm still the head of this clan!"

"No one's arguing about that, Father," Noah said, speaking as calmly as he could. "But all of us need counsel from time to time."

"I've *had* counsel! As a matter of fact, all of the leaders agree with what I want to do about Ur-Baal." A line appeared between Lamech's eyebrows, and his lips drew together like a knife-edge. "You don't know the first thing about how hard it is to be chief over a clan like this! The town has grown like mushrooms, and everybody wants something different. Sometimes I think they'll drive me crazy!"

"I know it's hard, but—"

"You don't know *anything*! You live with that crazy seer and an old woman, you piddle around building houses, cutting down trees—and you don't have a family. You don't know the first thing about what life is really about!"

Noah forced himself to remain silent for a moment. He rarely allowed his temper to escape, but now it threatened to boil over. Gritting his teeth, he said, "I've always tried to honor you as my father and as chief of the clan, but this thing that you're doing is wrong! Ask Mother. She'll tell you."

"Oh, so now you'd have a woman rule the clan, eh? That shows how much sense you've got!"

Noah sighed in frustration. "Don't you know what Ur-Baal is like,

Father? Have you ever been to one of their ceremonies? Don't you know they burn babies alive to honor that awful god?"

Lamech blinked, not able to meet Noah's hard gaze. "Yes, I know all about that," he muttered.

"And you're *still* willing to let our people worship this god?"

Lamech threw his hands apart in a gesture of futility. "I tell you, you don't know what the world's like! Ur-Baal is a strong god. Look around you if you don't think so."

"He's an *evil* god—if he's a god at all, which I doubt!"

"Well, then, why do so many people worship him?" Lamech challenged.

"Because they like to be free to lie together as they please!" Noah fumed. "They like to drink their evil potions and indulge in drunken orgies! They're willing to destroy themselves for the pleasures that Ur-Baal offers!"

Lamech shook his head stubbornly as Noah ranted about the evils of such worship. Then he threw up his hand in Noah's face. "That's enough! This conversation is over!" He rose abruptly and began to leave the room. When he reached the door he turned back, however, his eyes pleading for understanding. "Look, son, I know you honor the Strong One. So do I—believe it or not. I'm not suggesting we forsake Him. All I'm saying is that we can do both. Let those who want to worship Ur-Baal do so. And those who want to worship the Ancient One are free to do that. I can't tell a man which god to serve."

"Your father could! He knew better than to let people make their own decisions about something so important. They're like stupid animals at times—and you, as their leader, need to tell them what is best for them. If they choose not to listen to you, then so be it. But don't *encourage* their evil choices by approving them! You know Methuselah will never sanction this. What does he say about it?"

Anger and pain were mixed in Lamech's eyes. "He's an old man. His days of leading are over. The sooner you realize that the better."

Noah watched sadly as his father stalked out of the house. He was frustrated by his failure to convince his father to take a different path. But he also knew that rarely had anyone ever dissuaded Lamech from doing whatever he had made up his mind to do.

Noah then left his father's house, not even saying good-bye to his mother. He knew she was grieved, as was Methuselah, about Lamech's decision. But the three of them together would never change his mind.

Ur-Baal was what the people wanted, evil or not, so that was what they would have.

Noah made his way through the town to the river path. He spoke to no one on the way and was oblivious to the glances people were giving him. He had long ago ceased to care what people said of him—or so he convinced himself. Actually, it hurt him to be considered eccentric or even crazy, but he had chosen his way and now he would follow it.

When he reached the river, he sat for a long time watching the reed boats as they plied their way up and down. He turned to see Methuselah hobbling down the path and rose to smile at him. "Hello, Grandfather."

"Noah—how are you?" The old man sat down heavily and stared out at the river. "I overheard the conversation between you and Lamech."

"You were eavesdropping, then."

"My hearing is still good."

"Can't you do anything with him, Grandfather? He's dead wrong."

"No. He thinks I'm too old to have a wise thought in my head."

"But you've *got* to make him listen to reason!"

"I think he's past that, Noah. I grieve over my son, and I regret my failure as a father. I should have made a stronger man out of him."

Noah was not surprised by Methuselah's response. He had long known that his grandfather was ashamed of Lamech. Not sure how to respond, he sat silently, watching the boats.

Methuselah broke the silence. "Are you still working on that wooden boat?"

"Yes. It's almost ready."

"When are you planning to try it out?"

"Tomorrow," Noah said. "I'm going to take it upstream. Why don't you come with me?"

"Me, get in that thing? I don't think so," Methuselah said, shaking his head.

Noah laughed. "As far as we know, you're the oldest man who ever lived. If you drown, you'll give another man the chance to beat your record. Come along. I'd like your company."

Methuselah hesitated. "Where are you going upriver?"

"To Yaphet's village. Boz tells me the man wants me to build him a house. He's got plenty of money, so I'll charge him a high fee. Then I can buy you a new pair of sandals."

"Nothing wrong with these," Methuselah said indignantly, looking down at the worn leather sandals and nodding. "No need to get new sandals when the old ones are still good."

"All right. We'll buy you a jug of wine."

"Oh, so now you want to make your old grandfather drunk!"

"You have never been drunk in your life, and you know it. Come with me."

"All right, I will." Methuselah smiled, pleased at the invitation, but then he frowned. "Fool boat will probably drown us both! I've seen lots of changes in my time—and I've been against every last one of them!"

The next day it took all morning to get the heavy vessel from Noah's house to the river. Noah hired some strong men to help pull it along on logs. They could move it only a length before they'd have to stop and move the back logs to the front. The method worked well, but it was a long and tedious procedure.

The sun was high overhead by the time the boat was finally launched. Noah helped Methuselah take a place in the front, and Noah took the stern. When he was situated he called out, "Are you ready, Grandfather?"

"Let's get this bucket going," Methuselah yelled back. "It'll probably sink, but there's no sense in just sitting here."

Noah laughed. He felt good this day. The sun was hot, and white clouds tumbled across the sky like huge mounds of cotton. He shoved the boat off with a paddle, but as soon as it was in the river, he moved to the middle of the craft, where a central post was mounted, and unfurled a sail made out of old linen tunics. The breeze filled it at once, and the boat surged forward. Noah sat down in the back again and grasped the rudder. "Now *this* is the way to travel," he said, smiling.

Methuselah turned around and saw his grandson, white teeth gleaming against his bronze skin, his eyes alive with pleasure. "Well, what do you know? The fool thing works!" he exclaimed with some surprise. "I'm shocked!"

"I don't know why you would be shocked. I told you it would work."

"So you were right for once."

The two men continued their teasing banter throughout the pleasant upriver trip. A goodly breeze blew, and all Noah had to do was steer with the rudder. He was delighted that his idea worked. Often while boating on the river he had felt a stiff breeze move his reed craft along without his having to pole or paddle it, and he had wondered long and hard if there was some way to capture the wind and put it to work more effectively. He had at times on windy days taken off his tunic and held it up, noting how the wind filling the tunic pushed him along more quickly. Since it was tiring to hold his arms up, the idea occurred to him to mount a piece of sturdy cloth to a pole in the middle of a boat. Then he devised a means of steering without having to use a pole or paddle. His thoughts led him to create a rudder that he could turn easily from a sitting position while the wind in the sail moved the boat along. The way it all came together and actually worked on this maiden voyage was almost magical to him. "I don't know why somebody didn't think of this a long time ago," he said, leaning back with one hand behind his head, enjoying the warmth of the sunshine.

"Imagine going *up*river without even working up a sweat!" Methuselah said, laughing. "No one was crazy enough to think of sticking a pole in the middle of a boat with old tunics on it! You're the only man I know who would think of it, much less actually try it."

Noah grinned, enjoying his grandfather's jibes. "We ought to be there pretty soon at this rate."

"I hope so. I'm hungry enough to eat the hide off a wild donkey," Methuselah complained.

"I imagine Yaphet will give us a good meal. He'll want to soften me up to beat the price down on his house."

"Are you really going to build it?"

"I don't know yet. I don't really need the money, but I will do it if his plans for the house are interesting enough. I like to try new things."

Both men were surprised at how quickly they reached the dock at Yaphet's village. Noah tied up the boat, and the villagers gathered around, curious about the odd-looking craft. Not only was it unusual, but the woodwork was beautiful as well—the work of a master craftsman. Noah had fitted every board together so tightly that the seams and joints were almost invisible.

He helped his grandfather out onto the dock and said to the gathered crowd, "I'm looking for the house of Yaphet. Can you tell me where he lives?"

"I'll show you," a little boy piped up, "if you'll take me for a ride in your boat!"

Noah laughed and ruffled the boy's black hair. "Of course I will, if you do as I ask."

A tall young man was watching, and Noah thought he looked honest.

He approached him and said, "I'd like to hire you to look out for our boat."

"I'll do it," the young man said eagerly. "Did you build it yourself?"

"Yes, he did," Methuselah spoke up. "You don't have anybody that clever in this village, do you?"

The young man laughed and shook his head. "No, we don't."

As Noah and Methuselah made their way through the village, the young boy was full of questions, most of which Noah tried to answer. As they reached the center of the village, they halted at the sight of a towering stone building that dominated the clearing. Methuselah felt there was something ominous about it, and he asked, "Boy, what is this tower?"

"That's the temple of Ur-Baal," the boy said, pointing up to it. "I'm going to get to go to the ceremonies next year. I'll be old enough then."

Methuselah just grunted at the boy's enthusiasm and the three continued on to Yaphet's house.

They found the potential employer at home. Yaphet was a small man, thin and nervous. He had close-set eyes and a stringy beard, but he was, according to all reports, the wealthiest man around. He greeted the pair warmly and seated them at a low table with elaborate carvings of snakes and vines interwoven along the edges. Clapping his hands, he shouted at the servants to bring food and drink at once. Then he too sat down and said, "I'm glad you're going to build my house."

"That's not settled yet," Noah said pleasantly.

Yaphet blinked with surprise. "But I thought you came for that reason."

"I came to talk about it. I don't build many houses, and I'm only interested in one that would be a challenge."

Yaphet's eyes glowed. "We will *make* it a challenge. It will be the finest house anyone has ever seen. You'll see."

After eating a meal of fruit, nuts, cheese, flatbread, and goat's milk, Noah asked, "Is there a place for my grandfather to rest?"

"Of course. Zeta, take this gentleman to the room with the window overlooking the river. See to it that he's comfortable."

Methuselah bowed to their host while the servant girl waited. "Thank you, sir. You are very kind." He hesitated before taking his leave, then said, "We noticed the temple in the village square. Do most of the people in your village worship Ur-Baal?"

"Oh yes, indeed! Almost all."

"Are there any who follow the Ancient One?"

Yaphet rubbed his chin. "Not too many of those now. When I was younger there were more."

Methuselah shook his head sadly and followed the servant out of the room.

As soon as he was gone, Noah said to Yaphet, "Now we can talk business. What sort of a house do you have in mind?"

Early the next morning Noah rose before Yaphet's servants had begun to stir. He slipped out of the house and noted that the dawn had already broken in the east. Crimson light shed itself on the earth, and he turned quickly and walked down toward the river. Very few people were to be seen at this early hour, but inside the houses the cooking fires had been started and spirals of smoke wound their way upward in the light breeze. Overhead the sky was a dark gray, but the sun highlighted the somber color as it rose higher over the hills in the east.

When he reached the river Noah was relieved to find the boat exactly where he had left it. The young man he had hired had made himself a bed in the middle of it and was sleeping peacefully. Noah smiled at him and nodded with satisfaction. Seeing that all was well, he turned and began to walk along the riverbank.

He loved the river at this time of the morning. He kept a close eye out for serpents and more than once saw one swim out over the river in a corkscrew fashion. He loved watching animals, even those who posed a threat to people. His years of careful observation of wildlife had taught him how to avoid danger from even the most harmful creatures.

He came upon some fishing lines tied out by early risers who had come to snag their breakfast. Some of the lines were already thrashing with a catch. Noah watched a crocodile surface—only his eyes above water—then lunge to take one of the caught fish. He ripped the strong line as if it were a thread and disappeared underwater again.

Noah ambled along, thinking of little except the beauty of the morning. He reached an area downstream where the reeds grew thicker. They rose up above his head, and as the sun shone through them, they made a lattice-shaped shadow on the water. He slowed his pace, then stopped suddenly when he heard splashing. He grew cautious, thinking it might be a river beast.

As he moved carefully down the bank, he stepped past a large clump of reeds and saw that the earth was beaten down. He realized with some relief that it was not a river beast he was hearing. This sign indicated human, not animal, activity—perhaps someone who had come to fish.

His curiosity getting the better of him, he stepped out of the tall growth of reeds to see who it was—and to his shock found himself face-to-face with Lomeen!

She was wearing a thin white tunic and had her arms lifted, holding up her wet hair. For a moment she stood stock-still in surprise at the sight of this man from her past. Then she smiled beguilingly, dropped her hair, and walked over to him. "Why, hello, Noah," she said, her eyes fixed on him. "Do you remember me?"

Yes, he certainly did remember! After all these years he had never forgotten her. She was older now, just as he was, but her beauty had been untouched by the years. If anything she appeared even more beautiful to him now. Her eyes were still large and almond shaped, the curves of her face delicate and inviting. As she moved closer something in Noah warned him to tear his eyes away and leave at once, but he could not budge. She put her hand lightly on his chest as he remembered her doing so many years ago and whispered, "It's been a long time, hasn't it, Noah?"

Noah's throat was so thick he could not answer. He barely nodded, then said hoarsely, "I . . . I didn't expect to see *you* here."

"I guess that *would* be quite a surprise for you. I've lived in this village for many years now. I married into this clan shortly after we met." Lomeen's lips curved upward in a smile. "I never forgot you, Noah. I think often of the time you came to our village when you were a young man. I never stopped hoping that you would return someday . . . but you never did. Why not, Noah? Did I not please you?"

Noah could not pull himself together to even answer her. He knew he had to get away, but before he could act on that impulse, she pulled herself even closer to him. He honestly thought he might faint. His desire for her was overcoming his reason, as if he were sixteen years old again. He had tried so hard all his life to put Lomeen behind him. She was a part of his past, the part he sincerely wanted to forget. But as she pressed against him, the invitation in her eyes was unmistakable. He muttered something unintelligible, pushed her away, then turned and ran like a skittish mouse escaping a house cat. He heard her laughter follow him and her teasing words on the breeze—"You were bolder once, Noah. Don't you remember. . . ?"

Noah was shaken to the core by his encounter with Lomeen. He thought he had put his memories of her out of reach, but the sight of her on the riverbank had brought them all back in a trembling flood of emotion. All that day he kept himself inside Yaphet's home and talked feverishly about plans for the new house.

Late in the afternoon Methuselah came to Noah and said, "You have a visitor."

"A v-visitor?" Noah panicked at the thought of facing Lomeen again.

His grandfather gave him a quizzical look. "It's Comir, the son of Jaalam. Do you remember him?"

Noah felt his hands tremble, and he held them together behind him. "Comir—what is he doing here? And what does he want?"

"He's visiting his sister Lomeen, who lives here now. He heard you were coming to do business with Yaphet and he wanted to talk to you. I guess word gets around quickly in these parts." Methuselah stared at Noah, then said bluntly, "He wants you to marry Lomeen."

"B-but she's already married . . . or so she said."

"She was, but her husband was killed in a hunting accident a while back."

Noah looked up with tortured eyes and faced his grandfather. "Why is this happening?"

Methuselah stared at his grandson, then said in a stern tone, "You must be very careful, Noah—very careful indeed!"

"I know, I know," Noah sputtered. "Y-you talk to Comir, then, Grandfather. Tell him it's impossible. I can't see him."

Methuselah examined Noah carefully. "Pull yourself together, my son. Do you want people to think you've completely lost your mind? You'll have to talk to Comir yourself—like the grown man that you are! It's the only courteous thing to do. Shall I send him in?"

Noah could only nod. With a sinking heart, he watched Methuselah disappear out the same door that Comir entered a moment later. Noah recognized the warrior instantly, though he was older now too, with gray flecks in his beard, and quite changed from the young hunter who had captured him years ago.

Without preamble Comir spoke. "Noah, your grandfather tells me he's informed you of my wishes."

"Yes . . . h-he said you want me to marry Lomeen."

The passing of years had not changed the fact that Comir was a strong man, not one that Noah wanted to disappoint or cross in any way.

Comir explained that his father, Jaalam, had died ten years earlier, and Comir was now chief of their clan. He often came to Yaphet's village on business, ever since his sister had married into this clan. When Yaphet had mentioned to him recently that Noah was coming to make house plans, Comir had immediately arranged to meet him there.

"Let me say only two things," said Comir, his tone terse. "I've heard much about you over the years, Noah. You are a strong man, and there's a need for strong men today. The Nephilim are more of a threat than ever. Not only do they still attack and steal from our people, but they also boast that they will wipe us off the face of the earth. They want to create a new race to people the earth—and there is no stopping them other than through force. I pride myself on being a man of heart, a man who believes in living in peace with others, but the Nephilim are giants, and they are merciless. If you were to marry Lomeen, our three clans would be joined together, and we could fight the Nephilim together. They would find such an alliance impossible to defeat. Is this not so?"

Noah was having difficulty thinking, but he finally nodded. "Yes. A three-fold cord is not easily broken."

"Good." Comir's eyes glowed, and he said, "Now, I've often wondered why you didn't come back and ask to marry Lomeen. You chose her that night at our religious festival, then you left and never returned. Why was that?"

"It . . . it was a long time ago."

Comir was an astute man, and as he stared into Noah's eyes, he said abruptly, "You cared for her then, but perhaps you have someone else now. Another woman you love?"

"No, I . . . I don't," Noah insisted.

"Good! She's always loved you, Noah. You could have had her years ago if you'd only asked."

Noah felt trapped. "I'll have to think about it, Comir."

"Fine. You think about it, but it makes sense." Comir came over and put his hand on Noah's shoulder. "We would be brothers. Together we could stand against anyone." He then touched his finger to his forehead, as if a new thought had occurred to him. "Not only are we strong men, Noah, but I serve Ur-Baal, and you serve the Strong One. The Nephilim could not stand against both of these gods!" He laughed heartily, then clapped Noah on the shoulder and left the room.

Noah felt like a helpless youth again, drained of any pretense of self-control or mature thinking. All of his youthful desire for Lomeen had rushed back like a flood—and now he had been offered the opportunity to have her. He thought of her standing on the riverbank after her bath. . . . Uttering a short, pitiful groan, he fled from the room.

Zorah stared across the table at Methuselah in Noah's home. They were talking together about Noah and Methuselah's visit to Yaphet's village over a snack of wild berries and wild-rice cakes. The old seer listened intently as Methuselah related the details concerning Lomeen and Comir, and dismay washed across his face. "That woman!" he groaned. "She'll be the death of Noah!"

"You may be right about that," Methuselah said gloomily. "We've got to do something. Noah's like a rat transfixed by a cobra. He just stares—he seems to have lost his mind."

"She has a power over him. He's never been able to forget her."

"Well, what are we going to do?"

The two men sat there, and finally Zorah said helplessly, "Women know that men are weak, and an evil woman like Lomeen will always find a man's weakest spot."

"Yes, and now we're old and weak. We can't keep protecting him forever. Who's going to help Noah after we're gone?"

The lives of these two old men revolved around Noah. Both of them knew that the Ancient One had marked him for something important, and both of them had devoted much of their lives to keeping Noah from evil. They thought that the victory had been won, but now, because of the wiles of a beautiful woman, all their efforts were crumbling about their feet.

Lamech stared at Noah and shook his head with shock and disgust. "You've got to take her as your wife, boy! You've wasted your life! You're a disgrace to the family living with that half-crazy old man." He paced the floor, his voice tense. Then he stopped and reached up to put his hand on Noah's shoulder. Despite his many failings, he loved his son, and now he said, "Noah, think of the clan." His voice had a plea in it as he urged, "We need sons and grandsons, strong men to defend us. And, Noah, you need a woman!"

Noah knew that his father loved him and that his intentions were good. But he had to convince him otherwise about Lomeen. Noah tried to explain. "Father, she's a worshiper of Ur-Baal, and so is Comir."

"But as I understand it, Comir's not going to demand that we serve Ur-Baal. He says that his tribe will continue to serve Ur-Baal while we can serve the Strong One. That ought to make you happy."

Noah closed his eyes and put his hands to his temples. "I'm too tired to think, Father."

"You think I'm blind, boy, but I remember how you loved Lomeen. Your mother told me about it, and I watched you. It's true, isn't it? You did love her."

"I . . . I suppose I did."

"That's why you haven't married," Lamech said suddenly as the idea seemed to explode in him. "Of course! You've *always* loved that woman! That's why you wouldn't have another one. But now she's yours, Noah. All you have to do is take her. I think the Ancient One has put this in our way to save us."

Although Lamech's reasoning seemed logical to Noah's mind, his heart told him this idea was not from the Ancient One. But he was too exhausted to try to explain that to his father. He had slept little since he had seen Lomeen on the riverbank at Yaphet's village, and now he shook his head and, without a word, left his father's house. As he walked wearily down the path he heard his father crying out, "She's yours! You've loved her, and now she's available! Take her, boy—take her!"

CHAPTER 10

For days Noah went through his duties like a man in a daze. Leaving the house before dawn, he would work all day, eating little, then leave his work when darkness fell. More than once he stayed out most of the night, seeking his bed only when he was exhausted.

Ofra and Zorah tried desperately to reach Noah by reasoning with him, but he seemed incapable of responding. Ofra said once, "He must be losing his mind. Why, he's acting like a crazy man!"

One afternoon Noah came in early from work and found his father waiting for him. Lamech met Noah in front of his house and said at once, "We have a message from Comir."

"From Comir? What does he want?"

Lamech shifted his feet and looked at the ground uncertainly for a moment. He and Dezia had been worried over their son's strange behavior, neither of them knowing what to make of it. "He wants you to come for a meeting."

This news brought Noah's head up. "What does he want? Why does he want me to come there?"

"The messenger said he wants to work toward a closeness between our clans."

"What does that mean?"

"It means just what you think," Lamech said, and here he lifted his eyes to stare at Noah. "He's still seeking a marriage between you and Lomeen."

Noah shook his head. "I never told him I would marry Lomeen. I can't go."

Lamech began to argue, but for once he kept his temper. He brought up all the advantages of the match, and finally Noah threw up his hands. "All right, Father. I'll at least go talk to him. Perhaps we can come to some agreement between our clans—but not because of any marriage."

Lamech watched Noah turn and go inside. "If only our son would just settle down and act like an ordinary man!" he muttered.

The next day Noah left early to make the trip to Comir's village and reached it just before nightfall. Like Noah's town, Comir's home was no longer just a village, having grown into a more extensive settlement. But not being on the river, it was not as large as Noah's town.

There were few people on the streets, but still Noah drew suspicious glances, for strangers were always suspect. He no longer recognized the village he had once visited as a young man, but when he reached the clearing that lay in the center of the town, he froze. The sight brought back painful memories. He stood with his eyes half closed, remembering the night he had seen the high priest of Ur-Baal throw the child into the blazing fire. The memory had never left him, and he knew it never would. Staring at the open space, which now had a permanent stone temple erected to the bloodthirsty god, he thought bitterly, *How many babies have they burned since I was here the last time?*

He wrenched himself away and went quickly to where he remembered Jaalam's hut had once stood. Now a sturdy house was in its place, occupied by the new chief, his son Comir. As Noah walked slowly toward the front of the house, a figure suddenly emerged. It was Lomeen.

Noah stopped, startled. "What are you doing here, Lomeen? I thought you lived in Yaphet's village now."

She came to him at once and stood before him, her face close to his. "Comir asked permission of my father-in-law to bring me back with him—so that I can marry again . . . a man of his choice."

Noah needed no further explanation. It appeared that marriage plans had been going ahead without his knowledge *or* his agreement. He wondered if there was any way to escape what so many others wanted him to do. Even his own parents were pushing this idea! They certainly would not have been in favor of such a union when he was a young man. Why had they changed their minds? It seemed they had changed their minds about a lot of things lately.

Lomeen's light, gauzy garment swirled about her enticingly in the breeze. Noah caught his breath as she stepped close and placed his hands around her waist, pulling herself close. Looking up at him, she whispered, "I knew you would come."

"Lomeen, I-I'm not here to—" Noah struggled to get the words out that he could not marry her, but before he could say any more, she flung her arms around his neck and pulled his head down. Feeling her warm breath mingling with his, Noah gave up all pretense of self-control and kissed her in a fiery rush. A distant voice seemed to warn him to stop, but the touch of her body against his toppled his defenses as surely as a mighty fortress breached by a persistent and riotous enemy. She clung to him with a passion beyond anything he had ever known. The world around him faded away—and with it the voice of reason—and he knew nothing but the woman he grasped in his arms. He had been alone so long. He wanted love like this, love that possessed him and made him surrender to its demands, love that could lift him into another world and make him feel alive.

Lomeen pulled away slightly, whispering against his lips, "I knew you would come, my love. I knew you would!"

Noah felt like a man caught in a powerful river, the force of it dragging him down against his will. He knew Lomeen's beliefs would never mesh with his own, but the power of the flesh had caught up with him at last, and he allowed himself to be led inside her brother's house.

Comir was waiting for them, and his eyes went to Lomeen, who squeezed Noah's arm and whispered, "I will wait for you."

Comir offered Noah a seat, and Noah, still shaken over the embrace and Lomeen's caresses, sat down like a man resigned to his fate. He took the cup Comir handed him and drank it without knowing or caring what it was.

Finally Comir studied Noah carefully. "You know why I sent for you?"

"You want a union between our clans."

"Exactly. You're next in line as chief of your clan. If we unite through your marriage to my sister, we can stand strong against any who would harm us. It would be a good thing." Then, as if anticipating Noah's protests, Comir said quickly, "I know you are a follower of the Ancient One, while our people follow Ur-Baal. That is a difficulty. But think of it like this, Noah—your marriage to Lomeen would join not only our two clans together but also Yaphet's clan, since Lomeen married into that clan. Think of it merely as a political alliance. Men have more than one wife. You can also marry one of the women of your own clan."

"I don't think I could—"

Comir lifted his hand and interrupted Noah. "I know how you feel about Lomeen. She has told me, and she's told me how she feels about you. She's always loved you." He went on speaking for some time, and Noah made no further effort to resist. "Stay with us for a time," Comir offered. "Get to know our people. You and I can get to know each other better. When your father dies, you will be chief, and we will be brothers, our clans united as one. Go talk with Lomeen."

Comir watched as the tall man rose, his shoulders stooped in defeat. He thought, *Noah's like a man who's taken a wound and doesn't even know it but keeps on moving anyway. But Lomeen can persuade him that this is best for all of us. My little sister can persuade any man to bend to her will—even the stubborn Noah, son of Lamech!*

Noah looked up at Lomeen, who had brought him a plate of roasted lamb, still sizzling and smoking from the fire. After putting it on the table in front of him, she laid her hand on his shoulder and smiled down at him. Her hand moved to his cheek, caressing him gently as he leaned his head against her and sighed.

For the past three days he had stayed at Comir's home. Much of the time he had spent with Comir himself. Comir was a powerful man with a great deal of knowledge, and though Noah had never been particularly interested in politics, he listened to what the man had to say. Comir was not like his father, whom Noah knew to be a man of unbridled passion. He was much smoother than that, and without appearing to do so, he had planted seeds in Noah's mind to make it easy for him to accept the union that Comir desired.

Lomeen had tried to persuade Comir to let her into Noah's room each night so she could lay with him, but Comir had the wisdom to know that if he wanted Noah as an ally, the man needed to believe he was choosing Lomeen of his own free will, not merely as a result of her powerful methods of seduction.

Not to be deterred, Lomeen had invited Noah on long walks in the woods, taking him to private places where she offered herself to him unreservedly. Noah wasn't sure what kept him from giving in to her advances on those long walks—perhaps the knowledge that Comir was always watching in the form of a servant sent along to chaperone from a respectful distance.

Now as he sat with her hand on his shoulder, he was confused. Lomeen caressed his cheek and then leaned over and whispered, "Eat your food. Then we'll go to the woods again before Comir knows we're gone. I know a place where we can be alone."

The mere promise of such a tryst in her husky whisper stirred Noah powerfully. He had to refuse, for he felt himself slipping, and reason told him that a total surrender to Lomeen would mean certain destruction, not only for him, but inexplicably, for many others as well.

"There isn't time, Lomeen. I must go back home," he managed to say.

Lomeen shook her head, momentarily disappointed but not deterred. "Home can wait, Noah. I can't lose you. We'll talk about it later." Before leaving, she planted a lingering kiss on his lips and stroked his cheek one last time before whispering, "Later..."

Lomeen was accustomed to handling men. She smiled to herself as she returned to her room, knowing that victory was within her grasp. For Comir this marriage was merely a political matter, but for her it was much more personal. She had always prided herself on her ability to control men, to bend them to her will with her well-practiced moves. But Noah was an enigma. Somehow this rough, powerful man, who had walked back into her life after so many years, was the one man she could not possess as she had so many others. She knew he wanted her, but there seemed to be some power working against her efforts to seduce him. Why wouldn't he give in to her completely? He'd done so years ago, but they were both very young then, and the hypnotic drink used at their worship ceremonies had the power to break down anyone's defenses. This man was the biggest challenge of her life. She would not rest till she had him firmly in her control. There was something about Noah that fascinated her. Despite his odd beliefs and behavior, she sensed he was destined for greatness. And before that happened, she *would* be his wife!

Later in the day Comir sent for Lomeen and Noah to join him in the great room for a discussion. Lomeen thanked the servant girl for bringing her the message and hurried to get herself ready for what she was certain would be an announcement of their betrothal.

"Hello, Noah," she said as she entered the room and sat down next to him, stroking his knee with her hand. "Comir will be here soon."

"Lomeen," Noah said to her, "I've made a decision—"

"Let's wait till Comir gets here before we talk, my love." She leaned over toward him and began to kiss him when he suddenly jumped up.

"What was that?" he asked, walking to the front window to see what was causing the sudden commotion in the street outside the house.

She followed him to the window. "I'm sure it's nothing. Let's go sit down again."

"No, Lomeen. It's not nothing," he said, pointing to a large and growing fight in the street. "It's the Nephilim."

Noah began to go outside, but Lomeen pulled him back. "No, Noah—don't go out there. They come often. They're powerful fighters. We need to hide—let our warriors deal with them!"

Noah did not heed her words, however, for he suddenly spotted a man among the Nephilim who caused him to draw in his breath sharply.

"What is it, Noah?"

"That man—it's Mak!"

Fear filled Lomeen as she remembered the story of how Mak had killed Noah's brother and taken his sister-in-law. She also knew the terrible strength of the man, and as she watched Noah's body grow tense, she pleaded with him, "I know he's your old enemy, but leave him alone. No one can beat him."

Noah appeared not to have heard. He stood watching, and then he saw that Mak was dragging a young woman.

"Who's that woman he's got?"

Lomeen stared at the pair. "She's a beggar girl. She was abandoned here. Nobody knows who her parents are."

Something about the young woman stirred Noah. She was not pretty, but nonetheless she reminded him of his lost sister-in-law. Throughout the years he had kept Tirzah alive in his memory, and as he watched, it seemed that Mak was dragging not some stranger but his own beloved sister-in-law, who had been like a mother to him in his youth, always gentle, always available. As the two women merged inexplicably in his mind, he uttered a strange guttural sound and turned toward the door in a frenzy.

"Noah!" Lomeen cried. She tried to hold him back, but he shook her off. "You can't fight them!"

Noah did not even hear her. He stepped outside the door and stood still, contemplating what to do. Mak was older now and heavier, but still the mighty arms and mountainlike shoulders were there. Noah's gaze went to the young woman, who was barely more than a child and dressed in rags. Terror-filled eyes stared from her thin face as the giant reached out and cuffed her, shouting, "Shut up, you sniveling girl, or I'll give you something to cry about!"

And then—when he least expected it—Noah heard what he had been waiting for, for so long! A voice echoed inside his heart and then his brain. It was a quiet voice, but strong and powerful—it said only three words: *Save that woman.*

Instantly Noah knew it was the voice of the Ancient One! He had been begging for years to hear the Ancient One speak, and now at this unexpected moment he had.

Ignoring Lomeen's pleas to come back inside, Noah marched right up to the giant, his attention riveted on the form and face of Mak, the killer of Jodak and kidnapper of Tirzah.

Stopping a few feet away from Mak, Noah lifted his voice. "You're brave, fighting children." The giant looked around in a befuddled manner, his eyes glazed. *He's been drinking,* Noah thought. *That's good. He'll be slower.* "Why don't you fight a man?" Noah demanded.

Mak was still the strongest of the Nephilim. For many years no man had stood against him. He had lost count of the men he had slain and the women he had taken. He was feared even by his own kind, for he was a cruel man, seeking his own gratification and bound to have it.

"What's that you say?" Mak shook his head and tried to focus his eyes on the man standing before him. "What do you want? Get away before I squash you like a bug!"

Noah took two steps closer. He was now no more than five feet away. The giant towered over him like a tree, but Noah knew no fear. A great calmness had come over him, a stillness that filled his soul. He could see the evil in the man's eyes, but he smiled and said, "You're nothing but a child killer. You couldn't stand for a minute before a real man. Let that girl go."

It had been many years since Mak had been challenged head-on, and then it was only by the biggest and strongest member of the Nephilim. Mak had beaten him after a fierce battle, and no one had dared stand up to him like this since. With a savage laugh, he shook his head. "You dumb beetle! Get out of my sight, or I'll rip your eyes out!"

"You killed my brother and stole his wife!"

Mak laughed harshly, as if to say he would enjoy smashing this measly man before him. "So? I've killed many men and taken their wives." Mak sneered down at Noah.

Noah wanted the giant to remember him. "It was in a village not far from here. I was just a boy then, and after you killed my brother, I came at you with a spear. You won that day, but I was only a stripling."

Mak was weaving back and forth like a huge animal. He nodded, exposing his yellowish fangs in a travesty of a smile. "Yes, I remember—you were the only boy who was ever foolish enough to fight me. I split your brother's head, and I took his woman. I thought I'd killed you too, but I can still do that."

"Where is the woman you stole?" Noah demanded.

Mak laughed again, as if enjoying the memory. "She served me well . . . until she ceased to amuse me and I wrung her neck!"

It took all of Noah's strength to keep from flying at the giant in a fury, but he knew he needed to move cautiously and wisely.

A crowd had gathered around the two. Everyone in the village was afraid of Mak and his fellow Nephilim, but Noah's brave confrontation gave them the courage to at least watch. Comir approached and stepped nervously beside Noah, Lomeen with him. Urgently Comir said, "Don't pay any attention to him, Mak."

"Who are you to tell me what to do?" Mak bellowed.

Comir was not a coward, but he knew his limitations. He grabbed Noah's arm and whispered to him, "Come on, Noah. Don't be a fool."

Lomeen urged him too, with desperation in her voice and grabbing his other arm. "Please, Noah, don't fight him! He'll kill you!"

Noah shook them both off and took two steps forward. He was within a foot of the giant now and could smell his terrible odor. He lifted his head and spat right in Mak's face, then backed away and laughed. "You're nothing, Mak! You're not a man!"

Mak stood there stunned, the spittle running down his face into his beard. He reached up, touched it, and stared at his fingers in disbelief.

"Look around you, Mak," Noah said. "Look at the sky and the earth and the trees. It's the last time you'll ever see them, because you'll be dead in a few minutes."

A shudder ran through the body of the giant, and he cried out, "I'll rip you apart with my bare hands! I don't need a sword or a spear for a pup like you!"

This was exactly what Noah was hoping for. He did not have a weapon, and even if he had, he was not as expert as the giant. But once again he could hear that inner voice telling him to *Save that woman,* and he knew he could not lose. "Come to me, you miserable wretch! I will kill *you* with my bare hands!"

With a roar, Mak loosed his grip on the girl, who sprawled in the dirt, her eyes enormous as she watched the giant throw himself at Noah. Noah could hear Lomeen screaming, but he had no time to think of that now. As he had guessed, Mak was ponderous and slow. With ease, Noah simply moved his head away as the giant's enormous fist cut the air beside him. Noah kicked the giant's ankle, and Mak lost his balance, falling into the dust. Noah waited until Mak rolled over, and as he rose to a half crouch, Noah kicked him full in the face. He heard the crunching of teeth as his heel struck the giant's mouth and Mak fell over backward.

An astonished gasp ran through the crowd. Even some of the Nephilim had joined the crowd and were watching the fight. One of them whispered, "Shall we help him?"

The other giant muttered, "No. If he can't handle a weakling like that, he's not fit to be our leader anymore."

Mak struggled to his feet. There was now a bloody gap in his teeth, and blood ran down his smashed lips over his beard. To the spectators it seemed an unequal battle, for Mak was huge and had been a fighting man all his life. Noah, however, was taller than any man in his clan, and his labor in the fields and with heavy timbers had built up a solid layer of muscle. He looked frail against the giant's bulk, but he was still in the prime of his life. Now looking at the wounded warrior, Noah was certain he could kill the giant.

Mak moved forward more cautiously this time. He was aware that this man confronting him was more dangerous than any he had faced in years. He had the strength in his hands and arms to crush Noah, but he had seen the speed with which the man moved. And now, instead of striking out, he put his arms in a half circle, reaching out to enfold Noah. He did not rush in blindly but moved slowly.

Noah knew what was in Mak's mind. If he fell into those mighty arms, he would be crushed. He circled, moving easily, and the giant followed doggedly. Blood covered his beard, and his eyes glittered with the desire to kill.

Noah waited, and finally Mak lunged again. But once again he was much too slow. Noah struck out for the giant's face, but his blow missed, and he struck Mak in the throat instead. It was a terrible blow and would have killed most men, for the full weight of Noah's powerful muscles was behind it. It stopped Mak in his tracks, and he began to gag.

Noah taunted him. "What's the matter? I've only hit you once. Come on, Mak. Kill me!"

Mak tried again to get Noah in his grip, but Noah's hands were half lifted to avoid that maneuver. The two moved around in a circle, Mak plodding ahead, and Noah jumping quickly from one side to the other, causing the giant to make sudden, awkward turns.

Mak struck out, and the blow caught Noah in the chest. The power of it brought a coldness over him, and he staggered backward and fell.

Mak gave a cry of triumph and surged forward to stomp him to death. Noah rolled to one side and lashed out with a kick that took the giant on the thigh and slowed him long enough for Noah to roll over again—but Mak was after him, moving faster. His eyes glinted with hatred, and his hands, like mighty talons, were almost on Noah.

Noah grabbed a handful of sandy dirt and threw it directly into Mak's face.

The giant uttered a cry of pain and began to claw at his eyes. Noah, coming to his feet, deliberately kicked him in the groin with every bit of his force and heard Mak utter a terrible high-pitched cry. The giant leaned forward, clutching himself in agony.

Noah clasped both hands together and brought them down in a tremendous blow on the back of Mak's neck. It drove the giant to the ground and would have broken the neck of a lesser man. Noah whipped his arm around the giant's neck, tightening his powerful muscles against Mak's throat. With his other hand he grasped his own wrist and squeezed the giant's neck, cutting off his air.

Uttering choking cries, Mak struggled to stand upright. He reached behind him, trying to grab his enemy's head, but Noah ducked and clung to the giant's back like a burr. He whipped his legs around the giant's waist and locked them. He would hold on until one of them died!

Mak struggled, his face turning first crimson, then purple. His eyes began to bulge as he frantically tried to dislodge Noah.

As for Noah, he had no other thought than to hang on until the man was dead. He had never killed anyone in his life, but he had heard the voice of the Strong One telling him to save the girl. And there was no way to save her without killing Mak.

Like a tall tree, Mak began to sway. He tried to keep his balance and pulled feebly at Noah's arm, but his strength was gone. Noah whispered in his ear, "You have killed your last man and raped your last woman,

Mak. You die at the order of the Strong One."

And then Mak fell to the ground, his legs kicking in a wild contortion. Noah held on until long after the legs had grown still. Mak was a mighty man, but the Strong One had given Noah the power to overcome him.

Finally Noah loosed his grip. He stood to his feet, his chest heaving from the effort, his face crimson. The dead eyes of the giant stared up at the blue heavens that he would never see again. Noah looked over at the band of Nephilim, expecting them to take up the fight, but one of them merely laughed. "So the mighty Mak is not so mighty after all. Feed him to the crows." Then he turned and walked away, followed by the others.

Noah gasped for breath, aware that everyone was staring at him. He heard Lomeen and felt her touch. "Are you all right, Noah?"

Noah turned to look at her and knew without question that he had to get away. His weakness for this woman had nearly destroyed him, and it occurred to him that perhaps Mak had saved his life. The burst of terrible violence and the slaying of the giant had purged him of his desire for Lomeen, and he knew what he had to do. "Good-bye, Lomeen," he said quietly.

He did not wait for her response. He walked over to the young woman Mak had tried to capture. She still lay on the ground, fear in her face and eyes. Noah asked her quietly, "What's your name, child?"

"Adah, sir."

"Come with me, Adah. I will see that you're safe." He helped her up, and supporting her with his arm, he turned and walked away.

Comir was in shock over the results of the fight. He said to his sister, "That man can do anything. You must marry him!"

Lomeen nodded. "I'll make a vow to Ur-Baal, brother. He will give me this man!"

CHAPTER

II

Ofra hobbled back to the table and stood looking down, her face twisted into a frown. "What's wrong with you, Zorah?" When the old man did not even look up, she shook her head. "I know what it is. You're worried about Noah."

Zorah shifted uncomfortably on the bench and, leaning forward, placed his forehead in his hands. He had eaten little for the past two days and had hardly slept at all. Shaking his head, he muttered, "I don't want anything to eat."

"You've got to eat something," Ofra insisted. "You'll starve yourself to death. You're nothing but a bag of bones as it is."

Zorah looked up and smiled slightly, for the old woman was nothing but a bag of bones herself. He did not know how old she was, but it was a source of constant wonder to him that so frail and aged a creature could care for two men so well.

"Won't the Ancient One take care of Noah?" Ofra asked. "That's what He's for, isn't He? To help His servants."

Zorah found this amusing. He smiled sourly and shook his head. "That's what people think, but it isn't that way."

"Well, what is He for then, if not to help us?"

Long ago the old man had given up trying to explain the ways of his God to Ofra. In all truth, even after long, arduous years of service, he himself did not understand the Ancient One. He now said wearily, "Sometimes, Ofra, He will allow His favorites to go through very hard times."

"Why does He do that?" Ofra demanded indignantly. "What's the use of serving Him if He doesn't help us?"

"He *will* help us, Ofra, but sometimes His help comes in a pretty rough form." Heaving a sigh, he added sourly, "Serving the Ancient One is not all honey and sweet cakes!"

The distant, plaintive cry of a wild dog brought Noah out of a fitful sleep. He awakened with a start, not knowing for the moment where he was; then he looked over at the remains of the dead fire, next to which the young woman, Adah, was curled up. She seemed so defenseless, so vulnerable, and it touched him.

Sitting up, Noah stretched and wondered what in the world he would do with her. *Perhaps Mother would take her as a servant—or Boz. He needs help with all those babies of his. His wives would be glad for another servant girl.* His thoughts moved slowly, for the battle with Mak had dulled his senses. Behind every thought was the question of Lomeen, whom he still kept thinking about, even though he had said good-bye to her for what he thought was the last time. But as he sat waiting for the morning sun to warm the earth, he knew he was not through with her. Even miles away, she still had a hold over him, and he felt like an insect caught in a spider's web, unable to free himself.

Getting slowly to his feet, he walked over to where Adah lay sleeping. Reaching out, he touched her shoulder and said, "Get up, girl."

He was shocked at her reaction, for she uttered a shrill cry and covered her head with her hands. She lay curled up in a small ball, as if awaiting the blow she must have endured many times. The sight of her fearfulness startled Noah, and he backed away a step.

"It's all right, Adah. Don't be afraid. I won't hurt you." He watched as she moved one arm and looked at him, her thin features tense with fear. She was not an attractive child, and poor diet and bad treatment had not helped. Her scraggly black hair had a tint of red in it like Noah's own. She came to her feet quickly, clutching her rags and shivering in the coolness of the morning. Noah wished he had a cloak to give her for warmth, but he had nothing with him.

"Come along, child," he said. "My home's not far from here. It'll be warm, and we'll get some food into our bellies." He smiled to encourage her, but she was too frightened to smile back. *Poor thing has been mistreated until there's nothing left of her,* Noah thought. Aloud he told her again, "You don't have to be afraid. No one's going to hurt you."

Adah looked at the huge man and could not believe what she was hearing. She had known little kindness in life—and none at all from men.

She fell into step beside him and noted that he adjusted his long strides to accommodate hers. This encouraged her, and a faint glow of hope stirred in her small body.

As for Noah, his thoughts returned to Lomeen. He realized she was the strongest force in his life and wondered how a woman could have such power over him. His mind seemed severed into two parts. One part cried out for Lomeen, while the other seemed to echo with the warnings of Methuselah and Zorah, the two strongest men in his life.

I wish life were simple! How wonderful it must be to have nothing to think about but work and taking care of a family. He thought with envy of his friends who had achieved this. *They're married and have families. They must be happy. But me—I have never been lonelier.* That realization was bitter, and he wrested his mind away from the thought as he saw his town come into view. He turned his attention to the girl trudging along beside him. "Tell me about yourself, Adah."

"About myself?" The question seemed to confuse the girl.

"Yes," Noah said cheerfully. "What about your parents?"

"I never had any."

"Well, where did you grow up?" Noah asked. He had to ask many questions to get much information out of her. As she struggled to tell him about her life, he got the sense that it was a miracle she had survived her childhood. She had never known her father or mother, brothers or sisters. She had been little more than a slave, living with daily blows and hard work.

"How old are you, Adah?"

"I . . . I think I'm about fifteen, but I'm not sure."

To Noah this was strange, for his clan kept birthdays carefully, and everyone knew exactly how old they were. This waif knew nothing about such things. He said no more, but as they entered Noah's town, they became a target for curious eyes. The members of his clan always watched Noah, and now with a young girl by his side, it was inevitable someone would come and question him. In this case it was Nophat, the huge hunter, who came to stare at him with his single eye.

"Hello, Noah."

"Hello, Nophat."

The single eye swiveled to stare at Adah. "Who's the plucked chicken?"

Noah saw Adah shrink back in fear, and he said quickly, "Just a girl I thought I'd find a place for. Maybe serving a good family."

Nophat stared at the girl and shook his head. His voice was a growl as he said, "She'll need some meat on her bones if she'll be any good to anybody." He turned back to face Noah and demanded, "What about Lomeen? Are you going to marry her?"

The abrupt question reminded Noah of how impossible it was to keep anything a secret within the clan. Everyone knew everyone else's business, and there was no place to hide. He realized that the news had somehow gotten all over town that he was going to talk about a possible marriage with Lomeen, and it angered him. He said curtly, "Don't you have any business of your own to look after? Come on, Adah."

Nophat was not offended. He knew his friend Noah to be a strange man, and he shook his head as the mismatched pair moved down the street. "He'll marry Lomeen," he growled. "From what I hear, his father's all for it, and it'll be good for Noah. A man can't live without a woman." He smiled grimly to himself and shook his head. "Can't live *with* 'em either."

"That's my house right there, Adah. Come along." Noah took a few more steps, then turned and saw that the girl had stopped. Her eyes were wide and she was trembling. He walked back. "What are you afraid of?"

"I . . . I don't know."

The girl was as stiff as a bronze bar, her fists clenched together. Noah wanted to encourage her, for it hurt him to see her in such abject fear. He himself knew something about fear and hated to see one so young beaten down and cowed by everything. "You don't have to be afraid. I live in that house with an old woman named Ofra and with an old man named Zorah. Ofra takes care of us. She sees that we have plenty to eat and washes our clothes."

"Will she beat me?"

"Beat you!" Noah said, shocked at the idea. "Why, of course not! Where did you get such an idea?"

"Everybody beats me. They always have."

Noah was struck by the tragedy in the girl's voice and wondered what it must be like to grow up with no love, only the wrath of those you are forced to serve. He realized how fortunate he had been to have a family that cared for him and loved him, and his heart went out to the girl again. He had a quick compassion that reached out to the helpless, to the downtrodden. He had always been an easy mark for beggars—a trait for which his father had often berated him. Now as he stood bent over, trying to find some way to assure Adah, he realized there were probably more people in the world like this abused girl than there were like him.

He determined to see to it that the girl had a good home and a peaceful life from here on.

"Look, Adah, how about this? My mother, Dezia, is a wonderful woman. She's kind, and she's never beaten a servant in her life. How would you like to go live with her?"

The girl dropped her eyes and did not speak.

"Do you think you'd like that?" Noah persisted.

Finally Adah lifted her head, and Noah noticed how well shaped her eyes were, dark brown and shaded by thick black lashes. "Couldn't . . . couldn't I stay with you?" she asked.

The simple request, and the heartache that filled the girl's face, decided it for Noah. "Of course you can, if that's what you want. You can stay as long as you'd like."

To Noah's surprise, Adah's eyes filled with tears, and her body shook with sobs. Nonplussed, he did not know what to do. Finally he put his hand lightly on her frail shoulder. "Nothing to cry about." He spoke gruffly and knew that the girl would need time to learn to trust people. He thought of Ofra and her sharp tongue. *The girl had better be prepared for her*. "Look, Adah," he explained, "Ofra is a good-hearted woman, but she's old and sometimes harsher than she means to be. She may seem a little unkind at first, but she's the same to me and to Zorah. But she means well, and if you'll just learn to put up with her ways, you two will get along fine." He thought of the girl's earlier words and added, "And she will never beat you. Now, come along."

Ofra met them as the two entered Noah's house. She looked at the girl, her lips drawn together in a tight line. "And who is this you brought home, may I ask?"

Noah immediately put his arm around the frail old woman and smiled. "I've got a surprise for you, Ofra. This is Adah. She's had a hard time, but she's going to help you with some of the work around here. It'll make life a little easier for you. Now, I want you two to be good friends. All right?"

Ofra stared at the young woman, saw the fear that was etched plainly on her thin face, and noted that the girl's hands were trembling so violently she had to hold them together tightly. Ofra suddenly had a memory of how she herself had been alone, helpless and filled with fear, when Noah had appeared from nowhere to rescue her. She had been half sick with dread, unable to sleep because of her fear. Noah had brought her to this house, had given her a room, had laughed with and encouraged her, and had given her a new life. Now when she saw this child's face, it was not hard to figure out that life had treated her harshly.

"Well, I can always use another pair of hands," Ofra said. "Your name is Adah?"

"Yes."

"I'm Ofra. You come along now, and I think I can find you a better dress than that one."

"Thank you, Ofra." Noah smiled at the old woman and winked. "Just take care of her half as well as you do Zorah and me, and you'll have her spoiled in no time." He turned to the girl and said, "You go along now. Ofra will take care of you."

Adah stood unmoving, with tears glimmering in her eyes from the kindness that was being shown her.

Ofra understood how overwhelmed the girl must have felt at this change of fortune. "Come along now," she said gently. "We'll get you cleaned up and put some clothes on you, then you can help me with dinner."

Noah turned and a sense of relief filled him, for he had been in a quandary over what to do with the girl. Now it was settled. It was typical of Noah not to think of all the consequences of his decisions. The girl needed help, and he could give it—that was all there was to it. He did, however, enjoy a sense of relief now that Ofra had taken the burden of caring for the girl from his shoulders.

He went quickly to wash his face and hands, and when he returned to the large room, he found Zorah seated at the table. "You look worn out," he said, seating himself across from the seer. "Haven't you been sleeping?"

Zorah ignored the question. "Who's the girl?" he asked, for he had seen Noah bringing the young woman into the house.

"Her name's Adah."

"Where did you pick her up?"

The memory of the past day came to Noah, and with it a sense of apprehension. "I've got some things to tell you, Zorah. I don't know what you'll think. . . ."

Zorah sat back and listened. He saw that Noah was tense, and as the tale unfolded, he found it almost incredible. When Noah had finished he said, "You mean you killed Mak, the Nephilim?"

"It was what the Ancient One told me to do. He said as plainly as if you were speaking to me, 'Save the girl,' and I did. It was a miracle! Mak did not have the strength he once had, but the Nephilim still have great power."

"Were you thinking of your brother and of Tirzah?"

Noah tried to remember. "I was," he confessed. "But it wasn't just revenge."

"No, I can see that. What about the girl?"

"She had no place to go. Mak had abused her, and so has everybody else, from what she tells me. She's a pitiful creature."

"And you're going to keep her here in the house?"

"She can help us. Ofra's getting on in years."

"Yes, she is, and so am I."

Noah reached out and squeezed the arm of the old seer. "You'll outlive Methuselah."

"I doubt that," Zorah said dryly.

The two sat talking, and Noah noticed that Zorah did not mention Lomeen. Noah was very glad of that, for he did not know his own mind about the woman. She hung over him like a cloud, yet at the same time she was able to draw him to her like a lodestone, in spite of all his efforts to resist.

Finally Ofra came in with the girl beside her. Each of them had a plate of food, and as they sat down Noah said, "Adah, this is my dear friend Zorah. You must be very kind to him, for he is a good man."

"Yes, sir," Adah whispered.

Noah was looking at her with interest. Ofra had pulled out a woven dress of her own for the girl to wear. Her face was washed and her hair combed and tied back. He said, "You must be as hungry as I am. Get two more plates, one for yourself and one for Ofra."

"Yes, sir," Adah whispered, obviously glad to have something to do.

"Sit down, Ofra. It's time you had someone waiting on you for a change."

"How old is the girl?" Zorah asked.

"She thinks about fifteen, but she isn't sure."

Zorah sat quietly while the young woman brought the food back, and then they all ate. He was relieved that Noah was back, but he knew that the problem of Lomeen was not yet solved. What troubled him was the fact that he had dreamed twice since Noah had left—and both times a young woman had been in his dream. He had been shocked to see Adah, for she was clearly the girl in the dreams!

Now as the old seer sat eating slowly, his eyes were fixed on Adah's face. Her presence here was not by accident. During his long life Zorah had learned to see the hand of God in things, and now he studied the girl and wondered what part she would play in the days to come.

CHAPTER

12

Noah breathed in the aroma of freshly roasted meat as he arrived home. Adah came out of the smaller room to greet him. "I've got your food ready," she said.

"Where is everybody?"

"Zorah and Ofra have gone to bed."

"You should have gone also. It's late."

"I wasn't sleepy. Come along and eat, master."

Noah was very hungry. Except for a few morsels at dawn, he had eaten nothing all day, and now he sat down eagerly at the table. He silently watched Adah move back and forth bringing the food, and when it was set before him, he looked at her and tried to smile. "How was your day?"

"Oh, it was very good! Ofra's teaching me how to cook the way you like it."

Noah looked down at the meat and pulled off a chunk with his fingers. Popping it into his mouth, he chewed it and asked, "Did you cook this?"

"Yes. Is it all right?"

"Why, it's better than all right," Noah said heartily. "It's fine. Now, you sit down there and talk to me while I eat."

Adah slipped onto a bench across from the big man and said breathlessly, "What will I talk about?"

"Oh, anything. Just what you did today." He listened as the girl spoke somewhat haltingly at first. He had noticed during the days she had been living in his house that at times she would almost slip back into the paralyzing fear he had first seen in her. Now, however, she seemed more at ease, and he noted with approval how bright her eyes were and how clean she kept herself. There was color in her cheeks now, and her eyes glowed as she spoke of how Zorah had talked to her for a long time.

"What did he say, Adah?"

"Oh, he told me all about the Ancient One."

"Had you never heard of Him before?"

"No, I don't think so. I've heard about Ur-Baal, but—" She broke off suddenly, fear once again in her eyes. "I don't like Ur-Baal."

"You're very wise. I don't like him either. What did Zorah tell you about the Strong One?"

Adah's face glowed as she spoke about her conversation with Zorah. "I love to listen to him talk. He's so wise."

"Yes, he is. I'm glad you two are getting along."

Noah said no more. He seemed to have lost his appetite as he pushed the last remaining morsels of meat around on his plate with a piece of bread. Adah watched him carefully, noting the joyless expression on his face. Timidly she asked, "Can I ask you something, master?"

Noah looked up with surprise. "Of course. What is it?"

"You're so sad. Is it because you killed that man, Mak, who was hurting me?"

"No. Don't ever think that. I am a little sad, but it's not your fault."

Adah gave a sigh of relief. She leaned forward and locked her hands together, then said, "Your grandfather came by today."

"Methuselah? Did you like him?"

"Oh yes! He's so kind. He took me for a walk and showed me some interesting places along the river."

"My grandfather is a very good man."

"So are you."

Noah stared at the girl, then laughed. "Well, I'm glad you think so. Now, you go to bed. I'm going myself."

"Good night, master," Adah said. She turned and left the room as silently as a ghost.

Noah leaned back and shook his head. "Strange child," he muttered.

Finally he arose and went to his bed. He slipped off his sandals, lay down, and for a time, stared up at the ceiling. Though his thoughts were confused, he prayed to the Ancient One as his grandfather and Zorah had taught him—simply speaking what was on his heart—until he finally fell asleep.

Methuselah was sitting in Noah's house when Noah stepped inside the door. Seeing his grandson's expression, Methuselah knew something was wrong. Two full moons had come and gone since Noah had killed Mak and brought Adah home. During that time the whole family had watched him, for Noah was behaving strangely—even for *him.* He was even quieter than usual and worked harder than ever. From early dawn until late at night he labored building a house for a wealthy member of the clan. He drove his workers so hard they threatened to walk out on the job, but he ignored their protests.

Now Methuselah stared at his grandson and waited for him to speak. Noah was nervous, twisting his hands together and trying to find some way to express himself. Finally he took a deep breath and blurted out, "Grandfather, I've got to have something more in my life."

"Something more in your life?" Methuselah repeated with surprise. "What do you mean by that?"

"Well, every man I grew up with married long ago. They all have families. Boz, Kul, Ruea—they all have children about their feet. And I have nothing."

"You could have married. It was your choice not to take a wife."

Noah flushed. "I suppose you're right, but now I've changed my mind."

Methuselah felt a chill grip his heart. He knew instantly what Noah intended. "So you're going to marry Lomeen after all, aren't you?"

"My father says it's what I should do."

A touch of anger swept over Methuselah, and he shook his head, saying roughly, "Don't blame your weakness for that woman on your father! She's got a power over you that makes you pitiful. You've wasted half your life pining after her!"

Noah rose and said angrily, "I don't see it like that. I've tried and tried to turn away from her, but the truth is I love her, and I'm going to have her as my wife. I've got a right to have a family as well as the next man!"

"You're making the worst mistake of your life, Noah!"

Noah turned on his heel and headed out of the room. As he reached the door, he looked back and said, "I'm going to Lomeen's village tomorrow to tell Comir that I'll marry her. It's all settled."

Methuselah felt that his world was falling apart. He and Zorah had been fearful of this for so long—had tried so hard to prevent it—and now it was happening. The old man lifted his hands and cried out, "O Strong One, don't let him do this thing! It's wrong. He will destroy himself and all your plans for him!"

Noah left at dawn to walk to Lomeen's village. As the sun rose higher, the skies were blue at first, but by midmorning they turned to a slate gray, and a low rumbling in the west told Noah that bad weather was approaching. He forged ahead, but dark clouds rolled in, and soon white bolts of lightning were reaching down with fiery arms to touch the earth. The rain began all at once, falling from the sky like a waterfall.

There was no place to take refuge, so Noah trudged on in the deluge. Before long he saw a rock overhang that would give him some protection. It was scant shelter in such a storm, but he sat down and leaned back against the rock cliff, staying out of the rain as well as he could. The rain fell with relentless power, and tremendous blasts of thunder rocked the ground Noah sat on. He had never seen such a storm and sat there helpless and trembling in the face of the elements.

As always, his imagination began to create scenes in his mind. He thought of Lomeen and how his desire for her never went away, no matter how hard he tried to ignore his feelings. He shoved aside thoughts of his grandfather and Zorah, for he knew they were adamantly opposed to his marrying her, a worshiper of Ur-Baal.

It seemed the rain would never stop, and Noah huddled against the bank in his sodden tunic. Eventually he found himself being lulled by the rhythm of the drops drumming on the ground. He was almost asleep when he was startled by a strange occurrence.

He stiffened and sat up straight, staring at a mysterious glow in the darkness. He stood up cautiously, stepping out of his shelter into the rain to get a better look.

"Who is it?" Noah whispered hoarsely. He waited for a reply, but he heard nothing. He had never *seen* a light like this. It had no solid shape but appeared to be fluid, changing and flowing as he watched. It pulsed with color—like those in a rainbow but with more variety. The luminous colors blended and separated constantly in a complex pattern. Noah blinked his eyes, closed them, and shook his head, thinking that he was dreaming, but when he opened his eyes the bright shape still moved before him.

And then Noah knew! This was what he had prayed for, for years. The Ancient One was showing himself!

Noah cried out toward the light, "O Strong One, who lives forever! Speak to me, for I am filled with fear!"

"Fear not, Noah, for my eye has been on you."

Noah heard the voice clearly. It was not simply in his mind; he knew he was hearing it with his own ears. It was an unfamiliar voice, powerful yet quiet, stern yet gentle. Noah felt himself shaking so much he could barely keep from falling to the ground. He bowed his head and whispered, "What would you have me do?"

The light surrounded Noah, holding him in a warmth such as he had never known. He lost all sense of the cold rain and felt he was being held in a loving and kind embrace. Engulfed by the light, he heard the voice speak again.

"Before you were born, I chose you to be my servant. For years I have watched over you, although you did not know I was there. I have heard every word you spoke, and I know your every thought. I know those times when you doubted my existence, but I did not punish you, for all men and women have those thoughts. But you came to believe in me and have remained faithful, and now I have come to speak with you out of love. You ask what I would have you do, but I have come to tell you what you must not *do. Noah, I forbid you to marry the woman Lomeen."*

The startling words drove all of the warmth and comfort away from Noah, and he clearly saw the wickedness of his own heart. Here was the Strong One, the Ancient One, telling him what *not* to do. And it was the very thing he wanted most of all!

The coldness around Noah intensified as he thought of Lomeen and how much he wanted her. The sense of love and compassion that had surrounded him just moments before was gone. He grasped at the light that now receded in the darkness, wanting to feel once again that warmth embracing him, but in his heart, Noah could not give up the woman that so bound him. His desire for Lomeen seemed to cancel out the closeness to the Ancient One he had just felt. He knew he must choose between them—yet how could he, when he wanted both!

Irrationally he thought to bargain with God to let him have his way in just this one thing. "O Ancient One," he pleaded, "is it so much to ask to let me have her for my wife? I will do anything else you say, but please do not make me give up Lomeen. I am so lonely."

The light faded and the voice spoke no more. He found himself standing, with the cold rain soaking his body, plastering his hair and beard, more alone than ever. He sank to the ground and wept.

The rain finally abated as the storm passed, and Noah dragged himself to his feet and made his way back home. It was dark when he got there, and he went silently to his room. He stripped off his damp mud-splattered clothes, washed himself, and put on a clean, dry tunic. He lay down on the bed, but sleep evaded him. He took no comfort in the fact that the Ancient One had finally granted his request. Noah had actually seen Him and spoken with Him! But this great blessing was turned to despair when he thought of the commandment of the Ancient One: *"I forbid you to marry the woman Lomeen."*

Noah knew that everyone was worried about him, for he had told no one why he returned home without carrying through on his plan to marry Lomeen. It might have been good news for those who opposed the marriage, but they could see that Noah was depressed, going about his work in silent gloom.

Noah did not even tell Zorah about the Ancient One's appearance, not wanting to confess that he did not want to obey God's one commandment to him. He went about his work mechanically, ate when food was put before him, and slept badly at night, his mind filled with mysterious and troubling dreams.

As the days passed, his parents, brothers, sisters, and most of all, Methuselah and Zorah, were sick with worry. He tried to find some way to tell them what had happened to him, to give them a measure of assurance, but he had none to give. His heart was as cold as a stone, and all he could think of was his loss.

Despite his meeting with the Ancient One and the overwhelming sense of goodness and love that had surrounded him in that moment, Noah felt he had no power to resist the woman and obey God's clear commandment. He struggled terribly with this, and each day brought him one step closer to disobeying the Ancient One and marrying Lomeen.

He was thinking of this very thing when he had an unexpected visitor. As he worked in his shop he heard someone call his name. Glancing up, he was shocked to see Comir. He looked quickly past the tall man to see if Lomeen had accompanied him, but Comir was alone. Putting down his tools, he went forward and greeted his visitor. "Hello, Comir."

"Noah . . ." Comir began, but then the words seemed to fail him.

Noah stared at Comir and said, "What's wrong? Why have you come?" He suspected, and even hoped, that Comir had come to press the matter of his marriage with Lomeen. As Noah waited for Comir to speak, he decided, *I'll marry her today if he asks me to.*

But Comir was held by some emotion that twisted his face into lines of strain. Noah stared at him, then suddenly realized something was terribly wrong. "What is it, Comir? What's happened?"

"It's Lomeen."

"Is she sick?" Noah demanded.

Comir put his hands on Noah's shoulders. "I am filled with grief, and you shall be too when I tell you."

And then Noah, feeling the pressure of Comir's hands, knew everything. He whispered hoarsely, "Is she dead?"

"Yes, my friend. She died two days ago."

Noah could not take the news in. But when he stared into Comir's eyes, he saw the truth there. "What was it?"

"No one knows. It wasn't an accident, and she had no sickness. She was happy and cheerful the night before, as always." Comir's voice broke as he added, "But the next morning we found her dead. There . . . there was not a mark on her."

Noah turned cold. His mind raced with thoughts of his planned disobedience to the Ancient One's order. Could it be that he himself had caused her death through his rebelliousness? Would God have taken her life so he would not be able to marry her?

"I wanted to tell you at once," Comir said, "for I know you cared for her."

"I did. . . ." Noah whispered, his heart wrenching inside. He fell on his knees sobbing, grieving for her loss, and grieving over his own weakness. *I loved her as I will never love another woman!*

News of Lomeen's death traveled swiftly through town. Noah's mother came at once to him and put her arms around him. "I know you loved her, and you will grieve." Dezia tried to comfort him, but it was like holding a piece of wood. The light had vanished from his eyes, and he could not speak, so great was his grief. Dezia left, but others came, all with the same reaction from Noah when they tried to comfort him. It was like talking to a dead man.

Day after day passed, and Noah made no pretense of going to work.

He stayed outdoors down by the river most of the time. He did not get into his boat but simply walked back and forth along the riverbank, often staying out all night.

Methuselah and Zorah were beside themselves with sorrow—not over Lomeen's death but for what had happened to Noah. "It's like he's *died,* Zorah," Methuselah moaned. "What will happen to him?"

"It was the will of the Ancient One," Zorah whispered. "Noah told me yesterday he considers himself responsible for her death."

Methuselah stared at Zorah. "How can he believe that? He wasn't even there."

"He thinks the Ancient One took her so that he wouldn't marry her. He told me the Ancient One appeared to him in the storm, telling him not to marry Lomeen. He had come home, trying to obey, but he knew in his heart he was going to disobey when suddenly this happened."

Methuselah's eyes narrowed, and he nodded slowly. "What will he do now?"

"I cannot say," Zorah said. "First he needs to be healed of his sin—but such a healing must come from the Strong One himself."

Adah had watched Noah for days now. Her heart went out to him, and she tried to do little things to cheer him up, such as fixing his favorite foods, but nothing touched the big man. She had been so happy in her new home, and she knew it was all due to Noah. But now he looked like a man about to die, and it frightened her.

She was lying awake one night trying to pray the way Zorah had taught her, when she heard someone entering the house. Quickly she rose and dressed and went into the great room to find Noah, who was standing in the middle of the floor. He seemed dazed; he looked at her, his eyes filled with pain. Adah did not know what to do, but she had come to love this man who had changed her life so completely. She went to him and, looking up into his face, whispered, "Are you all right, master?"

Noah had to focus his eyes deliberately. His hair was uncombed, and he had wandered all day beside the river. The smell of it was still on him, and he could not speak. Suddenly his shoulders began to shake, and he felt tears rising in his eyes. The enormity of his loss overcame him, and like a very old man, he slumped down in a chair. He put his arms on the table, then lowered his head and wept like a small child. He was aware of a light touch on his shoulder, and with one big hand he reached back and covered Adah's small one.

Adah stood there not knowing what to say, but the sight of the man's grief wrung her heart. He turned to her, his eyes red with weeping. He said, "I have lost someone I loved very much, Adah."

"I know," Adah whispered. She could think of nothing else to say, but then she suddenly did something she would never ordinarily have done. She put her arms around him and whispered, "I will grieve with you, master."

Noah held the young woman tightly. After a time he patted her shoulder and stood up. "Go to bed, child," he whispered.

"Can I do anything for you?"

"You've done much. You have a good heart, Adah." He turned and left the room, and the young woman could barely see for the tears in her own eyes.

CHAPTER 13

Jukka never tired of watching Adah go about her work. He was a tall, spindly lad of twenty who had of late begun to hang around Noah's house in hopes of winning Adah's admiration. When Noah had first brought Adah home to their town five years earlier, she had been such a scrawny girl, the boys did not take much notice. But with the good care she received in Noah's home, it wasn't long before Adah began to fill out. And in time, the little girl who had been as skinny as a rail and pale as a ghost blossomed into a full-figured woman of grace, with smooth, lustrous skin of olive hue. Jukka could not keep his eyes off her. Nor could he keep his hands off her, whenever the opportunity arose to get that close.

Now, seeing that Adah's back was turned to him, Jukka grinned broadly as he tiptoed across the floor and threw his arms around her. He did not, however, have time to delight in the soft contours of her figure, for the girl twisted like an eel in his grasp, drew her arm back, and struck him hard in the mouth.

Reeling backward, Jukka yelled, "What'd you do that for?" He glared at the girl and held his lip as it puffed up. "What's the matter with you? All I wanted was a kiss."

Adah opened her mouth to answer, her face flushed with anger, but at that moment a faint voice called out from a small room off the great room in which they stood. Shoving the young man out of her way, she went to answer Ofra's request.

The old woman was sitting in a chair in her bedroom, her eyes alert. They were the only part of her body that *was* alert, for her limbs had stiffened so much her working days were over.

"What was that?" Ofra asked. "Who's making all that noise?"

Adah sighed. "It's just Jukka—as usual."

"What's he yelling about?" Ofra demanded. She waited expectantly, but then Adah giggled.

"He can't keep his hands to himself, so I hit him in the mouth."

Ofra stared at the girl, then let loose with a high cackle. "Serves him right! Don't even *think* of marrying him. He's got no sense."

"Don't worry about that! I'd sooner marry a toad. Now, do you need anything?" Adah put her hand on the aged woman's frail shoulder. She had a great affection for Ofra, and she remembered, with a touch of sadness, how hard Ofra had worked when Noah first brought Adah to this place. Now it was Adah who had to take care of Ofra, as well as Noah and Zorah. She patted the thin shoulder. "Don't worry, Ofra. I'll get rid of him. He's nothing but a pest anyway."

Returning to the great room, she found Jukka eating figs out of a bowl. She slapped his hand and said, "Stay out of those! They're for supper."

Jukka could not understand why Adah treated him so badly. He did, after all, come from a wealthy family, and he figured he was quite a catch for any young girl—but especially for a woman with no family at all, such as Adah.

Adah stared at Jukka, hands on hips, waiting for him to put the figs back. She found him not just unattractive but downright repulsive. He possessed a wealth of bushy black hair that seemed to stick out in every direction no matter what he did. He had once slicked it down with pitch, but that had made him look even worse. His eyes were close together, and he had a petulant lower lip that made him look as if he were constantly pouting. The pout was further exaggerated by his now very swollen lip. He was also cursed with a weak chin and terrible posture.

Jukka reluctantly put the figs back and followed Adah into the kitchen. Staring at her as she worked, he thought about what a puzzle she was to all the young men of the town who followed her around at festivals and in the marketplace. She seemed to care for none of them, and Jukka often boasted to the others that she was waiting for a suitor with money—like him. He did not admit to them, of course, that she had turned down every one of his marriage proposals.

He was a persistent young man, however, and sought to wear her down eventually. Now he said impulsively, "Adah, what's wrong with you?

I want to marry you, and you act like a wildcat every time I put my hands on you."

Adah paused in her work and turned to face him. For a fleeting moment she felt a wave of pity for Jukka. He was indeed a pathetic character. The only incentive he could offer a young woman was his family's money, and Adah was certain that someday he would find a woman willing to settle for that. "I don't know how to say it any plainer, Jukka. I don't love you, and I don't want to marry you."

"You'll love me after we're married, Adah. I'll give you a nice house. You can have a servant of your own. And clothes—I'll buy you the very best there is, and you can have any kind of jewelry you want."

"You're a fool, Jukka." Adah shook her head wearily. "Now, get out of here. I've got my work to do."

Jukka was not to be deterred. "You're nothing but a slave here! A hired servant at best. Think what you'd have if you married me."

She stopped and crossed her arms, appearing to be in deep thought. Jukka waited anxiously, hoping that she was finally going to agree to his proposal.

Then she said very slowly, "Jukka, if I ever do something really, really bad—I mean *awful*—then I will atone for it by marrying you. Now, off with you."

Jukka's anger flared at her insult. "All right, then! Go ahead and be a slave for the rest of your life. See if I care!"

Adah laughed as he stomped out of the house, glad to be rid of him for now, but knowing he would be back. She leaned down in front of the clay oven and pulled out a loaf of freshly baked bread. She set it down on the worktable, took a bronze knife, and sliced off a piece. She poured some honey out of a large jar into a small one, then carried both into Ofra's room.

"Here, Ofra, fresh bread and the honey you like so much." She sat down beside the old woman, pulled up a tray, and began to break the bread into small pieces.

Ofra had lost almost all her teeth, but she could eat the soft bread and honey. She eagerly dipped the bits in the honey and stuffed them into her mouth. "Did you get rid of that sniveling Jukka?"

"Yes. I don't think he'll be back for a while."

"Good!" Ofra dipped another morsel of the bread in the honey and put it into her mouth. Her eyes glowed as she rolled it around on her tongue. "This is *good!*" she exclaimed. "Your bread is almost as good as mine!"

"Never as good as yours, Ofra," Adah said, patting the old woman's knee.

In truth, Adah had become a far better cook than Ofra had ever been. She was clever and had thought up new ways to make food tastier, hunting for wild herbs to give it a richer flavor. By the time Ofra had begun to fail, the young woman had learned the ways of the house perfectly well. She did all the bartering for food and other items. She cooked, cleaned the house, washed the clothes, and made new ones for all of them. She was, in effect, mistress of the house, but everyone carried on the pretense that Ofra still held that position.

As Ofra savored the honey and bread, she gazed at the young woman. Beneath her crusty surface dwelled a real love for Adah, which her eyes revealed as she watched the young woman.

When Ofra had eaten all she wanted, Adah said, "I'm going to start cooking the evening meal. Why don't you lie down awhile?"

"I think I will. I'm a little tired."

Adah reached down and pulled Ofra to her feet. The pain in the old woman's knees and hips was dreadful, and she survived only by drinking various concoctions of herbs. It was not the herbs, however, that provided most of the pain-killing effect of the drink, but the fermented fruit juice Adah included as well. The beverage proved to be quite soporific, and Ofra spent much of her time sleeping. Adah guided her slowly across the room. She helped her sit on the bed, then lifted her legs, noting that the pain seemed to be worse today. When the old woman was down, she said, "I'll go get you an herb drink."

She quickly left the room but was soon back with a small clay tumbler. She helped the old woman drink the brewed herbs and wine, then carefully placed her head back. "Now, you sleep. I'll come in and check on you later."

"Thank you, Adah."

Adah then went about preparing the evening meal. She was still busy at it when Zorah came in and sat down on a stool to watch her.

"Noah should be here soon," Adah remarked.

"I think so." Zorah watched her cut up the meat skillfully with a bronze butcher knife and said, "Talk to me, Adah. I'm lonesome."

Adah turned to him and smiled. "Talk about what?"

"Something sensible."

"You never think a woman talks about anything sensible."

"Most of them don't, but you do. How about this pack of suitors that come looking for you with their tongues hanging out. Are you going to have any of them?"

"I doubt it. I've been around real men like you and Noah too long. Those boys all seem like addlebrained puppies."

The remark pleased Zorah, but then almost everything Adah said pleased him. He listened to her speak of everyday things and of people in the town. She was not a gossip, but she knew everyone's business.

She stopped cutting the meat and looked up. "You know, Zorah, sometimes I think I'd like to live out in the wilderness without everyone knowing exactly what goes on in my life."

Zorah chuckled softly. "What do you do that's so private?"

"Oh, nothing really, but it's aggravating that everyone knows everything about us. There are too many people in the world!"

Zorah laughed, then changed the subject. "How is Ofra today?"

"She's not good. In a lot of pain. I have to give her more and more of that drink. It makes her so sleepy, but she can't stand the pain without it."

"It's sad. She always loved to work so much, and now she can't. All she can do is watch you. You've been good for her, daughter."

"No, she's been good to *me*. When I first came here, she made me nervous. But then I learned quickly what a kind heart she has—just like Noah told me—despite that sharp tongue of hers."

The two talked easily, as they had for years. They had become great friends, and the old man was like a father to Adah. While they talked Zorah remembered the dreams he'd had of her before she came. He had never been able to sort them out, but somehow he knew that this young woman was born to play a part in his life. He had watched her grow up from a spindly-legged, gangly girl into a mature woman of wit, intelligence, and some beauty. He was also well aware of how she practically worshiped Noah—although the big man had not the slightest idea about this.

Even as this thought went through Zorah's mind, Adah turned to him, her face serious, and asked, "Do you think Noah will ever be happy?"

Zorah sighed and shook his head.

When he said nothing, Adah went on. "He's still grieving over that woman Lomeen, isn't he?"

Zorah was not surprised that she should see this. "Yes," he agreed. "I thought when she died everything would be better for Noah—but it's even worse. Now Noah's bound by some invisible chains to a dead woman!"

At that moment a sound drew both of their heads around, and they waited silently as Noah came in the door. Zorah did not miss how Adah looked at him. There was a look in her eyes that was not there for anyone else. But Noah, he knew, still thought of her as the small girl he had brought home five years ago, not the lovely young woman she had become.

"You're late," Adah said. "Sit down. I'll bring your food."

"Good," Noah said, settling into a chair and patting his stomach. "I could eat a whole river beast." He leaned back and stretched. "I finished that house, so I'm taking some time off.'

"You deserve it," Zorah said. "You've never learned how to relax."

"I guess you're right." Noah sat idly in his chair, and the flame from the oil lamp brightened the surface of his eyes. It accented the bridge of his large nose and deepened the ruddy coloring of his skin. He smiled across the table at Zorah. "What have you been doing all day?"

"Nothing, as usual. I'm too old to do much."

The two men spoke quietly until Adah brought the food in and sat down with them. She ate slowly, and at a pause in the conversation, she turned to Noah. "Don't forget. The harvest festival is next week." He grinned broadly at her, and Adah thought his smile made him look much younger.

"Are you working on a new dress?" he asked.

"I've already finished my dress, and I've made a new tunic for you. You look like a beggar in those old clothes of yours."

"No one will be looking at me." He winked at Zorah and asked innocently, "I guess Jukka will be coming by to take you, huh?"

"That pest has already been here . . . and I sent him away," Adah said, disgusted.

Noah nodded as he took a bite of his dinner, but he wasn't really paying attention and had missed her remark. "You see, Zorah," he went on, "we'll be losing this one soon."

"Never to Jukka!" Adah cried, making a face.

Noah reached across the table and captured her hand. She looked up in surprise and saw that he was staring at her in a rather odd fashion. "What is it?" she asked. "Why are you staring at me like that?"

Noah cocked his head and studied her. "Where is that scared little rabbit I brought home five years ago, I wonder?" He squeezed her hand and nodded. "You're growing up."

Adah yanked her hand free, got up, and stormed out of the room.

"What's wrong with her?" Noah said. "What did I say to upset her?"

Zorah leaned back in his chair and stared at Noah. "For a man as smart as you, sometimes you're dumb as dirt!"

"I've never claimed to be smart—especially when it comes to women. It seems I've hurt her feelings. What's wrong with her?"

"If you don't know, I can't tell you," Zorah said half angrily. Then he leaned forward and asked, "When are you going to forget Lomeen, Noah? She's been dead five years now, and you're still crippled by the memory of her."

Noah's face contorted, and he ran his hand through his thick hair. "Do you think I don't know that, Zorah? She's always with me somehow. I'll be working on a piece of wood and suddenly it's like she's standing right there. I can smell her and feel her presence—and at night it's worse. She comes to me in dreams, but when I reach out for her, she's gone. She's *always* with me, Zorah. I'll never get rid of her!"

Adah put on the dress she had made especially for the harvest festival. The loose-fitting garment was dyed a bright blue and trimmed in scarlet. She looked down at it and turned around, wishing she could see herself. Ofra, sitting across the room, said, "That dress cost enough to buy five or six sheep."

Adah laughed. "So? I can't wear sheep to the festival, can I, Ofra?" She went over to the old woman and kissed her on the cheek. "I wish you could go," she whispered.

"I'm past all that, but when you come home I want to hear all about it."

Adah agreed at once. "If you're asleep, I'll tell you about it tomorrow."

She left Ofra's room and found Zorah sitting on a bench with his arms folded, leaning back against the wall, his eyes half closed. They opened as she entered, and he sat up. "Well, look at you," he said, pleased with her appearance. "Turn around. Let me see." He watched as she whirled around and said, "What'd you do to your hair?"

"I washed it. It wouldn't be a bad idea for you too."

"I don't hold with washing all that much."

Adah laughed and went over and put her hand on his cheek. "Do you really like my dress?"

"I do. Never saw one any prettier."

Noah had been outside putting up his tools, and when he came in, she saw that he was filthy from the hard work. "Noah, go get ready!"

"Naw . . . I'm not going. I've been to festivals before."

Zorah saw the hurt in Adah's eyes, and he spoke up. "Don't talk like a fool, Noah! You promised Adah—you've got to go. You act like you're as old as Methuselah. Go get cleaned up."

Noah grinned. He glanced at Adah and shook his head. "I won't be as pretty as she is, though."

While Noah was washing up, Adah walked back and forth, enjoying the comfortable feel of the dress. She had become an expert weaver since Noah had made her the finest loom in the clan. She knew she could make a lucrative business of selling the garments, but she never made the effort. She was happy just to keep her small family well clothed and make gifts for a few special friends.

"Well, Adah," Zorah said while they waited for Noah, "you're a woman now and ready for a man, but I don't think you'll have any of those eager young men at the festival." He hesitated for a moment, then went on, "Not when you've got your eyes on another man."

Adah turned pale. Zorah was the wisest man she knew, and she whispered, "What do you mean?"

"You know what I mean. I may be old, but I'm not blind. Your eyes follow Noah wherever he goes."

Adah dropped her eyes, her shoulders stooped. "He'll never look at me, Zorah. He'll always love Lomeen—even though she's dead."

"I'd not be too quick to say that," Zorah said slowly. "You're a young woman, and you've got a long life ahead of you. I decided a long time ago that the Ancient One is also the Wise One. He does things with our lives that we don't dream about—and I think He's going to do something with yours."

Adah was caught by the seriousness of his words. She stared at him, not smiling.

Then Noah sauntered in and said, "I'm ready. Who's going?"

Zorah stood up and clapped Noah on the back. "You two young folks go have a good time. I'll stay here and look after Ofra."

As they left the house Noah asked idly, "What were you and Zorah talking about?"

Adah hid her eyes from his gaze. "Oh, nothing. . . ."

The harvest festival was the most joyous time of the year for everyone in the clan. The hard work of bringing in the crops was over, and the grain was safely stored. Starvation would not come this year, for the harvest had been especially good.

Adah enjoyed the festival and so did Noah. He teased her about the young men who followed her around trying to get her away from him. "Why don't you go with that one right over there? He looks like he's got a little sense, and he's a fine-looking fellow."

"I *did* go with him. Don't you remember? He hung around our house so long, Zorah finally had to kick him out."

"Why did he do that?"

Adah looked up at Noah and laughed. "Because he fancies himself a musician. He sings love songs, but he sounds like a dog howling at the moon. None of us could stand it."

The two walked around, enjoying the music and sampling the food. Noah turned to look down at Adah and found himself admiring her. "I was teasing you last week about how you've changed, and you got upset. But I didn't mean to make you angry."

"It's all right. I'm too hot-tempered."

Noah suddenly laughed and took her arm. "You have the easiest temper of anybody in the house. I was just trying to say how wonderful it is that you've grown into such a fine young woman. You don't know how often I give thanks that you came to take care of us all."

"Noah, it's you who takes care of me."

"That may have been true five years ago, but it's not now. Why, where would poor Ofra be if you weren't there? She knows how helpless she is, but you never mention it."

Adah was very conscious of Noah's hand on her arm. He was so large, she had to tilt her head back to look in his face, even though she herself had grown to be quite tall. "It's nice to hear that, Noah," she whispered.

The music changed to a lively tempo and some young people started a wild dance. Adah laughed and pulled on Noah's arm. "It's time to be foolish, you and me. Come on."

"Me, dance?"

"Why not?"

"I . . . I don't know how. My feet are so big I'd probably trample you."

"I'll stay out of your way. Come on, Noah, please."

"All right. You asked for it, but you've been warned."

The two joined in the circle of dancers and went around and around with the others. For such a large man, Noah was actually quite nimble on his feet, and he picked up the dance steps easily. Adah was pleased that Noah seemed to have put his troubles behind him. His eyes were flashing, and he laughed, his lips red under his mustache. He had a good voice too, and when the songs began they both joined in.

After several dances, the two retired to the refreshment tables. "I don't know how I can be hungry again so soon. I've eaten enough for five men," Noah said.

"It's the harvest festival, Noah. It's the time to overeat and overdance and oversing." She smiled up at him, and he returned the smile. Then he said, "You ought to be with young people—not an old dead stump like me."

"Don't talk about yourself like that. You're the strongest man in the clan . . . and the smartest too."

She would have said more, but Noah suddenly lifted his eyes. She saw him look over her shoulder, then freeze. "What is it, Noah?" she whispered. She turned when he did not answer and saw a tall broad-shouldered man standing beside a young dark-haired woman.

"Who are they, Noah? I never saw them before. Do you know them?"

Noah's voice was hoarse and barely above a whisper. "Yes, I know them. One is a spirit from the dead."

Shocked by his words, Adah looked back and saw that the man was coming toward them, while the woman remained where she was. The man greeted Noah immediately. "Hello, Noah."

"Hello, Comir."

Comir saw that Noah's eyes were fixed on the young woman behind him, and he said quickly, "You're not seeing a ghost, but I know how you must feel. Have you ever seen her before?"

"No. Who is she?"

"She is Lomeen's daughter, Meira. She was raised by our older sister."

"I can't believe it. I didn't know Lomeen even had a daughter. It's like—"

"I know. It's like Lomeen risen from the dead. Meira's heard much about you. She wants to meet you."

Adah was forgotten as Noah's attention was now riveted on the willowy young beauty with Comir. Adah could see that Noah was in another world. She watched as Comir led him to the woman. Meira was wearing a white tunic that left her slender arms bare. She had glossy black hair that fell to her waist. Her eyes glowed as she looked up and spoke to Noah. Adah could not hear the words, but she saw that Noah was stiff and that Comir was watching the pair carefully.

As for Noah himself, he was stunned. When Comir introduced them, Meira said, "I'm delighted to meet you at last."

Noah could not speak, so great was the resemblance. "Sorry if I . . . seem speechless, but . . ."

"I know. I look so much like my mother. She spoke of you often and obviously thought very highly of you."

Before Noah could say anything, Comir said, "Would you watch out for Meira? I have to go speak to your father."

"Yes. Of course." Noah did not even watch Comir go; his eyes were wholly on the face of the young woman. "You'll have to pardon me. I'm not myself."

"It's happened before." Meira smiled. "I must be very like her."

"As like as she was to herself. Have you eaten? Would you care for something to drink?"

"Yes, please. And I want to hear all about you." She put her hand on Noah's arm, and the two moved away to the tables.

Adah stood stiffly, numb with shock. *The daughter of Lomeen!* She forced herself to watch the two as long as she could. Finally she could stand it no longer and turned to leave the festival. She walked almost blindly, and when she reached home, she found Zorah sitting outside watching the moon.

"Where's Noah?" he asked, surprised.

"I . . ." She could say no more. Her throat was tight, her lips paralyzed.

Seeing her distress, Zorah rose and came to her. "What's wrong, child?"

"It's that woman—Lomeen!"

"Lomeen? What about her? She's been dead for years."

"Her daughter—she came to the festival with a man called Comir."

"I had heard she had a daughter that she did not raise herself. Comir brought her here?"

"Yes, and she looks exactly like her mother. That's what Noah said. He went off with her and left me."

New trouble seemed to rise in Zorah's mind, and he said, "Come tell me about it, Adah." They sat down, and he listened as the girl explained. Zorah was horrified, for even though he had not seen the woman, he knew what was happening. He whispered, "He's always been a fool about that woman, and now he thinks he can have the daughter."

"You should have seen him, Zorah," Adah wailed. "He was like a man struck by a spear. Just one look at her—"

"I know," Zorah said. Then he whispered, "He's a lost man, daughter, unless the Strong One helps him." He saw tears running down Adah's face. He wanted to comfort her, but no words came to him, and he cried out in his spirit, *O Ancient One, show yourself strong on behalf of Noah. Don't let him destroy himself because of this woman.*

CHAPTER 14

Adah sat alone beside a grove of trees on the outskirts of town. The sun reached long fingers of light through the branches and touched her face. Overhead a green-and-white bird perched on a limb, proudly enlivening the air with his song. Adah looked up and thought, *I wish I had a song as happy as yours, little bird.* She dropped her head, then drew her legs up, enclosing them with her arms. She thought back to the day Noah had saved her from Mak and what a miserable creature she had been then. She kept all memories of her days before that imprisoned inside herself, refusing to let them come out. But the days since then had been full of joy. Her life had taken on a different shape, as a tree grows new branches and the old branches are trimmed and fall to earth. She had been happy with the constant pattern of discard and growth her life had taken, and grateful for the new things that had come.

A movement caught her eye, and she turned to see Methuselah hobbling along, leaning heavily on his staff. He wore a tattered gray robe, and his silver beard and hair ruffled in the light breeze. As he drew closer she rose to stand, facing him.

"Good morning, daughter," Methuselah greeted her.

"Good morning, sir."

"You are out early this morning." He studied her for a moment, taking in the clear skin and the troubled eyes. He had grown to appreciate this young woman and had been especially interested in her since Zorah had told him of his dreams about her and his feeling that she would play an important role in the days to come.

Methuselah had sought her out deliberately but did not want to be too abrupt. "It's a good day, is it not?" he said. "Here, sit beside me for a while. We haven't talked in a long time." He led her to a fallen tree, and the two sat down on the trunk. She was silent, so he came to the point. "I can see that you are very troubled, Adah."

Adah had long ago learned of the wisdom of this ancient man. He had talked to her many times of the old days—old days that went back so far she could not comprehend it. Hundreds of years. She knew of his attachment to Noah, and that endeared him to her. Finally she whispered, "Yes. I am grieving."

"Grief is always a terrible thing. Many times I've been so overwhelmed with it I didn't know which way to turn."

Adah looked up, startled, for she had never imagined that this man, who was so strong despite his age, had ever suffered from trouble. "You, sir?"

"Why, of course! How many times have I been caught in deep troubles? At times I've been like a man stuck on a rock in the middle of a raging river who can't see any way across. At such times all I could do was look down at the troubled water surging around me and pray that the Strong One would bring me safely ashore."

"I never thought of you like that."

"We're all the same, and I have lived so long. I suppose I've experienced as much grief and trouble as any man. I've watched many dear friends and loved ones die." He gazed warmly into her eyes and said softly, "And I too have loved with all my heart, only to have that person not return my love."

Adah's eyes brimmed with tears and she hung her head. He impulsively reached for her hand. "When life is hard for us, child, it seems that the pain will last forever. But things are never hopeless. You're worried about Noah, aren't you?"

"Yes . . ." She choked back her tears and swallowed hard. "When he left to go to that woman, I thought my heart was going to break." Now as she confessed her feelings, she remembered the day Noah left to go visit Comir's village—to see Meira. His parting words still rang in her ears: *"I must do this thing, Adah. I love her, and I must go to her."*

"He loves her, sir."

"No, he doesn't love her," Methuselah said, shaking his head grimly. "He *wants* her!" He tightened his grip on Adah's hand and said, "Wanting is not loving. Loving is giving."

She considered his words but was so deeply enmeshed in her grief she could make nothing of them. "I don't understand that," she said simply.

"People who love rarely do understand it. They just do it. Ever since you've come to live here, you've given to others."

"Oh no, I'm the one everyone has given to!"

Releasing her hand, Methuselah nodded. "You've given to everyone you've come in contact with. To Noah. To Zorah. To me. And to poor Ofra. Where would she be without you?"

Startled, Adah gazed up at the old man. "How have I given to all of you?"

"By being kind. By giving yourself for the comfort of others. Noah's been too blind to see this. He's got that woman in his heart—or at least in his flesh." His words were bitter, and he shook his head angrily.

"Everyone says he'll marry her. I've got to get away from here," Adah said suddenly. It was something she had made up her mind to do. If Noah came back with a bride, it would be more than she could bear to watch his happiness with another woman. "I've got to leave."

"No. You must stay here, Adah. To run away from trouble is fruitless. Wait and see."

"Wait for what?" Adah said desperately. "There's nothing for me here."

"We never know what's here for us, but Zorah knows something. He believes the Ancient One has a plan for you, though he can't see what it is. Promise me you won't go for a while."

Adah nodded reluctantly. "All right. If that's what you want."

"Good. Now, we will ask the Ancient One, who is also the Strong One, to give Noah what he *needs*—not what he wants."

Adah listened as Methuselah began to pray. He prayed gently at first, thanking the Ancient One for all the blessings he had received in his long life. When he began to pray for Noah, however, he was like a man beating on a door, demanding entrance. She was shocked that anyone could pray to God with such courage and fervency. When he was finished, she rose with him and smiled shyly. "Thank you, sir. You've been a help to me."

"Always remember this, Adah. Most people want greatness, but it's better to have human warmth than greatness—and you have as much of that quality as anyone I've ever seen. Don't give up! The Ancient One will have the final word!"

Noah glanced down at Meira, who was walking along beside him. She had been at his side much during his visit to her village. He had arrived full of doubts and fears, but over the last few days she had acted so warmly toward him that he was feeling almost happy. They were taking a midday walk in the woods, where it was cooler. Noah noticed a flight of gaily colored butterflies and pointed at them. "Look at those butterflies. Their wings are so delicate the light passes right through them."

Meira turned to look and studied the large red butterflies. She smiled up at him. "You notice so many things, Noah. I've never known a man so conscious of the world about him as you are."

"Doesn't everyone see these things?" Noah asked.

"Not like you do," Meira said, a small smile touching her lips.

Noah watched her as she spoke, intrigued by the intricate arrangement of her glossy black hair. She went on, "You see the birds, the animals. You smell things that most people don't notice. You even stop and taste plants every once in a while." She laughed at him, and the sound of it was a delight to the big man. "You're a man of senses, always touching things, smelling things. I wish I were like that."

Her words pleased Noah, and he took her hand and squeezed it as they continued their walk along the cool, shaded path. They reached a pond in a clearing, where he said, "Look over there, Meira. There's a heron. He acts like a high priest, all dressed in gray. How fierce he looks."

"Why, he just looks like a heron to me. You do have a vivid imagination! I expect you have vivid dreams too, don't you?"

Noah blinked, surprised. "Yes, I do," he said. "How could you know that?"

"Anybody who sees as much as you do must have dreams."

What Meira said about Noah was true. He was always conscious of smells, of textures, of unusual shapes in the rocks and landscape around him.

Noah noted the arrival of four crows to a patch of tall grass at the edge of the pond. They shook their heavy wings and took off again, making their way high into the sky. Even though he continuously watched nature around him, he was at this moment mostly conscious of the woman beside him. He had felt such grief over Lomeen's death that he could hardly believe his good fortune in meeting her daughter—Lomeen's very own flesh and blood, and in appearance, the woman herself. In one sense Meira was even better than Lomeen, for the daughter had a gentler spirit than her mother had.

The two slowed down and stopped in the path to watch two squirrels chasing each other through the treetops. Without warning she turned and grew serious. "What is it you want, Noah?"

Noah, taken off guard, smiled nervously. "I don't know. I don't suppose most of us know what we want."

"You've lived a long time. Why haven't you ever married?"

The reference to the difference in their ages bothered Noah, but older men married young women all the time. He blurted out the truth without meaning to. "I think it has something to do with your mother."

The expression on Meira's face darkened. "Am I as much like her as people say?"

Noah held up his hands. "More alike than these two hands."

He paused with his hands in the air and gazed into her eyes as she watched him. Her clean, fresh scent touched his senses and stirred his emotions, and he let his hands drop to her shoulders. Then he pulled her forward and kissed her. She did not resist him, so he held her in a long embrace. When he gently released her, she smiled up at him, her eyes expectant. Noah asked haltingly, "Meira ... would you marry me if I asked?"

Meira seemed to have a ready answer to his question, as though she had expected it. "I will do what my uncle says."

It wasn't the answer Noah wanted to hear. "But would you ... *could* you ever love me as I loved your mother ... and as I think I love you too?"

An enigmatic light glowed in Meira's eyes. She was quiet for a moment, then shook her head slightly. "I'm not sure I know what love is. You're a strong man, and I know my uncle wants us to marry. I'll do as he says."

The two stood silently in the shade, not sure what else to say to each other. The heron dipped his long neck in the pond, then turned his cold eyes toward them as if disturbed by what he saw. He unfolded his wings and beat his way into the sky. The pair watched as he disappeared over the treetops.

Noah cleared his throat and said formally, "Then I will ask your uncle."

Comir was delighted when Noah came to him and asked to marry Meira. He slapped the big man on the back and said, "It will be a good thing. We will be brothers. Our two clans will be as one."

Noah shook his head. "I wish I were sure this was the right thing to do."

Comir stared curiously at the big man. "None of us are sure at all times. What's bothering you?"

Noah could not speak the truth aloud. He had prayed for two days, asking the Ancient One to speak, to tell him what to do. He had received no answer, and in despair he had finally said, "All right. You haven't said yes or no, Holy One, so I will assume the answer is *yes*." Despite his decision, the uncertainty over it lurked in his heart, leaving him without the peace he desired.

Comir saw the trouble in Noah's eyes and said, "Look at it this way, Noah. You loved a woman with all your heart once. Everybody saw that, and Lomeen loved you. But you missed your chance with her." His brow furrowed, and he said, "All of us miss chances. Every man looks back on his life and wishes he had done something he failed to do." He smiled then and slapped Noah again on the shoulder. "You missed your chance at happiness once, but now it's in your grasp. Not many men have a second chance."

"Give me a few more days to be sure of this," Noah said. "I must go home and think about it some more. When I settle it in my mind, I will send you word or come myself."

Comir was disappointed that Noah seemed to be changing his mind. He had hoped to settle the matter that day. Still, he was too wise to pursue it, for he knew Noah was a stubborn man. Hiding his feelings, Comir smiled confidently and again slapped Noah on the shoulder. "Go, brother. I will await your decision. I hope it will be a positive one, for I know this marriage will make you very happy."

CHAPTER 15

After getting home late, Noah arose early in the morning and found Adah already up preparing loaves of bread to put in the oven. Her face was usually cheerful, and she always had a ready smile, but this morning she stared at him without expression, and without even a greeting. He wasn't sure how to take this unusual side of the young woman he thought he knew so well. Without thinking, he blurted out, "I . . . I think I'm going to marry Meira."

He could not understand the shadow that passed over Adah's face at his sudden pronouncement. He felt he had to say more, to explain to her. He moved closer and put his hands out with a pleading gesture. "I know you think this may not be right, and I know that my grandfather and Zorah will be opposed to it. But I'm getting older, Adah. All of my other friends have families, and I have nothing, really. I want sons. I've never said much about it, but I've always had a longing for a family. What else is a man for except to have a family?"

Adah felt as if a cold bronze fist were clasped about her heart. She had prayed desperately that Noah would not make this decision. She knew that Zorah and Methuselah were praying also, but now she saw that it had all come to nothing.

"I'll be leaving here, Noah."

Her words struck against Noah like a punch to his gut. He stared at her, not comprehending. "Leaving here!" he cried. He stepped forward to put his hands on her, as he often did, but she drew back, obviously rejecting him. "Where will you go?" he asked. "This is your home."

"Now it will be another woman's home," Adah said coldly.

"But what will happen to Ofra? And what about Zorah? He's getting old. All of us need you!"

"Your new wife can take care of them."

Noah watched in disbelief as Adah turned her back on him and began kneading the dough fiercely. He had expected that she would not approve, but he had not thought she would be this upset. In all the years she had been here, he had never seen a single instance of such hardness, and he tried desperately to think of a way to change her mind. But no words came, and he stood watching her helplessly.

Without looking at him, Adah said, "In the meantime, you'd better find somebody to come in and help with the work—because I won't be here."

"Is there anything I can say to make you change your mind?" Noah pleaded.

Adah's lips were drawn together so tightly they were pale. "I thank you for all you've done for me, Noah. I would have still been a slave, or even dead by now, if you hadn't saved me. I'll always be grateful to you—but I can't stay in this house now."

Noah began to speak, but she cut him off. "Don't say any more! My mind's made up!"

The house seemed abysmally empty without Adah. In desperation, Noah hired a woman named Jachil to take care of things. She was a small, dumpy woman with a quick tongue and a vast store of impatience. Zorah had been showing signs of illness for some time and required much care, and Ofra, of course, was totally helpless now.

Jachil, after the first three days, came to Noah and said, "I've got to have more money. This is more work than I thought."

"All right, Jachil. Just take care of the house and Ofra, and I'll pay whatever you ask."

Noah took over the care of Zorah, who appeared to be failing fast. Noah was alarmed at how quickly his illness was dragging him down. He sought the advice of anyone who had a reputation for healing, trying an array of herbal remedies and poultices, but nothing helped.

One day, a week after Adah had left, he sat down beside Zorah, who was lying on his bed. "How are you today, old friend?"

Zorah turned his skull-like face toward Noah. His eyes were deeply sunken, and his lips were wrinkled and dry. "I must go soon to be with my fathers, Noah."

"Not for a long time yet, Zorah," Noah pleaded.

"I'm old enough to know when my time has come."

Noah sat there stunned. Zorah had been, for so many years, a fixed point in his life—someone he trusted and could go to for anything and ask for help. But he clearly saw the truth in the old man's words. He knew that Zorah was unhappy about his intention to marry Meira, and for a moment, Noah thought about telling him that he would do whatever Zorah advised. But he knew well what Zorah would say. He had made his mind clear on the matter. A follower of the Ancient One could never marry a worshiper of Ur-Baal without bringing much grief into his life.

Noah did not want to hear that lecture, so instead he said lamely, "I wish Adah were here to take care of you. She would know what to do to make you better." He waited for Zorah to answer, but the old man merely shook his head. His breath was so faint it barely stirred his chest, and for a long time Noah just sat quietly. Then he said almost in despair, "I don't see why Adah had to leave."

Zorah's old, tired eyes suddenly burned like new coals. "You're a fool, Noah, if you don't know that."

"Why, what do you mean?"

"You're so aware of things in the world—birds, fish, snakes, animals. You look at a tree and almost compose a poem about it. I've never seen a man more aware of his world—but you're stone blind where women are concerned!"

Noah was confused. "I'm not very good at it, I'll admit, but—"

"All these years, and you don't know how Adah feels about you?"

As Zorah spoke these words, Noah was struck dumb. He stared at the dying old man, and memories passed through his mind. He thought of Adah's warm smile whenever he spoke to her and how eagerly she used to cling to him when she was little more than a child. As she had grown older and matured into a woman, there was still a childlike way about her. He had never stopped to consider that her emotions had also matured into those of a woman. Suddenly he swallowed hard and whispered, "I never thought of her like that."

"No. That's because you're blind, as I said. You've been blinded by the beauty of another woman's body," Zorah snapped. "And now you're in love with a ghost. It's not Meira you love. It's Lomeen! And it's not even love, Noah—it's the lust of the flesh that has shackled you since you were a young man. That woman has reached out from the grave to pull you down with her to your doom! You're a fool, Noah, and not worthy of the Ancient One!"

Noah could not bear to look into Zorah's eyes. He dropped his head and clasped his hands together, squeezing them hard. An unbearable silence fell between them.

Zorah's eyes closed, and his breathing became labored. "I'm sorry to be so harsh, Noah. You've been the son I never had in the flesh, and I've loved you all your life. I say these things *because* I love you."

Noah was touched by the whispered words. He opened his eyes, overflowing now with tears, leaned forward, and took the old man's hand. "Tell me what to do, Zorah. I've lost my way." His voice was stark with pain, and he clung to the old man's frail hand.

Zorah mustered the strength to open his eyes and look deeply into Noah's. "Do you mean that, my son?"

"Yes, oh yes!" Noah sobbed. "Just tell me. I can't make any decisions anymore. Everything I do is wrong."

"No . . . not everything. Just *one* thing." Zorah gasped for breath, trying to say these last important words. "Go tell your grandfather that I said it's time you should know. . . . Then bring him back here."

"Time I should know what?" Noah asked, leaning forward.

But Zorah shook his head. His lips moved in and out with his breath, and then he whispered, "Hurry. My time is short!"

Methuselah stared at Noah. "What did you say, son?"

"Zorah is dying, and he said for me to come for you." Noah hesitated, then went on, "He told me to tell you that it's time for me to know. What did he mean by that?"

Methuselah stared at his tall grandson, then said quietly, "I will go. Just a moment." He moved across his room swiftly and opened a chest that was in a niche in the wall. Noah watched as he moved several objects aside, then pulled out a small box. Then he said simply, "Let us go."

They made their way slowly, for Methuselah's joints were stiff and he could not move fast. Noah was frantic, fearing that Zorah might die while they were gone. When they finally arrived at Noah's house, Jachil met them at the door.

"The old man's dying," she said. "You'd better hurry."

"I know. Leave us alone, Jachil."

Offended, the servant moved away, but Noah did not notice her indignation. He accompanied Methuselah to the small room where Zorah lay. He watched his grandfather hobble over and sit down on a stool beside the bed. Methuselah spoke to the sick man, and Zorah's eyes opened.

"I'm glad you are here, old friend," Zorah said. "I was not sure . . . I could wait."

Methuselah put his hand on the old man's forehead in a gesture of affection. "We are agreed, then, that it is time for him to know?"

"Yes. He is the one. Tell him quickly, for I feel the darkness gathering."

Methuselah turned to Noah, and he held out the box in both hands. "I have something for you."

He opened the lid, and Noah moved closer so he could see in the dim light. The single oil lamp in the room flickered, twisting shadows into tortured shapes and shedding pale yellow light on the walls and floors. He stared at Methuselah's twisted fingers as he unfolded a piece of soft leather, obviously very old. "What is it, Grandfather?"

Methuselah did not answer. He took something shiny out of the leather casing and held it for a moment in his hands, his head bowed. When he lifted his head, his eyes were bright, and he said to Noah, "This is for you."

Noah reached out and took the object. He held it close to the lamp and saw that it was a piece of yellow metal. Engraved on it was a beautifully executed carving of a lion. The beast was lifelike and had one paw uplifted as in victory, but it was the eyes that caught Noah's attention. They were inlaid with a gemstone such as he had never seen. Even in the dim light the jeweled eyes glittered like the stars overhead, as if they had life of their own. Noah stared at the engraving and said, "What is it?"

His fingers felt the raised surface on the opposite side, and turning the medallion over, he saw a lamb.

"What is it?" he asked again. He looked up and saw that his grandfather was smiling.

"My father, Enoch, gave this to me before he went to be with God." Methuselah's voice was quiet in the stillness. The only other sound in the room was Zorah's erratic breathing. "He told me to be careful whom I showed it to and to keep it secret. The only one who has ever seen it is Zorah. It was a burden for me, because I could not make the right decision about it."

"What decision?" Noah urged.

"My father told me to give it to one of my blood kin who would be faithful to the Ancient One even to death. He was very strict about that. He told me, 'He may not look like a victor. He may not be a great soldier or a warrior, but he must be one who will obey God's voice no matter what the cost.'"

Zorah turned and reached his hand out, and Noah knelt, taking it in both of his large ones. It was only bone and skin, the muscle having all withered away. "Enoch was a seer, a prophet," Zorah said. "He saw what would happen in days to come. Be *very* careful, Noah. This is a great trust that your grandfather puts in you."

Noah could not understand what was happening. He turned to Methuselah and asked, "What does this medallion mean, Grandfather?"

"My father was often puzzled by what the Ancient One showed him, but he knew God as no other man ever has. He called this the 'sign of the lion.' Why a lion, he did not know. He just knew that somewhere in the future, after he had left this earth, his descendants would have a task to do for the Ancient One. I myself have done nothing of note, except to grow older than any other man, and that's not much of a triumph." His eyes glowed then, and he reached forward and put his hand on Noah's head. He stroked the thick hair and said, "I think you are the man who must bear the sign of the lion. You will pass it on after you have finished your work. My father said there would always be a man to do God's work, and that man will bear the sign of the lion."

Noah was trembling now, for he knew his life would never be the same. He listened as Methuselah went on speaking of his father's words. "Enoch said that the Ancient One would not leave mankind to be destroyed, and he often told me that one day He would send a deliverer who would rid the world of all evil. I and you also, Noah, are in the bloodline through which that one will come."

Noah's hands shook as he held the medallion. He stared at it, suddenly frightened at what it stood for. "But why me? I am nothing!" he protested.

"You are the chosen one." Zorah's voice, suddenly strong, drew Noah's head around. The old man had raised himself up on one elbow, and he reached out his hand in a familiar gesture. "You will bear the sign of the lion. We do not know what that lion means, but it is the will of the Ancient One. Be faithful to Him, and He will make of you a deliverer."

The old man opened his eyes wide and stared across the room. He appeared to see something the other two could not. Then he whispered a few unintelligible words and fell back on the bed.

Noah leaned forward and cried out his name, but Methuselah knew there would be no answer. "He has gone to be with Enoch and the Ancient One—wherever that is, my son."

Noah did not move or speak, nor did Methuselah. They sat still and quiet until the oil in the lamp grew low, and the light burned so feebly that Noah could hardly see the face of the dead seer.

And then, without warning, the room was filled with light. Noah blinked, and when he turned he saw that Methuselah was on his knees. He knelt down also, holding his grandfather, who was about to fall to the floor. He saw that Methuselah was unconscious, and he himself felt as if he could not bear the light. And then he heard the voice that he had heard before in the rainstorm—the voice of the Ancient One. There was no mistaking it; it was warm and vibrant and more living than any human voice could ever be. It was also very still and quiet, yet Noah heard every word.

"I have chosen you to be my servant, Noah, and you must obey me even when you are afraid. You must marry and have sons—and one day I will come to you again. I will be silent for many years, but never forget you are my servant. One day I will do a work through you such as the world has never known."

Noah trembled as if he had a fever. The light seemed to flood every organ of his body and flow through his veins. He felt both warm and cold, and he shook so violently that the medallion nearly slipped from his hand. He grasped it harder, and finally he whispered, "I will do as you command, Holy One."

"You are a good son. I am pleased with you, Noah. Now, hear my word. You must marry Adah, for I have created her to be your helper. You do not love her now. You have turned aside to unworthy women who do not believe in me, but this is my commandment to you. Will you obey?"

And then Noah, the son of Lamech, the descendant of Enoch, the one who had walked with God, knew that all of the life he had known till now must be abandoned. He did not know what lay ahead, but neither did he fear it. As he bowed before the light that seemed to emanate from nowhere yet permeate his very soul, he fell on his face and cried out with all his might, "I will obey, O Holy One. . . !"

CHAPTER 16

Adah sat on a bench outside the small home she had come to share with Methuselah's granddaughter. The late afternoon sun threw its last beams down across the village where she was staying. When she left Noah's home, she did not know where to go, so Methuselah had sent her here, saying, "You will go stay with my granddaughter Edel. She is a widow and she's lonely. Go there until I send word to you."

Adah had found Edel to be quiet and gentle. She helped with the household chores, but there was little work needed for just two women. Hence the days seemed to crawl by, and now as she watched the setting sun, she fought against the hopelessness that weighed her down, the despair she felt at having left the only real home she'd ever known.

Looking up, she noticed the moon had made a premature appearance. It looked aged and scarred, cloaked by a veil of drifting clouds. The distant hills in the east brooded in a sullen haze, and the landscape took on a tawny hue.

She watched the villagers passing by. Several children had been playing in the road, but as the sky grew darker they went inside, leaving her to gaze up at the moon. As darkness covered her, she welcomed it. Life here held no meaning for her. She could see nothing ahead but boredom and unhappiness.

Peering down the darkened road to a spot where the moon had freed itself of the clouds and now threw its silver beams down, she was startled to see a man appear. There was no mistaking the huge figure. She knew his shape, his every gesture. She would have recognized him in almost total darkness. Her heart began to beat quickly, and she stood up. He was looking from side to side, and she knew that he was searching for her. Lifting her voice, she called out, "Noah, I'm over here."

"Adah!" Noah ran toward her with his hands out, and she extended her own. She felt the warmth and strength of his hands as he took hers. She looked into his face, lit by the pale moonlight, and studied the features that were so familiar to her.

"What are you doing here?" she whispered.

"I had to come."

"I wish you hadn't. I told you I had to leave, and I didn't want to see you again."

"Will you let me speak with you, Adah?"

"As you like," she said stiffly, withdrawing her hands. She sat down on the bench, and Noah sat beside her. He was quiet for a long time, and she waited for him to speak. When he did not, she finally said almost harshly, "Are you married yet?"

Noah turned to face her. She could smell the outdoorsy scent he always had with him. "Adah," he said. "Will you listen while I tell you what happened?"

Curiosity stirred her, and she nodded. "All right. Tell me."

"I have to tell you first that Zorah is gone. He died three days ago."

"Oh, dear Zorah!" Adah felt tears rise to her eyes, and she brushed them away with her hands. "I will miss him so much."

"So will I. He spoke of you often after you left. He loved you greatly."

"I had to leave. I couldn't help it."

"I'm not blaming you," Noah said quickly. "I just wanted you to know how he felt about you. It wouldn't have made any difference if you were there. It was his time to go. But he missed you greatly and so does Ofra."

"Why did you come to tell me these things?"

"I thought you ought to know, but I also wanted to tell you what has happened to me." He began to speak about Zorah's death and some of the events that happened that night. Finally he said, "I was there in the room, and the Ancient One came. He told me many things I can't share with you now. Many I do not understand myself." He searched her eyes, and she saw a light in his that she could not understand. "Part of it," he said, "was about you."

Adah was shocked. "The Ancient One? He spoke of me?"

"Yes. Did you know Zorah had dreams about you, even before you came to live with us? He felt it was no accident that we met."

"I remember. He told me that."

Noah hesitated, reluctant to go on, not certain what Adah's reaction would be. Zorah had told him that Adah loved him, but she had also left, and he did not know if she would be willing to come back. Since God had given him a clear commandment, however, his only choice was to tell her the truth.

"The Ancient One told me that . . . that I was not to marry Meira."

Noah's words struck Adah almost physically. She straightened up and turned to stare at him. Her eyes were large, her lips trembling. "You're not to marry Meira?"

"No." Noah reached out and took her hand again.

This time she felt his huge hands trembling, and she knew that for some reason he was afraid. "What is it, Noah?" She took his big hand in both of hers. "What is it? Why are you so afraid?"

"I'm afraid of what you will say."

"You're afraid of me? You must *never* be afraid of me. What is it? You can tell me."

"The Ancient One said that I was . . . I was to marry you. He said that He made you for that purpose."

Adah felt her heart beating. It pounded like a drum in her ears, and without warning, a deep happiness drove away the despair that had been hers. She squeezed his hand and leaned forward. "Is that what you came to tell me?"

Noah stood up and put his hand over the two of hers. The moonlight fell on her face, and he saw tears in her eyes. "Please don't weep, Adah. I've come to ask you to be my wife. It's the will of the Holy One."

"But you don't love me."

"You're wrong," Noah said quickly. "I've cared deeply for you since the first day I saw you. And over the years I've come to love you . . . I've just been too thickheaded to see it. You're the finest woman I've ever known, but the choice must be yours."

And then Adah knew both joy and sadness. The sadness rose from the knowledge that Noah did not love her with the passion she knew he'd had for Lomeen. She had always wanted that kind of love from a man; it was what she had hoped for from a husband. Still, she had seen a miracle, and a tiny thought took root in her at that moment: *I can make him love me.* She freed her hands then, leaned against him, and felt his arms go around her. Lifting her face to his, she received his kiss. It was gentle and tender, like the man she knew, and she felt safe and secure.

Noah held her quietly, pressing his face to her hair, smelling the sweet fragrance of it. He whispered, "Our lives together will be difficult. Zorah said so. But at last I have found out what the Holy One wishes for me to do, and I'm glad."

Adah felt his lips caress her hair and then her cheek, and she looked up and whispered, "Yes. We may have hard times, but we will have each other."

As Noah held Adah in his arms, he knew that his old life was over. He was happy, for at last, after all these years, he had found the will of the Ancient One. Noah had heard His voice, and now he put aside the fleshly desires he had known for Lomeen and her daughter. He saw clearly now that his desire for the daughter had been as wrong as his desire for her mother. He regretted he could not give Adah the same fierce, passionate feelings as he'd had for Lomeen, but there was a steady joy that grew in him as he thought, *I've found the way. I'm not lost anymore.*

Smiling down at the woman in his arms, he had never known such peace before in his life. "Come, Adah. We will go home now."

PART THREE

CHAPTER 17

Adah shuffled slowly across the floor, leaning backward slightly, for the child she bore rode high within her. Her movements were cautious, as her time was very near. A shaft of brilliant sunlight slanted through the single window, and as she turned her eyes away from the glare, she thought of the ordeal that was to come. Carrying this baby had been no easier than carrying her first two sons. She had borne Noah two sons, and each birth had brought her to death's door. The birth of her firstborn, Shem, had been a terrible ordeal she never expected to survive. That birth had been twenty years ago, but she still remembered the tearing pains and frightful struggle she had bringing her firstborn into the world. The birth of her second son two years later had been even worse. Ham's entrance into the world had caused Adah a nightmare of tearing pain and agony.

Now as she walked slowly, Adah felt life stirring within her. This child had been more active in her womb, it seemed to her, than the first two. She knew with a quiet certainty that he would be a strong son, and her mother-in-law agreed. "You're carrying him high," Dezia had said. "And that means you're going to have another fine son to present to your husband."

Simply moving across the floor was difficult. Adah reached the table, then halted in midstride, bit her lower lip, and locked her hands over her swollen belly. The kicks were hard and insistent, as if the infant were banging at the doors of her flesh, demanding to be released. The fanciful thought made Adah smile despite the discomfort. "That's what comes of having a dreamer for a husband." She spoke the words aloud, and her thoughts, even as she stood there bracing herself against the movements of the child within, went to her life with Noah. She had always known he was a dreamer, but she had not known until after their marriage how deep this trait lay within him. Sometimes his eyes would glaze over even when she was speaking to him. She had come to accept his preoccupation, just as she accepted his oversized hands and warm brown eyes. During her first years as his wife, however, his daydreaming had troubled her, for she felt shut out of his life. Now she understood that these episodes were a part of him. She could not change his disposition any more than she could change the color of his eyes or his height—and it was not the worst trait one could have in a husband. This thought comforted her, and she stood still until the baby's movements subsided, then began peeling a bowl of apples with a bronze paring knife.

She felt more comfortable standing up, and as she worked on the food, a quiet peace came to her. It had not always been so, for marriage to Noah had been a difficult thing in some ways. Not that he had not provided for her; indeed, he had done very well in that respect. His fame as a woodworker, a carpenter, and also the finest grower of grapes in the region had brought them prosperity. There was no need to scrimp and save, nor was there any need to worry about the future as far as material possessions were concerned. Adah sent her gaze around the room, noting with satisfaction the luxuries other women did not have. The furniture was all very fine, made by Noah's own hand. Food of every sort was plentiful, with dried beans and grain in bins stuffed to overflowing and dried onions hanging from the ceiling beams along with an abundance of herbs. Adah enjoyed the sense of well-being that came from having enough, not only for today but also for the future.

She smiled at how fortunate she was and whispered, "Thank you, Holy One, for all you have given your servant. . . ." She had developed the habit of giving thanks constantly for small things, even for a drink of cool water or the sight of fruit bursting on the trees or vegetables pushing their way through the earth's crust.

As she began to slice the carrots that Noah had tended carefully in his garden, her smile faded, however. Despite the prosperity that had come to her through Noah and the fact that she had borne him two sons—which had made him very proud—something was missing in her life. A vague and disturbing spirit of discontent haunted her at times, as it did now. She knew the source of this troublesome mood and now tried to drive it away, but it refused to go. *How foolish to be jealous of a woman long dead! Hasn't God been good to you?* Even knowing that her resentment of

Lomeen was futile and stupid, Adah had never been able to put it aside. She was acutely aware that Noah's early love for Lomeen was still a part of him. The name was never mentioned between the two of them, but Lomeen's daughter, Meira, still lived in Comir's village, only a day's journey away. From time to time over the years, Noah and Adah had encountered her as she traveled with her uncle. Always upon seeing her, Noah had been unable to conceal his reactions from Adah.

He still loves that woman after all these years—and after all the love I've given him! Adah could not control the rush of anger that shot through her at the thought of Noah's weakness. Without thinking, she began chopping the carrots too quickly and then cried out as the sharp knife sliced the end of her forefinger. She dropped the knife, popped her finger in her mouth, and stood there brooding, angry with herself for allowing a dead woman to trouble her so much.

The cut was deep, and she moved over to another part of the kitchen, where she cut a small piece of cloth and tied her finger up with it. Moving back to the worktable, where the various ingredients of the meal were spread out, she glanced down at the floor. The knife lay where it had fallen. She was as awkward now as she would ever be, and as she leaned over, a sudden dizziness struck her. She tried to stand up, but the room turned black, and fiery stars danced before her eyes. She felt herself falling, and in order to protect the child, she simply folded up, put her hands out, and let herself down to the floor. Rolling over on her back, she put her hands over her stomach again, as if to protect the child, and for a time she simply lay there.

The dizzy spell was passing, and she knew it was not serious. The sound of a familiar heavy tread came into the room, and she heard Noah's voice call out with alarm, "Adah! What's the matter?"

Opening her eyes, Adah saw Noah rush over to her and kneel down. His hands were on her, and she said quickly, "Oh, it's nothing."

"Nothing! You're lying here in the middle of the floor, and you say it's *nothing!*" Noah put his big hand on her stomach and said, "Is it the baby? Is he coming?"

Even then Adah noticed that Noah said *he,* for this husband of hers wanted another son. "No, it's not that. I just dropped the knife, and when I bent to pick it up I got dizzy."

Noah's strong hands were under her shoulders, pulling her up to a sitting position. She felt like a fool and said so. "I shouldn't have tried to pick it up. I get dizzy every time I bend over."

"Are you sure you're all right?" Noah asked. "You look pale." He spotted her bloody finger and cried with alarm, "What have you done to your finger?"

Adah was pleased at his concern. Sometimes he got so involved with his many endeavors and activities that she got lost in the shuffle. Even when they were in bed at night, his mind would go off into deep thoughts and dreams she could not enter. But now as he held her, she was content, and the thought of Lomeen and Meira was momentarily pushed away.

"Help me up," she said. "I'm all right." She felt his hands under her, and he lifted her as easily as if she were a child. "Now," she said, leaning against him and smiling, "that's fine. It's just a little cut."

Noah's eyes were filled with concern. "I don't know why you won't mind me. I hired Edra so you wouldn't have to do all this work, and now I come home and find you flat on your back. You ought to be more careful, Adah."

Adah reached up and put her hand on his cheek. His beard was soft and luxuriant, and she loved to run her fingers through it. It was no longer the reddish color he had gotten from his mother but was now, after many centuries of life, a silvery white. "I get so bored," she said, "doing nothing all day long."

"Well, you're going to do nothing now! Come here and sit down." He led her to a chair that he had made especially for her. It fit her perfectly, and she relaxed as she eased herself into it. Her legs ached, and even as she sat down, the sudden drumming of the child made her put her hands over her stomach.

"Anything wrong?" Noah asked quickly, seeing the gesture.

"No. It's just your son making a fuss. Here . . . feel." She took Noah's hand and held it over her belly, then watched the pleased expression on his face. "He's a lively one, isn't he?"

"Even more than Shem or Ham, I think, although I didn't believe that was possible."

She liked when Noah showed her special attention, and now as he knelt beside her, one hand on her stomach and the other over her shoulder, she felt secure and warm and sheltered. Her mind, for some reason, went back in time to her youth when she had been so abused by Mak. She had never forgotten that day when Noah fought the giant and killed him for her sake under the command of the Strong One. She had been but a child then, yet she had learned to love this big, awkward man with all of her heart. And now as she covered his hand that was sensing the movement of the unborn child, a feeling of well-being filled her.

Noah saw that she was smiling and asked with surprise, "What are laughing about?"

"Just thinking how lucky I am to have such a handsome husband."

Noah laughed, and when he did, his eyes were almost hidden. It was a family trait, and both of their sons now had it. Despite his age, Noah's teeth were still white and strong against his bronzed face as he laughed. "You must be losing your eyesight. I may be big, but nobody ever accused me of being handsome."

"You are to me. You're everything I ever wanted in a husband."

Noah blinked with surprise. Adah had been a fine wife to him, but such statements from her were rare indeed. He knew that she loved him, and he returned that love with a deep desire to protect her. "Well, now, I'm glad you think so, but let's pray that this boy will be far better looking and stronger than his father. And we'll pray that he'll be good like his mother."

A warmth flowed through Adah, for if she had difficulty expressing her affection in words, Noah did even more so. His compliment pleased her, and she was content to sit there being comforted, until finally he rose and said, "I'll get Edra to finish the meal. I don't want you to move."

"How's your work going?"

Noah was building a fine new home for a wealthy member of the clan, and she watched as he shrugged his shoulders. "Very slowly," he admitted. "I need more help."

"Ham and Shem aren't enough?"

Noah pulled up the chair and sat down in front of her. His face was troubled. "Well, you know how they are. I've got them working, but if I'm not right there watching them, who knows what they'll do?"

"They're good sons, Noah," Adah said defensively. "But they're young."

"Shem's twenty and Ham's eighteen. They're old enough to have outgrown some of their childish ways." A thought was reflected on his sunburned face. "Ham is stubborn. No matter what I tell him to do, he argues about it." A streak of humor ran through this big man, and he said with a straight face, "I think that must come from you."

Adah was startled, and then she saw he was teasing her. "I doubt that. More than likely from your father."

"Yes, Ham is very like him, isn't he?"

"Yes, he is." This was true, for Ham resembled Lamech in many ways. He was a big man, very dark in complexion, with the same wiry black hair his grandfather had had as a young man. He was also, as Noah had well learned, stubborn and prone to argue with anyone who told him what to do.

"He's a hard worker," Noah finally said, "but only when he wants to be." His thoughts went to his other son, Shem, and an exasperated look crossed his face. "Our firstborn isn't stubborn, but he's such a dreamer, he's more likely to write a poem than he is to build a house."

"He's a lot like you in that respect."

Noah looked up sharply. "Like me! What makes you say that?"

"Why, you're the biggest dreamer I ever saw! Sometimes right in the middle of a conversation you forget the person you're talking to and go off into your own world. You may not be writing a poem, but you're building a house or a chair in your mind or thinking about your vineyard."

Noah ran his hands through his snowy white hair and shook his head. Ruefully he nodded. "I expect you're right about that. And the truth is, Shem is different from most."

"He's always been a good boy, and he has a great love for the Ancient One, just as you do."

"I'm thankful for that," Noah said. His mind then went to Ham, and his thoughts troubled him, for Ham was not as dedicated to the Ancient One as Noah would have liked. "Well, we'll get the job done. I'll stay with you this afternoon. We'll see how much work those two get done when I'm not there watching them every second."

Ham picked up a wooden mallet and drove a peg into a hole that he had drilled to fasten the beam. His strength was prodigious, and he drove the peg home with three sharp blows. He might have found pleasure in his accomplishment, but when the peg was in place he stared at it with a grim dissatisfaction. It was part of the mood he was in, and the unhappiness showed plainly in his rough features. He was a big man, as tall as his father, and he towered over his older brother, Shem. He was feared by many of the young men, for in the fights that inevitably arose, he demolished all who stood before him with a massive strength and fury that seemed to come from deep within. He had a temper that was not always evident, and now as he turned and walked over to where Shem was chiseling another timber, he said loudly, "I've had enough of this for one day."

Shem looked up, surprised. No one would ever have taken the two for brothers, for physically they were completely different. Ham was large and bulky, with well-developed muscles, while Shem was less-than-average height and slender. Although he was strong enough to do the work required, his muscles were long rather than bulky. His hair was exactly the same shade his father's had been in his youth, a light brown with the reddish tinge that came from his grandmother Dezia. His eyes were a strange color, much lighter than the eyes of other members of his family, and with a bluish tint that gave him a rather innocent expression. He had high cheekbones and a thin, narrow nose like his mother's. In fact, he resembled her in some ways. He was a thoughtful young man given to solitude, and now as he stared at Ham, he asked, "What's the matter? I think the house is going well."

"The house is all right. I'm just tired of it," Ham growled. He looked down at the beam and shook his head. "You're cutting that beam wrong."

Shem looked down and studied the beam. "What's wrong with it?"

"You'll never make it fit in that notch. Here. Let me show you."

Willingly, Shem rose and watched as Ham drove the chisel into the wood with his mallet. The chips flew as they usually did when Ham put his hand to a chisel. Shem noticed that Ham attacked the wood as if he were angry with it, and he wondered why his brother was so upset. He himself was mild mannered, prone to smile easily, and had none of the dark moods that Ham displayed from time to time.

"That's the way it's supposed to look."

"Yes. I can see that. You've got a real knack with wood, just like Father."

The compliment pleased Ham, and he reached out and grabbed a handful of his brother's hair and shook his head. "I know what you were doing," he said. "You were dreaming about something. Maybe writing a poem."

"I was not!"

"Of course you were! You're always off in some dreamworld—just like Father. You two make a pretty pair!"

"Well, that's not all bad."

"It didn't get that beam cut right." Ham grinned. Then he put the chisel down and said, "I'm going hunting."

Alarmed, Shem stared at his brother. "Father said we were to stay here until he got back."

"I've done enough work for one day. Tell him I'll be back in the morning." He turned and walked away before Shem had a chance to protest. The impulsive act was characteristic of the big man. He could outwork any three men whenever he chose, but now and then he would simply walk away and disappear. He was the best hunter in the clan now, a man who understood wild animals almost as if he were one of them. He always knew where the water holes were and how best to stalk any game. He never came home empty-handed.

Shem shook his head and muttered, "Father won't like that." He picked up the chisel, moved to the other end of the beam, and started cutting away the material. He was not a bad workman by any means. He simply lacked Ham's strength, and he was not particularly interested in building. He worked willingly enough and was a fair carpenter, but he would never have his father's expertise nor his brother's strength. In all truth, he would much rather spend his time talking with his great-grandfather about the Ancient One.

Shem worked steadily for the rest of the afternoon, and while he was working, he felt the words to a song growing within him. He could never explain to others how he created these songs. It was different from building a house. In building with wood, one always had to have a plan, and each timber had to go in a certain place. There was a method in it that any competent workman could reason and figure out.

Creating songs was different. Sometimes they would come to him so fully completed that all he had to do was simply speak them and they were birthed without effort. At other times, however, a mere word or a single image would come to him, and he might struggle for days to put the words and images together. Oftentimes he failed, and he simply had to set the effort aside. He had once watched as Emmer, the potter, had spoiled a bowl on the wheel. "What are you going to do with it?" Shem had demanded. "It's ruined now."

"Start all over again," Emmer had replied. "That's all you can do when something's ruined."

Many of Shem's songs were like that. They had begun and had failed to come to birth, but somehow the words and images would come floating back inside his head, perhaps at night when he lay on his bed or when he was working on a piece of furniture or planting in the vineyard. He could not explain the creative process, nor did he try. Most people were not really interested in that part of his songs anyway.

Sitting on the roughhewn beam, Shem's bluish eyes glazed over. He did not move outwardly, but inside, a furious mental activity was at work that few would have dreamed of. He was thinking and pushing words about as if they were parts of a puzzle. Occasionally the words would come together in a pattern that fit exactly. Then he would smile and nod his head with pleasure.

Shem was suddenly accosted by his father's voice. His eyes flew open, and he jumped to his feet. "Oh, hello, Father."

Ignoring the greeting, Noah looked around, then demanded, "Where's your brother?"

"Why, he left some time ago."

"Where did he go?"

Shem hated to speak evil of anyone, so he answered reluctantly. "He went hunting."

"Hunting!" Noah looked around, and anger flared in his eyes. "With all this work to do, he's gone hunting?"

"He's really worked very hard, and I think he needed to get away for a while."

Noah clamped his lips together. It was not the first time this had happened, but there was no point in taking it out on Shem. His older son did not have the physical capability of his younger brother, but he, at least, was faithful to stay on the job. Noah looked fondly at Shem and said, "Well, I'm glad you're here, but the day's almost gone now." He flashed a smile. "I'll bet you made up one of your songs today, didn't you?"

Shem nodded eagerly. "I did. It's been floating around in my head all day long. Would you like to hear it?"

"Yes," Noah said. He sat down on one of the beams and smiled as Shem began to sing.

Sometimes Shem merely spoke the words that formed in his mind, but this time he sang the words with his clear voice:

"O Ancient One, most mighty God
You have caused the grass to grow
So the beasts of the earth may be fed.
You have touched the hills and they smoke;
The sun rises at your bidding,
And the moon and stars obey your voice.

Let heaven rejoice!
Let everything that breathes praise the Holy One!"

As Noah listened to the song he felt a surge of pride that a son of his could create such a thing. He himself had no gift for composing and was only a mediocre singer. Shem, however, had whatever quality exists that draws people's attention. Whenever he began to sing or speak the words of his poems, everyone stopped to listen. Sometimes Shem would get so carried away that tears would roll down his cheeks, and he would have to stop, overcome with emotion. Noah suddenly thought, *This son of mine loves God more than any of us!*

Shem's face shone with pleasure. His features were finer, more chiseled, than Noah's or Ham's, and there was a glow about him that revealed his warm spirit.

"Come along, Shem. Gather up the tools, and we'll let you go sing this song to your mother."

Noah leaned forward and spoke with pride to Methuselah. "You must have Shem sing the new song he made up today. It's a beautiful one about the Ancient One, His power, and His might."

Methuselah nodded. "It's amazing what can come out of that boy's head. You remember how he started doing that when he was no more than five or six years old? I saw something in him even then that was different."

Noah pulled the medallion out from beneath his garment and stared at it for a moment. "I've been wondering if, perhaps, Shem will be the one to bear this sign of the lion."

"It's too soon to tell. You may have many more sons. You must wait to learn who may be the one to carry on from my father." The two men had talked often about the medallion and what it meant. Neither of them really understood it, nor had Zorah. They both studied its round face, admiring the fine etching of the lion, wondering what kind of gemstones made up the eyes of the beast and who had found them and where.

As Noah slipped the medallion back under his garment, he shook his head sadly. "The world's changing so fast—and not for the better."

"It certainly is," Methuselah agreed with a heavy sigh. His voice had grown weaker over the years, as had he himself. He could only hobble about now for a short distance, but his eyes were still clear and his mind sharp. "I don't know what's happening, but it's something terrible."

"You're right, Grandfather. Evil seems to be spreading everywhere. Once it was just among Jaalam's clan, but now many of our own people worship Ur-Baal. The next thing, they'll be wanting us to have human sacrifices."

"You must never permit that!"

"That would be up to Father, wouldn't it?"

"Your father is not a strong man. He's easily swayed. You are the one who must proclaim the truth."

Noah shook his head. "I'm no Zorah."

"Of course not. But someone has to stand against this evil. It's like a plague, a fever, that passes from person to person. What's going to become of us, my son?"

Noah reached out and took his grandfather's hand. It was frail and thin, feeling almost like fragile sticks that he could snap if he were not careful. He held the hand for a moment, and the two men were silent. He touched the medallion as it lay close to his skin and wished that Zorah were alive to give him comfort. "What do the lion and the lamb mean?"

Methuselah shook his head, and his voice was faint as he answered. "Time will tell, my son. You must wait until the Ancient One speaks."

CHAPTER 18

It was market day and the streets were packed as Noah and Adah pushed through the jostling crowd on their way to see his parents. The marketplace resounded with the shrill voices of the vendors crying out the virtues of their goods. The stalls provided a riot of color with green vegetables neatly stacked on tables and yellow squashes banked by red berries. There was a riotous element about the crowd too. Noah frowned, noting with displeasure that many were already drunk, though it was not yet noon.

"It didn't used to be like this," he murmured to Adah. "If people were going to get drunk, they'd do it in the privacy of their homes. Now look at them!" Indeed, there was a raw element to the shouts, and the obscenities angered Noah. "A man can't even bring his family to town on market day without hearing this," he said bitterly.

"It's all right," Adah said. "We'll soon be—"

She never finished her sentence, for two red-faced, bleary-eyed drunks came barreling out of a shop, shouting at each other. One of them crashed into Adah with such force, she spun around and gave a gasp of pain.

Noah swiftly reached out and grabbed him by the neck. "You drunken fool!" he snapped. "Why don't you watch where you're going!"

The drunk writhed in his grasp and flung out his fist, striking Noah on the side of the neck. His friend shouted as if it were all a bit of fun and joined in the fray. If Noah had been alone, he probably would have ignored the men and gone his way, but the danger to Adah, who was close to giving birth, infuriated him. His fist shot out, and he caught the oncoming drunk squarely in the mouth, driving him backward as if he had been struck by a timber. He hit the ground and never moved. Noah cuffed the other drunk roughly, then, grasping the man in his mighty hand, continued to slap his face.

"That's enough, Noah!" Adah cried out.

He shoved the drunk away, and the man tripped over his fallen friend, who lay in the road with blood streaming from his mouth. A crowd had gathered to watch the fight, and Noah glared at the spectators in disgust. He took Adah's arm and growled, "Come on. Let's get out of here." They had taken only a few steps when another figure stopped in front of them. "Get out of the way!" Noah shouted.

"You're not going to beat me up too, are you, Noah?"

Noah halted abruptly, not sure if he knew the man in front of him, though the voice was familiar.

"It's Kul, Noah! Don't you remember?"

"Ah yes . . . Kul. We haven't seen each other since our youth. I barely recognized you."

Kul had swelled up over the years. His huge body was loosely covered with rich clothing, but he couldn't hide the rolls of fat around his neck, which protruded from his gold-threaded tunic. Noah immediately recognized the woman standing next to him as Benei. Though she too had aged over the centuries, she had maintained her slim figure, and her face still reflected the beauty she once boasted. Noah had not seen her since the day they had met at Jaalam's village for the festival of Ur-Baal. Kul and Benei had eventually married, but Kul's family had never blessed the union, so they had settled into Benei's village, where they could worship Ur-Baal freely.

Noah started to step around the couple. "You'll have to excuse me, Kul, but I want to get Adah out of this crowd."

"What's your hurry? Come along, we'll all have a drink together."

"No, Kul. We don't care to drink. My wife is expecting, as you can see, and I need to get her off her feet and out of this heat. We're going to my parents' house."

"Well, you've at least got to come to our village sometime and see us, Noah. I hear you're the best builder in the world. I want a new house for my wife."

Noah glanced at Benei. She still seemed to be a lascivious woman, despite her age. Her face had changed, but from the alluring look in her eyes, Noah could see that she remained the same woman inside. Her now-wrinkled face was heavily painted, and she held herself haughtily with gemstones flashing from her earrings and from rings on her fingers. She smiled at Noah, a smile that was both enticing and cruel. "I remember you all right—from that night you and Kul first came to our village. There's somebody back there I'll bet you'd like to see."

"No, I don't think so," Noah said, again attempting to go around the couple.

"And I *know* she'd like to see you." Benei laughed and grabbed Noah by the arm. "Meira speaks about you all the time, Noah—she's never forgotten you."

Noah's face flamed at the mention of the name, and Adah did not miss his reaction.

Benei continued in a taunting voice. "She's still beautiful, Noah—and she still wants you. You could have her anytime you'd like."

Adah had stiffened beside Noah, her anger getting the best of her over Benei's audacity and at the painful reminders of her husband's past attachments. "Please, husband . . . I need to rest. Let's go from here quickly."

"Yes, excuse us," Noah said to Kul and Benei. "I need to get my wife out of the heat."

As they left the couple and pushed on through the crowd, a young woman began to call to Noah from a window just above the street. He looked up and gasped at the vision before him. It was Meira, her painted eyes fixed on Noah. Dressed in a silky red garment, she gestured for him to come up, her black hair glistening under the sun, black as the darkest thing in nature. He stared at her in disbelief, then reality dawned on him as he realized this young woman could not be Meira. After all, Meira was old now too. No, this goddess draped in red silk was simply a young harlot who sought the opportunity to make some good money from a prosperous old businessman.

"Noah, let's go!"

Adah tugged on his arm, fire in her eyes.

"I'm sorry, Adah," Noah said, his voice oddly strained. "I thought I knew that woman . . . b-but it was nothing . . . just a ghost from the past."

Adah grabbed his hand and began pulling him from the marketplace. He glanced down at her and saw that her face was set and her jaw clenched as she dragged him from the scene.

She should not have to see all these things, Noah thought sadly. She was such a good woman—in sharp contrast to the violent and immoral world around them, a world that seemed to grow worse with every passing day.

He wished in his heart that he could be as good a husband to her as she was a wife to him, but it was never to be. He knew he was a weak man. He had tried for a lifetime to keep his mind focused solely on God and his family, but always there were reminders of his past, of the women he had so desired. He tried to say lightly, "Kul is getting fat as a butterball, isn't he? Looks like he's quite rich now, huh?"

Adah did not answer. In fact, she kept silent all the way to Lamech's house. When they reached the door, Dezia opened it. She smiled broadly and embraced Adah, having to lean over, so enormous was the pregnant woman's stomach. "You don't need to be out in this heat, Adah." She kissed her daughter-in-law and then saw instantly that something was wrong. She shot a glance at Noah, who did not speak, and she quickly said, "Why don't you go talk to your father, Noah? I'll take Adah into the back room. It's cooler there."

"All right, Mother," Noah said, feeling guilty. He left at once to find his father while Dezia gently escorted Adah down the hall to a small back room. Adah allowed Dezia to fuss over her, settle her into a long chair where she could put her feet up, and then bring her a refreshing fruit drink. "We'll be eating later," Dezia said. "How are you feeling?"

"Very well" was all Adah said.

Dezia knew her daughter-in-law had been hurt, and she wondered if she and Noah had had a quarrel. Having too much tact to ask directly, she carefully led the conversation toward finding out what was wrong. "The streets are so crowded these days, aren't they?" she said. "I hate to go out on market days. The crowds are so horribly uncouth."

Adah took a sip of the cool juice and then looked frankly at Dezia. "We saw Noah's old friend Kul and his wife."

"Oh yes. They travel here once a month to visit our market."

"They invited us to go see them"—Adah nervously brushed back a lock of hair from her face—"and then they told Noah that Meira would love to see him."

"So *that's* it!" Dezia said. She knew the whole story then, for the two women were good friends and did not keep many secrets. She understood that Adah was still jealous of Lomeen's memory and of her daughter, whom Noah had almost married. "I don't hear anything good about Meira, Adah. She has spent her life sleeping with men from everywhere. Doesn't matter if she's married to them or not!"

Adah's eyes welled up with tears, and Dezia immediately walked over and held her close. "You don't have to worry about that woman. She's old and wicked. I am so very thankful that Noah did not marry her. *You* are the only woman for Noah, Adah, the one he loves very much."

"No, he doesn't!" Adah wailed, letting the tears flow freely, her shoulders shaking with violent sobs. "He's never loved me as he loved that woman! Don't tell me that he does! I know him!"

Dezia did her best to calm Adah. In truth, she knew that there were some grounds for Adah's accusation. It was not that she thought Noah had ever touched the woman, but still she knew him well enough to understand her son's emotional attachment to Lomeen and later to her daughter, Meira. Dezia comforted her daughter-in-law as well as she could, then changed the subject to speak of the child that was to come.

Noah found his father in the field out back, looking over some new cattle he had bought. Lamech greeted him warmly, and when he had finished examining his new purchase, he said, "Let's go inside and have a drink."

Knowing that Lamech drank too much, Noah did not really want to drink with him, but he was too polite to say so. When Lamech called for wine and the servant brought it, Noah only sipped it. He listened as his father spoke loudly and tossed back three goblets in a row. Noah was greatly disturbed at how quickly Lamech was getting drunk. Ever since his father had agreed to let the clan worship Ur-Baal if they wanted to, he had sunk ever deeper into a moral pit himself. For many years he had remained faithful to the Ancient One, but eventually he had found he enjoyed some of the festivities associated with Ur-Baal worship and decided there was no harm in joining in . . . "just for fun." That began a steady decline into more and more involvement. Noah had been hearing rumors for years that Lamech had been participating in the sexual side of those ceremonies as well. Noah hoped that his father had never given in to sanctioning human sacrifices, but he could not be sure of anything.

Noah had a hard time remembering what his father was like when he was younger, for Lamech had not aged well. He had put on weight much like Kul; his eyes were bloodshot, and his hands trembled constantly. He had always been an impetuous, overbearing sort, but there had once been a kindness in him that seemed to have disappeared.

After allowing his father to finish talking, Noah tried his best to caution him. But he had no sooner begun to speak out about the dangers of going to the religious festivals of Ur-Baal than his father turned crimson and shouted, "You shut your mouth, Noah! You're nothing but a religious fanatic! You're no better than your grandfather!"

"I didn't mean to offend you, Father, but you must see how bad things are getting. You may not think it has anything to do with Ur-Baal worship, but that's where you're wrong. Violence is so common now—men killing each other over women or even over a bet."

"Men are men," Lamech said hoarsely. "They always fight. You're just like my father—seeing evil in everyone."

Noah soon realized it was useless to try to reason with Lamech. He stood up and excused himself, then climbed the steps to the flat rooftop. He found his grandfather there, sitting in the shade of a large potted plant, his eyes closed.

Methuselah opened his eyes when he heard Noah approach and smiled. "Hello, grandson. Sit down." He pointed to a bench and added as Noah took his seat, "This is the only place there's any peace and quiet around here. Look at them down there." He waved toward the street. "Nothing but a drunken mob every market day."

Noah nodded but said nothing. What could one say about the present state of the world? Instead he asked, "How are you feeling, Grandfather?"

"How would you expect me to feel? As old as I am, I'm lucky to be feeling at all."

Noah smiled at the gentle rebuke, and the two men sat quietly. Methuselah was one of the few men Noah could talk to in a straightforward way. They were bound together by their devotion to the Holy One. Methuselah listened with pleasure as Noah spoke of Shem and his latest songs. "Send him over to see me," Methuselah said. "I'd love to see him. He's one of the few young men left in the world that has any sense!"

"We're very proud of him."

"What about Ham? Is he as stubborn as ever?"

Noah said carefully, "He's very different from his brother. He's impulsive."

"He's like your father, then, but he's young. He can change."

"Yes he can," Noah said, nodding.

Suddenly a servant came rushing up the stone stairway, his eyes wide. "Sir," he said. "Come quickly."

"What is it?" Noah gasped as he rose, but he already knew.

"It's your wife. The child is coming!"

Darkness had come, and the lamps had been lit. By the yellow, flickering light Noah peered into the red, wrinkled face of the child in his arms. He stood beside Adah, who lay soaking wet with sweat, utterly exhausted. Her labor had been hard but had not lasted as long as with the other two boys. Now she lifted her hand. "Come closer, husband."

Noah knelt beside the bed and held the child up for her to see. With deep pride in his heart, he reached over with his free hand and laid it on her shoulder. "You did well, Adah. You've given me another fine son!"

"Is he perfect?"

"Yes. He's going to be a joy to us. We shall name him Japheth."

Before Adah dropped off to sleep, she whispered, "We must ask the Strong One to make him a good man."

Noah knelt on the floor, held the child up, and began to pray, "O Strong and Holy One, bless this child and let him be a faithful man, a man wholly devoted to your service. . . ."

CHAPTER 19

The sun was sinking low in the west as Ham trudged wearily along a faint pathway leading through the wild country. He moved slowly, for he was weary in body and also disgusted. He had been on a three-day hunt and, except for very small game, had bagged nothing. He shifted the bronze knife in his belt and adjusted the leather strap that bound the quiver of arrows to his back. In his left hand he grasped a bow that his brother Japheth had made, the best weapon he'd ever had. He held it lightly, thinking of Japheth, who had reached his eighteenth birthday the previous week. At the age of thirty-six, Ham felt more like a father to the youngster than a brother.

His older brother, Shem, was now thirty-eight, yet he showed no signs of assuming any authority over his younger brothers. He had never even tried. Ham had known from the time they were young that Shem would never attempt to rule over him. Fortunately for Ham, Shem was more interested in singing songs than in ruling over anyone!

A movement caught Ham's eyes, and he reached for an arrow, but it was only a very small rabbit not worthy of a shot. Game was scarce this year, and he hated to go home empty-handed. The trip had been good for him in other ways, however. He had left after one of his frequent conflicts with his father. Ham admired his father in many ways, but he had a stubborn streak in him that would not submit to authority. He got along much better with his mother, whose gentleness he admired. Deep down he loved Noah too, but his father made the mistake of trying to force Ham to serve the Ancient One with a better spirit. Ham resisted his efforts, and at the height of their last argument before he left, he shouted, "I may go serve Ur-Baal! At least I can *see* him!" His taunt had hurt his father, and now as Ham moved toward the sharp-pointed hill that marked the trail leading to his home, he regretted his statement. The truth was, he had no use for Ur-Baal, and he did respect the Ancient One. He didn't make up songs to Him as Shem did, but then neither did Japheth.

A smile came to Ham's lips as he thought of Japheth. He loved his happy-go-lucky young brother a great deal. The two got along very well, for Japheth loved having fun. He was very clever with his hands, always inventing something—or trying to. Many of his devices did not work, but failure never daunted him.

Next time I'll bring Japheth with me, Ham thought to himself. *We get along well together.* He frowned. *Why do I have to be the odd one in the family? I have some gloomy spells, but I can't help that.* He knew his brothers were far more pleasant to be around than he was, but even when he tried to control his stubbornness, it rarely worked.

As he reached the main trail, he turned his head and stood still. "Voices," he muttered. "Somebody's on the road." Robbers were a constant threat in the world that Ham inhabited. He was never afraid, for he was skilled with knife, spear, and bow. But reports of wild men reached his family often, and Noah had warned them to be very careful.

The road was shielded by scrub bushes and small trees, which grew thickly at this point. He hid in the bushes and glanced to the right. His eyes narrowed, and he grew perfectly still. Not fifty feet away a man lay on the ground, dead, his face and breast covered with blood. Near the dead man four rough-looking thugs surrounded a young woman. Their ribald laughter and obscene talk prevented them from hearing Ham as he stepped out of the bushes.

One of the men was holding the girl, and another, the largest of the men, reached out and grabbed the girl's garment, ripping it open. She screamed, and the big man said, "Scream all you please. There's nobody to hear you." He began pawing at the girl, laughing at her ineffectual cries and struggles as two men held her.

Ham silently lifted his bow, drew an arrow from his quiver, and nocked it on the string. Carefully he drew the string back to his ear, froze for a moment, then released the arrow. It hissed through the air and struck the back of one of the men holding the girl. The strength of Ham's arm and the powerful bow released the arrow with such force it sank into the man's body up to the feathers on the shaft. The man gave a choking cry, half turned, and grasped the arrow as it stuck six inches out of his chest. He leaned forward and slowly fell on his face, crying out a name Ham did not know.

The biggest of the remaining three robbers whirled around and saw Ham. He shouted in rage and, pulling his knife, ran straight for him. Ham reached back, plucked out another arrow, and nocked it. He drew the arrow back, released it, and saw it catch the big man right in the throat. Again, the arrow sank to its feathers, and Ham watched as his victim fell, making a strange gurgling cry and pulling futilely at the arrow.

The other two men charged toward Ham and were on him before he could draw another arrow. Both of them carried long, wicked-looking knives that glinted in the sun. Ham tried to turn away, but a sweeping blow caught him across the upper arm. He felt the flesh tear, and pain shot through him. Ham managed to grab the wrist of his attacker and threw him backward so that he collided with the other robber. Ham drew his knife, but the two separated, coming at him from both sides. Ham knew that if he turned his back on either one, he would be slain instantly. He threw himself at the smaller of the two men and parried his thrusts with his right arm, then threw a wicked left-handed blow at the other man, catching him full in the face with his fist. He heard the bones crunch as the nose broke, and the man stumbled backward.

The smaller robber reacted quick as a weasel, lunging at him with his knife. Ham felt the searing heat of the blade slash his side, and he had time only to turn. He parried another thrust and lunged at the man with his own knife, but his opponent was swift. His face was filled with fury as he circled Ham and screamed, "You're a dead man! You killed my brother!"

Ham felt weakened by the blood that was dripping from his side and arm, and he knew he would grow weaker. Throwing caution aside, he flung himself forward, inviting another thrust. His opponent's blade slashed at him, and he felt it make a narrow cut across his left forearm. But then he drove forward with his own blade and saw it slice across the man's thin face. He drew it back again, and his next cut slashed across the chest, leaving a bloody track.

The man staggered back with a wild cry and fled, holding his face, and Ham turned to see the other man he had smashed in the nose get up and follow him, his face streaming blood. Ham felt a wave of dizziness and he stood there swaying. The two men with the arrow wounds lay still, and the two fleeing robbers had disappeared around a bend. He looked up and saw the young woman coming toward him. She was holding her torn garment together at her throat, and her eyes were wide with terror. Her voice trembled as she asked, "Can you walk?"

"Walk where?" Ham gasped. The pain of his wounds and the loss of blood were draining him.

"You're going to bleed to death. Sit down."

Ham abruptly sat down and heard the ripping of cloth. He glanced over to see that she was tearing her dress from around the hem, and soon he felt her hands as she bound his arm and then his side.

"If you can walk a little way, my home is just over there. You can almost see it from here. Or should I go get help?"

"No," Ham said hoarsely. "I can walk."

He got to his feet unsteadily, and she said, "Lean on me."

This amused him, for she was not a large woman. Her hair had been loosened in the struggle and hung down her back, and she clung to the torn fabric of her dress, covering herself. He obeyed her, however, putting his hand on her shoulder and letting her help him walk. As he did so, he caught a hint of perfume.

As they passed the dead man he'd seen first, the young woman whispered, "He was one of our servants. His name was Joffi. He was so faithful to take care of me!" She shook her head and shuddered. "They would have killed me too if you hadn't come."

Ham was so dizzy he was not sure what direction they were heading. It seemed like a long way, but the young woman encouraged him every step.

"What's your name?" he whispered.

"Kefira. Look, here come the servants. They know something's wrong."

And then Ham was surrounded by people. He vaguely heard the young woman urging the men to help, and then he felt himself being lifted by strong hands. They had come just in time, for his world was fading out. As darkness closed over him, easing the pain, he heard the young woman's voice saying, "Be careful with him. He saved my life. . . ."

A cool breeze filtered through the lattice that held a wall of thick, heavy vines. Ham carefully stretched his arms out and noted that the pain that had at first been excruciating was now bearable. For the past two days he had been recuperating at the home of Kefira. He had been unconscious for hours, but when he had awakened, the first face he had seen was that of the young woman. He had been confused, but then it had all come rushing back. She had laid her hand on his cheek and smiled at him, saying, "You are better. You are going to be all right."

The day's heat had passed away, and now the coolness of the earth felt good as he sat back in the walled garden and quietly thought of how strange it was to be staying in the house of Jaal and Dalit, Kefira's parents. The house was luxurious, and its gardens luscious and well cared for. Now as Ham looked up at the gray light of early evening, he found himself feeling strangely relaxed. This was unusual, for he normally craved activity. Now it was enough to lean back and relax, staring up at the few pale stars that had begun to pierce the sky. For him the night was like a timeless swing, a vast rhythm that caught him up and bore him away from the activities of the day. Even now as he rested, the darkness provided an undertone of mystery to his thoughts. It strangely humbled him, which was unusual, for he was not a humble man. But as he sat there, he was conscious of thoughts that might have come to Shem instead of to him—thoughts of a faint, immortal flame that no earthly night could quench.

He sat very still, thinking about the strangeness of this adventure, until a crescent moon arose, turned butter yellow by a haze in the air. As he watched, the stars became great masses of light. They seemed close enough for him to touch as they glistened, and then the scented wind lifted and the night air, crisp and sharp, touched him.

He had almost drifted off to sleep when a voice awoke him. Then Kefira was there, her white gown giving off a peculiar sheen under the soft moonlight.

"Come. It's time to eat." She waited until he stood up and then smiled at him. "You're moving much more easily now."

"Yes. I always heal quickly. My mother says I heal quicker than an animal."

Kefira laughed a little, and as she said "Come and eat," he heard the strange falling cadence of her voice. The top of her dark head seemed to glow from the moonlight, and a fragrance rose sweetly from her. He followed her inside the house, which was brightly illuminated by many oil lamps. When they reached the large dining area, he saw that the table overflowed with food, and hunger stirred him. Jaal, Kefira's father, was a short, heavy man with sharp black eyes and a balding head. He was not old, yet there was the suggestion of age about him. "Sit down, friend Ham. You must eat and recover your strength."

"Thank you." Ham sat down and noted that Dalit, Kefira's mother, had a much darker complexion and eyes than her daughter. She was wearing a robe with a rose-colored sheen, and a ring on her finger glittered with a pale blue stone such as Ham had never seen. The dress of both the man and the woman was rich and spoke of wealth, as did everything in the room. Ham cared little for riches; still, he found himself impressed with the opulence of the home and the richness of the food.

The meal included several kinds of meat, with chicken fixed in a way he had never tasted before and steaming cuts of mutton that were his favorite. The mutton had a pungent, tangy taste and gave off an aroma that piqued his hunger. During the meal, three different kinds of wine were offered, and he sampled each liberally. He noted that Jaal ate steadily, while his wife was more restrained. Kefira ate very little and kept her eyes on him throughout the meal.

When they were finished, Jaal said, "I have heard of your family. Lamech is your grandfather, I believe."

"Yes. My father is Noah."

Jaal nodded, acknowledging his acquaintance with the name. Actually, he knew a great deal about Ham's family, for he was a man of broad knowledge of people and places. He knew the heads of all the clans in the area and was ambitious to know more.

Dalit sipped at the pale wine in front of her, merely tasting it, and studied the dark-featured young man. She had thoughts of her own that were reflected in her bright black eyes, and finally she said, "I must thank you again for what you did for our daughter. I shudder to think what would have happened if you hadn't come along."

Jaal put in eagerly, "Yes. We are most thankful that you were there."

"It was more or less an accident," Ham murmured.

"No, it was not. It was the will of Ur-Baal," Dalit said firmly.

"You'll have to forgive my wife," Jaal smiled. "She's very religious. Every good thing that happens she attributes to Ur-Baal."

"Be quiet, Jaal, you will offend him!" Dalit cautioned.

Ham's eyes lit up with interest. He knew something about Ur-Baal and the orgies that took place at the ceremonies and festivals where people worshiped him, but he had been brought up to believe that Ur-Baal was evil. He glanced toward Kefira to see her reaction, but her face was expressionless, and something stirred within him. *She doesn't like this Ur-Baal nonsense,* he thought. Aloud he said, "I don't know much about things like that."

"You should," Dalit insisted quickly. "There are powers bigger than us, and Ur-Baal is powerful."

Ham did not answer, and he noted that Kefira turned the conversation away, asking him about his family. He talked about his parents, his two brothers, and his grandfather Methuselah.

Finally Jaal said expansively, "When you go home, you must carry an invitation. We want your whole family to come so that we may celebrate your courageous rescue."

"I'm sure they will be happy to," Ham said, nodding. Actually, he was not at all sure of this, but he saw it as an opportunity to see Kefira again.

After the meal Kefira and Ham walked outside to enjoy the stars and the night air. He listened as she spoke softly of unimportant things. Looking down at her, Ham found himself entranced and was both amused and alarmed by his reaction. Ham had known many women in his life, but he had not truly cared for any of them. Unlike his brothers, he had sought out the loose women of their own clan and of other nearby clans, women who loved the worship and rituals of Ur-Baal, and who did not hold back around men. But he had to admit that he had tired of those coarse women with their loud laughter and easy ways. Something about the gentleness and sweet beauty of Kefira drew him, and as the two gazed up at the stars, Ham found himself behaving in a most peculiar fashion. When a woman attracted him, he usually approached her with rough ardor. But he found he could not do this with Kefira. She looked too fragile and innocent—like a delicate flower that needed to be handled tenderly. As they talked on, watching the yellow crescent moon rise higher in the sky, Ham knew that something unusual was happening to him. He had heard love songs before but had known only the passion of sex. Now, for the first time, he realized there was much more to love!

CHAPTER 20

"What in the world is *that* thing supposed to do?"

Shem had stopped to stare at a strange device that Japheth was working on. Normally Shem had little interest in mechanical things, being of a more artistic nature. But the apparatus Japheth had worked on so diligently for weeks was at last near completion. Shem shook his head in puzzlement. "I never saw anything like it."

Japheth turned and grinned at Shem. He was a bright-eyed young man with enormous energy, always throwing himself into any activity like a whirlwind. It mattered not whether it was hunting, fishing, dancing, or inventing. He gave his older brother a look of pity and said, "It's a waterwheel. Can't you see that?"

The wheel Japheth had made had spokes in the center that circled an axle, and at the outer edge were fastened small buckets made of woven reeds and plastered inside with clay.

"A waterwheel! What in the world is it for?"

"Don't you ever get tired of carrying water in buckets to water the crops?"

"Of course I do, but it's got to be done."

"Well, it'll be easy with this waterwheel."

Shem was helpless where mechanical things were concerned. He stared at the device and said, "Show me how it works."

"All right. Watch this." At right angles to the wheel, six boards were fastened to form a rough circle. Japheth stepped on one, and the wheel moved slightly. One of the baskets dipped into the water, and as Japheth continued to walk on the treadmill, the water-filled basket was lifted up. Behind it another basket was immersed, and then finally the original basket reached the top. It poured the water out in a stream, and the second followed and then the third. Soon a steady stream of water was flowing into a wooden vat that caught the overflow.

"Well, it works, but what's it good for?"

"Can't you *see*?" Japheth said in disgust. "It picks the water up out of the river, lifts it high, and then we run it in wooden troughs over to the crops. It fills up the ditches we make there. Instead of hauling those buckets until our arms get pulled out of their sockets, we just walk like this."

Shem's eyes glowed. "You sure are a smart one, Japheth. Does Father know about this?"

"He didn't think it would work. He's like all old people. They don't trust new things. You just wait. After it's been in operation for a while, he'll claim he knew all along that it was what should have been done."

Shem grew interested and took his turn walking on the treadmill. "Why, it's easy!" he said.

"That's because your legs are so much stronger than your arms," Japheth replied. He lifted his eyes and said, "Look. Here comes Ham."

Shem stepped off the waterwheel, and the tinkling of the water as it poured out tapered off to a small, muted sound. "He's going to get it," Shem murmured. "Mother and Father have been worried sick about him. He shouldn't go off like that and stay away without letting us know where he is."

Japheth shrugged. "Well, you know Ham. He does what he wants to do." He peered closer at Ham and said, "He's all bandaged up! Looks like he's been hurt."

The two left the river and quickly walked up the dirt road that ran alongside it. As Ham got closer, Shem asked, "What happened to you? Did you get chewed up by a bear?"

Ham stood before his brothers, towering over both of them. His dark eyes gleamed, and he shook his head. "I'll tell you all about it later."

"That's right," Shem said. "You'd better go to Father at once. He's likely to give you quite a lecture."

Japheth grinned. "I'll bet you got into a fight over some girl, didn't you? Mother will *love* that!"

"You don't know everything," Ham sneered. "I got these wounds saving a beautiful young woman from being killed by a band of robbers."

Both brothers stared at Ham doubtfully. "Aw, come on, now," Japheth said. "Tell us the truth."

"If you know so much, then, you figure it out." Ham laughed, turning from them and walking on toward the house, leaving the two brothers staring after him with puzzlement in their eyes.

"You never can tell about Ham," Japheth said doubtfully.

"You can always count on him to do the unexpected. Maybe he really *did* save some woman."

Japheth grinned and poked Shem in the ribs. "I'll bet he made her give him a *reward* for saving her! Come on, I want to show you some more about how we're going to water the crops from now on."

Noah looked up as Ham entered the house, and a frown furrowed his brow. "Where have you been?" he demanded, getting to his feet. "Your mother's been worried sick about you, and so have I. How did you get hurt?"

Ham had prepared his speech. He had known that his parents would be upset with him, and now he held up his hand. "Hold on, Father. This time it wasn't my fault. Where's Mother?"

"Right here." Adah came in, her displeasure evident in her stern features. "You shouldn't go off without telling us where you're going. You could have been badly hurt." Then her eyes opened wide. "What are those bandages? What happened to you?"

"That's what I want to tell you about. Come and sit down. This is important."

Noah cast a doubtful look at Adah, then shrugged. "All right. Let's hear it. You've had time to invent a good story by this time."

Ham waited until his parents were seated; then he paced back and forth and began by telling them how he had hunted far from home and found no game. His eyes glowing, he stopped pacing and stood before them to relate how he had seen the young woman being attacked by four men after they had killed her guardian. His voice grew excited as he told how he killed two of them and fought the other two until they ran away. "They cut me up pretty badly, and I nearly passed out. But the young woman took me to her home."

"What was her name?"

"Kefira. I was pretty weak, and they took good care of me—she and her parents and the servants."

"Who are her parents? Where do they live?"

"Her father's name is Jaal. He says he knows all about you. And her mother's name is Dalit. They are very wealthy people," he added. "Pretty influential, I think. Do you know them?"

"I've heard of them," Noah said, nodding briefly. "Are you all right?" he asked.

"Yes, I am now. But something's happened to me. I want to marry the girl."

Noah stared at Ham, then turned to face Adah. "Did you hear that? He's seen her one time, and he wants to marry her."

"But, son," Adah said quickly, "we don't know anything about them."

"I know a little about her parents," Noah said. "I've never met them, but I know they're worshipers of Ur-Baal. He's a little too sharp in business dealings. Some even call him a thief, although he does it in a very sly way."

"I don't care about them," Ham objected. "I'm not marrying her parents. It's the girl I want for my wife." He turned to his mother and said in a pleading voice, "You'd like her, Mother, I know you would."

Adah did not answer, and Noah said sharply, "We know the kind of women you run with, son. I haven't seen any yet that your mother would like."

"But this one's different."

The argument went on for some time, and both Noah and Adah were apprehensive. Ham finally said, "At least go see them. I'm going to marry her if I can. It'd be better if you two would be in favor of the match. I could tell that her parents like me."

"But they worship Ur-Baal," Noah said. "You know what your mother and I think about that."

"Her parents may, but I don't think Kefira does. I watched her pretty closely while they were talking, and she didn't say a word. I had the feeling that she didn't agree with them."

"All right. We'll go visit them," Noah said. "But I'm warning you, son. I don't think anything will come of it."

"It will. She's different. You'll see." Ham laughed and then turned and left the room.

"What do you think of that, Adah?"

"I've never seen him like this before."

"I don't like it," Noah said. "Ham's never been a very hearty follower of the Ancient One, and that family may demand that he worship Ur-Baal."

Adah remained silent for a time, and Noah came over and sat beside her. "It'll be all right," he said, putting his arm around her. "We'll go meet them, at least."

Noah looked around the table, his eyes resting on his three sons and Adah; then he put his gaze on Jaal, his host, and his wife, Dalit. They had waited a week after Ham had brought the invitation, but both Adah and Noah had dreaded the visit. They'd had no choice, however, for Ham had been tense and more demanding each day that they go.

Now as they all sat there, Noah studied their host. He had made inquiries about Jaal and had heard nothing that pleased him. True enough, Jaal was a wealthy man, but there were rather sinister rumors of how he had accumulated his possessions. Noah had learned to judge men fairly well, and there was something about Jaal he did not like, although he could not put his finger on it. Dalit, his wife, was a proud woman, and Noah always distrusted proud people. His eyes went to the girl, and here he had to relent. Kefira, from all he could pick up in their evening visit, was a sweet young woman, not at all like her parents. Indeed, Noah whispered once to Adah, "I think she must be an orphan they found. She doesn't look like them or act like them."

"No, she doesn't," Adah had whispered back. "And she has no interest in worshiping Ur-Baal. Of course, she has to do what her parents say."

The meal was in midcourse, and Noah, who ordinarily had a good appetite, was so upset that he ate only enough so as not to appear unfriendly. He listened as Jaal talked about big business deals he had in mind, and finally Dalit said, casting a fond look at Ham, "We have told your son how grateful we are, and now we must say it again. Kefira's our only child, and if anything had happened to her, I would have died."

"That's right," Jaal put in. "That son of yours is quite a hero around here. Taking on four strong men! I wouldn't have thought even one of the Nephilim could have done that."

Shem spoke up quickly. "My brother is the best warrior in our clan. I think he could defeat anybody with any weapon." He turned then and smiled at Kefira. "I'm glad he arrived in time to help you."

Kefira returned Shem's smile. She had a soft voice and said quickly, "I had given up all hope, and then suddenly I was saved." Her eyes went to Ham, and she bowed slightly. "I'll never cease being grateful to you, Ham."

Ham's face lit up. "I'm glad I was there."

Japheth had been studying their host also and now spoke up. "I understand you have extensive holdings around here, sir."

"Oh yes. We've built up quite a little kingdom here with land and servants and slaves." Jaal was obviously proud of his "little kingdom," and for some time he boasted of his activities.

Noah listened without speaking, but finally Dalit said, "We give thanks to Ur-Baal. He has favored us."

Adah and all three of Noah's sons instantly turned to him. He knew they were expecting him to challenge this statement, and he did. "We do not worship Ur-Baal. We worship the Ancient One," he said firmly.

Dalit laughed shrilly. "I'm surprised, Noah! There are so few people who hold to that old fable anymore. Everyone that I know has given up their faith in the so-called Ancient One."

"Not everyone," Adah said quietly. "We believe that He is the Creator, and we give Him our loyalty."

Shem had been watching Kefira and saw something that caught his attention. *She truly doesn't believe in Ur-Baal. She's interested in the Ancient One.* The thought flickered through his mind, and he filed it away, determined to find out more about her interest.

The meal ended, and Shem had a moment alone with Kefira. The others were in another room looking at some possessions their host wanted to show off, and Shem quickly went over and smiled at the girl. "That was a wonderful meal, Kefira," he said.

"I'm glad you liked it, Shem." She studied him and shook her head. "You're very different from Ham. You don't look like brothers at all."

"No, and I'm not like Japheth either."

"I can tell you're different. It's very obvious."

"That's right," he grinned. "I'm the lesser son of Noah."

"Lesser in what way?"

"Pretty much every way, I guess."

"That's not what your mother thinks." Kefira smiled sweetly at him. "She thinks you're wonderful."

"Well, mothers are prejudiced." Shem shrugged. "Japheth can do anything with his hands or with any kind of tool. I can't put two nails together! And as for Ham, no one can stand against him. He's the strongest man in our clan. All I can do is sing songs."

"Your mother told me about that. I'd like to hear one. What do you sing about?"

"Oh, everything. But mostly about the Holy One."

"You mean the Strong One? Is that what you call Him?"

"Yes, we call Him by different names." Shem studied the girl's serene face. Now as he spoke with her, he saw that there was, deep down, a fire in her that she kept well hidden. A love of life seemed to lie impatiently behind her eyes and lips, as if it were, somehow, waiting for release.

"Are you interested in the Ancient One?" Shem asked.

"Oh yes, very much!"

Shem hesitated, not wanting to offend her. "I suppose you picked up on the fact that we don't think much of Ur-Baal."

"My parents do, but—"

"But you don't?"

"He's a cruel god—if he's a god at all." Her face grew stern, and Shem realized that beneath the curtain of reserve, she was a complex and striking young woman. "I despise the very idea of sacrificing helpless babies! No true god would demand a thing like that. It's evil, not good. But your god is good, isn't He?"

"I believe so." Shem smiled. "You should talk to my grandfather Methuselah. He's lived longer than anyone, and his father was Enoch, who was probably the best man who ever lived."

"Maybe I'll get to meet him someday."

"I'm sure you will. Ham's already made my father promise that you'll come for a visit."

A rich color tinted Kefira's cheeks. "I'm not sure I could do that."

"I wish you would. We'd love to have you."

Kefira studied the young man. He was much smaller than his brother Ham but strong and with a liveliness that appealed to her. "I will if my parents will let me," she said.

Shem had no time to answer, for Ham had come in. "What are you two talking about?" he asked.

"I've done you a service, brother."

"It's about time. What is it?"

"I've told Kefira we'd all love to have her come for a visit, and she's almost said yes."

"Good," Ham said, his eyes glowing. "When?"

"My parents will have to decide that. I'll have to bring my aunt Noli with me too."

"Noli? Who is she?"

"Just a widow, my uncle's wife. They'd never let me go alone."

"Bring her along," Ham said heartily. He reached over and clapped

Shem on the shoulder. "I see you're good for something besides writing songs. I was surprised you didn't burst out singing right in the middle of the meal."

"I wanted to," Shem said, laughing, "but I'm saving it for later."

As Shem turned and walked away, Kefira said, "He's so different from anybody I've ever met."

"Oh, he's a dreamer. He forgets what he's doing when he gets to writing his poems and songs." Ham reached out and touched her arm, wanting to do more but showing restraint. "Try to come as soon as you can," he said. "I'm anxious for us to know each other better."

Kefira did come, and she brought her aunt Noli, a short woman with a jolly temperament. Noli was more interested in drinking wine than in watching after Kefira, and most of the time she stayed in a half stupor, smiling and talking to herself.

"That woman Noli is a joke as a companion for a young woman," Noah complained. "I wouldn't trust her to go to the market and buy a melon."

"She's not very suitable," Adah agreed. The two were sitting in the cool of the evening and speaking of the girl's visit. Both of them were pleased with Kefira. She was gentle, soft-spoken, and eager to please. Her quiet beauty pleased them both, but now Adah said tentatively and with some doubt, "She's not at all the kind of young woman I would have expected Ham to choose."

"I agree with you. He's always liked the more earthy sort."

Adah knew exactly what he meant by that. "He's been with a lot of easy women, but I don't think this young woman is like that."

"No. And have you noticed she's spending more time with Shem than she is with Ham? That's strange, isn't it?"

"Shem tells me it's because she's very interested in the Strong One and wants to hear more about Him. Shem tells me she has an open mind and a very quick one too. She hates Ur-Baal with all her heart."

"How could that have happened? Her growing up in a house where her parents worship Ur-Baal—I'm surprised."

"It happens like that sometimes. You've noticed it, I'm sure," Adah said. "Look at us. We worship the Strong One with all our hearts, and Ham doesn't. Not the way Shem does."

Not fifty feet away on the other side of the house, Ham and Kefira were sitting on a bench. Kefira looked around at the garden and said, "You have so many flowers. Who grows them all?"

"Oh, my mother's crazy about flowers. She brings the wild flowers in and puts them in pots. Shem likes them too."

"They're very beautiful, and they smell delightful."

Ham turned to her and grinned. "That's what Shem's good for—singing songs and picking flowers, but he's really impressed with you."

Kefira laughed. "He's a fine young man, and so is your brother Japheth. I like them both very much."

Ham had been waiting for an opportunity to speak to Kefira alone. He was unaccustomed to gentle women and believed that he had shown proper restraint, but there was a brusqueness in him that now surfaced. He suddenly reached over and took her arms and pulled her to her feet. "Kefira," he said with determination in his voice and in his dark eyes, "I've never met anyone like you."

Kefira suddenly felt helpless in his powerful hands. He pulled her closer, and she began to grow frightened. "Please, don't hold me so tight!"

Ham laughed. "I'd like to hold you even tighter. You must have guessed by this time."

"Guessed what?"

"Why, that I want you for my wife." And then Ham pulled her so close she could scarcely breathe. She tried to turn her head away, but he kissed her roughly, ignoring her attempts to escape. Finally she freed one arm and twisted her head away.

"Please, let me go!"

Ham released her but held on to her arm. "What's wrong with you?"

"I . . . I don't like to be touched like that."

Ham was puzzled by her reluctance. "I've never known anyone like you, Kefira. I want you to marry me."

"I can't do that, Ham."

Ham blinked with surprise. It had never once occurred to him that she would refuse him. After all, he had saved her life, and she owed him. He kept his hold fast on her arm despite her attempts to pull away. "You're just young and not accustomed to men, but you'll learn to love me."

"No, Ham, I really—"

Ham's anger erupted. His temper always lay under a thin veneer of manners, and now he said harshly, "What's the matter? I'm not good enough for you?"

"It's not that. You know how grateful I am that you risked your life to save mine. I'll never forget that, Ham. But . . . well, you and I aren't suited. We'd make each other miserable."

Ham laughed sharply. "You wouldn't make *me* miserable. Come here." He tried to hold her and kiss her again, but she struggled so wildly that he turned her loose.

"Please don't do that again," she whispered, then turned and walked away as Ham stared after her. His fiery temper caused him to jerk around, and he stalked away, muttering, "Does she think she's too good for me? Is that it? I'll change her mind. Her parents want her to marry me, and that'll be enough for a while."

Ham was unable to conceal his foul mood, and very quickly everyone in the household knew that there had been a misunderstanding between him and Kefira. Adah had gone to the girl at once and gotten the story. She had listened carefully and then assured Kefira, "Ham is so rough, he may not be right for you at all. You're free to choose the man you'll marry."

Next, Adah had sought Ham out and tried to speak sensibly to him. "She's a very gentle young woman. You frightened her with your rough ways."

"Why, I just kissed her. What's the matter with that?"

Adah shook her head. "You're rougher than you know, Ham. She'll not respond to anything but gentleness."

"I can't change what I am."

Adah stared at her son and felt hopeless. Neither she nor Noah understood this man, who seemed like a stranger to all of them. She tried to instruct him, but as usual, he would not listen.

She went to Noah and said, "I've tried to talk to Ham about Kefira."

"She'll never have him now," Noah said. He was not the best judge of women in the world, but he had been quick to see Kefira's quiet, gentle spirit. "Ham would tire of her soon enough. He needs a woman of his own temperament."

The two talked for some time, and then Adah said tentatively, "You know, I think Kefira really likes Shem. Perhaps because he's so interested in the Ancient One."

Noah shook his head regretfully. "She's Ham's choice of a wife."

Adah straightened her back and looked deep into Noah's eyes. "I know that, but Ham may not be *her* choice of a husband!"

CHAPTER 21

"Girl, you've got to come to your senses! You think you can do just as you please, but you'll find out soon enough that you can't!"

Kefira's parents had summoned her from her room, and as soon as she walked in, she recognized that they were both determined to force their will upon her. She was not really afraid of her parents, for they had been kind to her in their fashion, never making any unusual demands. But lately they had both given strong hints that she must agree to the marriage with Ham, the son of Noah. Standing before them, she suddenly felt like the small child she had once been, and she tried hard to keep her feelings from showing on her face. This was almost impossible, for she was a very open young woman whose countenance usually revealed her heart.

"I'm sorry, Father. I . . . I just don't feel like it would be the right thing to do."

"Why, you fool girl! Are you telling me that *I* don't know the right thing to do?" Jaal was accustomed to getting his own way. He loved his daughter, but he was very self-centered. His face grew red as he continued to harangue her. "You've got to marry *someone*. Even you should understand that."

"Just a minute, Jaal. Let me speak to her." Dalit was a proud woman. She prized her place in society, and this marriage had seemed to her an excellent alliance. She turned to her daughter and said, "Noah's family is very prominent, Kefira. You know that. His father, Lamech, is the head of the entire clan, and Noah himself has grown very prosperous with his building skills. Of course, I don't agree with his getting out and sweating like a slave when he could hire others to do the work, but that's his choice. The important thing is, you need a husband who has already established himself, not some young man who has to make his way."

Kefira listened quietly, forcing herself to keep her head up and meet her parents' eyes.

Jaal said flatly, "So you've got to marry Ham, and that's all there is to it!"

"But, Father, I don't really care for him."

"Care for him!" Jaal shouted. "What difference does that make? He'll be a good husband. That's all that matters."

"But don't you think a husband and wife should be suited to each other?" Kefira asked.

"A wife learns what her husband wants, and she gives it to him. That's all the suiting you need!" Jaal snapped.

Frostily Dalit stared at her husband. "I think there's a *little* more to it than that." Her tone was cold, and she waited until he guiltily mumbled something and looked down at the floor.

Then Dalit spoke to Kefira kindly, entreating her to accept her role in life. "Look at it this way, my dear. Women must marry—that's the way life is. They must bear children, and then those children will bear grandchildren. We all have to do a few things we don't like, but this isn't such an awful request to make of you. Why, look at your best friend, Meiva. The poor girl's parents forced her to marry old Seofit. He's as old as the hills and so crippled he can hardly get around. Ham, on the other hand, is a fine, strong young man. He will give you many children, and you will never want for anything. So I trust you will obey us in this matter and we won't have to have this conversation again."

Kefira ordinarily would have agreed with her parents' wishes, but after Ham tried to force himself on her, she knew she would have a hard time learning to love him. She was grateful for his courage in saving her life and had told him so, but he was not the sort of man who could bring her any joy. It troubled her that he was often moody and sullen. But she said no more, simply nodded to her parents and left.

When she was out of the room, Jaal snapped, "I thought we had raised her better than that."

"Don't worry, my dear," Dalit said, her lips set in a firm line. "She will come around. We will be allied to Lamech's family. Never fear."

"She asked to go to the market today. I'm hoping she'll meet Ham there," Jaal said.

"That's a good idea. The more she sees of him, the more likely it is that she'll be resigned to having him."

Shem juggled several bundles in his arms and complained, "Mother, it seems you could find a servant to do this. I feel foolish trotting along after you carrying all these things."

Adah turned and smiled at her son, thinking, not for the first time, how much pleasure he brought into her life and Noah's. "It will do you good to get accustomed to following a woman around the marketplace. When you get married, you'll be doing a lot of it."

"No, I won't." Shem smiled, but at his mother's upraised eyebrow, he added, "I really don't mind, Mother."

Adah had enlisted Shem's service in going to the market, and the two had spent a pleasant hour going from stall to stall. It occurred to Adah that neither of her other two sons would have been at all agreeable to such an arrangement. Ham, of course, was little company to her, since he was interested in hunting and manly pursuits, while Japheth was so caught up with his activities and inventions that he had little desire to go to market. Shem, on the other hand, was always available to do anything Adah asked.

The two stopped and inspected some fresh fruit, Adah bargaining with the toothless woman, who insisted in a shrill voice that her prices were absolutely fair. After buying a supply of fresh figs, Adah put them on top of Shem's other burdens and said, "They'll be good after supper tonight. They are delicious."

Shem managed to get his hand free and plucked one out. Popping it in his mouth, he nodded. "They *are* good."

He reached for another, but Adah slapped his hand. "Leave those alone! They're for after the evening meal." She turned and stopped abruptly. "Look, there's Kefira."

Shem turned to see that the young woman was examining a piece of cloth at one of the vendors. "Let's go speak to her," he said eagerly. "Maybe she'd like to shop with us."

"All right."

The two made their way to the young woman, who turned as Adah said warmly, "Kefira, how nice to see you!"

"Come along with us, Kefira," Shem smiled. "You can help me carry this stuff. I'd have brought a wagon along if I'd known Mother was going to buy out the market."

Kefira smiled and agreed. "I'd like to very much. Here, you can carry some of these things for *me*."

Shem groaned as she put several small purchases on top of his load.

"Have you been at the market long?" Adah asked as the three ambled along.

"No. I just got here."

"I know what," Shem said. "Why don't we go to Grandfather's house? We can put these things down, and you can meet the rest of our family."

Shyly Kefira said, "If you think it wouldn't be too much trouble for them."

"Oh, people come and go there all the time. They'll be delighted to see you."

The trio made their way to Lamech's house and were greeted by Dezia as they entered. She gave Adah a kiss on the cheek and took one from Shem, then said, "Who is this young woman?"

"This is Kefira," Adah said. "This is my mother-in-law, Dezia."

Kefira murmured a greeting, and Dezia said, "I've heard so much about you. I'm glad you've come." She looked over at Shem and shook her head. "You look like a beast of burden, Shem."

"That's all I am, just a slave, Grandmother! Now, where can I put these things down before my arms break?"

Dezia directed that operation, then led them to an inner room of the house where Lamech sat dozing, his head back against the wall, his mouth open. He was snoring slightly, and when Dezia touched him, he snorted and looked around wildly. Seeing the young visitor, he immediately stood up and said, "Well, who is this, Adah?"

"This is Kefira."

Lamech stared at the young woman, then laughed roughly. "So you're the one who's giving my grandson Ham so much trouble."

Seeing Kefira's look of distress, Dezia moved closer and touched her arm with reassurance. "Don't worry about him. He's always grumpy when he wakes up."

"I'm *never* grumpy!" Lamech proclaimed indignantly. He looked Kefira up and down and grunted as though pleased. "Well, you've driven my grandson to distraction, and I can see why! When's the wedding? Young Ham is going to lose his mind if you don't marry him."

Kefira could not think of a thing to say. She was half frightened by the huge, rough man, but Dezia was accustomed to smoothing the way before her husband. She guided Kefira into the hallway and whispered to Shem, "Why don't you show Kefira the rest of the house while Adah and I talk."

"Of course. Come along, Kefira."

Kefira willingly accompanied Shem. He showed her the house, which, he informed her, had been built by Noah, and she was duly impressed. In one of the rooms she saw a stringed instrument on the wall and asked, "Who plays the harp?"

"My mother plays a little."

"You play too, don't you? I think Ham told me about that."

"Oh yes. But not very well."

Kefira smiled and said, "I hear that you sing beautifully and make up your own songs."

"My father says I'm nothing but a dreamer. I guess he's right."

"I'd love to hear one of your songs."

Shem at once pulled the harp off the wall. "You asked for it," he said. "Here's one I just made up this morning:

"Great is the Ancient One!
His voice is in the winds,
And He causes the waves to break!
He has given to His children
The stars and moon and sun.
How I love to hear His voice,
For in the singing of the birds He speaks to me.
He has given the earth to man,
And when I see His mighty works I rejoice.
He is good and kind to all,
And none who trust in Him will be ashamed. . . ."

Kefira had taken a seat, and she listened wide-eyed and with her lips slightly parted. She did not know what an attractive picture she made for the young man! She was so caught up with his song that when he stopped, she clapped her hands together and cried, "How wonderful! I could never do anything like that. How long have you been making up songs, Shem?"

Pleased at her response, he said, "Ever since I can remember. Even when I was a little boy, I loved to make up songs." He was usually rather shy about his singing and songwriting, but he spoke freely about it to

Kefira, seeing that she liked it. While they talked, he could not help noticing her pleasing figure, the smooth ivory shading of her skin, and the turn of her lips. Her black hair lay rolled and heavy on her head, and the gray dress she wore brought out the color of her eyes. He leaned forward and said, "You have the strangest eyes. They're gray sometimes, and then at other times they're blue. And sometimes they're both."

Kefira dropped her eyes, then lifted them and laughed. "Next thing I know you'll be making a song to my eyes."

Shem liked this idea. "And so I will!" he declared.

"I'll bet you've written a lot of songs to young women."

Shem was embarrassed by this. "Well, I've been a fool once or twice, I must admit. Maybe when I get this song finished you'll let me come over and sing it to you."

"Of course. I'd like that very much."

He sang two more songs for her, then said, "Come along. You've got to meet my great-grandfather. There's nobody like him."

The two made their way to the rooftop, and as Shem expected, they found the old man sitting and staring out at the white fleecy clouds as they floated across the sky. A light breeze stirred his silver hair, and when he was introduced to the young woman, he smiled gently. "I'm glad to see you, child. Has this one been singing songs to you?"

"Why, as a matter of fact, he has."

"He sings them to me too. I like them."

"So do I."

The three sat together amiably, and Methuselah very soon began to speak of the Ancient One. It was his way; no matter what the subject or the occasion, sooner or later he would begin speaking of the wonders of the Strong One whom he served. At Shem's urging, he told some of the stories of the old days, and he saw that Kefira was taking it all in. "Are you a worshiper of the Ancient One, Kefira?"

"N-no, but I'd like to know more about Him."

"That's good! Not many young people are interested in such things. It's never too late to become a follower. He is the only true power and strength in this world. "

Shem said little, but he was aware how entranced Kefira was with his great-grandfather. He himself loved to talk with the old man or, more properly, listen. Finally Shem said, "We'd better get back to the market, Kefira."

Kefira arose and bowed before Methuselah. "Sir, it's been so wonderful to hear you talk. I hope I may come back."

"Why, of course, child. You be sure to bring her back, Shem."

"I promise."

The two went downstairs, and Kefira said, "He's such a wonderful man."

"Yes, he is." Shem hesitated, then said, "My family likes you very much. I can tell."

The words pleased Kefira, and she smiled at Shem. "I like them too."

When they reached the main room of the house, Kefira said, "I really think I must go." Impulsively, she held out her hand, and Shem took it. It felt soft and warm but strong, and he said without meaning to, "I've never met a woman like you, Kefira."

Kefira was confused by the compliment. She had heard other compliments before, but there was simplicity in Shem that she had never encountered in another man. She smiled as he held her hand and said, "I've never met a man like you."

At that moment they were interrupted by the voice of Ham, who had entered the house. Kefira quickly withdrew her hand, and Shem stepped back. "Hello, brother," he said. "It's good to see you."

Ham had bumped into his mother in the marketplace. Adah had gone back to get a few things with her mother-in-law, and they had told Ham about meeting Kefira. He had demanded to know where she was, and Adah had said, "Why, she and Shem are talking to Methuselah." Ham had gone at once to the house, and now as he stood before them, suspicion burned in his dark eyes. He missed nothing, even their looks of guilt, and anger stirred within him.

Kefira greeted him. "Hello, Ham. We've just been listening to your great-grandfather."

"I don't see him," Ham said, his eyes fixed on the pair.

Kefira felt the tension and said, "I must get back. I've been gone so long."

"All right. You go ahead. I'll be with you in a moment," Ham said. He waited until Kefira left, and then he turned to Shem and looked down at him. His anger was plain as he said in a harsh tone, "Find your own woman, Shem!" Then he wheeled and left the room.

Shem stared after his brother. All the joy of being with Kefira was gone, and he shook his head. "She mustn't marry him," he murmured. "She's not for him."

CHAPTER 22

The days passed slowly after Kefira's visit, for Ham was not a patient man. Time and again he tried to convince Kefira that they should marry, but she continued to refuse. Her refusals both puzzled and irritated him. Ham was a man who liked to have his own way, and he was not going to quit trying until he had gained Kefira's consent. He assumed any woman could be won eventually by dogged persistence. Finally one warm afternoon he came home from work and sought his father out.

"You've got to do something for me," he demanded without preamble. He stood before Noah, who was kneeling in the garden planting vegetables.

Noah's hands were dirty with the black loam, and he was startled by Ham's attitude. "What is it, son?"

"I'm tired of waiting for Kefira to make up her mind. It's been months now since I asked her to marry me, so I want you to go talk to her father."

"But what can I say?" Noah stood up, brushed the dirt off his hands, and stood facing his son. They were both big men, but there was a vast difference in their appearance. Noah's face was sharply planed with clean lines, and he usually had a pleasant expression. Ham, on the other hand, had a blunt face, a wide slash of a mouth, and a permanent scowl.

Now he shook his head and said in a sharp voice, "She doesn't know what she wants. She's too young. I'll make her happy, though. It'll be fine once we get married."

Noah had been expecting this moment, but now he was hesitant to speak frankly. While he thought carefully how to answer his son, he looked up and watched a flock of geese headed across the azure sky. He waited so long that Ham demanded impatiently, "Well, will you do it?"

"I think it might be a little premature, son."

"Why would you say that? I'm ready."

"I know you are, but it seems the girl isn't. And, to tell the truth, your mother and I have thought that she might not be . . ."

When Noah left his comment unfinished, Ham's eyes narrowed, and he asked aggressively, "Might not be what?"

"Well, it's possible that she's not . . . altogether suited for you. She's such a gentle girl, very inexperienced, as you say. And you're a pretty rough fellow."

"Are you telling me she's too good for me?"

"No, I'm not saying that at all. I'm just saying she's so young, she's having difficulty making up her mind. And she has to be treated gently. Even I can see that."

The discussion went on for some time, and Noah saw that there was no way to convince Ham to give up his quest. Throwing up his hands, Noah said, "All right, I'll go, but I still believe it's something you need to think about more."

"You just talk to her father. Get him to agree, and then it'll be settled."

Noah watched as Ham stalked away, then went inside and found Adah helping the servants prepare the evening meal. "Ham just told me he wanted me to ask Jaal to go ahead with the marriage."

Adah glanced at the servants and, not wanting to speak in front of them, took his arm. "Let's go outside. It's warm in here."

When they were out in the garden, Adah said, "What did you tell him?" She turned to face him and saw the concern on his face. "I see by your face you agreed."

"I didn't know what else I could do. I'm worried about it, but he was insistent."

Adah said slowly, "I've told Ham I don't think such a marriage would work out very well."

"That's what I told him too."

They were silent for a moment, and then Adah spoke what was on both their minds. "We haven't talked about it much, but it's not too difficult to see that she's not the kind of woman Ham needs."

Noah's eyes narrowed, and he said, "I've always thought that Kefira favored Shem."

"She does. She tries to keep it hidden, but it's there all right."

"This is a bad situation, Adah. I just don't know what to do."

"Maybe Jaal will refuse," Adah said hopefully. "He may be against the match by now."

"You know he's not. Both he and Dalit are for it," Noah said, shaking his head. "I'm afraid my going will only put more pressure on Kefira to agree to a marriage that's doomed to failure. But I have to go anyway," he added heavily. "I promised Ham."

Adah watched her husband turn and walk away with his shoulders stooped, and she wondered what it would all come to.

"When did he go see Kefira's parents?" Ham had come in to find his father, and Adah had informed him that he'd gone to Kefira's house.

"He left several hours ago. He should be back anytime."

Ham rubbed his big hands together and smiled. "You'll be a mother-in-law soon," he said. "How will you like that?"

"I'd like it fine," Adah said, smiling. She wanted to say more, but knowing Ham's temper, she refrained. "Why don't you go get cleaned up for supper?"

"All right, Mother."

By the time supper was served, the boys were all there, but Noah had not yet returned. They were almost finished eating when Ham's head jerked up. "I think I hear him now."

Noah appeared in the door, and Adah, who knew him so well, was aware right away that he did not bring good news. "Sit down, dear," she said. "I'll bring you some meat."

Noah, however, did not sit down. His eyes went to Ham, and he appeared to be having difficulty forming his words.

"Well, did you settle it?" Ham demanded. He leaned forward, his dark eyes on his father, his body rigid with expectation.

"Not exactly," Noah said slowly.

"What does that mean—not exactly?" Ham demanded.

"I have some news you won't like, Ham. I wish it were better for your sake."

"They refused the marriage?"

"No ... Jaal and his wife agreed, but ... well, Kefira said she won't marry you no matter what. She told us that she'd already turned you down many times."

"Why, that little ..." Ham's face grew dark with anger, and he stood up suddenly. Always an impetuous man, he threw the knife down on the table with such force that everyone in the room jumped. All of them had seen Ham angry before, so it was no surprise he took the news like this.

"Maybe she'll change her mind," Japheth said hopefully. "Give her a little more time, Ham."

But Ham was past reasoning. "She's had all the time in the world. I'll give her nothing!" he shouted. He turned and left the room, and a silence reigned over the entire family.

Finally Adah whispered, "I knew he'd take it like that."

"Did you talk to Kefira yourself, Father?" Shem asked.

"Yes, I did."

"Well, what did she say?"

"She just said that she didn't think she could make Ham happy. Which means, of course"—Noah shrugged his burly shoulders—"that she didn't think he could make *her* happy."

"I think she's done a very wise thing," Adah said. "But it must have been hard. Her parents were so set on the match."

Noah sat in his chair and slumped down. Shaking his head, he said, "They threw a fit, but nothing would change her mind. That girl's got more grit in her than I thought! She stood up to both of them."

"What will Ham do?" Japheth pondered. "He doesn't like to lose anything."

"I expect he'll be a pain," Noah said. "We'll just have to put up with him."

Shem was not through with his questions. "What did she look like when she talked with you?"

"Kefira? She was very pale, and I could tell it took a lot of courage for her to go against her parents. But she did what she thought was the right thing."

The boys got up and left quickly, and Noah went over to put his arm around Adah. "It was very hard, and it's going to get worse."

"I know. I see the end of this."

"You mean Shem and Kefira?"

"Yes. I thought of that. But I don't think Shem would ever come between Kefira and his brother."

"No, he wouldn't, but now that she's refused Ham once and for all, that may make things different."

Noah squeezed her and said, "You know, the older I get, the more I realize how fortunate I am to have a woman like you, Adah. Not many men are so blessed."

Adah looked at him, startled. Her husband had said very few things like that to her during their married life, and now as he held her, she was aware of his sincerity. "Thank you, Noah. It's good to know that."

"I guess this is a good time to tell you something about Lomeen."

Adah instantly grew stiff in his arms, but Noah went on. "It took me a long time to figure things out. I'm not all that smart, as you well know." He looked down at her, and his expression was gentle, with a warm glow in his eyes. "I made a fool of myself over that woman. I thought if I couldn't have her, I'd lost the world. And then when the Strong One told me to marry you, I was obedient."

"I knew you didn't love me, but I loved you," Adah said simply.

"I know, and that's made me feel bad. It still does. But during these last months something's happened to me, Adah. The Strong One's been showing me how foolish I was to give my heart to a woman like Lomeen. And He's also been telling me how He gave you to me as His own special gift, so what I want to tell you is . . ."

"Yes, Noah? What is it?"

"I love you now as a man ought to love his wife. I may not always show it, but I do, Adah. You're very dear to me, and I'm so thankful that I have you for a companion."

Adah could not contain her tears. They overflowed, and she threw her arms around him and buried her face in his chest. Noah held her, surprised at first by her tears. But then he squeezed her tightly and said, "Adah, please don't cry!"

"I can't help it. I've waited so long to hear you say that."

"Well, I've said it, and you may have to listen to it again. I'm way behind on talk like this."

"That's all right. I'll listen anytime you want to say it."

Noah chuckled then, and when she lifted her head he kissed her. "Don't expect me to start singing songs like Shem. I don't think I could handle that."

"Just keep telling me you love me. That's all I want, Noah."

Ham stayed away for three weeks. Noah wavered between worrying about him and being angry with him. "He shouldn't disturb his mother like this!" he protested to Shem.

"He was hurt pretty badly, Father. It'll take a little time for him to recover."

"He could have let us know where he was going," Noah insisted.

Finally early one morning, before Noah and the boys had gone to work, Adah heard Shem call out, "Here comes Ham!"

Putting down a pot of hot cereal she was stirring, Adah ran into the great room. "Where is he?" she asked Shem, who was looking out the window.

"There."

Noah appeared and came over to stand beside Adah. "I'd like to punch his head for worrying you like this!"

"Don't be angry with him. I'm just glad he's home." She turned and smiled at him when Ham's huge form filled the doorway. "Ham, I'm so glad to see you. Where—" She stopped abruptly, for Ham had stepped aside, revealing a woman who had been hidden behind him.

"This is Mendora," he said with a stubborn set to his mouth and a challenge in his eyes. "She's my wife."

A total silence fell over the family. They all stared in shock, for the woman who stood there was certainly noticeable, to say the least. She was very tall and much darker complected than Ham. Her hair was short and curly, and there was a savage look about her. It was the only way to describe her. Her eyes glinted with suspicion, and she stared at them, not with the embarrassment a bride would usually show in meeting her new family, but with arrogance.

"Hello," she said. "Ham's told me all about you." She took Ham's huge arm in hers and leaned against him. "This is some son you got here. He wouldn't take no for an answer."

"Well, aren't you going to welcome your new daughter?" Ham demanded.

"Of course," Adah cried and moved forward at once. She put out her hand and then had to reach up to kiss the woman on the cheek. "We're surprised, that's all."

Noah cleared his throat and forced a smile. "Glad you're back, son, and we're glad to welcome your new wife. Which clan are you from, Mendora?"

"From Comir's clan."

Shem and Japheth exchanged quick glances. Both of them were thinking the same thing. *It looks like Ham got a bride about as wild as he is.*

Adah was flustered, but she finally said, "Come now. I'm just getting breakfast ready. You must tell us all about it."

The breakfast was a strange affair. Mendora did most of the talking. There was a bold look about her as she studied her new family, and she laughed loudly. Once she said, "Ham told me about the girl he was going to marry. What's her name?"

"Kefira," Shem said quickly.

"Yes, that's it. Well, she sounds like a pale, washed out sort of woman to me." She reached over and pulled Ham's head down and kissed him passionately, then looked at the family with a sly smile. "I guess I know how to make him forget *her*."

Shem said almost nothing during the meal, but after it was over he walked outside and Japheth followed him. "What do you think of her!" Japheth exclaimed.

"She suits Ham," Shem answered dryly.

"She's been around some. I never saw a bolder-looking woman in my life. My guess is she'll be a handful."

Shem did not answer. He was not thinking of Mendora at all but rather of how this would affect him, and finally Japheth put his thoughts into words.

"Well, brother, it's no secret that you've had eyes for Kefira. I guess now you're free to go after her."

"It's too soon."

"Too soon! Why, the road's before you!" Japheth laughed. He hit Shem a sharp blow on the shoulder and winked. "It's time to quit singing songs and get yourself a woman."

Shem tried to smile, but he could not. His thoughts were all on Kefira, and deep down a joy was growing in him. Now he was free to go to her without restraint!

CHAPTER 23

Kefira had lain awake most of the night, tossing, unable to sleep. No one was stirring in the house, and she sat up and rubbed her eyes. She had slept poorly for several nights, and she knew her eyes were puffy and red from the lack of sleep. Swinging her legs over the bed, she sat still, thinking of the past four months. Ever since she had refused Ham, her life had been miserable. Her parents missed no opportunity to tell her what a fool she was to turn down such an advantageous marriage. They seemed incapable of understanding that she simply could not face the thought of spending the rest of her life lying beside a man she feared and who was her opposite in so many ways.

A scrabbling sound near the wall caught her attention, and she turned to see a mouse nibbling at the bit of bread she had left for her. Kefira had seen that she was a nursing mother and every night made certain to leave food out. It gave her pleasure to watch the mouse sit up and hold the bread crumb in its tiny paws, nibbling it and turning it around. The beady eyes were fixed on her, and Kefira wondered if she could tame the mouse to come to her hand for food. She had always had a heart for small creatures and had even nursed many wounded ones back to health. Now the thought leaped into her mind, *I wish my problems were as small as yours, Mother Mouse. All you have to worry about is getting something to eat and taking care of your little ones. You probably don't have any bad memories, as I do, and you certainly don't worry about the future.*

She rose and watched the sleek creature scurry under her clothes chest. Then Kefira dressed and left the room as silently as possible. She passed through the outer door and walked quickly away from the house. Her parents were not light sleepers, but the servants would be up soon, and she was not in a mood to talk with anyone.

Overhead the stars were cold and brilliant in the sky, faint pulses of light that had already begun to dilute the cold blackness of the earth. A night bird uttered a plaintive call, making a strange falling cadence on the air. She had the sudden disturbing thought that nothing in life was good. Usually a cheerful girl, full of hope and wonder at the things she saw, the future loomed before her like a dark phantom of doubt. Even the shadows in the sky and the patterns of the trees glimmering through the breaking dawn would never be quite the same. Her life before Ham showed up had been simple and innocent, but now she lived with powerful feelings from deep within. For the first time in her life she thought much about death. She hated the thought of being gone, having left no impression, not even a shadow, upon the greatness of the earth.

Disturbed by such thoughts, Kefira hastened toward the garden. It was the one place she could find a measure of peace, and as she entered, she could smell the heavy fragrance of the fresh flowers their gardener had planted the day before. She watched the light fingers of the sun touch the deep shadows, driving them away, bringing the colors of the flowers to life.

A few times in her past she had met men and women whose purpose in life was clear and uncomplicated and sweet. She envied those individuals and never gave up the steadfast hope that one day all of the complications that gnawed at her would fade as she found the secret of simplicity. She had felt of late, since the coming of Ham, that invisible forces were moving her about as a river or a stream will push a tiny chip this way and then that way. Somehow her close brush with disgrace, or even death, had made her think of life differently. She watched the world about her and saw suffering on every hand. True, she was sheltered from most of this by her parents' wealth and position, but she knew a time was coming that would bring her own suffering. She did not shrink from that. The only thing she feared was that she would be pushed aside or would live out her life in a meaningless manner, making no imprint on the world about her, shriveling up like a flower burned by a blistering sun without the blessings of rain.

The cry of a rooster startled her. She shrugged and smiled slightly, wondering if the rooster thought his call pulled the sun out of the darkness and made the day begin. She half turned, then abruptly halted, for a figure stood in the shadows of the garden. A man was watching her! Remembering the band of robbers, fear swept over her. She opened her mouth to cry out, but then the figure stepped forward into the light.

"Shem!"

"Hello, Kefira." He rushed toward her and whispered, "I had to see you."

Kefira stared at him in confusion. She had thought of him so often, but since his brother's marriage, she had seen him only twice, and both times he had looked at her with an unfathomable expression and confined his remarks to commonplace matters. Now, however, she saw that strain had sharpened his features. By the gray blades of light that sliced through the darkness, she read his face and stepped forward to meet him. "What is it? Is something wrong?"

"Yes. Something's wrong," he said.

"What is it?"

Shem reached forward, and she impulsively gave him her hands. As he closed his hands on hers, she was surprised to feel safe and secure—something she had sensed little of late. She waited, aware of the warmth and strength of his hands and puzzled as to what kept him struggling to find words. "What is it? Is something wrong with your family?"

"No. Nothing like that." Shem hesitated, then said, "Kefira, I've always sensed you've had something in your eyes for me. Is that true, or have I just wished for it?"

Kefira instantly knew what he meant. From the first time she had met Shem, she had responded to him in a way that both troubled and intrigued her. She was a gentle girl and had had little to do with men, but she had always felt at ease in this man's presence. She knew that other women would be more evasive and sophisticated, but she was a simple woman without guile. "Yes. It's true," she whispered.

"I knew it!" Shem said. He squeezed her hand so hard that it hurt, but she did not protest. "I've been caught in an awful trap. Ham found you and thought you would be his woman. I stepped back, even though I had strong feelings for you, because he's my brother, and I couldn't take that which is his. But things have changed now."

"What's changed, Shem?"

"Ham has been married for four months. I've waited all this time trying to puzzle it out." He smiled faintly and shook his head. "Would you believe I haven't written a song or a poem in four months? You've been so much on my mind that I can't think straight, Kefira."

Kefira suddenly felt like a hunter who had been lost for a long time and finally, after many dangers and hardships, came to his own place, his own home.

"I want you for my wife, Kefira. Will you marry me?"

She did not hesitate. "Yes," she said softly with a gladness that bubbled up unexpectedly.

Shem gave a quick, exultant cry, dropped her hands and put his arms around her. She put her arms around his neck, and when he lowered his face, she accepted his kiss. Ham's demanding kisses had frightened her, but Shem's lips were gentle and caring, and his arms about her gave her a stability and happiness she knew she had been seeking. Everything seemed to come together for her. All of the hopelessness vanished, and when he lifted his head, she said simply, "I think I loved you all this while, but I never thought you'd come to me."

"It may not be easy, Kefira," Shem said soberly. "Ham will take it wrong."

"But he's married."

Shem could not explain his brother, but he knew there would be trouble. "What about your parents?" he asked.

Kefira laughed, a soft, musical sound on the dawn air. "You don't need to worry about them. They want to ally themselves with your grandfather's family. They wouldn't care if I married you or Japheth. They really wouldn't."

"What time do they get up?" Shem asked, then laughed softly. "Let's go get them out of bed and catch them while they're only half awake."

"No, don't do that. Sit down and tell me what you've been doing." She pulled him down to the bench, and as the dawn broke in glorious crimson in the east, she listened as he spoke of his love for her.

As Noah bent over and pulled one of the grapes from the vine, he smiled, thinking of the upcoming wedding of Shem and Kefira. He and Adah had been caught off guard when, just a week earlier, Shem had told them that he and the young woman had pledged themselves to each other. It had disturbed them both, for they knew Ham's probable reaction. Still, Shem stood so straight and his eyes glowed with such happiness that they could not help but rejoice with him, and now the plans were all in place.

Noah put the grape in his mouth, crushed it between his heavy teeth, and savored the sweetness of the juice. "It will be a good year for the vineyard." He spoke the words aloud into the stillness of the evening.

Moving on down the row, his thoughts turned to Ham. As everyone had expected, Ham had been jealous. Mendora had thrown one of her fits, physically assaulting Ham. He had cuffed her to one side, and she had stopped attacking him but had made his life generally as miserable as possible.

She's a wild woman, Noah thought. *I wish he had found someone more suitable. Now I'm afraid Ham will never forget his desire for Kefira, but he must!*

He continued pruning the vines, pulling off dead leaves and sampling a grape from time to time. The evening was darkening, and as usual, he looked up and noted the positions of the stars. *Always in the same place at this time of year. But three months from now they will move.* The stars puzzled him, and he wished he knew more about them.

Finally he was ready to return to the house, but before he could move, a light suddenly glowed to his left. He turned and gasped. It was the same light he had seen years before when the Strong One had appeared to him in the rainstorm and had spoken. That had been centuries ago, but the incident was still always on his mind. Now he heard the voice again calling his name, and he fell to his knees, bowing his head to the earth and trembling. The voice spoke again, and it seemed warmer and more filled with affection than he remembered it.

"Rise up, Noah. Do not be afraid."

"O Holy One, is it you?"

"Noah, you have found grace in my sight. You are a man greatly beloved."

As he heard the words, something inexplicable happened. He had worshiped the Strong One for many years and had offered what he hoped were acceptable sacrifices. There had been a satisfaction in being faithful when it seemed that the whole world about him was falling into the worship of Ur-Baal. Now as he stood up and stared into the depths of the brilliant glow, squinting his eyes against its brightness, he felt something unexpected. For a time he did not understand what it was, but as the Strong One remained silent Noah suddenly knew. He burst out in a wild cry, "O Holy One, how I love you!"

And it *was* love, pure and untainted, rising from his heart. He had heard Zorah speak of his love for the Ancient One, and this had puzzled Noah, but now he knew exactly what the old man had meant. It gushed up in him like a fountain, and he began to weep without knowing it. All he could do was worship, crying out over and over again, "O Holy One, I love you! O Holy One, how I love you!"

Noah then felt as if something reached out to him from the brilliant light, almost like the touch of a hand. These were not human fingers that touched him, yet he felt the warmth and love of the Strong One as if it were physical.

"Your love pleases me, Noah. You have been a faithful servant."

"I have tried, O Strong One, to serve you."

"I know that, and because you love me, I now have a commandment for you. You must be strong, Noah, for a terrible thing is going to fall upon the earth. I have seen that the wickedness of man is great throughout the world. Every thought from the hearts of men is continually evil. I am sorry that I have made man. It grieves me to see what he has become."

Despite the love that Noah was feeling, a terrible fear also gripped him, a fear of what lay before him. "What will you do, O Strong One?"

"I will destroy man, whom I have created, from the face of the earth—not only man, but also every beast and creeping thing and the birds of the air—for I repent that I have made them."

Noah heard the words clearly, but they were so horrible, he doubted his senses. "You will destroy everyone, O God?"

"Not everyone. The end of all flesh must come, for the earth is filled with violence. But I will make a new beginning. I will preserve human life, and we'll begin again. From you and your line will come a Redeemer, for you have found grace in my sight."

"What will you do, Strong One?"

"I will bring a flood of waters upon the earth to destroy all flesh. Everything in the earth that has breath will die."

"But how can this be?"

"You cannot know my ways, Noah. You can only obey. With you I will establish my covenant, and one day from your line there will come One who will make the earth as it was in the beginning. Holy and without blemish."

Noah listened transfixed and finally whispered, "But how will I survive?"

"You are to make an ark of gopher wood. Make it three hundred cubits long, fifty cubits wide, and thirty cubits high. Inside, make lower, second, and third stories. Make rooms in the ark and seal it inside and out with pitch. Put one window up high and set a door in the side."

As Noah listened, trying to imagine such a thing, he finally blinked into the light and asked, "What about the animals, Holy One? Will they all die?"

"Of every living thing, you will bring two, male and female, into the ark to keep them alive with you. Every kind of bird, every kind of beast, every kind of creeping thing of the earth—two of every sort will come to you at my command so that you may keep

them alive. Gather enough food for them and for you and store it in the ark."

Trembling, Noah asked, "Will I be alone with the animals? Will any others be on the ark, Holy One?"

"I will establish my covenant with you, Noah, and you and your family will come into the ark—you and your sons, your wife, and your sons' wives."

Noah waited for Him to continue, but only silence roared in his ears. Then he gasped, "But no more than that? Just my family?"

The burning light faded then, and Noah again heard the voice of God, this time a soft whisper. *"You have found grace in my sight. I will come again and instruct you. It will take you many years to build the ark, and while you build it, you will warn the world of what I, the Strong One, will do."*

And then the light was gone, and Noah stood alone in the darkness. Overhead the pale stars glittered coldly, and Noah slumped to the ground on his face. His vivid imagination saw a multitude of people—friends, his own family, thousands he had never met—all dying in the calamity that was to come. He could not fathom the thought of the deaths of so many, and finally he cried out, "O Holy One, I cannot bear it!"

His shoulders shook with sobs, but as he lay prostrate in the darkness and quiet, Noah felt the presence of God. This time it came to him in his inner spirit, bringing peace in the midst of the deep sorrow that would now be his constant companion. He rose to his knees, looking toward the heavens, knowing that nothing would ever be the same again. He could only remember the words of the Strong One: *"You have found grace in my sight."* And there underneath the stars, Noah, the carpenter, bowed his head and surrendered himself to the task that the Strong One had laid upon his shoulders.

PART FOUR

CHAPTER

24

Shem was entering the kitchen, humming a tune under his breath, when he saw Kefira and stopped dead still. She was standing with her back to him, lost in thought as she peeled vegetables. With a mischievous twinkle in his eye, he crept silently toward her, then threw his arms around her, squeezing her hard and lifting her off her feet. "Gotcha!" he cried. He whirled her around, ignoring her cries of protest, then finally set her down and kissed her. He grinned at her, one eyebrow lifted.

"You crazy man!" Kefira laughed. She reached up a hand to strike him on the chest, but he pinioned it quickly, and she giggled in return. "You're acting like we just got married."

"I'll be acting like this a hundred years from now. Maybe two or three hundred. Who knows?" Shem said, kissing her again, then whispering in her ear, "That was an interesting evening we had last night, wasn't it?"

Kefira flushed and made a face at him, then reached up with her free hand and placed it on his cheek. "Yes, it was," she confessed. Her eyes sparkled brightly, and she laughed. "Proud of yourself, aren't you?"

"I'm proud of *you*. I don't know why we wasted so much time waiting to get married." He laid his hand on hers against his cheek and whispered, "I don't think I've told you today that I love you."

"Yes, you have—three times."

"Well, that takes care of the next two days, then."

He stood holding her, and the two whispered and laughed together, oblivious to anyone who might be listening or any work that had to be done. Marrying Shem had made Kefira happier than she could ever have imagined. Standing now in his embrace, she felt an inner glow and knew without a doubt that she had made the right choice.

Reluctantly, she pulled away with a sigh and said, "I've got to get this meal ready. Why don't you help?"

"All right," Shem agreed, and the couple worked together, stealing smiles and glances every time they passed each other. When it was ready, they carried the plates into the larger room where the family was gathered to eat. Shem glanced around and asked, "Is Father not here?"

"No," Adah said. "He's late."

"I don't know what's the matter with him," Ham muttered darkly from his place at the table. "He's touchy as a cat with a sore tail."

Adah did not respond to Ham's grumbling. After she served the food and everyone began to eat, she remained silent, her eyes occasionally touching on Shem and Kefira with a warm glow. They were two people in her family she didn't need to worry about. She did, however, worry about Noah, for he had been strangely quiet of late. She also worried about Ham and Mendora, whose volatile marriage was a source of constant friction for the family. She did not know from one day to the next whether they would be fighting or loving. She wished they could have a steadiness in their marriage like Shem and Kefira had found. Her thoughts were interrupted by approaching footsteps, and she lifted her head. "There's your father now," she said.

Everyone turned to watch Noah as he came into the room. He seemed haggard as he moved to take his seat on the bench at the end of the table. Adah at once began loading his plate, saying, "You must be starved. You've been eating like a bird lately."

Noah appeared not to have heard. He sat with his head down, and it became obvious to everyone he was troubled. Finally it was Shem who asked tentatively, "Is something wrong, Father? Don't you feel well?"

Noah shook his shoulders in a strange gesture, as if struggling to rid himself of a heavy burden. Lifting his head and moistening his lips, he stared around at the family. He seemed at a loss for words, and Adah knew that whatever had been troubling him and driving him into isolation for the past few days had grown to be too much. She could not imagine what it was, and now she laid her hand on his arm and said gently, "What's wrong, husband? Tell us about it."

Noah turned to her with a grateful look and put his large hand over hers. When he spoke, his voice was lower than usual, and he had to clear his throat before he could get the words out. "Something . . . something momentous . . . has happened," he said slowly, spacing the words out in an unnatural fashion. "I've been trying to find a way to tell you about it."

Ham turned his head to one side, studying his father. He had never seen him in this mood, and a worried look came to his brow. Despite his disagreements with his father, he loved him. "Is something wrong with the business, Father? Is that it?"

"No, nothing like that. I only wish it were something that simple, Ham. It's different from anything that's ever happened." He straightened up painfully and placed both hands flat on the table, letting his eyes go around the circle. For days now he had been walking by himself, sleeping almost not at all, and eating very little. Now he knew the time had come when he needed to lay this burden before his family. Slowly he began to speak. "The Strong One has spoken to me." Again he hesitated, as if afraid to go on, then turned, and his eyes met Adah's. "What He said has disturbed me more than I can explain. I've been trying to think of a way to tell you, but it's so hard. I haven't been able to find the words."

Japheth leaned forward. "Well, just tell us," he said urgently. "Is it bad news?"

"Yes, son, it's very bad news. Worse than anything you've ever dreamed!"

Mendora stared at Noah. She had not developed any great fondness for her father-in-law, although she had to admit he had been kind to her, as had Adah. She had listened carefully to everything her in-laws had to say about the Strong One. She had been, along with her entire family, a worshiper of Ur-Baal and had at first sneered at all this talk about their God. She had once made some slighting remark about the Strong One to Methuselah, and his gaze had fastened on her in a way that was most unsettling. She had mumbled her apologies and thereafter kept her thoughts to herself. Now she spoke up. "Does He want a better sacrifice? That's the message our priests usually get from Ur-Baal."

"Don't even breathe the name of that god and his unholy sacrifices in this house, Mendora!" Noah said harshly, then immediately closed his eyes and shook his head. "I'll tell you the whole thing." He began to speak haltingly as he related the Strong One's commands. He opened his eyes to see the mixed reactions in the faces of these whom he loved most on earth. In Ham and Mendora he saw incredulity. Ham even shook his head slightly with an involuntary gesture, and Noah was certain he was rejecting the whole thing. Shem was leaning forward, his whole expression intent and his eyes fixed on Noah's as he drank in every word. Adah, whom he glanced at as he finished his story, was watching him with an unreadable expression. Finally he ended, "... and so that is what He told me. He's going to destroy the world by water, and we are to build a boat—an ark, He called it—so that we of all the people on earth will not perish."

Ham was the first to break the shocked silence that fell on the room after Noah's voice ceased. "You must have heard Him wrong," he said, his eyes fixed on his father. "It *can't* be true! Why, Great-grandfather's been around for hundreds of years, and even he's never seen anything like that. Water just doesn't get that high."

"I know it sounds impossible," Noah answered, his eyes pleading for his son to believe what he was telling them. "But I know what I heard, and my heart's breaking because of it."

Adah was still in a state of shock. "You mean everyone's going to die except for us?"

"Yes. Everyone on the whole earth."

Mendora said loudly, "I've heard you call Ur-Baal wicked because he demands human sacrifice. Well, what do you call *this*? Your God's going to kill everybody on the earth except those of us in this room! How can you love a God like that?"

Noah had no answer for her. Indeed, he had been over that same question in his own mind. He said only, "Mendora, I can't explain it. I only know that he is the Strong One. He never lies. What I've told you is the truth, and I'm going to obey Him."

Ham rose abruptly from the table, his face flushed with anger. "People say we're strange now, but when this gets out—if you follow this impossible dream of yours—they'll think we're *all* crazy! And what's more, I think the whole thing is insane!" He got up and stalked out. Then Mendora, after glancing around, leaped up and followed him without a word.

Japheth had not said a word, but his mind had been working rapidly. "You say that we're to take two of every kind of animal onto the ark?"

"Yes, that is what He told me. Also that we're to take seven of the clean animals."

Japheth's brow furrowed as he figured in his mind for a moment, and then he shook his head. "There's never been a boat built like that, Father. The biggest boats I've ever seen are the wooden ones you have built for river travel."

Noah nodded as Japheth continued to figure this out in his head.

"But the river boats are only a few feet long," Japheth went on.

"According to what the Strong One says, this will be an enormous piece of work. Everything about it will be different. Tell me again what He said about the size of it."

He listened carefully as his father went over the size of the ark, then took a deep breath. "Well, the Strong One will have to give more instructions than that. You realize that no tree is long enough to reach the length of it? The timbers will have to be fastened together somehow. And it is to have *three* levels? Father, I don't want to question whether you heard this from the Strong One—because I believe you have—but just building the ark is going to be something that's beyond my imagination."

"And all those animals. How would you capture all of them?" Kefira asked.

"And how would you feed them?" Adah put in. "Just think of all the food it would take!"

"I don't know," Noah said defensively. "I don't really know anything except what I've told you. But one thing I'm sure of—if the Strong One has told us to do it, we must obey. I know I'll look like a fool and so will all of you, but I love Him, and I must obey His voice."

Noah suddenly walked out of the room, grief etched on his face. Adah watched him go, then turned to Shem and Japheth. "I'm going to offer all the help I can to your father, but it will be up to you boys and Ham to actually carry out what the Ancient One has commanded."

"We will, Mother. Don't worry," Japheth said. His eyes were electric with excitement at the thought of a project of such monstrous proportions. "I've got to think carefully about how we will do this."

Shem sat quietly, not speaking. His mind was occupied not so much with the difficulties of building a boat but with the enormity of what God had commanded. He knew that Japheth would occupy himself with the physical details of building the huge boat of deliverance. And Ham? Who could say what he would do? But Shem suddenly realized that everything from this point on would be different. He turned to Kefira and said, "I've got to go think about this. Maybe the Strong One will speak to me." Looking at his mother, he added, "I'm with you, Mother. We'll have to stay together as a family."

Adah watched her oldest son leave the room, then put her eyes on Kefira. "I've always wondered why God chose me to be Noah's wife. Now I know."

Kefira rose, put her hand on her mother-in-law's shoulder, and squeezed. "Why's that, Mother?"

"Because the woman he loved all those years would never have helped him with this."

"Why, that's right!" Kefira exclaimed. "And that's why the Holy One put Shem and me together, to be a part of all this." She hesitated and then said, "I don't know much about the Strong One. I've often wondered if He cares about small things."

"Yes, I believe He does," Adah said. She had gone through hard times in her life, and now she saw far more clearly than Kefira what all this would mean. "It's going to be very hard, daughter," she whispered. "Very hard indeed!"

Methuselah sat and listened as the words poured out of Noah. The old man's health had not been good, but his mind still worked perfectly well. Noah ended by saying, "I know it all sounds so . . . so *crazy*! But I couldn't make up a thing like this."

"His ways are not our ways, my son," Methuselah said. "He is God and not a man. I have seen this coming for some time. I've had dreams about it, but I haven't spoken to anyone of them."

"I just can't believe it. It's so terrible! Just one family out of all the earth to be saved."

"It is terrible, but what has happened to the earth is terrible as well. You just don't understand, Noah. You haven't lived long enough. I can think back to the time when the world was better. The world is like an apple that had just a tiny speck of rot, and the badness grew and grew until the whole earth is almost totally wicked."

Noah stared at his grandfather and whispered, "That's what the Strong One told me. He said the end of all flesh must come because the earth is filled with violence. I've been losing my mind over this. Think of it, Grandfather, everyone dying—my brothers and sisters and nephews and nieces! And all over, people we don't even know are going to die—and they don't even know it."

Methuselah listened as Noah blurted this out, seeing the anguish in his grandson's eyes. When Noah stopped, he said, "We cannot question the purposes of the Holy One, Noah—but God has chosen you, and I am proud. You are so different from other people. What did He say? You have found grace in His sight. What a wonderful thing to find grace in the eyes of the Almighty, the Holy One!"

"But this thing that's going to happen. It's terrible!"

"If the Strong One does it, Noah, it is right. He is just and good, and although *we* do not understand why suffering comes, He does. I've often seen terrible things happen and wondered why He allowed them, but He is a good God, and we must love Him no matter what happens to us or to others. He is the Strong One and the Wise One. He is altogether holy, and if this thing looks terrible to us, I think it must look terrible to Him. But then, iniquity always looks terrible to the Holy One."

Noah sat listening as his grandfather spoke softly for a long time. He respected this old man's wisdom, for no man on earth had seen more than he. He especially grasped at the words as Methuselah spoke of his father, Enoch, and what a righteous and holy man he was. "That's what the Holy One intends for us all to be." Methuselah sighed. "But we have failed." He looked up and said, "Let me see the lion."

Noah blinked and pulled the medallion out from under his garment. It was pierced, and he had tied a single piece of rawhide through it and always kept it suspended around his neck. He removed it and handed it to Methuselah, who stared at the image carved on it. "You and I do not understand what this lion means, but someday one of our descendants will. I know in my heart it has something to do with a great thing that lies far in the future. Zorah saw it, and he spoke of it often."

"What was it he said?"

"He spoke of one who will come to help us, and he spoke of how the Strong One is always working to change the hearts of men. I know that a day will come when He will fulfill His promise!"

Lamech stalked up to Noah as he and Japheth were hewing down a tree. Without preamble, Lamech said, "Have you lost your mind, son?" His voice crackled with anger, and his eyes flashed. He threw his hands apart in a wild gesture and said, "You're preaching that the world's going to be destroyed! I've tried to defend you when people said you were crazy, but I can't defend this!"

"I'm sorry you feel that way, Father."

Lamech had expected Noah to lash out at him, but when his son only replied meekly, he sighed deeply and shook his head in despair. "All right. Tell me all of it." He listened intently as Noah described what the Strong One had said to him, and finally he echoed the words of Mendora. "So your God is going to kill us all! I don't want to hear any more of your talk about Ur-Baal being cruel. What could be crueler than killing a whole world full of people?"

Noah listened as his father ranted on. His heart was tortured, but he had no answer.

Finally Lamech demanded, "What about your family? All of *us*? Will we all be on this boat if it's ever built?"

For Noah this was the hardest question of all. He did not answer his father, for the Holy One had said clearly that it would be only his wife and his sons and their wives who would be saved. Lamech stared at him, then huffed, "Well, that's just *fine*, isn't it? I'm glad you're going to be safe while the rest of us die!"

As Lamech stalked away, anger in every line of his figure, Japheth looked at his father and saw tears in his eyes. He had thought much of his father's vision, and although he had not heard from the Strong One personally, he trusted his father. He came closer and whispered, "No matter how hard it gets, Father, we must obey the voice of God."

When Kefira brought food to the men as they were working, she saw that Ham was not with them. Shem told her that he was out looking for new timber. She made her way home, and as she passed through a grove of trees, she came upon Ham around a bend in the path. He saw her and approached her at once. "Hello, Kefira," he said. "What are you doing here?"

"I brought some food. You'd better hurry back before the others eat it all."

Ham did not answer her, just stood staring, unsmiling. Kefira was uncomfortable in Ham's presence, as she had been ever since she had married Shem. "Well, I must go." She started to leave, but he put his hand on her arm.

"Do you believe all of this about a flood and everybody dying?" he asked.

"Yes. Don't you?"

"Father's always had dreams and visions. Most of them don't mean a thing."

Ham did not release her arm, and there was an odd light in his eyes that frightened her. She tried to pull away, but his strength was too great. He laughed, reaching out and taking her by the other forearm. He pulled her closer until she was pressed against him, and she cried out. "Please, Ham, turn me loose!"

Ham did not heed her cries. He held her effortlessly, and at that moment she knew she was in great danger. Then, to her surprise, he laughed roughly and turned away. Kefira did not speak, just ran down the path without looking back. She knew Ham was watching her, though, and she thought, *He's never forgotten that I refused him.*

Ham watched as Kefira disappeared around the bend. His anger at her refusal had festered, and he knew it would never leave him. With a grunt he turned and walked down the pathway, the dark side of his nature—the side that usually won—struggling to overcome him.

CHAPTER 25

"I think it's going to work," Japheth said, examining the rows of timbers that had been joined together with hardwood pegs to form the huge keel of the ark. Japheth had studied hard to figure out a way to make it strong enough to bear the weight of all the animals and their feed. It had been a painstaking business to join the timbers together strongly enough, but now that it was done, Japheth allowed himself a surge of pride as he ran his hand over the timbers.

"It's all nonsense, Japheth." Ham had worked diligently along with his two brothers, but he had no faith in the design. Now as he looked at it, he shook his head with disgust. "All the work that's gone into this—and for nothing!"

"I don't think it's for nothing, Ham," Japheth interjected. "I believe Father has heard the directions correctly from the Strong One."

"That's more than I know," Ham said. He was planing a board, and the muscles in his back moved smoothly. He enjoyed such work when it had a purpose—building furniture or a house—but this crazy idea of a monstrous boat that would carry enough animals to start a new world had never taken root in him.

"This thing doesn't even *look* like a boat!" Ham protested. He moved over and pointed at the plan Japheth had drawn on a large piece of tanned leather. "Every boat I've ever seen has a sharply pointed bow. This thing looks like a . . . a *block*!"

Japheth laughed. "Well, Ham, why do you think boats have sharply pointed bows?"

"To make them go through the water easier when you paddle them, of course!"

"Right—but the ark isn't going anyplace. All it will do is *float!* It's very difficult to build even a small boat with a curved front that comes to a point. You can bend reeds, but this boat has to carry a tremendous weight. The ark itself will be very heavy, and the animals and the food will weigh a lot. That's why the ark is really a floating box. It's easier to build—and a lot stronger this way."

"I still say it doesn't look like a boat," Ham said defiantly. He was smart enough to understand the reason for building the ark in this fashion, but as always, he hated to lose an argument. "It'll never float—and you know what? I don't think it matters. Nobody ever saw enough water to cover the high land."

Japheth gave up on Ham and walked over to where Noah was working thirty paces away. "It looks good, Father," he said.

Noah was boring a hole to join two timbers of gopher wood. It was hard work, and sweat glistened on his back and ran down his face. He picked up the tunic he had removed and wiped his face with it, then smiled briefly. "It's going well. We could never do it without you, Japheth." He looked at the outline of the ark and tried to see it in his mind as it would be when it was finished. Japheth had drawn out the plans for him, and Noah was proud of the young man's skills. "How long do you think it will take, son?"

"A long time. It's going very slowly, and with just our family working on it, it's going to be a slow business indeed." He looked at his father curiously, studying the craggy face and noting the age lines that were becoming more pronounced by the day, it seemed. He had always thought of his father as ageless, but now when he saw the stoop in the powerful frame, he realized that Noah was growing older. "Did God tell you when the flood would come?"

"No, He did not." Noah gripped his hands together behind him and contorted his brow as he thought back, bringing to memory the words of the Strong One. "He said very little about the time, but He'll wait until we get the ark built to give us any more instruction."

"Well, that will be many years. Gopher wood is hard to come by and even harder to work with."

The conversation between father and son then focused on the boat's design. While they talked, Noah was conscious of Ham working steadily. And beyond him, Shem was hewing a tree trunk into one of the timbers. Shem was not as handy as the other men, but he did keep at the work, usually singing under his breath or sometimes aloud.

"Shem tries hard, doesn't he?"

"Yes, he does, Father. He'd much rather be writing songs, and to tell the truth, I'd rather be working on my waterwheel. But this is what we must do."

Noah was pleased with Japheth's encouraging words. The young man had never had a visit from the Strong One, but Japheth trusted his father's words, and Noah was proud of him. Noah started to speak, but then he heard a noise and turned quickly. "Who's that?" he whispered.

Japheth turned and, following his father's glance, saw a ragged crowd approaching. His eyes narrowed as they came closer, and he shook his head. "Another bunch of drunkards coming to make fun of us."

Ham put down his plane and ambled over to stand beside the other two, and Shem quickly joined the small group. "They're all drunk," Ham sneered. "Look at them! Aren't they a pretty sight?"

"I know some of them. That's Zurton," Shem said. "They come from over in the east."

The four men waited until the crowd drew close. They all looked the worse for wear, Noah noted, and he suspected they had been drinking all night. He watched as the smallest man, Zurton, stepped forward and cried out, "Well, if it isn't the preacher! Give us a sermon, Preacher Noah!"

Noah had endured such taunting from the beginning. He had been instructed by the Ancient One to proclaim the tragedy that was to envelop the world, and he had done so. His announcement that the world would be destroyed brought looks of incredulity at first, then disbelief, and finally ridicule. Noah, despite his rough exterior, was a sensitive man, and he cringed each time something like this happened. His eyes ran over the crowd, and he saw the signs he had often seen—the heavy drunkenness even before midday, the lewd jesting, and the ribald laughter of the loose women who followed along with such crowds. A woman Noah thought was named Ziva sidled up to Zurton.

"Where's Abahaz?" Ham demanded of their leader. "He's usually with every bunch of drunks I see."

"He's dead!" Zurton laughed, his mouth wide and his eyes half glazed with the thought.

"Yes," Ziva said, her eyes glittering. She put her arms around Zurton and laughed wildly. "And this is the mighty warrior that killed him!"

Noah stood there listening with sadness as the woman took great delight in describing how the small man had killed Abahaz and his own wife. The crowd laughed along and seemed to find particular delight in hearing all the repulsive details. When the laughter died down, Noah knew he had to reproach them and warn them of God's displeasure, although he felt it would be to no avail.

"The Ancient One will not tolerate such behavior!" he pronounced boldly. "He demands holiness, and He will punish those who defile themselves." He felt awkward trying to proclaim the word of the Holy One, for he was not an eloquent man, but as he lifted his voice, despite the laughter and the jeers that punctuated his remarks, he continued to speak. "Turn from your evil ways, and perhaps He will spare us the judgment that is coming," he pleaded.

"Crazy Noah!" Zurton laughed loudly. "Everybody knows you've lost your mind. There is no Ancient One. Ur-Baal is God!"

"Ur-Baal is not God!" Noah raised his voice. "The Ancient One is the only true God, and He demands holiness."

Noah continued to speak for some time, despite the vulgar jeers and rude laughter from the crowd.

Ham finally grew angry and stepped up to Zurton. "Take your bunch of drunks and get out of here, Zurton!"

At once the smaller man was intimidated by Ham's size and strength. This son of Noah was known to be a man of action, and Zurton swallowed hard and attempted to smile. He turned to his followers, waving them away. "Come on. There's no fun here. Let these crazy preachers build their big boat."

As the rowdy bunch turned and stumbled away after Zurton, Shem stood beside Noah and put his arm around his shoulder. "I'm sorry you have to put up with that, Father."

"It's the will of God."

"What good does it do?" Shem whispered. "All this time you've been trying to warn people, and not a single one listens. Not even your own family."

This was a bitter truth for Noah, and he looked at Shem with sorrow in his eyes. "It is what God has laid upon us."

"What if no one *ever* believes you?" Shem asked.

"Then we alone will be the followers of the Most Holy One. Our race began with one man and one woman. What the Strong One has done once, He can do again."

Shem wiped the sweat from his face, and his eyes grew thoughtful. He alone of Noah's sons had received some of the visionary qualities of his father. He had dreams as Noah did and a vivid imagination. Along with this he was possessed of a true devotion to the Ancient One, and this united him with his father as nothing else did.

He finally left his father's side and went over to begin working with Japheth. The two spoke about the drunken mob, and Japheth shrugged. "I don't think any of them will ever change. They are an unholy bunch."

"I wonder," Shem said, straightening up and arching his back to ease the strain, "if there are any other people, anywhere in the world, that are different. It seems, even in our lifetime, that men and women have gone crazy. They're all rushing to worship Ur-Baal. Burning babies alive. Stealing wives. Fighting and killing most savagely."

"These are violent times. That's what the Holy One said to Father when He spoke to him," Japheth said, nodding. "I don't know about other people in other parts of the world, but around here I don't see anything but corruption in the hearts of men."

The two worked together in silence for some time, and finally Shem stopped and turned to his brother. "Japheth, I've been thinking about something."

"What's that?"

"God said that the ark would be for our father and mother, for their sons, and for their sons' wives. But you don't have a wife. Don't you ever think about that?"

Japheth shrugged. "Doesn't seem to be time to find one. I spend all my days working on this ark."

"There's more to life than working, you know."

Japheth had gone over this with Shem many times, and now he stopped working and looked his brother full in the face. "I don't have dreams like you and Father do, and I don't suppose the Holy One will ever speak to me face-to-face as He has to Father. But He's given me one gift—I'm able to build things. It seems to me that the most important thing right now is to get this ark built. It's going to take all the strength I have. It's a challenge, Shem. Nothing like this has ever been done before!"

CHAPTER 26

The tall tree rose high into the sky, shutting off the rays of the blistering sun. Underneath it Noah stood looking up through the leafy fringes and taking some pleasure in the lacy shadows that covered the ground beneath the magnificent specimen. The girth of the tree was tremendous, and now as Noah leaned forward and put his hand on the rough bark, a shock of memory ran through him. It was a way he had of going back in time and pulling forth a scene in all of its details and colors and textures.

He had thought the scene long forgotten, but now it came to him as clearly as any reality. The memory of the distant event was so real he could even smell the crisp morning air and see the azure color of the sky as it had been that morning so many years ago. He half closed his eyes at the memory of the drunken crowd led by Zurton that made fun of him and his family. In his mind's eye he could see their faces. Especially those of Zurton and the woman. *What was her name? Yes. Ziva. That was it.*

Although there had been many such crowds over the decades, he particularly recalled that day because of one small detail. After the crowd had left, he remembered sitting down beside a small sapling no higher than his waist. The sapling had pushed its way out of the ground and had put on a few tiny branches. He could recall having admired the golden color of the tiny leaves that would soon be green, and he remembered plucking a leaf and tasting it.

The simple pleasure of that time long gone by filled his mind. Then he became conscious of the roughness of the bark underneath his hand, a sensation that ran through his whole being. He opened his eyes to look at the mighty tree that towered above him. What was once just that tiny sapling now rose over a hundred feet in the air, with its massive trunk sturdily fixed in the earth, the root systems running for hundreds of feet beneath the ground. It had grown slowly, and the years had rolled on with each added ring. Noah wondered how many rings there were. He did not know for sure, but he looked up again at the leafy patterns above him and thought of all the decades that had passed since that day when the tree was no higher than his waist. He murmured his thoughts aloud, as he often did nowadays. "Well, old friend. I remember the day when you were little more than a twig. You only came up to my waist—and now look at you!"

And then a torrent of memories flooded his mind of all the days and months and years and decades that had passed since he had sat beside this once-small sapling. The years had furrowed his face with lines and drained him of much of the mighty strength he had possessed as a young man. He had watched his family grow older, and their faces appeared to him now—his wife, Adah . . . his sons, Shem, Ham, and Japheth . . . his two daughters-in-law, Kefira and Mendora. Neither had borne children, and Noah knew deep in his soul that there was some purpose in this. In the natural order of things, both women would have borne many children during these long years, but they had remained barren.

Adah and he had spoken of it often, and Adah had finally shaken her head. "It is the will of the Holy One. We will see our grandchildren someday, but the time is not yet."

A sudden breeze caused the leaves overhead to whisper, and Noah turned and looked at the framework of the ark. He remembered that on the day he had sat beside the sapling there had been only a keel, just the foundation of the ark. Now the structure rose high over his head, the massive timbers fastened together with gopher wood, the hardest wood that could be found. Japheth had learned to make clever joints that were extremely strong yet fit so tightly together, one could barely see them. The skeleton of the ark was braced and kept in place by long timbers that fanned out from each side, holding the ribs, and as Noah walked slowly toward the ark, he thought of the monumental labor and sweat and painstaking care that had gone into its construction.

"It has not been easy, O Holy One," Noah whispered aloud. "But we have obeyed." It had been especially difficult since Noah and his sons had been forced to do almost all the work alone. Noah hired timber cutters from time to time, but this meant he had to work at his trade as a carpenter or build a house in order to pay them.

Noah walked under the shadow of the framework and noted that the shadow made a latticed pattern on the ground. His heart grew heavy then, and he shook his head. "So much to do! The work is so *slow,* Holy One."

The heat beat down upon the earth, which had become parched and cracked. The thought passed through Noah's mind, *One day all this will be under water. The fish will be swimming up at the top of that big tree.* He had let the big tree grow for some reason he himself did not understand. When it had become large enough to serve as timber, Japheth had urged him to cut it, since it was handy, but Noah had said, "No. Let it stay. It furnishes shade and gives us something green to look at."

As the years had passed, the Strong One had been strangely silent. From time to time He had appeared to Noah and given further instructions, but those times had been rare indeed. And in the intervals between the Holy One's appearances, Noah would periodically fall into melancholy and even doubt. But when the doubt grew intolerable, the Strong One would appear again and restore him. Once the silence had lasted over ten years, and Noah had watched the earth grow more violent, the crimes bloodier, and the sins of men and women more vile. It had been Adah who had strengthened him during these times, who, along with Shem and Kefira, had great faith.

"Where have the years gone?" Noah muttered. He glanced back at the tree and thought of the sapling, then looked back to the framework of the unfinished ark, and his spirit, for the moment, was almost quenched.

"There you are, Noah."

Noah turned to see Adah coming. She was wearing a light blue dress, and he noticed that she walked swiftly, with a strong stride. The years had been good to her, and she was still strong and able. She drew near to him and looked up with an anxious smile. "I've been worried about you. You said you'd be home before this."

"I know. I just forgot."

"Your sons are back."

"Did they get much new timber?"

"Japheth says it was a good haul. They have to go so much farther now to find exactly what he wants."

"I don't think we could have accomplished all this without Japheth. It wouldn't have been possible."

"No. He's so good at big challenges—and this is certainly the biggest challenge he's ever had!"

Noah nodded and then sighed deeply, his eyes troubled.

"What's wrong, Noah?"

"The same old thing, Adah. I haven't heard from God in so long. I have done everything I can think of. I've cried and begged and fasted, but all I get is silence. Where *is* He? Why does He leave me alone for so long?"

Adah stepped forward and put herself against Noah. She felt his arms go around her, and she laid her head on his chest. They were quiet for a moment, and then she looked up into his face. "You have found grace in His sight, husband. He is the Strong One. We must wait and be faithful."

Noah smiled, two large deep creases appearing at the edges of his mouth. His skin was burned very dark by years of working out of doors, and he seemed somehow younger as he bent down and kissed her. "What would I do without you, Adah?"

These were sweet words to Adah. She had, over the years, learned the ways of this man, what went on in his heart, more than anyone else. She knew the heartache he carried as he grieved over the sins of the world and as he saw with his vivid imagination the tragedy that would sooner or later befall them.

"Come along," she whispered. "You need something to eat and you must rest."

By the time they got back home, the food was ready. Kefira patted Noah's arm and gently scolded him. "You're working too hard. Come and sit down."

Noah reached out and ran his hand over Kefira's light brown hair. She was still a beautiful woman, and now he gave thanks once again that Shem had found such a wife. "All right," he said. "I am hungry."

Shem was already at the table with Japheth. Ham and Mendora did not speak as Noah entered, and he saw that the two were having one of their sullen arguments. Noah took his seat, and when Adah put the food before him, he stared at it unseeingly. He was gripped with a grim sense of futility that fell on him from time to time. He only awakened when Mendora's voice cut through to his attention. He glanced up and saw Ham staring at Mendora—anger settling in the lines of his face, and his heart sank. Noah's eyes met Adah's, and he saw that she too was pained by the scene.

"You think I didn't see you watching that woman?" Mendora cried, her voice rising shrilly. She was jealous to the bone, and all that was needed to set her off was for Ham to pay even passing attention to any other woman.

Ham shouted, "Shut your mouth, woman, or I'll shut it for you!"

Mendora reacted to his roughness as she always did. She flew at him, screaming, and he caught her with his big hands and held her as she attempted to claw his face. Panting in anger, he said roughly, "If you were a real woman, you'd give me a son!" He shoved her backward, and Noah watched in shock as she picked up a bowl of hot soup and flung it in his face. Ham reeled back, clawing at his eyes, then roared and started for her. Mendora fled, screaming, and Ham followed, rage carved into his features.

Noah listened to the fading screams as Ham pursued her beyond hearing distance. He lowered his head, then said quietly, "Nothing like a quiet evening at home."

Japheth stared at the door where the two had disappeared. "That woman is wild as a lion! Ham should never have married her."

Everyone at the table had made up his or her mind to this long ago. Mendora's family was noted for its wild savageness, and they were completely unable to get along with the people around them. Her father had been a hot-blooded man with no control whatsoever over his temper, and her mother had been little better.

Kefira seemed to have lost her appetite. She waited until the unpleasant meal was almost over, then said, "Ham shouldn't have thrown that up to Mendora about not having children. It's not her fault."

Kefira's eyes revealed her own pain, and Shem reached over and put his hand on hers. They had both grieved over the fact that they had not conceived a child, and when she turned to look at him, he smiled at her and whispered, "It's all right. You'll have a child yet."

Kefira tried to return his smile, but the joy was gone from her. She was usually a happy woman and loved her family very much. She was even fond of Mendora. "I don't understand it," she whispered. "All the women in my family and most of yours have had babies, but Mendora and I, nothing. It's almost like—"

Adah knew she was about to say, *It's almost like a curse.* To cut her off, she said loudly, "You mustn't grieve over it. You still have time."

Noah sighed heavily. "I don't know why the Strong One has not blessed our family with fruitfulness." He got up and left, and they all heard him murmur, "Who can understand the Ancient One?"

Japheth was touched by Shem and Kefira's pain. "If you don't have children," he said to them, "it's probably because the Strong One wants us to put all of our strength into building the ark. Children do take up time and energy."

"Yes, that's probably it. Japheth is right," Adah said. She did not believe it for one moment but was searching desperately to find a way to console Kefira.

Japheth looked thoughtful and said, "If I had a wife, I wouldn't be able to put all the time into the ark that I have."

Shem turned to his brother and studied him thoughtfully. He was very close to Japheth, much closer than he was to Ham, and it troubled him that Japheth was still alone. He had been thinking deeply about this, and now he said, "Have you ever thought about what will happen after everyone on the earth is destroyed except our family?"

Japheth *had* thought about this—many times—but he did not answer. He sat there silently, and Shem pressed the issue. "God is going to destroy *everyone* who is not on the ark."

"I know that," Japheth said seriously.

"That means there will be no woman alive for you to marry. That bothers me, brother. You have many years to live, and after the flood you would be all alone."

Japheth stirred uneasily in his seat. He had indeed thought many times of marrying, and more than once had looked carefully at a woman. But now he expressed what was on his heart. "You know what most women are like. They have no shame at all. I haven't seen one yet that I'd want for a wife." He hesitated and then looked up defiantly. "Besides, they all think we're crazy! What woman would want to marry into a crazy man's family?"

Kefira was burdened with her own sense of futility, but she was fond of Japheth. Leaning over, she put her hand over his, and when he turned to her, she smiled at him. "There's a woman for you somewhere, Japheth. I know there is! I think the Strong One wants every man to have a wife and every woman to have a husband."

Japheth smiled faintly and shook his head. "Well, if He wants me to get married, then He'll just have to bring me a wife. I'm too busy building an ark to hunt for one!"

CHAPTER 27

The newborn kid butted against Roma's legs, bleating urgently. The tall woman looked down with a smile and, leaning over, ran her hand over the animal's rough head. As the kid nudged against her, she laughed. "You've already been fed. Now, don't be so greedy."

Roma wore the simplest of garments, a shapeless affair made of softened animal skins. She was strongly built, and her features would never be called beautiful. She had an appealing face, however, and a fairness of complexion that set her apart from her family. She was *different,* and in the world Roma inhabited, being different meant being ugly. With her paleness and strangely colored blue eyes, she had been ridiculed all of her life for her unusual looks. Her hair was not the ebony black of her family but a light tawny shade with blond streaks that glowed in the afternoon sun. It was soft and wavy, and she had it tied back with a simple rawhide thong so it would not interfere with her movements.

The kid bleated again, and this time Roma leaned over and swooped the animal up in her arms. As he tried to reach her face and butted at her with his embryonic horns, she merely laughed and squeezed him. "You're a beautiful thing," she crooned, stroking the rough fur. Roma thought all animals were beautiful, and she felt an affinity with almost anything that breathed. The only exceptions were snakes and crocodiles, of which she was not particularly fond, but any warm-blooded creature was sure to find a friend in this robust woman. She stood there enjoying the nuzzling and the smell of the tiny kid, a half smile on her broad lips. Then the sad thought occurred to her that sooner or later this animal, like all the others on her family's farm, would be slaughtered for meat. She pushed the troubling thought aside, for though she would work hard at any task, including cooking the meat, she had flatly refused to kill any animal herself. This had infuriated her father and her family, but it was the one point on which she would not bend.

Glancing up, she followed a flock of geese winging across the sky and delighted in the orderliness of their passage. They were lined up in a raggedy V shape, and she kept her eyes on them until they shrank to mere dots and then disappeared. The kid in her arms struggled to get down, and stooping over, she released it with a loving pat on its back. As she straightened up she heard a voice and turned quickly. Seeing her father, she felt a stab of reluctance. As always, she would rather have stayed outdoors with the animals than go into the house to her work. But she had schooled herself to this duty, and now as her father approached, she walked quickly toward him. "I'm coming, Father."

Arvad, Roma's father, was a very large man with a huge girth and several chins. He loved eating more than any other pleasure, and his excesses showed in the rolls of fat that covered him and in his protruding eyes. At times when he ate they would bulge out even more as he crammed food down as fast as he could possibly swallow it. His voice now was harsh and rough, and he gestured angrily toward the house. "What are you doing out here, girl? Are we supposed to wait forever for supper? We're all starving to death!"

Roma nodded obediently and moved toward the house. "I'm sorry. The nanny is going to deliver her kid at any time."

"She can take care of that without your help! Get in the house and get to work! You should have been born a boy. Then you could have been more help around this place."

Arvad often made this statement about his youngest daughter. He was grieved never to have had any sons, only three daughters. The other two daughters were small and feminine, but Roma had always looked and acted more like a boy, so Arvad had raised her accordingly. The bulk of the heavy work fell on Roma, and she had learned to accept it as her way of life. No one had ever heard her complain that she had a harder lot than her two sisters; if she ever had complained, her pleas would have fallen on deaf ears.

Arvad was not a rich man, and at one time he'd had hopes of marrying off all three of his daughters to wealthy men so that he might have an easier life. This had not happened, however. Although the two older daughters had husbands, both men were lazy louts, perfectly willing to be supported by their father-in-law.

As Roma entered the house, she was met by her sister Hadar. A small woman with rather attractive dark hair and eyes, Hadar was proud of having captured a husband. Gad, her husband, was handsome enough but had no talent for anything except gambling and drinking wine. Hadar snapped irritably at her youngest sister, "Where have you been?"

"I had to take care of the animals, Hadar."

"Why isn't the meal ready?" Hadar was a waspish woman and had a feud with the world. It all stemmed from the fact that although she had captured a burly and handsome husband, he had not brought her the comfort she desired. She often took out her disappointment on those around her, and now she stood there defiantly, her black eyes snapping, as Roma hurried toward the cooking area.

Roma had built the fire earlier, and the meat was roasting on a spit. She tested the meat and, finding it done, began carving off thin slices. From time to time she paused to look at the vegetables simmering in a large clay pot over hot coals. Any other woman would have been furious at the two able-bodied sisters doing nothing, but Roma had been trained to think of herself as practically a slave. She worked from dawn until long past dark, and no one ever bothered to thank her for her labors. She had once expected at least a little gratitude, but that time had passed long ago. Now she simply toiled long hours with all her strength, taking whatever was left in the way of clothing or food.

Moving into the larger room used mostly for eating and social purposes, she saw that the family was all seated. Urit, the sister next to her in age, was a small, thin woman. Her husband, Ebar, was correspondingly small. She was as dissatisfied in marriage as her sister Hadar, for her catch of a husband had been no more successful. Ebar spent most of his time off with other men on hunts or drinking binges, and Urit's voice could be heard whenever he was in range, criticizing him for his failure as a husband. Now she raised her voice sharply to her younger sister. "You're going to have to do better, Roma! If we had to wait any longer for supper, we'd all have starved."

"I'm sorry, Urit," Roma said contritely.

While Roma began placing the meat on the wooden slabs used for plates, Ebar said lazily to his wife, "It wouldn't hurt you to help her a little, Urit."

"Why don't *you* help her?" Urit snapped back, her eyes flashing. "All you do is go out having fun with those cronies of yours! It wouldn't hurt you to work a little either!"

Ebar gave her a furious glance and applied himself to his meal. The others followed suit, and for a time Roma was busy moving back and forth from the cooking area to the dining area. When it appeared everyone had all they required, she cut another portion of the meat for herself, put it on a wooden slab, and spooned out some vegetables. She sat down and listened as the others talked. Her sisters were mostly complaining that they needed new garments, and Arvad stared at them, stoutly declaring he didn't have the means to dress them in the fine clothes they demanded.

Roma had taken no more than three bites when they all heard a child's cry. Urit snapped, "See what's wrong with that baby, Roma. He's driving me crazy."

"I think he's cutting teeth," Roma said, rising to attend to the child. Along with her heavier outside duties, which included tending the garden and the animals and cutting the wood, she took care of her sisters' four children. They were all very little, Urit's youngest being only a few months old. Secretly, this was another part of her work that Roma loved, for she adored children. She reached the screaming, red-faced infant and picked him up. "Now, little one," she crooned, cradling him and speaking in soft, soothing tones and giving him loving pats. She smiled and laughed softly as the infant stopped crying and gave her a toothless grin. "You just wanted some attention, didn't you? Well, I don't blame you. A pretty fellow like you deserves attention!"

It grieved Roma that her sisters lacked proper love for their children—a boy and a girl for Urit, and two girls for Hadar. They despised dirty work, so any troublesome tasks concerning the children fell to Roma to do. When the babies were clean and bathed and ready to be shown off, both of her sisters would smile proudly and take the credit. Their fathers might take some pride in them when they grew old enough to be interesting, but neither of them paid much heed to their children now.

Roma walked back and forth rocking the child, feeding him, then putting him back to sleep. She returned to her food, which was no longer hot, and had no sooner started to eat than Urit said, "You're going to have to wash clothes tonight. The children don't have a thing to wear."

Roma gave her sister a pleading glance. "But I must be with the nanny goat tonight. She's going to have her kid, and it'll be a hard delivery."

"That's just like you, Roma! You care more about those goats than you do about your nephews and nieces! I'm ashamed of you!" Hadar exclaimed, shaking her head in disgust. "No wonder you can't get a man! Homely as you are and always complaining."

As usual, Roma had no answer for this. How could she argue with lies and accusations? She sat with her head bowed, trying to ignore her sister's comments as she ate. While the others moved away, no one bothered to help clean up the mess, nor did she expect it. Her father turned as he left the room to say, "You'll have to get up early in the morning, girl. There's lots of work to be done around here. If that fence isn't repaired right away, I'll lose my goats."

"All right, Father. I'll be up early."

Roma rose and began to clean up. By the time she was finished, she was bone tired, for it had been a long day. But rather than sit down and rest, she kept working, preparing as much as she could for the morning meal. She was the only one who would be up early, and the family would expect her to have breakfast ready for them when they finally did arise. When finished, she washed her hands and face in a basin. She would have little sleep that night, for she was worried about the nanny goat. She knew the animal was bearing twins and would require much help.

Going to the corner of the room, where she slept on a small, hard cot, she picked up the worn coverlet and made her way outside to the stable. As she approached the nanny goat, the animal lifted her head and uttered soft noises. Roma stroked her and said, "It's all right, mother. I'll stay right here with you. You're going to be just fine." She could not have told anyone how she knew that the animal was bearing twins. Like much of her other knowledge, it was both instinctive *and* gained by years of staying in close contact with the animals.

She lay down and stretched herself out wearily in the straw, pulling the worn coverlet over her. She shivered slightly in the chilly night air but went to sleep almost at once.

The twin kids staggered on wobbly legs, but Roma knew that within a few hours they would be bounding around in a delightful fashion. As Roma had suspected, it had been a hard birth, and now she sat beside the nanny, stroking her head. "You did fine, mother," she said. "Just fine! Look what nice kids you've brought into the world!"

Roma had slept very little that night. The dawn was still an hour away, but she was afraid to sleep now—there was too much to do before the others arose. The thought of the long day's work ahead of her dulled her mind, and she sat with her back against the wall half dozing, half dreaming—drifting between sleep and consciousness. The goat made a plaintive sound, and Roma opened her eyes but saw that the animal was all right. She leaned her head back against the hard surface of the wall again and tried to let the exhaustion flow away.

She drifted off into an exhausted half sleep, but a nagging thought kept pulling at her mind. And then she heard something disturbing, and her limbs twitched slightly.

Her eyes opened to mere slits, thinking someone was calling her from far away. She could not understand the words and did not recognize the voice, but the call became more insistent. *It must be a dream—or maybe Father's calling me into the house to start breakfast.*

Roma was not a highly imaginative girl, and she did not usually have distinctive dreams. She could not even remember most of them when she awoke. They were usually unpleasant, and she was glad to forget them. But now, as she stirred uneasily, she had a sense that the voice calling her was not a dream at all. Yet neither did it seem real. It was very like a voice, but it did not enter through her ears, being birthed instead deep within her breast. She was more curious than anything else, and she sat there half asleep, or so she thought, as the voice grew clearer.

Roma!

Roma half smiled. *It must be a dream. I'm dreaming that someone is calling my name.*

Roma, my daughter, wake up and listen.

And then sudden fear gripped her and she fully awoke. *This is no dream!* She stiffened and tried to get to her feet but found she could not move.

The voice was clear and definite, and it had called her "my daughter." No one had ever called her that! The voice was also kind and warm, yet Roma was frightened by it. She squeezed her eyes tightly together to shut it out, but her name was called persistently. She finally struggled to her feet and turned to flee from the barn.

Do not be afraid, my daughter.

The words were kind, as was the voice, but the strangeness of it made her weak. She felt she could not run away but was being held where she was in the half-light of the candle. Roma had been frightened many times by dangers. Once she had looked down to see a snake at her feet poised to strike, and she recalled the cold, paralyzing fear that had gone through her. She had almost drowned once and had known the terror of not being able to breathe. But this fear was altogether different. Whatever was happening to her, she knew she was in no danger.

You must not be afraid, my daughter.

"Who is it?" Roma whispered. "Who is speaking to me?"

I have many names, but for now you may know that I am called the Holy One.

Roma's family worshiped Ur-Baal, yet she herself had nothing but disgust for what went on at the ceremonies. They were dark and terrible, and they frightened her. But this voice was comforting, and she said, "What do you want of me, O Holy One?"

I have chosen you, my daughter. You will be used in my service.

"Surely not me," Roma protested, whispering the words so softly that even the nanny goat did not react. "I am only a poor girl. I cannot help a god!"

I will always use those who are worthy to be my servants. I do not want you to be afraid. I want you to love me and obey me.

Roma somehow took comfort from these words, yet she was confused. "But I don't know you, Holy One. How can I love someone I don't know?"

I will reveal myself to you more clearly in the days ahead. But first you must obey me. Are you willing to do what I command?

Roma discovered that the fear had left her. In its place she felt an inexplicable peace. Perhaps it was the warmth and love she felt in the voice of the Holy One. All her life she had been starved for love and affection, and now in the dimly lit barn she had found it! "What is it you would have me do, O Holy One?"

I want you to leave your home and go to a place that I will show you.

"Leave my home?"

Yes.

The voice was absolute, firm. There was no room for evasion. Roma stood perfectly still, conscious that within her something strange and new was happening. She did not look forward to the future, having given up on hope long ago. She had no dreams or visions of happiness—how could she have? She had given little thought to any gods other than Ur-Baal, but now she knew that a God calling himself by name had entered the stable and was speaking to her, asking something of her she could not understand. And she knew she loved Him, and whatever He commanded she would do!

"But where will I go? What will I do?"

I will show you where you will go, and I will teach you what you must do. The command that I give you now is simply to leave this place. I promise I will take you to the place I have designed for you. I will keep you safe.

For some time Roma sat absolutely still. Arguments darted through her mind: *I'm just dreaming . . . this can't be real . . . I can't leave here . . . I don't know any other place!*

The voice remained silent, and Roma somehow understood that He was waiting for her response. Despite the struggle that went on inside her, this Holy One who spoke to her gave her a hope she had never had. She waited for Him to speak again, but He did not. She gathered her resolve and whispered, "I will obey you, O Holy One. Tell me what to do."

I am pleased with you, daughter, and I will care for you. Go gather your things and leave. I will show you which way to go.

Roma suddenly awakened, as if she had been asleep, and looked wildly about her. Had she been dreaming? she wondered. But no . . . the words of the voice that had spoken within her burned in her mind. It was real—not a dream. She fought back the doubts and fears, then desperately ran out of the barn. Everyone in the house was still sound asleep. She moved as quietly as possible, gathering her meager possessions into a sack. They were so pitifully few, she had no difficulty carrying them.

Stepping out of the house, she looked up and saw the first light beginning to brighten the east. She stood uncertainly, not knowing which way to go—then a thought came to her so definitely she knew it was not from her own mind.

Take the east road.

Without question Roma headed to her right. She knew if she faltered, all would be lost. She had no intention of speaking with her family, for they would protest vehemently and call her crazy. She hastened toward the road as dawn began to fire the tops of the eastern trees. She knew nothing except that she was to take the east road. The future lay blank before her. "I must trust the Holy One! He has called me," she whispered to herself, and picking up her pace, she made her way down the road as the crimson light of the sun dispersed the darkness.

With her eyes on the road ahead, she did not once look back.

CHAPTER 28

Roma had reached the end of her frightening journey. Never had she been so far from her birthplace, and the strangeness of all she had seen was enough to terrify her. She had made her way along many roads, most of them mere paths, and more than once had been accosted by crude, rough men who terrorized her with threats. She learned very quickly to run from any man she encountered. In so doing she amused some and angered others. But amazingly, she managed to escape harm every time.

Now, at her journey's end, she stared at a massive and strange wooden structure that lay in the middle of a large open space. She could not understand what it was, but by some mysterious means, she knew she had arrived at the place the Holy One intended for her to stay. No voice spoke to her this time, but rather she felt a completeness and peace within her. She was as certain that the Holy One had led her to this exact place as if she had heard the words spoken aloud.

This conviction had occurred many times on her journey. More than once she had approached a house and a quiet sense within her had whispered, *Stop here. These people will be kind to you.* And it had never failed! She had been fed and shown courtesy such as she had never known.

The same certainty had occurred whenever she came to a fork in the road. As she had stood there uncertainly, not knowing whether to go to the right or the left, without her even asking, the knowledge would suddenly be in her, as solid and palpable as a stone, so that she would turn confidently and take one of the pathways. She never felt any doubt when she did this but always had a sense of wonder and awe.

The journey had taught her that the Holy One could be trusted completely. She had been cared for and given food and lodging, and now as she stood looking at the end of the road, she uttered a prayer of thanksgiving. "Thank you, Holy One, for keeping me safe on my journey."

Then the voice spoke again—this time clearly. *Go and speak to the man called Noah. Tell him I have sent you and that he is to take you in.* There was a momentary silence, and then the voice spoke again: *You have been obedient. I am pleased with you, my daughter.*

The words brought a fresh sense of joy to Roma. She had received little, if any, praise in her life, and now to be commended by a god thrilled her. Hurrying forward, she saw a man working on the huge building—for such it appeared to be, although she could not understand its function. Close beside him, sitting on a timber, was a young woman. Roma stopped, not knowing how to address the man. The woman looked at her strangely, then said to the man, "You have an admirer, Japheth."

Roma blinked with surprise at her comment, then shrank back when the man turned around and saw her standing there. Roma was an inhibited young woman, having been made so through hard trials. She could not think of a thing to say, but the man smiled and asked, "Are you looking for someone?"

"Yes. I'm . . . I need to see Noah."

"Why, that's my father."

Roma felt her heart leap. She had found the right family! "Is he here? Could I speak with him?"

"He'll be back soon," Japheth replied. He examined her closely, then asked, "Have you come a long way?"

"Yes. A very long way."

Japheth turned to the woman beside him and said, "Peninah, I think our friend here could use a drink."

The young woman, who had been watching Roma carefully, did not smile. Roma felt her antagonism as she shrugged and pointed toward the horizon. "There's water over there in the stream," she said indifferently.

"Oh, we can do better than that!" Japheth said, smiling. He went over to a tree and picked up a jug. As he shook it, Roma could hear the contents sloshing about. "Fresh milk," he said. "If you like goat's milk." When Roma hesitated, the man smiled and pushed the jug at her. "I'm sure you can use it. You look tired."

Roma gratefully took the jug and removed the wooden stopper. She lifted it to her lips and at first drank slowly, but she was hungry and thirsty, and it tasted so good she began to drink heartily. She heard the woman called Peninah say, "I'd hate to have to feed her. She eats like a hog."

Embarrassed, Roma lowered the jug. She handed it to the man. "Thank you," she said shyly. "That was very good."

"Are you going far?"

Japheth took the jug and looked at the young woman curiously. Roma assumed he was thinking she must look very strange, especially since the woman beside him had a very unpleasant sneer on her face. Roma noted that she was a very beautiful young woman, despite the sneer. She watched Peninah put her hand possessively on the arm of the man called Japheth. "What do you want to see Japheth's father about?" she demanded.

Roma could not answer. She knew instinctively she should not speak to this woman. The man looked uncomfortable, and Roma said simply, "I have to speak to him. That's all."

"Why don't you go over in the shade of that big tree and rest," Japheth suggested. "He's not here right now, but he'll be back soon." He smiled warmly at her.

"Thank you," Roma said, grateful for the man's kindness.

The pair watched as the young woman walked over and sat down at the base of the huge tree. She sat quietly, looking up at the ark, which towered even higher than the tree, with its massive framework and partially planked hull.

"What a strange person," Peninah said. "She's big and tough-looking enough to be a man."

"She is large, yet there's something rather winsome about her."

"Winsome! Why, she's covered with dust—just look at her hair! I don't think she's ever combed it in her life."

Japheth did not answer. He smiled at Peninah and said, "I think she'd clean up pretty well. I wonder what she wants with Father?"

Peninah wondered too, but she did not voice her thoughts, for she was more interested in turning Japheth's mind to other channels. She was a fetching young woman and had become quite interested in Noah's youngest son. She came from a well-to-do family, so marrying the son of crazy Noah would not be to her advantage. However, Peninah had a plan. If she could wean Japheth away from his father's insane scheme to build a boat to escape from a destruction that would never happen, he had possibilities. Everyone said that Japheth was a brilliant man, a man who could do anything he set out to do. It had occurred to her that she could make something of him. Now Peninah began to speak of other matters with Japheth, ignoring the woman under the tree.

Weary from her journey and soothed by the warm milk, Roma fell asleep in the cool shade of the tree. She knew the Holy One had brought her to the spot He had intended, but she was almost too weary to wonder what would happen next. Instead, she was content to rest quietly.

She awoke to hear a different voice and sat up to see that a man had joined the couple she'd spoken with—a tall man wearing a rough gray tunic and leather work apron. His hair was silver, and he had a beard he appeared to have cropped himself. Roma rose to her feet as she saw the man named Japheth pointing toward her. She waited as the big man in the gray tunic approached her. He stopped and examined her carefully, his eyes warm and filled with curiosity. "My name is Noah. My son says you are looking for me."

"Yes, sir, I am."

Noah waited for the young woman to speak. He had difficulty judging her age and was thinking what a strange-looking creature she was. Although not in the least beautiful, she showed a strength in her face and body that he admired. His eyes touched on the light-colored hair and the unusual light blue eyes, an eye color he had rarely seen. Noticing that she was frightened, he said warmly, "Don't be afraid, girl. Just tell me what it is you've come for."

Roma swallowed hard, knowing she should explain simply and truthfully. "The Holy One, sir. He spoke to me several days ago."

Instantly Noah's eyes narrowed. "What did He say to you?" Noah was suspicious of her claim. He had never heard of the Holy One speaking to a woman directly. But the girl had an innocent and vulnerable look, and he could not imagine why she would make up such a story—or how she would even know the name of the Holy One.

"He . . . He told me to leave my home and come here."

"Here? Why did He tell you that?"

"I do not know, sir. But He said that I was to tell you He had sent me and that you were to take me in."

For an instant Noah thought the girl was joking, but he saw she was totally serious. His next thought was that she was taking part in a trick. It would not be the first time men like Zurton had sent strangers to pull elaborate practical jokes on Noah. But as he studied the young woman, he saw no sign that she was of this sort. The strong impression he got of her was that she was a simple young woman who was telling the truth. He sensed a purity in her rarely seen in women these days. He stood for a long time trying to understand what was happening, and finally he asked, "When did the Holy One tell you this?"

Roma could barely meet the eyes of the tall, strong-looking man. He seemed to look down into her very heart, and she whispered, "He . . . He told me to leave my home four days ago, and He said He would show me the way. And He has. I don't know Him, but He speaks to me. When I arrived here, He gave me your name and said just what I have told you."

Noah was completely puzzled then, but he knew he must not send her away. He nodded and smiled. "We will talk more about this. You must come to my home."

"Yes, sir."

Noah said, "Follow me." Then he walked over to where Japheth and Peninah were watching them, and he noted that farther down the building site Ham and Shem had approached too. They were all curious about the strange woman. Noah regretted that he had not asked the young woman her name, and now he whispered, "What's your name?"

"Roma."

Noah nodded, and when they got to the small group, he said, "This is Roma. She will be staying with us for a while."

Peninah's eyes glinted, and she said sharply, "You're very generous, sir, to take in strangers."

Noah's eyes touched on Peninah briefly, and she could not meet his gaze. He nodded and said, "I will take Roma to the house. Then I will return, and we will see if we can get some more work done today."

As Noah left with Roma by his side, Ham shook his head. "Father's too gullible. He doesn't even know who that woman is—or who sent her."

"She looks all right to me," Shem said agreeably.

"Why, yes. I hardly think she's much of a danger." Japheth was looking after the pair and shrugged as he remarked, "Maybe she can be of some help to Mother around the house."

"She looks more like she could work in the fields," Peninah snapped.

Ham heaved a deep sigh. "Well, let's get back to work. This job will never be done—that's my opinion."

Japheth piped up, "Oh, yes it will! It's going very well indeed."

Ham shook his head in disgust and walked back to his tools, where he began shaping a timber. Shem lingered to say, "What does the girl want?"

"She just wanted to see Father," Japheth replied.

"Your father ought to be careful about taking in strange women," Peninah groused.

"Oh, I think she's harmless enough." Japheth smiled and said, "Why don't you go on to the house, Peninah? Maybe you can make her feel at home."

But Peninah had other ideas. "No, I'd rather stay and watch you." She smiled and moved closer to Japheth. Shem watched this carefully but said nothing. He just turned and went back to work.

Adah stared at Noah. "You mean she just appeared and told you that the Holy One had sent her to you?"

"That's what she said." Noah seemed perplexed. He had introduced Roma to his wife, and Adah had turned the young woman over to Kefira. Now Adah shook her head doubtfully. "Why would He do a thing like that?"

"I don't know, Adah," Noah said. "I thought at first it could be a practical joke, but the girl doesn't seem that sort."

"No. She seems harmless enough. But what will we do with her?"

"Just feed her and let her stay with us. I suppose she can work." Then he added, without much confidence, "Sooner or later, I guess the Holy One will tell me what He has in mind for her. I can't imagine, but I stopped trying to understand His ways long ago."

Adah was always suspicious of strangers. The family had been hurt so much during the long years of building the ark that her soft, gentle nature had been somewhat hardened. "I'll keep an eye on her," she said.

"Good. I'm going back to work," Noah said, walking out the door.

As Adah watched him go, a worried frown creased her brow. She went about her work, but later she found an opportunity to speak with Kefira. "Where is the girl—what's her name?"

"Her name is Roma," Kefira said. Her eyes were thoughtful, and she added, "She's a bit strange. Why did you say she came here?"

"She claims the Strong One spoke to her and told her to come."

"Why would He do that?"

"I don't know, of course," Adah replied. "You'll have to talk more about it with Noah."

"Roma asked if there was any work to be done," Kefira said. "I looked at her hands. They're as hard as a man's! She's done a lot of work somewhere."

"Yes," Adah agreed. "It appears she's had a hard life. Well, we'll just have to see about her staying here. In the meantime, we'll let her help with the work. There's plenty to go around."

As Kefira turned and left the room, Adah stood still, puzzled by this new turn of events. She whispered, "O Holy One, if you spoke to Roma, why will you not speak to me? Why has she come here, and what does it all mean?" She shook her head, her lips tight. Life had been very hard since Noah had been commanded to build the ark. Their neighbors had ostracized them, and even Noah's own family would have little to do with him anymore. Now this woman appears, claiming to be sent by the Strong One!

"We'll have to see," Adah whispered. "We must be very careful."

Japheth stared out the window and shook his head. "Roma's the hardest worker I've ever seen. She hasn't slowed down since she got here."

Adah had been watching Roma carefully too. It had been a little over a month since she had appeared. Both Adah and Noah had questioned her, but she had no more idea than they of why she would be commanded to leave her home and come to this place.

"Yes, she is a hard worker. She's so good with the animals and a fine gardener too."

"I'll go out and give her a hand," Japheth said. He left his mother and went outside, narrowing his eyes in the bright sunlight. He went out into the field where Roma was feeding the oxen, measuring out their food. She did not hear him coming, and he had an opportunity to study her face as he slowly approached. She was half turned away, and he saw the strong profile that had caught his attention the first time he had seen her. She had been wearing a worn leather garment when she arrived, but now Kefira and Adah had clothed her with a soft woven work dress. She was so quiet it was hard to get to know her, and he had wondered, along with the rest of the family, about her background. She had done little other than work, eat, and sleep, but he had discovered she was not unintelligent.

"I'm glad you've come to take some of the work off of my mother—and Kefira and Mendora."

Startled, Roma turned and stared at Japheth with surprise. She smiled shyly and said, "I'm glad I've been able to help a little."

"A little! Why, you've done more than that," Japheth said quickly. "You must have been used to hard work."

"Oh, I like to work outside. I've always liked that better than working in the house. My father wished I was a boy, and he tried to make a man out of me."

"Well, I'm glad he didn't succeed. We've got plenty of men around here—and most of them are too ugly for my liking!" Japheth smiled at her and added, "We need more women to dress the place up—something attractive to look at."

His remark confused her, and a flush touched her cheek. Surprised at her embarrassment, Japheth studied her more closely. *She must not have heard many compliments in her life.* Aloud he said, "Are you going to come down to the ark this afternoon? I could use a little more help when you finish here."

"Oh yes!" Roma said, her eyes bright. "I don't know much about that kind of work, but—"

"You're a great help just moving the boards around."

"Maybe I can work in the sawpit today."

The sawpit, which Japheth had invented, was an ingenious design. The timbers for the ark could be hewn out of solid tree trunks with an ax, but sawing thin boards from the large timbers had been a problem. Japheth had solved it by designing a sawpit. After the logs were hewn into a rough square, they were placed on a rack. One man would get down in a hole that was dug in the ground. A saw made of bronze, with sharp teeth and a handle on each end, was positioned over the timber. One worker would stand on the platform grasping the upper end of the long saw while another stood in a pit beneath guiding the other end. The work was backbreaking, and the man in the pit got the worst of it as his eyes, ears, and hair were filled with sawdust. Still, it was the only way to make the planking for the ark.

"No, that's too rough for you," Japheth protested.

"I could stand on the top and pull the saw. It would give some of the men a rest."

"No," Japheth said, shaking his head. "There's plenty for you to do that isn't so dangerous. You can peg some more timbers."

"All right," Roma said, smiling. "I like doing that. How did you ever think of that tool that puts a hole through the timbers and into the frame?"

"It just made sense to me," Japheth replied. "I don't know how I think of these things. I was just looking at a board one day and wishing there was a hole in it when I got this idea of a tool you could turn around and it would cut a hole in the board. Don't ask me how I thought of it."

"It must be wonderful to build something like this ark! And your family will be safe when the flood comes."

Japheth stared at her. The young woman had accepted Noah's explanation that the ark was built to save the animals and his family. It occurred to him then that this young woman, although she obviously believed in the Strong One, had no idea whether she would be saved from the disaster. To test her, he asked, "Do you really think there's going to be a great flood and everyone not on the ark will die?"

"That's what your father says the Strong One told him. Yes, I believe it. Don't you?"

"Yes, I do. I've obeyed my father and done the best I could, but God has never spoken to me."

"He spoke to me when He brought me here, and I've listened to your father talk about how He has spoken to him. It's easy to love a god like that. He's not like Ur-Baal at all."

"No, He's not."

The two stood speaking for a time, and finally Japheth asked curiously, "Do you have a husband?"

Confusion swept across Roma's features. "Me? No!"

"Why are you so surprised?"

"Why, no one would have me for a wife."

"I don't know why you'd think that."

"Because I have two nice-looking sisters, so I know what an attractive woman looks like."

Japheth had never met a woman exactly like this. He thought most women would die rather than admit they weren't attractive.

As he studied her face, she suddenly asked, "Why haven't *you* ever married, Japheth?"

Laughing, Japheth shook his head. "I'm too spoiled. No woman would ever put up with me."

Roma did not answer but smiled and turned away so he could not see her face. "Come on," she said. "I can go down to the ark now, and I can work all afternoon."

The two made their way down to the building site, and soon Roma was using the bore that Japheth had invented. It was simply a rod of bronze with a sharp tooth cut in one end and a wooden handle at the other end. One leaned against the board and turned the handle, and the tooth bit in. As it bit deeper, it brought forth a curled shaving. It was difficult work, for the wood was the hardest that could be found, but Japheth and Roma worked at it together and soon were laughing. "It's good to hear you laugh," Japheth said to her.

Roma, once again, was confused. She studied Japheth's face, seeing his open smile and his rough good looks, and she said, "It's a beautiful day to be out, isn't it?"

"Yes, it is."

Roma started to ask another question but turned at a noise she heard behind them. Her eyes flew open.

"What is it, Roma?"

"It's . . . it's my father and my sisters' husbands."

Japheth turned, and his eyes narrowed as three men appeared, walking steadfastly down the road. "It looks like they're angry."

"They've come to make me go back," Roma said, shrinking behind Japheth as if to hide. "Somehow they must have heard where I was. I . . . I do most of the work at home, so that's why they're angry I left."

"Do you want to go back, Roma?"

"No! The Holy One brought me here. I want to stay."

Japheth put his arm around her shoulder. "Then you'll stay," he said.

Roma looked at him with fear in her eyes. "They might make me go."

"Not if you don't want to. Come along."

Noah, Shem, and Ham had also seen the strangers coming. They had stopped work and formed a small group. "Looks like trouble," Ham said. "Those fellows mean business."

Neither Noah nor Shem answered, but Noah noticed that Japheth had approached with Roma beside him, and he saw also that the woman looked frightened.

The oldest of the three men suddenly turned, shouting to the others, "There she is!" He had spotted Roma, and now he bellowed at her, "All right, girl, you're going home where you belong."

"Just a minute. Not so fast. Who are you and what do you want?" Noah demanded. He stood directly in front of the three men, and his sons fell into line beside him.

"That's my daughter there," Arvad gruffed. "And you stole her!"

"You're mistaken about that. My name is Noah, and the girl came of her own free will."

"Well, she's going back, free will or not! Take her, Gad."

The biggest man grinned and started toward Roma, but Ham blocked his way. The two men were about the same size, but where Ham was hard and muscular, Gad was merely large. Ham put his hand on the big man's chest and sneered. "Back where you came from, tadpole."

Gad was used to bullying people. He started to pull his knife from his belt, but Ham simply swung a huge fist that caught him right in the throat. It was the worst place to hit a man, and Gad fell to the ground choking and trying to cry out.

Ebar was a much smaller man than Gad. He was armed, but he saw the rough-looking men before him and loosed the grip on the short sword he had started to pull. "She belongs to us!" he protested.

"Is she a slave?" Japheth demanded.

Arvad stepped forward. "I'm her father! She belongs to me!"

"She's not going anywhere with you," Japheth said, "unless she wants to." He turned and said, "This man is your father, Roma?"

"Yes, sir."

"Do you want to go with him?"

Roma swallowed hard, then shook her head. "No, I don't."

"Then that's all there is to it. You three have a choice," he addressed Roma's family, "you can either go back down that road under your own power, or we'll give you some help."

Ham laughed. He was watching as Gad got to his feet, his face crimson. "I think you'd better go under your own power," Ham said. "Otherwise you're going to get hurt."

Roma's father began to shout, but it was all bluff. Noah let it go on for a few moments, then stepped forward and said, "You've heard the woman's answer. We mean her no harm. She's free to go if she wants to, but she's free to stay if that's her choice."

"I'll be back!" Arvad huffed. "You wait and see! I'll bring enough men and we'll take her!"

"You'd better bring plenty if they're all like these two," Ham said, laughing. He had enjoyed the encounter, and as the three men left, he could still hear the big man gagging.

Noah walked over to Roma and said, "I meant what I said. You can go if you wish, but you don't have to."

Roma cast a quick look at Japheth, who gave her a reassuring smile.

Then she turned to Noah and asked in a tremulous voice, "Can I stay here for always?"

Noah was touched by the young woman. Though she was taller and stronger than most women, there was a childlike quality about her. "Of course you can. We need all the help we can get."

After this they all went back to work. The incident had livened their day, and Japheth said as they went back to boring holes and pegging timbers, "I'm glad you didn't go, Roma."

"Are you, Japheth?"

"Very glad! As Father said, we need all the help we can get."

Roma smiled then, a full, complete smile, the first Japheth had seen from her. She almost looked pretty, and he reached out and touched her light hair. "Come on. Let's get to work, and I'll show you how I'm going to design the floors that will go in this ark. . . ."

CHAPTER 29

Roma stirred the black mixture in the wooden bucket and wrinkled up her nose. "This stuff smells awful, Japheth! Why do we have to use it?"

Japheth, who was applying a black, oily coat of pitch to the planks that partially covered the side of the ark, glanced at Roma. She was wearing an old dress, already soiled with the tarlike substance. Japheth held up the applicator, a stick with a rag knotted around the end soaked with the shiny black goo. "Because the Strong One told us to! We're to apply pitch on both the inside and the outside of the ark. It's a good thing it's plentiful around here."

"But what's it for and where does it come from?"

"Well, it's for two things," Japheth answered. "In the first place it preserves the wood. Some of this wood was cut nearly a hundred years ago, and it would have rotted by now if we hadn't sealed it."

"But does it have to smell so bad?" Roma made a face and held the evil-smelling applicator out as far as possible.

"I don't know about the smell, but I do know that without this pitch to seal all the gaps where the boards are joined together, the ark would leak. And that would not be a good thing! As for where it comes from, it oozes up out of the ground about a half-day's walk from here. It's an ugly, smelly place. People say it's evil, so they stay away from there. Which makes this smelly, precious goo absolutely free!" He grinned crookedly at her, adding, "It's a dirty job, but you've stuck with it well, Roma."

Roma returned his smile. Since coming to this place, she had spent much of her time working with Japheth on the ark. She was a great help to the women at home too, assisting with the household chores, but at every free moment, she would come to the building site to help. Even though much of the work was backbreaking, she found it exciting. Besides, she secretly treasured the hours with Japheth. Now she craned her neck, looking up at the frame of the ark, which rose high into the air. The bottom section was already planked, but the bare ribs of the upper stories were outlined against the afternoon sky. Looking down at the lattice-like shadow it threw on the ground, she shook her head. "It's more like a building than a boat, Japheth."

"I guess you could call it a floating building. It's got to be strongly built. When the flood comes it's liable to be pretty wild."

Roma turned and scanned the horizon. She could see the buildings and houses along the river, and on the other side the flat farm fields. In the far distance were mountains she had never visited. "It seems impossible there could be enough water to cover those mountaintops."

Japheth shrugged. "I guess it does seem unlikely, but Father's pretty specific about the commands he got from the Strong One."

The two continued speaking quietly as they applied the pitch. Once Japheth stopped and looked fondly over the work that had occupied him for so many years. "You know, Roma, no man alive could have designed this boat! I wouldn't have known how to start, but the Strong One has guided me all the way."

"I know your father's thankful he has a son like you. You always know just what to do."

"Well, I don't really. Sometimes I just stare and wonder what to do next, and then the answer jumps into my mind."

"I think the Strong One puts it there."

"I guess you're right. I'm certainly not smart enough to build this thing by myself."

Roma dabbed the end of the applicator into the pitch, swirled it around, and then applied another layer to the seam she was working on. Then suddenly, without premeditation, she blurted out, "I love the Strong One!"

The forthright statement brought Japheth's gaze to her at once. It pleased him that she could say such a simple thing, and he knew she meant it with all of her heart. He had noted all the hours she had spent with his father and grandfather since she came to them, soaking up everything they had to say about the Strong One. Especially when Methuselah was speaking, Roma would sit at his feet, her eyes bright, drinking in his words. This pleased the old man greatly, of course, and he in return had become immensely fond of the young woman.

"Roma, do you ever miss your home?" Japheth asked.

Immediately she shook her head. "No. Not ever."

"Nothing about it?"

"Well, for a long time I missed my nieces and nephews. They were just babies when I left, and I loved taking care of them. But you know, Japheth, it seems my life really began when I came to be with you—" Suddenly Roma's cheeks flushed. She was so fair that whenever she was embarrassed it showed in the rosy countenance of her cheeks. "I mean, with you and your family." She hastened to tell him about the babies she had left and then said wistfully, "I doubt if I would even know them, and they wouldn't remember me."

Japheth said quietly, "You love children so much. You should have your own."

The remark confused Roma, and she turned her head away to hide her face.

Japheth went on quickly, "Of course I mean that you should marry first. What about Penez? Would you have him if he asked?"

Penez was an old man who had visited Noah's house often over the past few months. He obviously liked Roma, and everyone knew he would eventually ask her to marry him.

"No, I'll never marry him," she said, slapping on another dollop of pitch.

"Why not? He's pretty well off."

"That's not what's important, Japheth. He's not a good man. He really doesn't love anybody except himself."

Japheth nodded knowingly. "Yes, I expect you're right about that, but he's not a cruel man either."

Roma stopped working and eyed Japheth directly. "When two people share a life, it ought to be based on more than that!" she exclaimed, turning away again with a frustrated sigh and applying more pitch to her seam.

The two fell into an awkward silence as they worked, each occupied with their own thoughts. Japheth realized he had opened up a tender subject, and now he was not sure what to say to smooth things over.

As Roma thought about Japheth's suggestion that she marry, she found she couldn't help thinking about him. From time to time while they worked, she would steal a glance at him. He had been very kind to her since the very first day she came here. Being the only unmarried son, Japheth always found time to spend with her. He often took her fishing or hunting or to the market while shopping for the family. She had assumed that he did so because he liked being with her, but now this conversation made her feel uncertain. Roma never spoke of it to anyone, but in her heart she treasured a special feeling for this man. Dared she call it love? She had so little experience with love, she did not know how to define it. All she knew was that when she was in his presence, the world appeared brighter, and when he was absent, it was as if the light went out and she had to wait in the darkness for his return.

Japheth had no idea of the depth of feeling this young woman had developed for him. He liked her immensely, and they had spent much time talking together. He found they could discuss anything. She, more than anyone else, loved to hear him tell about inventions he hoped to work on in the future. She was an apt listener and would sit for long periods as he spoke dreamily of what he would like to accomplish in his life.

Suddenly it occurred to Japheth that this woman was very close to being his best friend. Not only was she a good listener and a hard worker, but she also had a quick wit and could take a joke. A playful thought came to mind, and he took his finger and dipped it into the shiny black pitch. Stealthily he turned to her, then with a sharp cry of "There!" he reached around her and touched the end of her nose. He laughed when she turned to face him with a pitch-covered nose.

"You've got a black nose," he said, grinning.

Roma's eyes sparkled, and her hand darted into her own bucket. When it came up coated, she slapped him across the forehead with it, leaving a black mark. She laughed. "Now you look absolutely silly!"

Japheth made a grab at her, and when she leaped backward, he caught her by the ankle. She tried to get away, crying out, "You let me go, Japheth! Don't you dare put any more of that stuff on me!"

Japheth, holding on to her ankle, reached and got the pitch-covered applicator out of the bucket. He made a lunge and pinned her to the earth flat on her back and cried out, "Now I'm going to give you a bath in this stuff!"

Roma screamed and tried to throw him off, but he held her tight, and his eyes were laughing as he brought the dripping rag close to her face.

"Don't you dare put that on me!" she hollered. "If you do, I'll wait until you're asleep and pour it all over your hair!"

The two wrestled on the ground until Japheth suddenly realized this was not one of his brothers he was struggling with! The soft contours of her body pressed against him, and his face was only inches from hers. He looked into her blue eyes and saw something he had not seen before, something he had missed. He quickly leaned back and took her hand, pulling her up to a sitting position. He sat beside her on the ground and laughed. "Aren't we a pair of fools?" he said, grinning from ear to ear.

"One of us is, anyway! And you're the one with that stuff all over your face."

"And you've still got it on the end of your nose. Come along. Let's try to clean it off."

Together they found a clean cloth, and Japheth mopped the black substance from her nose with one hand while his other hand rested on her shoulder. "Now you can clean me up," he said. "You made the mess—you fix it."

Roma took the cloth, aware of his hand still resting on her shoulder. She wiped the pitch away as well as she could and said, "There, that's the best I can do for now."

"Would you really have poured it all over me if I hadn't stopped?"

"You'll never know now, Japheth."

He laughed and removed his hand. "I think we've worked enough for today. As a matter of fact, you work too hard." He studied her countenance, which reflected a hint of willfulness. He liked her strong independence. That's why he could be such good friends with her, because she felt like his equal. He also liked her openness and expressiveness. To Japheth she was a woman without guile, her face always mirroring her changing feelings. Despite her ingenuousness, Roma was also a mystery to Japheth. She was tall and shapely in a way that had caught the attention of many men, yet she never sought out their company the way other women did. Now he wondered what the playful smile on her lips was telling him.

"You've grown up, Roma."

"I was so afraid of everything when I first came, Japheth. But do you know what made things easier for me?"

"No, what was that?"

"You were so kind to me that first day I arrived. I remember everything about it! It was midday, and Peninah was with you and she clearly didn't like me. But you got me some goat's milk because you saw I was hungry and thirsty. I still remember how good it tasted, but most of all I remember your kindness."

"You still remember all that?" Japheth asked, amazed.

"Yes, I do. And I remember so many fine times we've had together. If it weren't for you, it would have been very hard for me here."

Japheth dropped his head for a moment and thought, *I could have been kinder and more thoughtful. She's very much alone. No family or friends. I'll have to do better.* Lifting his head, he smiled. "Let's go down to the river. There should be some fish in the traps."

The two cleaned up their tools and put them away, then walked down toward the river. It was growing dark by the time they reached it, and they found four good-sized fish in the traps. Both of them splashed into the shallows and pulled up the trap. Roma couldn't resist the urge to splash water on Japheth, and he threatened her with a playful warning. "I'm going to stick you in the mud like an eel if you don't behave."

"I'm not afraid of you," she said, laughing.

When they had collected the fish and killed them with a blow on the head, Japheth grabbed her hand and pulled her to a large flat rock on the riverbank. "Let's sit and watch the moon rise. It's too early to go back, and it's such a beautiful night."

Roma happily sat down beside him, and they talked quietly as the moon lifted itself up over the distant hills. "I'm glad Methuselah came to live with us," Roma whispered.

"I'm glad he did too. I'd rather listen to him talk than anyone."

Methuselah had finally been unable to stand the godless atmosphere of Lamech's house, and Noah had been happy to take him in. Though very feeble physically, Methuselah's mind was still sharp, and he spoke often of the Ancient One in a familiar and endearing way.

The moon cleared the hills and rose like a huge silver lamp. It was so bright they could see the disfiguration of the surface. "I wonder all the time about the moon and the sun and the stars," Japheth murmured. "There are so many of them! No one could ever count them all."

"They are beautiful."

"Where do you think they came from?"

Roma turned to him in surprise. "Why, the Strong One made them! He made *everything*. You've heard your great-grandfather say that, and your father too."

"Just think of making all of those fellows up there! Look how they sparkle!"

Whether by accident or not—Roma could not tell—Japheth leaned against her as he spoke, and his very touch caused her to fall silent. Despite her strong feelings for him, he had never reciprocated her feelings in the way she desperately wanted. Never once had he made any move toward her as a man will who cares deeply about a woman, though she had waited patiently for it. Had she been more experienced with men, she might have found a way to draw him in—with a touch or a certain look in her eye. But she had no talent for this, nor did she want any—not in the brazen way she saw most women enticing men.

As they sat leaning against each other, she was as content as she had ever been in her life. She listened as he spoke eagerly of innovations he would bring to the ark, and from time to time she answered or questioned him briefly. His eyes were wide, and he used his hands to illustrate his ideas. The one thought that repeated itself in her mind and heart as she sat with Japheth in the silver light of the moon was, *I wish we could just stay here forever.*

"Japheth has done a marvelous job, hasn't he, Noah?" Adah said, looking around proudly at her son's handiwork.

Noah nodded. The two were standing on the lower floor of the ark, which was now partitioned with beams and timbers and panels made of boards laboriously sawed in the pit. "Look at this," Noah said, pointing. "He's made different-sized partitions—larger ones for the big animals and some much smaller. And down here, you see, he's made a place to store the food so it won't have to be carried very far." His eyes grew warm as he continued to point out the work as it now stood.

Adah listened, glad that she had come to see how the work was progressing. The ark smelled of pitch and wood, and there were shavings and half-finished beams everywhere. It had been divided up well, and now she said, "Without Japheth, I don't think this could have happened."

"No, I don't either. Ham and Shem both work hard, but there's a quality in Japheth that's not in either of his brothers."

"Now, Noah, let's not go comparing your sons again. They're just different," Adah said, shaking her head. "Shem and Ham both have good traits that Japheth doesn't have either. Why, Shem is closer to the Ancient One than anyone except his great-grandfather or maybe you."

"Not me," Noah said, denying her words.

"You always think the worst of yourself," Adah scolded. "Look what you've accomplished."

Noah looked around the ark and shook his head. "It's hard to believe we've been working on this for so many years."

"How long do you think it will be before it's finished?"

"I don't know, and I don't know where we're going to get enough food to feed all the animals and ourselves. And how are we going to gather all the animals together? We can't go out and trap them and keep building this ark at the same time." He turned to her and sighed. "I guess the Strong One will just have to show us when the time is right. Now come up here and I'll show you where we'll be staying."

He led her up a stairway to the top story. All the planking was not on yet, but the partitions were framed out. Noah said, "There'll be a window for air and light at the very top."

She listened closely to his explanations, then said, "I'm glad I came to see this today, Noah, but now I've got to go help Mendora and Kefira with the evening meal."

Noah nodded. He reached out and passed his hand over her hair. "We've come a long way, Adah. I often think of that skinny little girl I saw for the first time so long ago. Little did I know how much you'd come to mean to me."

His words pleased Adah. She reached up and touched his cheek. "You come home early," she said softly. "You need to rest more."

After Adah left, Noah walked through the ark, trying to picture what it would be like to live in a world where nothing was visible in any direction but water. He had a vivid imagination, but even he could not imagine a thing like that. Unconsciously he slipped the medallion of the lion out from under his tunic and rubbed the surface of it with his thumb and forefinger. It had grown to be a comfort to him throughout the years. Day by day and year by year, the world around him had grown more viciously wicked, so that now it barely resembled the world of his childhood. Methuselah had given up on it long ago. He still talked of the days when men were still close to the Strong One, but now all that was gone, passed away, and the world was only a wicked, violent, sinful place.

Noah heard a familiar noise approaching the building site. A frown crossed his face, and he climbed down off the ark. He saw the usual riotous crowd drawing near to make fun of crazy Noah. It had ceased to bother him that everyone thought he was insane. The Holy One had appeared many times to comfort him, and now Noah did what he knew God wanted of him. He lifted his voice and began to speak to the crowd. He had developed a powerful voice over many years of speaking, and now he spoke of justice and goodness and temperance—qualities that had almost completely vanished from the world of his day. He spoke also of judgment, but sadly his words had little effect on the crowd, which found more pleasure in jeering and throwing rotten vegetables than in taking concern for their souls. True, many of the listeners were so drunk they could barely stand up, and others were so occupied with shouting at him they couldn't have heard a word he said anyway. But Noah was accustomed to all this. He was merely a messenger, and God had given him the words to say. He said them every time he met people, whether they came in crowds or he met them individually. He warned them of the great flood that was coming to destroy all life on the face of the earth, but not a single person in all these years had turned from their ways and confessed their sins.

Suddenly Noah faltered, for he saw a familiar face in the crowd. He blinked with surprise to see Meira, the daughter of Lomeen, the woman he had loved to distraction so many years ago. He remembered with shame how he had even tried to find love with Meira. She was so much older now, but the face was unmistakable. Her presence was so distracting he could not continue, and finishing up his words of warning, he turned and walked away.

The crowd left, jeering the same taunts—"There'll never be enough water to make that thing float, and even if there is, it won't float anyway! You're crazy, Noah! You've gone mad! The Strong One is nobody! Ur-Baal is god!"

Noah simply wanted to get away, but he kept seeing Meira's face in his mind and memory. He walked along the base of the ark, bowing his head and praying, *O Holy One, I am not worthy. I still have wrong feelings about that woman. What a fool I am! What an utter fool!*

Suddenly a sultry voice spoke so close by it startled him. He turned to see Meira standing there, older, but still with the same beauty that had captured him years ago, the same beauty he had seen in her mother, Lomeen. It was as if he had stepped back in time.

"Hello, Noah. It's good to see you."

Noah's voice was strained as he answered her greeting. "Hello, Meira. I haven't seen you in a long time."

"No, you haven't." She came so close he could smell her perfume. She was still the image of Lomeen, but an aged Lomeen. She stood before him, an enigmatic look in her eye and her lips curving upward. "I've thought about you so many times," she whispered.

Noah did not know what to say, so he said nothing.

Meira laughed. "Well, I see you haven't changed."

"N-neither have you," Noah stammered. "You're looking very well."

A bitter smile touched her lips. "I've lost my husband, my second one."

"I . . . I'm sorry, Meira."

"Don't be. I'm not. I couldn't stand the man!" Laughing, she tossed back her hair, still black in places but with wide gray streaks now.

Noah was unsettled by her callousness. He had once thought her innocent and kind. He wanted to walk away, but he sensed that she had something on her mind she wanted to say. She seemed troubled, and the silence grew between them.

Finally she looked up at him and said soberly, "You once had something in your heart for me, Noah."

"That was a long time ago."

"But it was there."

"Yes . . . it was," he admitted.

"I think something is still there. That's why I came to see you."

Noah stared at the woman, and she stared back at him with directness, her lips pressed together willfully.

"What do you want, Meira?"

"You'll laugh when I tell you."

"I doubt that."

"Have you ever thought of taking a second wife?"

Noah stared at Meira in disbelief. If she had asked him to fly to the moon, he could not have been more astonished! "What are you talking about, woman?"

"It's not uncommon. Some men have half a dozen wives."

Noah's head swam as she moved close to him and looked into his eyes. "I want you to take me as another wife. Adah can be your first wife, but I want to be with you."

"Why? Why would you want a thing like that?"

Meira's expression broke, and she bit her lip. "I don't know," she said. "I've been listening to you for a long time. I know everybody says you're crazy, but I don't think you are. If everything's going to be destroyed, I don't want to die."

Noah could not believe what he was hearing. He shook his head and asked, "Do you really believe that God's judgment is coming, Meira?"

"Oh yes, I do. And I know if I'm with you I'll be safe. Please marry me, Noah."

Noah sadly shook his head. "It's impossible for me to marry you, Meira."

"I don't ask you to care for me like you do your first wife, but I believe something is still in your heart for me, Noah. You loved my mother, and you loved me once." Moving closer, she put herself against him. She lifted her hands and laid them on his cheeks. "I'll do *anything* for you, Noah! Please take me."

Temptation struck Noah at that moment with a force he had not imagined possible. She was in his arms, available. He had thought all his feelings for her had died long ago, but now they surged back like a tidal wave. He had to keep his hands at his sides, his fists clenched, to keep from embracing her. A nagging voice inside said, *Why deny yourself this pleasure? Many men have more than one wife.*

But then abruptly, as if he had been struck by a fist, Noah knew this must not be. He stepped back and shook his head. "No, I cannot marry you, Meira. The Strong One has directed me to have and love only one wife, and it would be wrong of me. But if you truly believe in the coming destruction and wish to escape, God will also make a way of salvation for any who renounce their sins and their false gods and embrace Him, the Ancient and Wise One. But I cannot be your savior by marrying you—it is you who must accept the Strong One's only offer of escape. Will you renounce Ur-Baal and ask the true God to rescue you?"

Meira stared at him for a long time, her eyes narrowed into slits. It was not really Noah's god she wanted, it was Noah himself. She stood there for a moment longer, then lowered her voice seductively, "You don't even *have* to marry me, Noah. You can just have me—anytime you want. All you have to do is ask and I'll be there for you. There'll be plenty of time before the flood comes to enjoy your god's good gifts. Is He such an unfeeling god that He would deny you that simple pleasure? Think about it. You know I'm right."

Noah shook his head, not able to speak. His throat was constricted, and as she walked away, glancing back every so often with an inviting smile, he had to almost physically restrain himself from rushing after her.

He watched as she disappeared around the framework of the ark, and then blindly he turned and made his way home.

When he reached the house, he found Adah outside at the well. He went straight to her and took her hands. She looked up startled, seeing the pain in his face. "What is it, Noah?"

Noah wanted desperately to keep from revealing what had happened, but he knew he could not. Speaking hoarsely and in fits and starts, he told her about his encounter with Meira. He saw the pain in Adah's eyes, for he was brutally honest, not hiding the effect that Meira had had upon him.

When Noah stopped, Adah stood stiffly, not speaking. Then she asked, "Why did you tell me this, Noah? Did you want to hurt me?"

"No, not ever that!" he exclaimed quickly. Squeezing both of her hands more tightly in his, he swallowed hard. "I don't want there to be any secrets between us, Adah. You know I am not a perfect man, and I'm so very weak in many ways. I could have taken her and said nothing to you, but then as she stood before me, I could think of only one thing—all the years of love you have given me, and how much I've come to love you. I love you more than anyone except the Strong One."

A warm glow began deep inside Adah because she knew he was speaking the truth. She put her face against his chest, and he held her as she whispered, "Not many men would have told their wives a thing like that. Thank you for being so honest with me, Noah." She lifted her head then and said, "For all these years I've feared that something like this might happen, and I might lose you. I'll never think that again."

Noah kissed her, and the two stood quietly in each other's arms, aware that the bond between them had actually been strengthened by what had happened. It was strange that a temptation could bind them closer together, but Noah knew that the Strong One had given him the strength to resist it, and he gave silent thanks as he encircled his wife in his arms.

CHAPTER 30

The long grapevines were burdened with fruit, plump and juicy, and a dark, purplish haze covered them. The heavy clusters dragged the vines downward, and from time to time Roma, instead of putting one of the juicy morsels into the basket she carried, popped it into her mouth, smiling with pleasure at the sweetness of the juice that ran down her throat.

Far to the west, the sun had almost dropped behind the low-lying hills. A late afternoon breeze blew a lock of Roma's fair hair over her forehead. She brushed it back with her free hand; then, noting that the basket was almost full, she placed it with the others in a small cart.

The night was almost upon her, but Roma was in no hurry. She knew the other women were preparing the evening meal, and a feeling of satisfaction filled her as she thought briefly of her old life. How hard that had been—and how happy her days were now! She glanced at the cart filled high with fruit and smiled at the memory of how the useful tool had come into being. She had been carrying two heavy baskets of fruit, and Japheth had come to take one of them. He'd said, "There must be an easier way than this to get the grapes to the press." He had said nothing more at the time, but one morning he'd walked up to her with a smile on his face. "I've got a present for you, Roma." She remembered her delight in the cart and his pleasure at her joy. He had made the wheels out of leftover pieces of board, sawing them in a circle, then used a gopher-wood sapling for an axle. Even as Roma placed the basket into the cart, she thought, *How good that day was! We had such a good time as he showed off his invention!* Instead of picking up the tongue and starting homeward, she stretched her arms high over her head. Arching her back, she exhaled a sigh of relief, and a prayer of thanksgiving rose in her: *Holy One, I thank you for all you've done for me!*

At that instant, Roma felt a presence at her side. She cried aloud and turned to her left, half expecting to see Japheth, but no figure met her eyes. She saw instead a glimmering of unearthly light—and knew at once that she was in the presence of the Strong One! Much time had passed since she had heard His voice, but she had never forgotten her encounter, nor had she ceased to hope that He would appear to her again. She remembered the voice well and fell to her knees, bowing low. "O Holy One, speak, for your servant hears."

The words that came to her were quiet yet possessed power and strength. Somehow it reminded Roma of a forceful wind, but with a softness and gentleness that brought joy to her heart.

My daughter, you have been faithful and obedient. I am pleased with you.

Roma bowed deeper and tears sprang to her eyes. Gladness and joy spread through her, for she did indeed love the Holy One. Now she lifted her head and looked directly into the light. All the colors of the rainbow swirled in it, dazzling her, light so brilliant she was forced to keep her eyes half shut. She waited until the voice spoke again.

I have a command for you. As you have been faithful to obey me in the past, now I command you to be obedient to whatever thing I shall say to you.

"I will obey, O Strong One. What is it you would have me to do?"

I have brought you to this place for a purpose. You are to become a wife. It is my will that you should make this known to Noah and to the family.

Roma's mind went blank. She thought at first she had misunderstood the Holy One, but the words had been clear and definite. Her throat was tight as she whispered, "Who is it that I will marry, O Holy One?"

That will be revealed to you in time. You must obey me step-by-step. Go at once and tell the family that you will soon be married.

The voice faded, and the light grew brighter for just an instant, and then it too faded. The luminosity gave way to the dusky hues of twilight. Roma still knelt, her eyes half closed, her spirit filled with wonder and awe.

Slowly she got to her feet and picked up the handle of the cart. She had no doubt at all that the God of all creation had spoken to her, but His commandment confused her. An agonizing fear gripped her—fear that God would have her marry old Penez! He already had two wives and had buried another that he had literally worked to death.

Then it occurred to her that the Holy One might test her faith by marrying her to an awful man like this. So she said in her heart, *If it is your will that I marry Penez, I will obey.* After this submission, she knew she had no choice. Pulling the cart loaded with the heavy fruit, Roma made her way steadily through the duskiness, determined to obey the Strong One at any cost.

"You're going to get *married*?" Noah stared with amazement at Roma, as did everyone else at the table. She had waited until the meal was almost finished before blurting out the details of her meeting with the Strong One. Her face was pale with anxiety, for they were all staring at her as if she had lost her mind. She said quietly but firmly, "I know it sounds strange, but that's exactly what the Holy One told me."

"But marry *whom*?" Adah was as surprised as the rest of the family and shook her head in disbelief. "What man did the Strong One command you to marry?"

"I . . . I don't know. I mean, He didn't tell me that yet."

Ham laughed abruptly. "You're going to get married, but you don't know who your husband will be? I think you had a dream, Roma."

Japheth, however, leaned forward and said quietly, "Roma, are you sure you didn't make a mistake?"

"Oh no! It was the Holy One. He appeared to me just as He did when He commanded me to leave my home and come here. He was as real as the fingers on this hand." Roma held up her hand and looked appealingly toward Japheth. If he didn't believe her, who would?

Mendora reached over and squeezed Roma's arm. She was smiling broadly, and her eyes sparkled. "You just want a man," she said loudly. "A woman doesn't need a visit from God to get a husband. You and I will have a little talk. I can show you how to catch a man!"

"I expect it will be Penez, then," Noah said quietly, ignoring Mendora.

"Not that old man!"

Everyone turned to stare at Japheth, who had spoken loudly and with great indignation.

"Why, he's older than dirt—and he works his wives too hard!"

"He's rich, though," Ham said, shrugging. "We could use some help with the ark. It's getting harder all the time to get materials."

Shem shook his head. "He would never give anything for a purpose like that. He worships Ur-Baal. You know that, Ham."

Roma sat quietly, fighting an impulse to flee from the room as the others talked about what had happened to her. She could sense their unbelief and displeasure, and it hurt her. It had been hard for her to bring herself to tell of her experience, and she was glad when the meal was finally over and she was able to start clearing away the dishes. None of them said anything more to her about her announcement, though she could see in their expressions they were unhappy with her.

After she had finished her work, Roma stepped outside and leaned back against the house. She felt weak, almost as if she were ill, and was glad to be alone. She caught a movement to her right, and she turned to see Japheth. He stepped close and stood beside her, saying, "Lots of pretty stars tonight."

"Yes. They are beautiful."

Japheth was silent for a time, then he turned to her and asked curiously, "What did He sound like, Roma? The Strong One, I mean."

"I can't tell you. It's not like anybody's voice I've ever heard. I don't know that it was a sound. It seemed to come from within me."

Japheth turned to face her, and in the moonlight his features were clear. "I wish He'd speak to me. I'm a little bit jealous of you."

"I don't think you should be. He's asked me to do a very hard thing."

"Oh, surely it won't be old Penez!"

"I think it might be. You've heard Methuselah say that the Strong One demands hard things of those He speaks to."

Japheth considered this, then asked curiously, "Suppose He does? Would you marry that old buzzard?"

"Yes, I would—if it was the Strong One's will."

Japheth moved restlessly, shifting his feet, and for a time the two simply stood there drinking in the silence. Overhead the night canopy was spread with brilliant stars, like glowing white sparks. They had talked often about the stars, but now neither one of them was particularly thinking of the heavens. Roma did not know what Japheth was thinking. She was certain he had no idea how much she loved him. Except for a few instances where he showed her special affection, he had continued to treat her only as a friend. She remembered how they had gone to the fish traps, how they had wrestled once and he had fallen against her. Even though that had been weeks ago, she thought of it almost every day, his body pressed against hers, his face only inches away. Now she yearned for him to love her, but she knew that her life was in the hands of the Strong One.

"I'd better go inside," she said abruptly.

She turned and left without another word, and Japheth stared after her with surprise. *She's so different from other women! I wonder what I said to hurt her feelings? Anyway, she can't marry old Penez. That will never do!*

In the days that followed her meeting with the Strong One, Roma endured a great deal. Ham and Mendora did not take her so-called "visitation" seriously, and they teased her unmercifully. Shem and Kefira were curious but not entirely convinced. More than once Kefira talked with Roma about her experience. She was a godly young woman, and the two had become fast friends, but she had no idea about Roma's feelings for Japheth.

More than once Noah and Adah questioned Roma closely, but it was Methuselah who offered her the most comfort. The old man was very feeble now but still fiercely interested in anything to do with the Strong One. He had Roma tell her experience over and over again, until Roma eventually had said, "Why is He doing this, sir? I don't understand it."

"I don't understand it either." Methuselah spoke in a voice not quite steady. "But you may believe *one* thing—if the Strong One commands a thing, then it must be done. He knows our lives, child—everything about us. My father believed that He was the God of the future as well as the God of the past and the present."

"What does that mean?"

"It means that He knows all things that are going to happen as if they already had."

Roma wrestled with this concept, but it was too difficult for her. To think of a God that already knew of the future was strange indeed! She knew that the priests of Ur-Baal often prophesied what would come to pass—and were often wrong. She'd never had any confidence in them at all.

"I have noticed, Roma, that the Strong One tests people in a special way. If He wants them to do something really difficult—and important—he doesn't tell them everything that is to come. He gives them just a piece of it, then waits to see if they will obey Him in that small thing. If they are faithful in the small thing, He gives them more knowledge. So you must obey the Holy One in the next step of His plan, as you have obeyed His first command."

Roma heeded Methuselah's words, and as the days passed, she pondered these things and waited. Of one thing she was confident—the Holy One would speak to her again, and then she would know His will!

CHAPTER

31

The sun overhead looked like a pale ship sailing across a tawny sky. Noah glanced up at it, paused in his walk, and wondered how many more suns would pass over the earth before the flood came and destroyed everything. He shook his head, depressed at his gloomy thought, then moved on along the path that led down to the ark.

Struggling to rid himself of terrible thoughts of judgment, Noah savored the pristine sweetness of the morning. He glanced over the bars of pale gold sunlight that bathed the earth, then turned to observe the hills to the west. They were still covered with a haze and seemed to be brooding like huge animals, much like the dark thoughts he could not get away from. He shook his shoulders before moving swiftly along the hard-beaten earth.

The days had passed rapidly of late, and he wondered at it. It seemed that times and places were gone forever. He knew it was impossible to go back to former days; still, he sometimes dreamed vividly of the past. What if he could go back and rediscover an old path and wander in it? He might even say, "Ah yes, I know this way," but he knew it was a futile dream. He had forgotten many valleys and knew that the valleys had forgotten him. He moved past a group of tall trees that stood in disorganized ranks, throwing their shadows on the ground in long lines; the sun stretched fingers of light through them, touching the earth with a gentleness that pleased him.

Of late he had thought much about the future world, but it was always with fear and dread. It would all be so different! *After the Strong One brings His judgment on the earth,* he thought, *the world I know and love will be gone. Yet I have to believe the new world will be a better one. I must bury the past quickly and leave it as deeply buried as I can. I must never turn back—and above all I must never believe that the past is better. It is the present and the future I must think about now.*

His dark thoughts were as unfriendly and injurious as a wound that would not heal, so now with a clear-cut force of will, he turned his thoughts to other things. He thought of Roma and her announcement that the Strong One had commanded her to marry but had not identified her future husband. The family had questioned the young woman, and Ham and Mendora had made fun of Roma, causing her great pain. He himself could not understand it, yet he was certain she had spoken the truth. The visitation from the Strong One, according to her description, had been very much like those of his own experience.

He hurried on, passing a heron that stood in a swamplike recess bordering a group of trees. The bird glared at him with a cold amber eye, then turned proudly away, as if he could not bear the sight of the man. It gave Noah a queer, eerie feeling, and then he heard a familiar sound.

"Get out! Get out!"

Noah knew this bird call. He saw it as he rounded a bend in the path, a small bird with gray feathers and a bright blue helmet of plumage rising in a crest from his head. The bird stared at Noah and lifted his shrill cry. It sounded exactly like human speech. "Get out! Get out!" Noah had laughed at this many times, telling his sons that the bird was protecting its mate and its nest—telling unwanted visitors to leave. Now, however, there was a prophetic strain in the bird's cry, and something almost abnormal about the way the yellowish eyes stared at him. And again the cry echoed, "Get out! Get out!" For some reason it made Noah think of the admonitions of the Strong One—as if he were, in effect, being commanded to get out of the world.

Noah skirted a small pond covered with lily pads, and as he stepped across it, a frog cried out and plunged with a noisy splash into the still waters. Concentric rings expanded over the surface, and Noah splashed through the shallows, then moved across the green meadow toward the ark. As he approached, he heard voices and identified them as belonging to a group of young people who were chasing each other in the shadow of the ark. This was not unusual, for every day many visitors would gather. Young people made a game out of it all, and Noah sighed as he drew near the site, knowing that they would show no reverence.

About twenty of them had gathered around the ark, all the way from a youngster no more than eight or nine up to a strapping young man of about sixteen. He was evidently the leader, for he suddenly yelled, "Look! There's the preacher. Come on!"

Noah was surrounded by the group. The leader had a glistening dark tan. His eyes were as black as the pitch that covered the ark, and a look of reckless abandon characterized his features. "Hey, preacher, give us a sermon!"

As if part of a chorus, all the youngsters began laughing and dancing around, echoing the leader's command. "Yeah, come on! Preach to us! Tell us how we're all going to die."

Noah towered over them all. Though somewhat bent and stooped now, he was still massive and under other circumstances would have been a rather frightening character to a child. But to these youngsters, he was merely a figure of fun, an object of their derision. He waited until they quieted down before he said, "You've come to hear a sermon, have you?"

"Sure," the leader said, grinning rashly. "Tell us how the water's going to be so deep we'll all drown in it."

"That don't scare me. I can swim." This was from a young girl no more than twelve. Though only just beginning to show the signs of early adolescence, there was boldness in her eyes that grieved Noah. Virtue among the young was almost nonexistent, and now as he looked at her, she wiggled her hips and made an obscene gesture. "Come on, Grandpa. Let's you and me have a good time."

Rude, coarse laughter went up, and Noah stood there as the raw jokes—unthinkable in earlier days—fell from the lips of these young people.

He tried to speak, but a lump came to his throat, and he found himself grieving, knowing that these children were doomed. Doomed in youth, doomed forever, he feared, and it broke his heart.

For some time the group just stood around him, and he tried briefly to remind them that the path they were on led to nothing but unhappiness. But they only mocked him, and the leader finally waved his group away. "Let's go. The preacher's not going to give us a sermon today. So long, Grandpa."

The group filed away—except for one young boy no more than eight or nine, Noah estimated. He stood looking up at Noah, and something in his eyes caused Noah to ask gently, "What is it, son?"

"Is it true what you say, preacher? That everybody's going to die?"

The question pierced Noah's heart. The boy was no different from many others on the earth. He would soon be as crude and wicked as those who had just left; then he would grow to be a man, filled with evil and violence and all the wrong things that can come into a human heart.

But now his youthful eyes were troubled, and Noah went over and knelt beside him. He began to speak, but what could he say? Only the same thing he had been saying for many years, that the Strong One was good, but His justice would come. He would not put up with the world's sins anymore.

"But I haven't done anything bad," the boy said. "Not *very* bad anyway."

Noah felt a surge of hope for the youngster and began to pick him up to hold him to his breast. Perhaps this little one would receive the truth. . . .

But then a voice shouted, "Get yourself over here, Mahaz. Don't listen to that crazy old man." A boy of about twelve ran over and grabbed the child out of Noah's arms, cursed the preacher, and dragged the youngster away.

Noah watched them go, his heart heavy with the agony of not being able to help the boy. He was not ashamed of the tears spilling from his eyes and running into his beard at the thought of the lost world all around him.

Roma had said very little during the family's evening meal, but she was a quiet woman anyway so no one noticed it much. Except for Japheth. He fixed his eyes on her, seeing that she was pale and seemed troubled. "What's wrong, Roma? Are you feeling bad?"

Roma felt the eyes of everyone come around to her, and she said, "No, but . . ." She hesitated, then blurted out, "The Strong One came to me last night. He woke me up and said . . ."

Noah exchanged a glance with Adah, then asked, "What did He say, girl?"

"He said that I would be married within a month."

Ham laughed aloud. "Who is it? Is it old Penez?"

Roma was accustomed to Ham's rough teasing, and she said quietly, "He didn't say. He just told me it would happen in a month."

Japheth studied the girl and said no more, but later, after the family had dispersed, he talked to his father, asking him, "What do you think about these divine visits Roma tells us about?"

"I think they're real. What about you? You seem to know her better than anyone else. Do you think she's lying or is perhaps deceived?"

"No," Japheth said slowly, stroking his chin thoughtfully. "I don't think so. She's always been a truthful girl and not very fanciful either. But I'm worried about her. What if He tells her to marry old Penez? He'll make her life miserable and force her to worship Ur-Baal. Would the Strong One actually tell her to do that?"

Noah stared at his son. "I really don't know what to make of it, son. It doesn't make a lot of sense to me either—yet I sense truth in what she tells us. For all her gentleness, she's very determined, and I think she will do whatever she believes God is telling her to do."

Later still, when Noah talked with his wife, Adah said, "Is there a chance the girl's disturbed? She's listened to Methuselah a lot. Young girls are fanciful sometimes, and it's possible she's imagined this."

Noah shrugged. "I think a lot of her, but we'll just have to wait and see what happens."

The ark was rapidly approaching completion, although there were many details yet to be accomplished. The men had spent much effort during the past months collecting food, and the harvest had been tremendous, more abundant than anyone had ever dreamed possible. Noah's fields had given three magnificent harvests, one after another, so that now the barns he had built were crammed with food stores of every kind. He had said to Adah, "I guess I'm a rich man, but that doesn't matter now, does it?"

The grain had been packed into tightly woven reed baskets, which Noah was piling up to the ceiling when Adah rushed into the storehouse. "Come quickly, Noah!"

"What is it?" Noah saw the alarm in her eyes and asked, "Is someone hurt?"

"It's your grandfather. I think he's dying."

Noah gave her a disoriented look, then pushed by her and ran at full speed, breathing hard by the time he got to the house. He entered Methuselah's room and saw that his sons were all standing at a distance looking at the ancient man. "Is he still alive?" Noah demanded.

"Yes," Shem said. "But he's going fast."

"Come, all of you," Noah said. "His family needs to be with him."

They all gathered around the bed, and Noah knelt beside his grandfather. Adah moved to the other side and knelt also. She put her hand on his shoulder, and there were tears in her eyes. "He's been so good to me and to everyone."

Noah took the frail, almost skeletal hand and moved close to the old man's ear. "Can you hear me, Grandfather?"

Methuselah's eyes opened slowly, as if with a great effort. His lips moved, but Noah could not hear him. "Can you speak a little louder, Grandfather?" he pleaded.

Methuselah gathered his ebbing strength and spoke in a voice that was frail and cracked, but his words were clear. "It is time for my departure. I go now to be with my beloved."

Noah's eyes filled with tears. They ran off his cheeks and dropped down to the hand that he held. Methuselah turned his head slightly and focused his eyes. "Why, you must not grieve, grandson. I am old—the oldest of all men on earth, I do suppose, and I have had a good life. You have been a good grandson, and I am grateful to God for you."

The room was quiet except for the shallow breathing of the dying man. His breath rasped once and everyone thought he was gone. But he suddenly tightened his grip on Noah's hand, and his eyes went around to each of his family members. He stopped at Japheth and whispered, "Come here." When the younger man knelt beside his bed, he took his hand, saying, "Your descendants will be many. They will be strong and able, and they will rule the earth. Many kings shall come from your loins, Japheth." He went on to speak of Japheth's descendants, and finally he turned his eyes to Ham.

"What about me, Grandfather?" Ham cried out, coming to kneel beside the old man as Japheth rose. "Have you no blessing for me?"

"Your descendants will be like the sands of the sea. They will be like the wild donkey that cries in the wilderness. They will be strong and will bring forth many rulers, but they will not be as strong as those of your brothers."

Ham's face darkened, and as he rose and moved back, he shook his head, as if denying the prophecy.

Methuselah's eyes then went to Shem, and he held out his hand. When Shem took it, falling on his knees, Methuselah whispered, "In your loins there is a mighty deliverer! He will come and deliver his brethren from their burdens. He will bring peace and forgiveness to all. Your descendants will carry in them the seed that the Strong One has chosen."

Shem swallowed hard, and tears ran down his cheeks. He held the old man's frail hand, and then he heard Methuselah say, "He is like my father, Enoch. I think you may trust him with the sign of the lion, Noah."

No one knew exactly what this meant, for Noah had kept the meaning of the medallion he wore a secret. Now they all stood quietly waiting for Methuselah to say more, but he had grown silent. He looked up once, and they heard him call on the name of God. "O Strong One, O Holy One, I come to you!"

They all watched as the ancient man's breast convulsed once more . . . then the muscles relaxed.

Noah reached out and closed the dead man's eyes. "He has gone to be with God," he whispered. "And I would that I were with him."

A week after Methuselah's burial ritual, Roma awoke at dawn, thinking about him. She still missed him terribly. The old man had been a link to the past, going far back into time—many centuries—and now he was gone.

She got out of bed but stood absolutely still. She saw no light this time, but she did hear the voice speaking within her. *Daughter, the time has come for you to believe me again. You must tell everyone that you will be the wife of Japheth. You are to marry in one week.*

A startled look swept across Roma's face, and her heart seemed to stop. She pressed her hand against her breast and struggled for speech. The voice had been firm, and now a long silence surrounded her. Along with this came a rising joy and a knowledge that her faith had not been in vain. She knelt down beside her bed and for a long time simply lifted her heart to the Holy One. Faith had come to her, entire and complete. Somehow, in some way, God was going to give her the desire of her heart.

Finally she rose and helped with the preparation of the morning meal. She was quiet, but there was such a look of peace on her face that Adah said, "You look much better, Roma."

"Yes, you do," Kefira added. She walked over and put her arm around the young woman and said, "I've been worried about you. You've been so troubled."

Roma almost blurted out the truth to them, but she knew she must tell everyone at once, so she waited until after the meal. When the men started to rise, she said, "The Strong One came to me again this morning, and He told me whom I must marry."

Noah blinked with surprise and sat back down. "Who is it, Roma?"

Roma's heart beat very fast, like that of a bird. She had held a bird once and felt the tiny heart beating faster than seemed possible. Now her own seemed to beat even faster! She turned to face Japheth and for a moment was utterly quiet. Japheth's eyes locked with hers, and everyone stood waiting.

"I'm to be your wife, Japheth. I'm to marry you in one week."

Japheth's face was a study of confusion. He stared at the young woman and then grew red. He was usually a very pleasant man, but he did not like this turn of events and said loudly, "I'll marry you, all right—when God tells *me*. I haven't heard anything about marrying *anybody!*"

Mendora winked across the table at Roma and smiled, whispering, "That's the way to get a man. Trap him by bringing God into it."

Japheth was shocked beyond speech. He disappeared that day, and Noah understood why. *He's a good-hearted man—but he doesn't like feeling used in this way.* Noah hardly knew what to say to the young woman, but Japheth's reaction had been quite out of character for him. Noah came to her privately and said, "Are you absolutely *sure* about this, Roma?"

"Yes, Father. Very sure." She lifted her eyes to him, and he saw tears in them. "I know it's humiliating and embarrassing for Japheth, but I had to tell the truth."

Noah was confused. He put his hand on her head and nodded. "We will see. . . ."

The week that followed Roma's announcement was strained. Japheth stayed away from the house as much as possible. He was obviously avoiding Roma and did not speak to her at all when they had to be together.

Roma offered no word of rebuke, but she enlisted Adah's help in getting things ready for a wedding. As the days passed, she was even more silent than usual, but her faith grew stronger every day.

The word, of course, got out around town. It was probably Mendora who had divulged the secret, Roma figured, for she went into town more than anyone else. In any case, everywhere Roma went she was met with simpers and giggles and bad jokes. She took it all in a gentle spirit, but the day before the wedding, she came to Adah. Japheth had been gone for three days, and no one knew where he was.

It was late, and Adah was surprised when Roma said to her, "I know you must think I'm out of my mind."

Adah loved this young woman. She had a loving nature, and the girl's humility, her willingness to work hard, and her gentleness had pleased her from the beginning. She was worried about her now, however, and asked, "What will you do when tomorrow comes and Japheth isn't here?"

"He will come."

Adah stared at Roma. There was such assurance in her! Not one glimpse of doubt wavered in those strange light blue eyes. Roma was smiling now, and she nodded again. "He will come."

The wedding day dawned, and despite her reservations, Adah and her two daughters-in-law began to prepare a feast. Ham was having a fine time. He laughed a great deal and said more than once, "No matter how foolish the girl is, we're going to get a feast out of it."

Mendora, however, was less certain. She put her hand on Ham's arm and said, "Why are you so sure that Japheth won't come?"

"Because he won't be pushed around. I'll grant you he's not as independent as I am. Ever since he was a child, he's been very easy to persuade. But you just try pushing him into something, and he'll set his feet and bow his neck, and that's all there is to it!"

Mendora had not been as close to Roma as had Kefira. Still, she liked the girl well enough and had seen something in her that Ham had missed. "I don't know," she said doubtfully. "I wouldn't be surprised if he does come."

With all the festivities, Ham was in a good mood. He put his arm around his dusky wife and kissed her. "He'll not have her," he said. "You wait and see."

As for Roma, she hardly spoke at all, and the expression of peace on her face revealed a calm certainty. Even Ham was somewhat shaken by her unfailing confidence—especially after she put on her wedding dress, a purple-dyed woven dress with delicate embroidery she had been working on for a long time. Ham watched her as she helped set the food out and shook his head. "I don't know, Father. I've been laughing at her—but just look at her! Why, she acts like she doesn't have a care in the world. And Japheth hasn't shown his face in four days!"

"I know, Ham," Noah said rather shortly. "I don't know what to make of it myself."

"I'll tell you one thing. If he *does* come," Ham said vehemently, "I'll have a lot more faith in these visions and visitations than you people seem to have."

Most weddings, by tradition, occurred at midmorning, and when that time arrived, a large crowd gathered at Noah's house. Most of them were simply curiosity seekers, and there was a great deal of laughter and joking among them.

Ham growled, "Let me go run those people off, Father. They're just here to make fun."

"No, don't do that. Let them stay."

"They're nothing but a bunch of brainless geese!"

Noah looked across at Roma, who was standing quietly beside Kefira. Kefira was speaking to her, a worried look on her face. *Roma looks like she doesn't have a care in the world,* Noah thought. *Now, there's faith for you! But what if—* Noah's thoughts were interrupted by a wild shout outside. He whirled around and heard the words, "It's him! It's Japheth!" Noah turned and saw that Roma was standing between Adah and Kefira. The two were staring at her in wonder, and then they all turned to face the door.

There was a sound of footsteps and a woman cried out, "Well, the bridegroom comes at last!" A rough male voice jeered, "Are you going to let that woman make you marry her, Japheth?"

As Japheth entered the house, Noah saw the strain on his face. He was pale and shaken, and as he raised his hand to run it through his hair, Noah saw that it was trembling. He did not look around, but he walked straight across the room and stood before Roma.

"Roma," he said in a hoarse voice, "I have been so unkind to you."

"Oh no, you're never unkind, Japheth. You've just been confused," she whispered. She looked beautiful as she stood there in her purple dress, her eyes glowing, her light-colored hair flowing down her back. She was a large woman, strong and able, but feminine in every line of her body. She put her hands out, and Japheth took them. He spoke to her as if they were alone instead of being in the presence of the entire family.

"The Strong One . . . He came to me! I was running as far as I could away from here. I was proud, Roma, and now I know how much the Holy One hates pride! But then He stopped me as if I had run into a wall, and He . . . He spoke to me!"

"What did He say?" Roma asked quietly.

"He said, 'Take Roma for your wife. I have designed the two of you for each other.' "

Roma reached up and put her hand on Japheth's cheek. "It's not easy for you, Japheth. I have loved you for a long time, and I know you don't love me in the same way."

And then Japheth, the doer, the maker, the tinker, in one instant became a gentle lover. He stepped forward, took Roma in his arms, and kissed her, ignoring the entire family. "The Holy One," he said, "told me one more thing besides telling me to marry you. He said, 'I will put love in your heart for this woman so that you two will be as one.' "

Adah felt her eyes fill with tears and run down her cheeks. She came at once and put her arms around the two. Noah followed, and then the rest of the family, including Ham.

Japheth looked around and whispered, "The Strong One is also the Wise One. He has given me a great gift!"

CHAPTER 32

Leaning over, Roma picked up a large basket full of grain and set it on top of others stored against the wall. She was about to turn and pick up another when suddenly a pair of arms went around her. She uttered a squeal, but then the arms tightened and lifted her off her feet. She began to giggle. Pulling at the hands locked around her waist but unable to break the grip, she cried, "Put me down, you crazy man!"

Japheth laughed and held her easily. She was a strong woman, but Japheth, though not thick and muscular like Ham, was a man of great physical strength as well. He held her easily, then leaned forward and nibbled playfully at her neck.

"Japheth, don't do that! You know what it does to me!" Roma shivered. He lowered her until her feet touched the ground but held on gently with his teeth, moving his hands in an urgent caress over her body. He felt her stir at his touch, then released his grip and turned her around.

"You are a shameless woman, letting a man stir you up with just a little bite."

Reaching up, Roma took Japheth's thick hair with her two hands. "I ought to pull out every hair in your head. You know what that does to me. Now, stop it!"

The two stood there looking at each other, and Roma's eyes gleamed with happiness. They had been married for a little over six months, and life had been sweet to her—sweeter than she had ever thought possible. She had come to him innocent and knowing little of how to be a wife—but she had learned very quickly. At least that was what her husband told her! Now as she stood in his embrace, she was thoroughly content.

"I can't get over how we got married. If somebody had told me of a thing like this, I wouldn't have believed it."

"Neither would I."

He held her loosely in his arms, but his eyes were thoughtful. "Just think, Roma, the Strong One came to you when you had never heard of Him and told you to leave your family and go to a place you never even heard of. And you did it. I don't think I would have had the courage to do that."

"I didn't have anything to lose," Roma answered, "but you've always had a wonderful family. It would have been very hard for you to give up your family to come looking for me. Maybe that's why the Holy One appeared to me first."

He laughed aloud then and stroked her back gently with his fingertips, feeling the strength in her fine-toned muscles. "I must have looked like an idiot when you announced that God had told you to marry me."

"You did look pretty surprised, but I thought you took it fairly well."

The two stood holding each other, both marveling at how the Strong One had brought them together.

"Do you suppose God brings many men and women together as He did us?" Roma wondered.

"Not quite as dramatically, but I've been thinking about what Great-grandfather said—that our children and our grandchildren are going to bring forth many good rulers, and that Shem and Kefira's descendants will bring a man into the world who will make everything right."

"I thought the flood was going to do that," Roma said. "I find it all a little confusing."

"I don't understand it either, but I'll never forget what Great-grandfather said just before he died. The Strong One is trusting all of us for something important and wonderful."

"I know, and we must always be faithful to Him."

"I'm going into town," Noah said.

Adah looked up, surprised. "What for? It's getting late."

"I know, but I just feel restless. You remember that young boy I told you about—the one no more than eight or nine who was down at the ark, asking me questions?"

"Yes. I remember. You've never forgotten him, have you?"

"It's so sad, Adah. I thought I might see him again and tell him about the Strong One. I know God will provide some means of escape for any who will repent and believe."

"After all this time, you're still hoping for that? You've been preaching for years and years and not one single person has listened to you."

Noah shook his head. "I'm just a stubborn fellow, I suppose. It'll probably come to nothing, but I feel I must go and preach this message again." He hugged her and said, "You have to put up with a lot from me, don't you, wife?"

"No. You're the best husband who ever lived."

"Roma and Kefira would argue that with you, and maybe even Mendora."

"Go on, then, and don't stay long."

Noah left the house, and as he made his way to the marketplace in town, he wondered what impulse it was that moved him. Adah had spoken truly enough when she said that all his years of warning and preaching had produced no fruit whatsoever that he could see. Still, there were times when he felt moved to do things, and he had learned to obey the voice of the Holy One, even if it was very still and quiet.

When he reached the marketplace, he saw a celebration going on, and then he remembered that it was the festival feast of Ur-Baal. He almost turned and went back home, but he still had the nagging feeling that perhaps one person would hear him.

The festival was nearly over, and the streets were littered with drunks—men and women alike who had fallen in a drugged stupor. Those who could still walk either stepped on them or over them without paying heed. He saw other men and women engaged in shameless behavior, and his lips grew tight as he thought, *There was a time when people had the decency to do such things in private, but now they just don't care.*

He also saw the usual signs of violence. Some men and even women had been beaten, and more than one, he suspected, would never rise again. He remembered God's words to him, that the violence and the sins of men had sickened Him, and with the sights before him now, Noah could well understand.

He stopped in the middle of the open space used for public meetings and lifted his voice. "Listen to me and hear the word of the Strong One! He has seen your sins and your despicable acts, and He has said that He will destroy those who disobey Him! Turn from your ways. Believe in the Holy One, and He will save you from what you have become."

He continued to speak, but the crowd was rowdy and angry, shouting insults at him. Two burly men approached and shoved him so that he almost fell. He could smell the sour wine on their breath, but he did not fight back; rather, he continued to beg the crowd to turn away from their sins. He never saw the rock that hit him. He was in midsentence when something struck him in the temple.

When he regained consciousness, Noah had no idea how long he had been out. He felt hands on his face and a dampness, and he reached up to hold his hurting head. He found his hand covering another that was holding a damp cloth to the wound on the side of his head. The pain was terrible, and he simply lay there, unable to get up.

"Are you all right, Noah?"

He knew that voice! Opening his eyes, he could not focus for a moment, and then a face swam into view. It was Meira who held his head in her lap.

Noah tried to get up, but it was as if someone had driven a knife into his brain. Groaning, he fell back and felt her hands on his head. "Be still," she said. "You took an awful blow. I thought it might have killed you."

"How long . . . how long have I been here?"

"A long time. Nobody knows who threw the rock, but I think it frightened people. They've all backed away, but they're still watching from a distance."

Noah was aware of her softness as she held his head in an embrace. He gritted his teeth and pulled away, rising with difficulty. The pain struck him like a blow from a hammer, and he reached up and touched the raw wound on the side of his face. "Thank you, Meira," he said simply, turning to leave.

Meira caught his arm and stood before him, her light gown gently wafting in the breeze. Her eyes once again held that look of invitation Noah had found so hard to resist months earlier, the day she came to the ark. "Please don't go yet, Noah," she said. "I can't stop thinking about you."

Noah wanted to say *I've thought about you too,* but he knew that would be a mistake. He simply nodded and said, "I'm grateful for your care, but I must go now."

"Noah," she pleaded. "Take me into your home. I'll be anything—a servant, even a slave! You don't have to marry me. I just want to be near you."

Noah almost shivered with the temptation, and he cried out in his spirit, *O Holy One, will this last forever? I feel helpless before this woman. Strengthen me now.*

And then the voice of God came clearly and sharply into his heart: *Leave at once! This woman is not for you. Her concern for you is not innocent. She will lead your heart astray.*

Instantly Noah obeyed. He knew he had no choice. He turned and said, "I wish you well, Meira—but I cannot take you into my home."

His head beat with shattering waves of pain and he hastened out of town, aware that he was being watched. As he walked through the gathering darkness, the pain seemed to subside, and when he reached up and touched his head, he was shocked to find that the wound was gone! He could not understand the healing, and it troubled him greatly.

He was almost to his house when he sensed that something was different. He stopped dead still and waited, and then right before him appeared the familiar light that signaled the presence of God. He fell on his knees and put his forehead on the earth and worshiped. How long he stayed there he did not know, but then he felt himself enveloped by the presence of the Strong One. And he heard the voice of his beloved God.

The time has come, Noah, when I will destroy all flesh. Tomorrow the ark will be inhabited. You have wondered about how the animals could be captured. I myself will bring them in. You have been obedient and filled with grace, and I will honor you.

Noah was on his knees, and he held out his hands in a pleading gesture. "O Holy One, must you destroy them all?"

No answer came, but this in itself was an answer. The light faded, and Noah fell on his face and wept. He knew that nothing in this world would ever be the same again.

PART FIVE

CHAPTER 33

Lying beside Ham in their narrow bed, Mendora turned on her side and put her arm around him. She felt his powerful muscles relaxed in sleep. She drew closer and shook him, whispering loudly, "Ham, are you awake?"

He groaned and half opened his eyes. "I am now." He turned his head to smile at her, and by the pale light of morning that filtered through the small window, he could trace the outlines of her face. He had been drawn to her partially because of her fiery temperament, which matched his own, but also because of the strength and savage beauty of her features. He reached out and touched her cheek, moving his hand along the smoothness of her face to her shoulder, then down her side. She nuzzled closer to him and sighed. He stroked her long dark hair and lay silently, thinking of what their lives had been like since they had come together. Both of them were hot-tempered, impulsive, and controlling. From the beginning, their relationship had been a battlefield of strong wills, and they fought almost constantly. However, at other times—such as now—peace prevailed. He pulled her to him, squeezing her in his brawny arms. "You're a good-looking creature, woman!" He kissed her passionately and felt her respond in kind.

Mendora lifted her head and said, "Why can't we be like this all the time, Ham?"

"Because you want to rule me, and I'll never let a woman do that."

A hot reply rose to Mendora's lips, but she managed to stifle it. She pulled her hand through his thick, heavy locks, lay silently for a moment, then said, "I know I'm hard to live with."

Surprised at this admission, Ham rose up on his elbow. Looking down at her, he grinned. "That's the first time since we've been married that you've ever admitted something wasn't my fault."

Mendora laughed softly. "Maybe I'll change. Get all soft and cuddly like Kefira."

"That's not your way," Ham said shortly. He still had painful, deep-seated memories of his courtship of Kefira, and the bitterness of her rejection had never completely left him. It had also built a barrier between him and Shem, and now he fell silent, thinking of what might have been. In his heart he knew, however, that Mendora was a better match for him than Kefira would ever have been. He grudgingly admitted this to himself, but the memory of being refused in favor of his brother still rankled.

"Do you think we'll ever get enough food on the ark for all the animals Noah says will be on it?" Mendora asked.

The question touched a sore spot in Ham. He had helped his father and his brothers store food for the animals until he was sick of it. "Who knows?" he grunted. "Sometimes I think the whole thing is just some crazy idea my father has dreamed up." He thought of the huge supplies of food stored in jars and baskets and fell silent again. It troubled him that he had doubts, for Shem and Japheth never seemed to entertain such feelings.

Suddenly Mendora sat up. "I hear someone—is that Noah?"

Ham rolled off the bed at once and began to dress. "He must have stayed out all night."

The two dressed hurriedly, and by the time they left their small room, they found the rest of the family gathered in the great room of the house. Ham took one look at Noah's face and demanded, "What's the matter? Is something wrong?"

Noah's eyes met Ham's, and he said briefly, "Not wrong, exactly—but I need to talk to everyone. I have something important to tell you all." He turned to Japheth and said, "Go bring Roma," and he waited silently until Japheth returned with Roma and stood with the rest.

Adah had greeted Noah when he came in, but now she spoke what all of them were wondering. "What is it, husband? What's wrong?"

Noah's face was drawn. His hair was tossed both by the wind and by his own digging into it with his hands. His eyes went from face to face, and each of them saw something very much like pain. None of them spoke, but all of them felt uneasy and fearful.

"The Strong One spoke to me on the way home. I've been out all night thinking about what is shortly to come." He straightened up, threw his shoulders back, and shook them, as if throwing off a burden. In a stronger voice, he said firmly, "The time has arrived that we've all been waiting for, for so many years."

"You mean the flood is going to come?" Japheth's voice was not quite steady, and he had to force himself to speak up. "Is that what He told you?"

"Yes."

Shem saw that his father was as shaken as he had ever seen him. That fear was communicated to everyone in the room. "When will it be, Father?"

"Right away."

"But what about the animals?"

"I don't know. The Strong One will have to bring them in. I've been out all night trying to get my heart ready for the thing that's going to happen." There was a tortured note in his voice, and they all saw that his hands were not steady as he raised them to push his hair back.

It frightened Adah considerably to see her husband so unnerved. She went to stand beside him and said firmly, "If the Strong One commands it, then we must obey."

Noah put his arm around her and tried to smile. "You're a good wife. I need all the help I can get to face up to this. We are all going to need each other." He looked around and said, "I don't understand the ways of the Strong One, but I know that He is good and that He has designed all of this. Now let us bow before Him and give Him pure hearts. We must ask that whatever happens, we might be faithful and courageous. We must get all the food on the ark immediately—but first we will pray."

Noah fell to his knees, and the others followed suit. The wives all clung to their husbands, and these eight people, alone together, knew that something momentous lay before them. They lifted up their voices as one, begging the Holy One to guide them and watch over them.

Dawn arrived with a strange shattered light breaking over the eastern hills. The sky was mottled, and a reddish glow emanated from the very heart of the light. Silence filled the land as Noah and his family arrived at the ark. They had scarcely spoken as they made the short journey, each of them caught up with his or her own thoughts.

Now as Noah glanced around, he saw fear and apprehension on

every face, and he knew he had to encourage them. He lifted his voice and spoke with all the confidence he could muster. "We must all put our faith and trust in Him who never lies. He has told us what to do. Remember what He said years ago when He first gave me the word that the world would be destroyed? He promised that He would preserve me and my house, and for that I give Him thanks. No matter how difficult or how terrible life becomes, we will cling to that word."

Japheth looked nervously toward the ark. He turned and walked over and put his hand on the side of it. Looking up, he measured the height and then ran his eye down the length of it. He had put his life into the building of this craft, but now strong doubt overcame him.

"What's wrong, Japheth?" Roma whispered.

He could only shake his head. "I don't know."

"Are you afraid?"

"Yes. I am very afraid."

"So am I, but your father is right. We are following the commands of the Strong One."

"But nothing like this has ever been done before," Japheth said, his throat tight. "We don't even know for certain that it will float."

"You have obeyed the Holy One, my dear husband. When we do that, we've done everything."

Ham had been listening to this conversation, and he shook his head as the doubt that was in him stirred. Shem, seeing this, went over and said, "All will be well, brother."

Ham turned and studied the features of his younger brother. There was a gentleness in Shem that Ham knew had come partially from their mother. Both he and Japheth lacked it, and now he said, "I envy you and Father, Shem."

"Envy me! Why in the world would you envy me?"

"Because the Strong One speaks to you."

Shem was shocked. It was the first time in his memory that Ham had ever admitted he was lacking in *anything*. There had always been such a driving insistence in this big man, who was so dark and so different from Shem himself that Shem could only shake his head. "He will speak to you one day."

"He's even spoken to the women, to Roma and to Mother. Why doesn't He speak to me? I can't understand it."

Shem desperately sought for an answer, but the best he could do was to lay his hand on Ham's shoulder and say, "I think the Holy One speaks to us at His own will. I know He cares for you, for I believe He cares for everyone."

Ham considered these words, and a bleak depression filled him. He had never confessed before that he was envious of those to whom the Strong One spoke, but now he realized that this envy had been lying deep in his heart for years. "I don't like what I am," he said finally. "But I'm too old to change."

"No one is too old to change. All you need is the desire."

Shem put his arm around Ham's shoulders, and the two men stood quietly, feeling a bond that had been missing for years, if not all their lives. It was an unusual moment. Shem was aware of Ham's resentment over Kefira. He and Kefira had talked about it many times, and he remembered how she had always said, *"I would have been a total failure as his wife, and he could not have made me happy either."*

Finally the two men parted as they saw their father trying to get their attention.

Noah lifted up his head and shouted, "Get the ramp in place! When the animals come, we must be ready."

Ham almost said sarcastically, *What animals?*—but he held his tongue, for there was something mysterious in the air. He could not explain it. It was as if everything seemed *tight* . . . as if the world were being compressed around them. The broken light of dawn threw its beams across the ark now, and the monstrous boat looked almost dangerous, coated with the pure black pitch. Still, Ham went along with his brothers, helping to secure the ramp in place.

Kefira watched the men work, then suddenly turned and stared off to the west. A movement had caught her eye, and she cried out, "Look! Look over there!"

Everyone turned at Kefira's insistence, and they all saw a scene that clutched their hearts with fear.

"It's two lions," Roma whispered. "A male and a female."

Indeed it was a pair of lions, the male with a heavy black mane and a sleek female. They walked steadily forward, moving at a pace that was neither fast nor slow, their pads making no sound as they approached.

Ham swallowed and began to search about for a weapon. He had killed lions as a hunter, but now with empty hands and the two magnificent specimens coming ever closer, fear washed over him. He looked wildly at Noah, but Noah's face was calm. In fact, he was smiling!

"Look at them!" Japheth whispered. "They're beautiful."

Mendora began to tremble. She had never even seen a living lion before, but now she saw the strength and power of the huge muscles, and she grasped wildly at Ham's arm. "They'll kill us," she whispered.

No one dared move for a moment, and then, to everyone's surprise, Roma stepped forward. They collectively held their breath as she advanced toward the huge cats. The female lion approached first, followed by the male. Roma had felt an inexplicable urge within her and knew that the Strong One was guiding her actions. She waited until the lioness was no more than five feet away, then looking into the eyes of the beast, she saw that there was no danger. The eyes of the lioness were half-lidded—indeed, she appeared almost asleep. It was as if the beasts were sleepwalking. Roma smiled as joy rushed through her. The Strong One had brought the first pair of animals!

She spoke out firmly, her voice sure. "Come, you beasts." She stepped forward, laid her hand on the head of the lioness, and began to walk toward the ramp. One end of the ramp rested on the earth, the other on the top deck of the ark. It was shored up with heavy timbers to take very heavy weights. Two shorter ramps had been built inside the ark, one leading from the third story to the second, the other from the second to the first. The female walked beside Roma, and the large, powerful male, his eyes glazed as if he were drugged, followed behind. Roma called out, "Come, Japheth, show me where they are to stay."

Japheth shook himself, for he had been standing stock-still, startled by his wife's bold actions. He rushed toward her, and when he saw the lion's eyes, he turned and called back to the others, "The Strong One has made them gentle!"

Noah lifted his hands in a spontaneous sign of thanksgiving. As the two beasts followed the pair up the ramp, they disappeared, and when Noah turned to face Adah, tears brimmed in his eyes.

"To think I ever doubted the Strong One. He will bring them all in!"

No sooner had he spoken than a pair of birds, the like of which Noah had never seen before, crossed the rosy skies broken by fragments of clouds. The birds descended on the ark, and Ham exclaimed, "I've never seen anything like those two. What are they?"

"I don't know, but God has sent them. Take them down, Ham."

Ham moved forward, and when he reached the birds and held out his hands, both of them lighted on his wrists. They had gray breasts, sharp talons, and the eyes of hunters. Ham recognized them as a type of hawk, but there was no fierceness in them now. They grasped his wrists, and he made his way up the ramp with them.

Inside the ark, Roma and Japheth led the lions down the ramp to the middle level. The ark had no windows except for one at the very top, and bronze oil lamps attached to the walls dimly illuminated the dark. The great beasts allowed themselves to be guided into the stout compartments, built of thick gopher-wood boards, and lay down like kittens. Roma laughed. "Look at them, Japheth! They're as gentle as lambs!" The two quickly returned to the ramp and made their way upward.

When they reached the top, they looked out at the land around them in amazement, for animals of all sorts were moving toward the ark. Roma grabbed Japheth's hand, and he squeezed hers. "No one has ever seen anything like this!" she whispered. "It proves that we are in the will of the only true God!"

They descended to the ground, and all eight threw themselves into the work of loading the ark. Male and female the animals came: rabbits hopping up to be picked up and carried aboard, shy deer coming with half-closed eyes, a pair of odd-looking mice that jumped on their large hind legs instead of walking on all fours. A pair of long green serpents slithered up to the ramp, and only Ham was willing to move forward and pluck them up. They wound themselves around his forearms as he gingerly and quickly ran up to deposit them in a snake cage.

Japheth watched this scene, then spoke to Shem with awe in his voice. "This is something we must remember to tell our children and our grandchildren."

Shem looked quickly at Japheth. Since none of their wives had borne children, the fear of barrenness had troubled all of them. But now it was from Japheth, the doer, the inventor, that the truth had come. Shem nodded and smiled, "Yes, brother, the great and powerful Holy One, who miraculously brings these animals in, will give us children as well."

Soon all were busy finding places for the animals, every one of which arrived as if in a trance. Noah himself went forward to greet the two huge river beasts. They were more powerful and fierce than any other creatures on earth. As he approached them, he remembered the day he had first hunted them as a young man—so many centuries ago! His mind went back to the accident on the river that day, and he could see his brother Jodak saving his life, pulling him into the small reed boat. He remembered taking the slain beasts home, and now as he stood beside the two monstrous animals, he knew he was seeing the power of the

Strong One as no one living had ever seen it. He stepped in front of the river beasts, then smiled and turned, leading the pair up the ramp.

A crowd had gathered, standing well back from the ark. Men, women, and children of all ages were enveloped in a strange silence. The loudest sounds were the whispers that went around and floated in the air when a new pair of animals would appear. Word had run like wildfire throughout the land. Many had come doubtful and disbelieving, but now they stood stunned by what they saw.

A tall, thin man, middle-aged and dressed in the finest of robes, watched as Noah went forward and led a pair of strange-looking wild dogs to the ark. They were desert dogs that would submit to no man, yet Noah led them quietly up the ramp and out of sight. The tall man watching this miracle turned to his companion, a shorter man with pale gray eyes and a full, bushy beard almost covering his face. "Does this make you think again, Joton?"

"I don't know what to make of it. Could it be that crazy Noah isn't crazy after all?"

The tall man did not answer. He was a priest of Ur-Baal, and he knew something was happening he could not possibly explain. "Come," he said. "We must get the people away from here. They will begin to doubt *our* god." He raised his voice and said, "Come away, all of you! This is not something that worshipers of Ur-Baal need to see."

A woman called out, "Why is this happening? Can Noah be right when he says a great flood is coming to destroy the earth?"

"It means nothing!" the tall man rebuked her. "Come! Come away from here! It is time to worship *our* god. Ur-Baal is stronger than any god you cannot see!"

The tall priest stalked away, and many followed him. But others soon took their places, and as the ingathering of the animals went on, more and more of those who had made fun of Noah and his family were filled with vexing doubt.

"I think this must be the end," Noah said wearily, turning to Adah, who had come to stand beside him. "The ark is filled." He was exhausted, for the strain of fitting so many living creatures into the ark had been great.

"I worried that there wouldn't be room for all of them," Adah said, sighing, "but they are all on board. There were exactly the right spaces. Japheth did well, didn't he, husband?"

"Yes, and now we will wait to see what the Strong One will do next."

Adah's eyes were searching the mob that had gathered. They stayed well back, as if there were some danger in coming too close. Usually such crowds called out insults and taunts, but now they were strangely quiet. She felt Noah stiffen and glance up, and she saw that his face had changed. His eyes were fixed on a certain place in the crowd, and when she followed his gaze, she saw the woman—Meira!

A pang seized Adah. She, for years, had been confident of her husband's love. Yet, at times doubts would come, and now she knew that she must, once and for all, free herself of any possessiveness that lay in her. She reached up and touched Noah's arm, and when he turned to face her, she said quietly, "Noah, if you want to bring Meira on the ark, I will understand."

Noah blinked with shock, and then with calm assurance, he put his hands on his wife's shoulders and said quietly, "I know what that cost you to say, and I rejoice in your sacrifice." Then his face grew stern, and he shook his head. "The Holy One has told me it is forbidden. She is not a believer, and she refuses to give her heart to the one true God. Come, we must go home one more time, I think."

Noah led his family down the ramp and through the crowd. As they approached Meira, he saw the pleading look in her eyes, though she did not move. This time Noah did not hesitate to obey what he knew was right, and he kept walking forward without so much as a comment to Meira. Adah looked with pity at the woman as they passed.

They made their way home, and Noah addressed his family. "Gather whatever things you can carry, for we will not come here again. This will be our last night in this place."

Noah did not sleep at all that night. Adah knew it and lay beside him quietly. From time to time he would toss restlessly, and she would put her hand on him, saying nothing but giving him comfort.

At dawn Noah was aware that the Holy One was speaking to him. He saw no light, but he heard the voice. He had been expecting it, but it still came as a shock.

Come now, Noah, you and all your house, into the ark. In you only have I seen righteousness in this generation. Seven days from now I will cause it to rain upon the earth forty days and forty nights, and I will destroy every living thing that I have made from the face of the earth.

Noah bowed and whispered, "I will obey, O Holy One." He turned to Adah, who was watching with her eyes wide, and said to her, "The Strong One has spoken. Come—it is time."

Noah found the rest of the family waiting, and he said without hesitation, "We must go." His face was fixed like stone, and no one dared speak to him. Adah, their sons, and their wives followed as he led the way. No crowds were gathered at the ark, but he knew they would come later. He moved up the ramp, and when he reached the upper deck, he stood as his family boarded the ark.

At the top, all of them turned to look out over the land, and suddenly Kefira began to weep. She turned to Shem, and her voice was muffled against his chest. "My family—oh, my poor family!"

The only comfort Shem could give her was to hold her, for he too was suffering at the thought of so many of his own family who would perish as well.

Ham moved over to stand beside his father. He did not speak for a moment, but when Noah looked at him, he uttered in a strained voice, "We're leaving our own people—all our family! They don't love us or the Strong One, yet I can't help grieving for them."

Noah's heart was so full of sorrow he could barely speak. He put his arm across Ham's broad shoulders and whispered brokenly, "I know it, my son, but it is the will of the Holy One."

Now that the ark was full, the men pushed the huge outer ramp away from the upper deck, allowing it to fall to earth with a resounding crash. The crowds watched in amazement as Noah's family now had no means of getting off the massive craft nor of allowing anyone else on. The time had come, and there was no turning back.

Every day the crowds gathered, and when nothing changed, their taunts and laughter carried to the upper deck, where the family awaited the coming storm. After the first few days, the mobs began to taper off, going back to their everyday routines, quickly forgetting the great miracle they had witnessed and assuming that Noah, his family, and all those animals would eventually die of starvation inside their self-imposed prison.

Noah had told his family that nothing would happen for seven days, so they waited patiently, speaking little, feeding the animals, all of them occupied with the immensity of what was about to occur. No one in the family doubted now—not even Ham—and every day each of the eight looked out of the upper window onto the earth. As they beheld farmers at work in the green fields, the birds of the air and the land animals gathering their daily food, the distant towns and villages where they knew their family and friends continued to live and work as if nothing were different, a great heaviness enveloped them.

On the night of the seventh day none of them were able to sleep. They gathered outside on the top deck and waited. Dawn came again, and the sun lifted up over the long line of trees to the east, but still nothing happened. They continued to wait, and finally Noah stiffened and lifted his arm, pointing. "Look there!" His voice was sharp, and everyone turned to look north.

A cloud had begun to gather, as yet small, but as they watched, it swelled and grew before their eyes. None of them had ever seen a cloud like this before, and Adah leaned against Noah so that he put his arm around her. "There's something frightening in that cloud," she whispered.

Noah did not answer. His eyes were fixed on the cloud, which now rose up like a huge column. There was no whiteness in it, only a terrifying ebony blackness. He stiffened and held Adah in the clasp of one arm, and as the cloud surged toward them with the speed of a running antelope, he knew that this was the hand of the Strong One.

Ham cried out, "Look! Look over there! The earth—it's breaking up!"

Noah whirled in the direction to which Ham gestured. He saw the startled and frightened expression on his middle son's face. This man, who all his life had been afraid of nothing, was now filled with terror.

Noah rushed to that side of the deck, seeing what his terrified son was witnessing. The earth was indeed splitting open, and as it did, a stream of water burst forth from the ground. Propelled by a mighty force, the water spewed out, spreading in all directions.

"Look over there!" Shem cried. "There's another one! The fountains of the deep are being broken up!"

The earth was shaking mightily now, and they saw their town in the distance shifting on the quaking surface, buildings and houses splitting apart and toppling into the river, which, once so peaceful, had become a raging torrent. They all stared wildly as the darkening clouds covered the sky, blotting out the daylight. In every direction, the subterranean fountains gushed forth water, which spread over the land in mighty streams.

Then Japheth cried out when a drop of rain struck him. He grasped his face as if it had been burned by a red-hot coal. The single drops were joined by myriad others, pouring down from the heavens like a mighty waterfall as the waters from beneath rose up and buffeted the ark on its moorings.

"Quickly, get inside!" Noah shouted to his family, clutching Adah as she clung to him. Their sons and their wives ran from the corners of the top deck to squeeze through the door together, all soaked to their skin. Japheth grabbed the boards they had reserved to close up the window and began to hammer them into place.

Noah reached for the handle of the large door to close it, but before he even touched it, the massive door swung shut of its own accord and latched. Noah stared at it, aware that the presence of the Strong One filled this place. Turning toward the frightened faces of his family, he felt all doubt leave his heart. He put his hands out as if to touch them, and his voice was clear and strong as he spoke.

"The Strong One is here!" He laughed and lifted his hands. "He has shut us in! We are safe from all harm!" And then tears came into his eyes and he dropped his hands. Falling to his knees, he wailed, both from fear and gratitude, "We are shut in—alone with the Strong One!"

The others knelt and all of them too cried aloud, weeping for the lost world but thankful that their God had delivered them. Adah clung to Noah, tears streaming down her face, and his arms tightened around her. They didn't speak, for the power of God filled the ark. They heard the mighty pounding of the waters from above and below, the unearthly screeching of the wind, the smashing of objects being hurled against the ark. At times they thought they heard people beating on the sides of the ark and screaming for entrance, but the power of the storm around them was too great to know for certain whether the noises were the voices of the living or if all around them were by now dead, swept away to their doom in the surging waters.

Again Noah lifted his voice in praise and gratitude to their Savior. "The Strong One has delivered us!"

And the fierce buffeting of the winds and waters grew ever stronger. . . .

CHAPTER 34

For five days the torrents of rain fell and the fountains of the deep flowed unceasingly. The earth was saturated, and the flat areas were covered with the muddy, swirling water. The eight people on the ark had gone about the business of taking care of the animals, glad to have something to occupy their minds. The steady drumming of fat raindrops falling on the ark and striking the water that now surrounded them threw a cloud over those inside.

Japheth had discovered that the pitch would burn, so to conserve their lamp oil, he had substituted pitch in many of the lamps. They burned poorly, casting feeble, ghostly shadows over the interior. Japheth had made lanterns for each floor, but they used them sparingly, partly because of the danger of fire, for the pitch-soaked, dry timbers of the ark could ignite easily.

Kefira and Shem had taken on the care of the animals in the lowest part of the ark. Below the water level outside, they felt sheltered from the incessant sound of the drenching rainfall. Kefira was a sensitive young woman, and as she pulled out bits of hay to feed the small deerlike antelope, Shem saw the grief on her face. As the tiny lamp flame flickered and smoked, he moved over and stood beside her. He looked down at the small antelope that stretched his neck forward and nibbled the food from her hand. "Beautiful creature, isn't he?"

"Yes. Very beautiful. I can't help thinking about all of his kind who have perished in this water." Kefira lifted her face to him, and as the shadows from the lamp flickered across her features, Shem saw that she looked tired and wan. "I also can't stop thinking about my family. They didn't love me or God, but I didn't want something like this to happen to them."

"It's very hard," he agreed. "I think about my family too. Uncles and aunts and nephews and nieces—now they're all gone. But we must learn to sing songs in the night."

"That's a nice thought," she said, repeating his words. "Songs in the night."

"But of course. Any fool can sing when the sun is shining bright and everything is going well. It's easy enough to be happy and even joyful under those conditions. But when it's dark, and the storm is raging, and things are bad, to be able to sing *then*—that's the test of a true believer in the Strong One."

"Sing me a song, Shem," Kefira whispered.

She turned to him and laid her head against his chest, and he began to sing softly.

"The Holy One is our God!
He will lead us as a shepherd leads his flock;
Though the crops all fail,
And though the herds perish,
Still I will come with joy to the altar!
As a bride is loved by her husband,
So the righteous are loved by the Strong One!
I will trust in the Holy One
And He will deliver me from all harm;
Power and beauty are His,
And He holds me in His arms forever!"

"That's beautiful," Kefira breathed. "It's marvelous how the Strong One gives you songs, and then when you sing them, it so encourages me."

The two embraced, wondering what lay ahead. They had only each other, Noah and Adah, Ham and Mendora, and Japheth and Roma. The very smallness of their number was daunting, but Shem began to sing another song of praise to the Strong One.

While Shem and Kefira were talking on the lowest deck, Ham and Mendora were working on the deck above them. They had fed the animals, and now Ham stood before the male lion. The creature fascinated him, for he knew well its strength and ferocity. Ham carried a wide scar on his side where he had been raked by the claws of a lion just like this one, but now as he stared into the eyes of the regal beast, he reached out and laid his hand gently on the creature's head. "So strong," he whispered in awe, "but now so mild!"

Mendora had gotten over her fear of the wild beasts. She came forward and looked into the eyes of the lion, which were half hooded. "He's so quiet, so docile."

"Yes, he is now. But if he were to roar, he would fill the whole ark with his powerful voice." Ham ran his hand down across the back of the lion, feeling the powerful muscles that could so easily kill a man. The lion did not move. It appeared to be half asleep, and Ham shook his head. "I never thought I would be able to touch a living lion like this. I've only touched dead ones."

Mendora had never felt fully accepted by the family, and now shut in so close with them, she felt especially cut off. She moved closer to Ham and leaned against him, needing his touch and assurance. Their marriage had been stormy, but now in her fear and in the doubt that assailed her, she needed to cling to someone. Her head lifted at the soft cooing of the birds filtering down from the upper deck. It was like gentle music to her in the midst of the terror outside of their dimly lit sanctuary.

Other small animal noises from the squirrels and a pair of pigs made her smile slightly, yet she shook her head in dismay. "I'm afraid, Ham. I can't help it."

Roughly Ham pressed her shoulder. "It's all right. We're going to live."

Mendora shivered, and she moved yet closer, her voice pitiful. "But we'll be all alone. My friends and my family are all dead by now. What kind of a world will it be? Will we even be able to get off this boat, or are we stuck on this thing forever?"

Ham had no answer that would satisfy her. He had felt the same thing himself, but it would do no good to let her know that. "We'll be all right." Roughly he put his arm around her and held her close, keeping his other hand on the lion's head. He seemed to draw strength from the magnificent creature, but he knew this was an illusion. He finally murmured, "I'm not even sure this thing we're in will float. It hasn't yet."

"It'll have to," Mendora cried out, "or we'll die like everybody else!"

Ham was not the only one with doubts about the ark. Japheth, who knew the structure better than anyone else, had been pacing the top story nervously. Roma sat against a wall watching him, her eyes filled with concern. "What's wrong?" she asked. "You haven't slept—and you're so nervous."

Japheth turned and spread his arms out with a gesture of either fear or doubt. "I don't know for sure if this thing will float!" he cried out. "I tried to build it exactly as the Strong One said, but it's never been done before. It may break up—then we'll all drown!"

Roma rose and drew close to him, laying her hands on his chest. "It will float," she said warmly. "You have been obedient to the Strong One, and He never fails."

Her calm words and demeanor assured Japheth. He expelled a huge breath and said, "I know. I've just kept all my fears bottled up."

"The Strong One does not intend for us to die along with everyone else," Roma said softly. "You'll see! All will go well for us."

No more than an hour after Roma had spoken these words, Japheth leaped to his feet. He had been sitting on a sack of feed, but now he cried, "Father—did you feel that?"

"Feel what?"

"The ark. It moved!"

Noah reached out and touched the wall of the ark. "I didn't feel anything," he said uncertainly.

"I did—it *moved!*"

The two men stood still, trying to feel the ark as a man would feel a tremor in the earth. From the sounds outside, they could tell that the water was over halfway up the ark and soon the buoyancy would be sufficient to raise the huge boat from its moorings so it would float free. But at first Noah felt nothing and thought that Japheth was mistaken.

"There!" Noah cried. "I did feel it that time!"

"It's moving! It's moving!" Japheth cried. He did a wild dance around and grabbed his father, and Adah, who was standing over to one side, came to join them.

Soon everyone on the ark felt the movement and heard the shouting and came running up to the top story. Before this, they had felt the ark shudder and shake in the wind and pounding waves, but it had still remained anchored to the earth. Now suddenly the floor lurched to one side. Noah staggered and grabbed the wall to gain his balance; then the ark shifted and rolled in the other direction as it was lifted clear of the land.

Everyone shouted and cried and hugged one another.

"It floats! It floats!" Japheth cried and grabbed Roma and swung her around.

Mendora felt a gush of relief. "We're not going to die!" she exclaimed.

"Of course not. When my brother builds something, he builds it right." Ham glanced with pride at Japheth and clapped him on the shoulder. "You did well, brother."

"We all did well," Japheth said, and at that moment he felt closer to his brother Ham than he'd ever felt in his life.

The ark floated, but it had nothing to give it direction. There was no motive power, no sails, no oars—nothing whatsoever to move it from one place to another. Noah, however, was content. He had said nothing to anyone about his doubts concerning the ark, and now a feeling of confidence filled him.

Days had passed, and the rains still poured down, the waters continuing to rise inexorably. The ark ponderously rose with the rising water, floating like a reed boat on the surface of a monstrous pond. Despite their earlier excitement and triumph over the ark floating, as the days wore on, the eight people in the ark felt, at times, like prisoners, shut into the dark, dank surroundings, unable to look out and occupied with holding desperately to their sanity.

Mendora, indeed, almost lost her mind. The movement of the ark now floating on the billowing waves outside had made them all sick to their stomachs, and she suffered worse than any of them. After several days of not being able to keep anything down, she collapsed in a fit of screaming, shouting that they were all going to die after all! She wailed that the Strong One had brought them through the flood alive only to kill them with sickness! Ham tried to calm her, but he himself was living on the edge of despair. As he held Mendora, who fought against him and screamed violently, Ham turned to Noah and said, "Who wants to live in a world like this? We have nothing now! No homes, no friends. And our wives are barren, so we're all going to die anyway."

Adah went to Ham and held her hand up. "Don't say that, son," she pleaded. "We're in the hands of the Strong One."

But Ham was almost as desperate as Mendora, and he shook his head sullenly and pulled away from his wife. She collapsed on the floor, beating it with her fists, then lying still. Ham stared at her helplessly, and when he left, Roma and Kefira went to their sister-in-law. Even though they were also still struggling with the debilitating motion sickness, they stayed with her for hours, bathing her face with a cloth and trying to soothe her. Adah also did what she could to help her distressed daughter-in-law.

Day followed day, and all of the ark's inhabitants were afflicted with their own form of suffering. The ark was silent except for the cries and sounds of the animals and a few curt words spoken by the survivors.

Adah felt the pressure as much as any, but what discouraged her most was Noah. He had been the strong one for her, and now he was so deeply grieved that he was a changed man. The burden of being one of only eight people alive in the world was more than he could bear. It tore at her heart to hear him weeping, mourning for the lost. She had heard him crying out names in his moments of fitful sleep—names of people he had cared about deeply who were now gone. In one mournful sob, he uttered the name of Meira. This especially brought tears to Adah's eyes, but she knew her husband was grieving not so much for what *he* had lost in not having her, but in the knowledge that Meira's soul was now lost forever and utterly beyond saving.

Knowing that his faith was at a low ebb, she tried to get him to talk, but he turned to her and said in a tortured voice, "I don't understand it, Adah."

"Understand what, Noah?"

"Why the Strong One saved *any* of us. I'm not a truly good man. I don't think there are any good men."

Adah's heart ached over the pain in Noah's voice and in the agonized expression that twisted his face. She knew that he wept much when he thought no one was around, that his heart was breaking over what had happened to their world. Now she clutched his arm and whispered fiercely, "It will be all right. The Holy One will take care of us."

But Noah was inconsolable. He was trembling now, and he whispered so softly that Adah could barely catch the words. "Surely there must have been other good men and good women who loved the Strong One!"

Adah could not answer this. She leaned against him, put her arms around him, and the two clung to each other in the midst of darkness and death.

CHAPTER 35

The rocking motion of the ark beneath her feet did not disturb Kefira as much as it had at first. Moving from a world that was stable and immovable into one that tilted and shifted, moved by waves and wind, had been a hard adjustment for her to make. She and Mendora had become deathly ill almost as soon as the boat had lifted off its base and began rocking, often wildly, as the strong winds and currents pushed it along.

The rain had fallen for forty days and forty nights without pity. Now, mercifully, it had stopped, and the family had been extremely grateful to escape the confines of their nautical prison and step out onto the upper deck of the ark into the sunshine. Japheth had unboarded the window, allowing fresh air and sunshine to flood the family's living quarters on the upper level. While it was raining they had kept everything closed up to keep the water out. Their only source of fresh air for those forty days and nights had been the narrow vents near the ceiling, angled in such a way that water could not gain entrance into the ark.

As Kefira stood holding on to the lower casement of the window, staring out at the endless space where the sky and the waters met in a seamless boundary, she thought of all those days of being shut in and the terrible sickness that ensued, and she uttered a fervent prayer of thanksgiving that at least the worst of their suffering was over.

Her mind went back to that moment when the rain had stopped. She had been with Adah, and the drumming of the rain had ceased so abruptly that the silence startled both of them more than if it had been a loud noise. They had stared at each other, then had dashed to the top floor to join the others, who had been shocked by that same sudden stillness. As they opened the door and stepped out, they were all filled with a sense of relief and joy as they watched the sun breaking through and the dark clouds lifting higher into the air. She had watched with the others until the dark clouds had completely disappeared, and the brilliant blue sky had offered great promise for the future. Mercifully they had seen no floating bodies, and Kefira had tried to put her mind as far as possible away from such things.

Since that day the ark had drifted slowly, but there was nothing to mark its progress—not an island, not a tree, not the tip of a mountain. Nothing could be seen but endless water. They had fed the animals and cleaned up after them. They cooked their own food—more now than when they were all sick—in the small kitchen Japheth had made.

Still gazing out of the window, Kefira saw nothing but sea and sky. It all seemed so peaceful. But the knowledge of the death and destruction that lay beneath the surface weighed heavy on her heart. A slight breeze stirred a lock of her hair, and reaching up, she pushed it back.

She began to turn back inside when a splashing caught her attention. Quickly she stood on tiptoe and looked out to see a school of fish jumping out of the water. The sign of life breaking through the monotonous covering that hid all she had held dear was a joyous sight. She relaxed and watched as the fish broke the water again and again, making silver flashes against the blue-gray surface. The sky overhead was intensely blue, and the weather was perfect. As the sun shared its warmth, Kefira felt complete and fulfilled.

With the arrival of the sun everyone else was feeling better, but Kefira had continued to feel sick and did not regain her appetite. Adah had kept a close eye on her and would not let her do any heavy work—only whatever she felt she could manage. She, more than anyone, had eased Kefira's fears and helped her realize that everything was eventually going to be fine. At first there was so much she had not understood, but now it all made sense to her. A slight smile touched her lips, and a warm light illuminated her fine eyes.

A sound caught her ear, and she turned and smiled as Shem approached her. She laughed as he crept up to her guardedly, as one might a dangerous wild animal.

"Is it safe to come near?" he asked, teasing her.

She went to him and put her hands on his chest. Looking up at him, she smiled. "I've been horrible to you, haven't I, Shem?"

"Why, no, I wouldn't say that *exactly*. . . ."

Kefira shook her head, and her light brown hair caught the reflection of the sun as it laid its golden bars through the window. She caressed his cheek and shook her head. "Yes, I've been terrible. I don't know why you didn't throw me over to the fish."

Shem was surprised to hear Kefira admit to her moodiness. She had indeed been almost impossible to live with for several weeks now. He had done his best to make things easier, but she had been more affected by all the hardships and the traumatic change of their world than the other women. Even Mendora had adjusted somewhat better once she got over the worst of her seasickness. Now, putting his arms around Kefira, Shem smiled and said, "You have been a little difficult, I must say."

Kefira whispered, "I know. I'm so sorry, husband! I love you very much. You've been so kind and understanding."

Shem smiled and, leaning forward, kissed her thoroughly. When she responded he held her more tightly. Lifting his lips from hers, he said, "Well, a man never knows how to act around a woman. They're always so blasted touchy."

Kefira locked her hands behind Shem's neck. Mischief sparkled in her eyes, and she said saucily, "Can't you think of any reason why a woman would be touchy and hard to get along with and sick to her stomach?"

"Why . . . other than being on a tossing boat . . . not really."

Kefira laughed softly. "You know so much about how to create songs, but you know so little about women."

Shem's brow furrowed. "I suppose you're right about that. So what's been bothering you?"

"A very common problem."

"Are you sick again?" Shem demanded in alarm.

"No . . . as a matter of fact, I feel *wonderful!*" She looked up at him, and a small dimple appeared to the left of her mouth. A light danced in her eyes, which mirrored some ancient wisdom. She held her head still and looked straight at him with only a hint of a smile at the corners of her mouth. Finally she laughed.

"Well, you *are* happy!" Shem exclaimed. "I'm glad of it."

"Shem, I'm going to have a baby!"

At first Shem thought he had misunderstood her. They had waited so long that this possibility was the furthest thing from his mind. He had known there was something almost mysterious about the way that three strong men with three young, healthy wives could not bring forth a single child into the world. But he had come to accept this as another work of the Strong One and that somehow, someday, they would be able to conceive. He just wasn't expecting it now!

He released his hold on her waist and put his hands on her shoulders. He gasped and shook his head, then whispered, "Are you *sure*?"

"I wasn't until yesterday, but I felt the baby move."

"Have you told anybody else?"

"No. Your mother suspects . . . but I wanted—" Her eyes suddenly blinked with surprise. Quickly she captured his hand and put it over the lower part of her abdomen. She watched his face and then whispered, "Do you feel that?"

His face registered shock, and he whispered huskily, "Yes! It's the most wonderful thing in the world, Kefira! We're going to have a son!"

"Maybe a daughter."

"No," he insisted. "A son."

"We will see one day."

He gave a glad cry and put his arms around her and held her gently. "I don't care whether it's a boy or a girl really. I'm so happy for us."

He released her and said, "Come along. Let's go tell Father and Mother. They'll be as happy as I am."

Shem led her to the forward part of the top level, where the birds were kept. As they entered, Shem saw his mother with the parrot she had made a pet perched on her arm. The parrot was saying, "Noah! Noah!" and then whistling shrilly.

Adah turned and laughed. "Isn't that smart? He can say your father's name."

Shem stopped and his face was alight with joy. Noah had been sitting watching his wife and the bird, and now he got up and asked, "What is it, son?"

"Kefira is carrying a child."

"Are you sure?" Adah cried, putting the parrot back on its perch and coming toward Kefira.

"Yes, Mother . . . you were right. I felt the baby move today!"

At this news, Adah let out a joyful wail, threw her arms around her daughter-in-law, and let her tears freely flow. She could not speak, and Kefira held her tightly, her own eyes wet with tears.

Noah stared at the two women, then shook his head and laughed loudly, a great booming laugh. He slapped Shem on the back hard enough to make him stagger forward. "I knew it would happen!" he cried out. "I knew it would! He's going to be a great boy."

"Kefira says it might be a girl."

"Nonsense! It's going to be a boy. Isn't that right, Adah?"

"Much you know about it!" Adah did not release her hold on Kefira, and she smiled through her tears at Noah. "A precious lot you know about babies."

"Well, I know it's a sign from the Holy One that He hasn't forgotten us. Imagine, the first child born in the new world." He turned to Adah and said, "Wife, I've got an order for you."

"You're getting awfully bossy now that you're going to be a grandfather," Adah said, laughing.

"I suppose I am, but a man has to celebrate. You women go and cook a banquet fit for kings. We're going to celebrate the coming birth of my grandson."

"And of my *son!*" Shem smiled.

Noah then put his hand on Kefira's shoulder. "I'm proud of you, daughter. You're a good child, and may the Strong One give His blessing on this baby and make you fruitful to have many more."

"Thank you, Father," Kefira whispered. She touched his cheek, then turned and said to her mother-in-law, "I'll go find Mendora and Roma, and we'll get the meal started."

"You go ahead. I'll help you shortly," Adah said.

Kefira and Shem headed for the lower decks, and Noah and Adah listened to their joyful laughter as they disappeared.

"They're so happy," Adah whispered, "and I thank the Holy One for His blessing."

"The Strong One is indeed good. He is not only strong, but He's filled with grace." Noah put his arm around Adah, and the two of them looked fondly at each other. "Did you ever doubt?" he asked.

"Yes. What about you?"

"I must confess that I have had doubts, but no more. This child is yet another sign that we're in the will of the Strong One."

They stood quietly for a moment, then Adah asked, "What sort of a world will he know, this new child?"

"Why, it will be a good world," Noah replied. "It'll be fresh and new. The old world was rotten and corrupt, filled with violence and idolatry."

Adah thought carefully about this and then ventured a tentative question. "But will this new one be any different?"

"We're not like all those people who worshiped Ur-Baal."

Adah was troubled despite her happiness. "But our descendants will have children, and those children will have children. They will scatter throughout the world. Will they do better than our fathers and mothers?"

Noah dropped his head, for this thought had occurred to him as well, not just once but many times. Finally he looked up at her. "Remember what the Strong One told me? He said that someday a man would descend from our family, a man who would make all things right."

Adah considered that thought, turning it over in her mind, then smiled and said, "A man who will change the world—and he will be of our blood." She pondered this for some time, then reached up and gave a half laugh as she touched Noah's cheek. "Let me go now and help them cook the meal. We'll let Shem make the announcement to his brothers after the feast."

The meal was suitable for a grand celebration. The women had worked hard on it, and Noah had agreed to sacrifice two of the chickens that they had brought on board for food. Fresh bread and a big pot of beans bubbled merrily, sending delightful odors throughout the kitchen.

When they all sat down, Japheth asked, not for the first time, "Why are we celebrating, Father?"

"Why, it's good for people to celebrate. I'm happy to be here with my family. Isn't that enough?"

Ham looked up from under his deep brows and shook his head. "There's more to it than that, isn't there?"

"Eat your meal. We'll save the good news until last." Then Noah went on, "Let us give thanks to our gracious God who has saved us and showered His blessings upon us." He waited until they had bowed their heads, and then he spoke tenderly, as he was wont to do when he prayed. "O Gracious One, we thank you for your deliverance. If it were not for you, we would not be here. Thank you for all you have done for our family. We love you, and we vow again to serve you, for you are a good and gracious and holy God of all the earth."

As soon as the prayer was over, they began eating noisily. Ham, suspicious by nature, ate as heartily as the rest, but he also kept his eyes moving, studying the faces of those about him. When they had all finished eating, Noah said, "I think Shem has an announcement to make."

Shem laughed and put his hands on the table. "I do. This is a time I will ask you, my brothers, to rejoice with me."

"Rejoice about what?" Japheth demanded.

"Kefira is with child. I'm going to be a father!"

Instantly Japheth and Roma cried out and jumped up. They hugged the pair, their faces beaming.

Ham rose also, but he did not seem happy. Mendora moved threateningly toward Kefira, anger flashing from her dark eyes. Her dusky skin made a startling contrast to Kefira's fairness, and she cried out in a voice shrill with anger, "Why you and not me?" All the bottled-up fears and depression that had plagued her exploded, and she reached out to strike Kefira.

Shem grabbed her, but she was strong, and he had to exert considerable force to push her back. He begged her, "Now, Mendora, don't be—"

Ham had seen Mendora stagger backward, and the pressures that had been building up in him exploded too. For a big man he moved fast, and he stepped up and struck Shem, his massive fist catching Shem in the chest and knocking him sprawling, gasping for breath.

Ham started forward to hit him again, his face dark with fury, but he found his father blocking his way. Noah was no longer the strong man he once had been, and Ham had always been the strongest man in their family. Still, the force of Noah's will held Ham as surely as if copper bands had bound him.

"He's your brother, Ham. Don't be like this."

Ham stared at his father and said bitterly, "Why do the others always get more than Mendora and I? You've always favored them."

"That isn't true," Adah said quickly, grasping Ham by the arm. She looked up at him and pleaded, "We love you as we love the others."

But Ham was beyond hearing. His voice was bitter, and his eyes glittered as he spat out, "Even the Strong One favors Shem! He will have a child, and we will not!"

"Oh, but that's not true!" Kefira cried, rushing to Mendora's side. She put her arms around the woman, who was much larger than she. The others half expected Mendora to strike her again, but she did not. Kefira looked up at her and said, "You *will* have children, Mendora, and so will Roma. We all will have many children. Don't you see? God has chosen us to bear children so that the new world will have people. Don't be angry." She turned to Ham and said, "Please, Ham, there are so few of us. We mustn't fight. We must love one another."

Ham looked down at the small woman, and his anger fled. His throat grew thick, and he had trouble speaking. He said, "Well, I'm too hot-tempered." He pulled Shem to his feet. "Sorry, brother," he mumbled.

Shem had regained his breath and was able to rise. He put his arm around Ham's shoulder, having to reach up to do it. "Why, we all lose our temper at times. But Kefira's right. We must love one another, brother. That's why we're here, to bring love into the world."

Noah watched Ham with sadness as the big man turned and walked away. He said nothing as he put his arm around Adah. They both knew their son would grieve over his violent outburst and think about this long after it was over.

Although Shem said no more about Ham's attack, he could not forget about it. After he went to bed that night, Kefira could feel him lying stiffly beside her. Usually he drifted off to sleep as easily as a baby, but she knew he was troubled. Finally she felt exhaustion coming on, for the scene had drained her as well. She drifted off to sleep and did not know when Shem rose and left the small bed they shared.

Moving as quietly as he could, Shem went to the top of the ark. The birds greeted him with mutterings, and he spoke to them gently. For a long time he stood looking out the window, fascinated, as always, by the stars, but his mind was still on what had taken place earlier with his brother. He was worried about Ham and began to pray for him. He knew the big man was unhappy, as was Mendora, and he prayed for a long time that the Holy One would touch Ham and give him the peace in his heart that he had always lacked.

As Shem stood admiring the glittering stars overhead a song came to him—fitting lines together, changing words, he lost himself in the act of creation. He never knew how he made songs. It seemed almost to happen by itself, but he delighted in the production of something that had not existed before. Japheth took this same pleasure in making a machine, an invention, or any physical thing, but Shem loved more the things of the spirit.

He became aware of the presence of the Holy One, almost as if a warm blanket was being wrapped around him. This had happened more often of late, and he waited patiently, knowing that soon he would hear the voice too.

He saw the glow and bowed, whispering, "O Holy One, Strong One, Maker of all things, I am your servant."

I am pleased with you, my son. I will use you in a mighty way. This child I am forming in Kefira's womb will be the first of your line. Now I will show you many things that will come to pass.

What happened next remained indelibly etched on Shem's mind. He could not tell whether he traveled in the body or in some other form, but the scenes that began to unfold appeared as clear to him as reality itself. He could not feel his flesh, and yet he was as alive as he had ever been in his entire life—possibly more so.

These are the people who will come from your seed. . . .

Shem saw a long line of people, stretching out as far as the eye could see. When he came to the first man, somehow he knew it was the face of the son Kefira now carried. Joy swept through him as he observed the noble features, the fine eyes, the determination, and the honor that was plainly etched on his face. Great joy like a fountain bubbled up within him, and he cried out with a voice filled with happiness.

You will name this boy Arphaxad. He is the first of your line, but there will be many others.

As Shem saw face after face, some men, some women, he knew he was being given the greatest gift he had ever received—seeing those of his own blood who were yet to come. He studied each face, and from time to time the Holy One would speak clearly, telling him something about the individual.

Two people he saw very clearly indeed were an old man and an old woman. The man was tall and lean, and his face was like that of a hawk. He was far past middle age and was somewhat stooped with the burden of years; his wife, though she was fair, was no longer in her youth either. Somehow Shem knew there was something very special about these two. Then the voice of the Holy One said, *I will make a covenant with this man. He will be a father of kings, and his descendants will be as the stars in the sky, and they will be your descendants as well.*

Shem could not speak but gazed earnestly into the faces of the man and the woman, and once again his heart swelled to think that from his own blood would come such godliness!

Further down the line he saw a young man with a rosy countenance, beautiful beyond description, with glossy black hair and eyes deep and black. The strong young man might have stepped from the world of the Holy One down to earth, seemingly untouched by the failures of ordinary men.

"Who is this one, O Holy One?"

He is a man after my own heart who will rule his people in righteousness, and he will come from your line.

Shem had no sense of time passing. It was as if he were suspended in a river of time. He could have gone on watching forever, seeing the long line of godly men and women who would descend from his loins, but finally he saw one so good and pure he made the others pale by comparison.

The face was neither handsome nor plain but seemed to be beyond such considerations. It was a face of compassion and love such as Shem had never dreamed could exist in a human being. There was joy in the warm brown eyes but also sorrow, so deep and so profound that Shem began to weep. "Oh, who is this, Strong One?"

Then the voice of God spoke softly, yet with a tone of triumph that rang out like a trumpet. *You have seen the one who will come to bring peace and justice and righteousness to the entire earth!*

CHAPTER 36

The news that Kefira was bearing a child had brought great joy to Noah. For several weeks after this happy event, Noah went about his work with a quiet satisfaction. But as the days rolled on—turning into weeks and finally into over four months—for some reason he could not fathom, he began to fall into doubt again. At first he tried to ignore it, passing it off as a mood. But as the days passed, his heart grew heavier and heavier, and he grew more silent, almost morose. He knew his behavior troubled Adah and the rest of the family, but he could not seem to shake it off.

Many times in the night he would leave his bed and go down to the bottom of the ark, where the larger animals were kept. He cried out and wept for the Strong One to take away the burden that had settled on him like a dark cloud. This gave some temporary relief, and finally, exhausted, he would fall asleep—but then the next day the black doubts would return to torment him. It was a terrible force he could not understand, and it drove all of the joy and happiness out of his spirit. This struggle continued, and Noah's face became lined with fatigue as he missed sleep and struggled within himself in a titanic battle against the torment of his soul.

Adah kept close watch over her husband, but like the others, she could not understand what was happening. Noah had always been strong spiritually, but now at times he would become unapproachable. She determined to speak with him, and one night when he did not come to bed, she sought him out. He was on the lower deck, sitting with his back against one of the pens. The tiny lamp threw out a feeble light, driving the darkness back for only a few feet. When Noah looked up and saw Adah, she said quickly, "I was worried about you."

"I'm all right. Just couldn't sleep."

Adah sat down and took his hand. He tried to smile but failed, for his eyes were so uneasy she knew no joy was in him.

"What's wrong, Noah?" she asked softly. "Can't you tell me?"

Noah had wanted many times to go to Adah with his pain, but what could he say? He was afraid of his own doubts, and now he shook his head. "I don't know what's the matter with me."

"Are you ill?"

"Not in body, but I'm sick in my spirit. I . . . I've prayed," he said brokenly, "but the Strong One only gives me momentary peace. The next day it starts all over again. I feel like I'm in a never-ending circle."

"Are you worried about what we will do when we get out of the ark?"

"I've thought about that a lot," Noah said. "But it's more than that." His face twitched with the emotion that boiled within him, and he turned to her and whispered hoarsely, "I've had terrible doubts about the Strong One, Adah. I don't know how to say it, but the thought comes over me that He's not a loving God. I think about all those who died and wonder why He did it."

Adah was thankful that Noah had at last come out with it. She listened as he poured out his heart to her, and when he fell silent she squeezed his hand and bent closer to look into his face. "Noah, the Strong One is good. You've always said that."

"But how could He cause the deaths of so many people, some of them just babies?"

"I can't answer that, and no man or woman could. Do you think I haven't thought about this? All of us have, Noah, even before this flood destroyed so many. I would wonder about why He would permit an innocent child to be slain by a wild beast or stricken with sickness. It's a terrible world we live in, but you are closer to the Holy One than any human being alive. You've found grace in His sight, and He has chosen you to do this great work."

"But why do I feel this despair? Why do I doubt Him?" Noah cried out, and he gripped her hand unconsciously, causing her pain, although she did not flinch.

"I think the Strong One chose you because you believe in Him greatly. No other man would have gotten this far. All those years of preaching and no one believing! Any other man would have given up, but you've been faithful to Him all these years."

Noah listened as Adah spoke quietly for some time, then shook his head. "I know you're right, Adah. Half of me knows that the Strong One is kind and good. When I'm in His presence I can *feel* His goodness. But then I see the terrible things in the world, and the doubts come."

"There are dark forces in our world, husband."

"What kind of forces?"

"You've seen it in the worship of Ur-Baal. You've seen helpless babies thrown into the fire to die. You've seen men, and women too, slay without mercy and then laugh at the dying. Violence and cruelty were everywhere in the world—but they didn't come from the Strong One," she said stoutly. "That means they came from someplace else. All evil that's in the world is against the Holy One. There are unholy things in this world, and we're part of the Strong One's plan to make the world fresh and new."

Noah sat there, conscious of the slow, rhythmic movement of the ark. He could smell the strong odor of animals closely packed together, and by the dimness of the single lamp he saw the pleading in Adah's eyes. He put his arm around her, drawing her close. She put her head on his shoulder and squeezed his hand as tightly as she could. "You're a blessing to this old man, wife," he said gently. "What would I do without you?"

Adah felt she had been a help, and she rejoiced in it. She held on to Noah, leaning against him as he began to pray.

"I know that you are good, O Holy One," Noah prayed. "Forgive me for my doubts, and even when they come, may I learn how to look to you and not to the evils in the world!"

Roma stroked the shoulder of the fox and smiled when he stretched out and nipped her on the arm. She had been feeding him by hand, and now she laughed and said, "You're a greedy thing, but you've had enough." She slapped him on the neck and started toward the next pen. She halted, however, when she heard her name called, and she turned to see Mendora.

"Hello, Mendora." Roma started to say more, but something in the woman's face stopped her. She had tried her best to be a good friend to Mendora. It was not easy. Still, Roma felt she had made some progress, and now she asked casually, "How are you feeling today?"

Mendora nervously ran her hand over her jet black hair and started to speak. Then she shook her head and fell silent.

Startled by Mendora's behavior, Roma said quickly, "What is it? Don't you feel well?"

"It's not that," Mendora said, and her voice, usually strident, was subdued.

"Well, what is it, then?"

Without warning, Mendora began to weep, and Roma moved forward quickly and put her arm around her. She patted the woman's heaving shoulders until the crying lessened, and then she waited, knowing that Mendora would speak when she was ready.

"I . . . I'm with child, Roma."

Instantly Roma exclaimed, "How wonderful!" She hugged Mendora and said, "But why are you crying? This is happy news."

"But I've been so *terrible*! I've hated Kefira because she was going to have a baby and I couldn't have one. I thought I never would."

"Well, now you *are* going to have a baby—so you can be happy."

Mendora clung to Roma, and her face was tense. "I'm not good like the rest of you, Roma."

"Why, of course you are."

"No I'm not. The rest of you all have such good, easy natures, and I've got a temper I can't control. It's a wonder Ham hasn't killed me, I'm so awful to him."

"Have you told him about the baby?"

"No. I've been waiting until I was sure."

"Well, if you're sure now, he needs to know. Go tell him at once."

"All right, I will." To Roma's surprise, Mendora hugged her. As Mendora left, a smile touched Roma's face. She laughed aloud and went in search of Japheth.

Japheth was repairing one of the birdcages on the upper story. The sunlight streamed in, and he greeted her with a smile as she came in and said, "I have news, but you can't tell anybody."

"There aren't too many bodies to tell," Japheth said, smiling. "What is it?"

"Mendora is going to have a baby."

"Why, that's wonderful!"

"Do you think so?"

Japheth stared at Roma. "Well, why wouldn't I think so? Aren't you happy for her?"

"Yes, I am, but I'm happier for someone else."

"You mean for Ham?"

"No, although I think he'll be glad to have a son."

"Who, then? Father and Mother?"

"I wasn't going to tell you so soon, but I think you and I are going to have a baby too."

Startled, Japheth threw his arms around her and asked, "Are you sure?"

"Not quite. I hadn't said anything yet because I didn't want you to be disappointed if I am wrong. But I know it's going to happen. I think it's all part of the Strong One's plan. He didn't want us to have children on the ark, but now that our time here is almost finished, I think He's quickened our wombs."

Japheth kissed her, and his eyes flashed. "A son! We'll have a son!"

"Maybe it will be a girl. This new world will need many mothers too. Would you be unhappy if it were a girl?"

"No. I hope we have a hundred of each, a hundred boys and a hundred girls!"

Roma laughed, and her eyes sparkled. "That will take some doing."

"I don't mind doing my part." He pulled her close and kissed her until she drew back, protesting.

"You're too rough, Japheth."

"Wait until later. I'll show you how gentle I can be. . . ."

After his talk with Adah, Noah was resting better, and he was grateful that the dark depression troubling him lately had lifted. He was encouraged by the news that both Mendora and Roma were expecting babies and insisted on another feast to celebrate. This time all went well, with no fights breaking out among the brothers.

One afternoon a sudden shudder ran through the ark. "What was that?" Noah cried out to Japheth. The two of them had been working together, and Japheth leaped to his feet. They both listened and looked around wildly as the grinding noise echoed throughout the ark.

"The water's gone down. We're touching solid ground!" Japheth shouted.

The two of them ran up to the window, and the ark suddenly tilted, but they saw nothing for a moment.

"Look over there!" Japheth shouted. "There's the top of a mountain. The water's going down."

Noah's heart leaped, and he gripped the sides of the window. The ark careened to one side, and he exclaimed, "We're not afloat anymore! The ark is at rest!"

"Where do you think we are?"

"I don't know, son, but the waters are going down rapidly now. It won't be long before we'll be able to leave."

The waters decreased day after day, and the tops of mountains began to break free all around them, especially over to the east. None of them had the slightest idea where their old home was, but they were all encouraged by the knowledge that soon they would be free to step on the earth again and spent hours looking at the dry land emerging all around them.

"We're on the top of some mountain," Shem observed as he and his two brothers were looking out.

Just then their father appeared with a black bird in his hand, and Ham blinked with surprise. "What are you going to do with that bird, Father?"

"I'm going to turn him loose and see what he does."

"That's a good idea," Japheth said as Noah put the bird out the window and cast him off. They watched as the glistening ebony bird rose higher and higher and finally disappeared.

"I think I'll send a dove too," Noah said. "They're gentler creatures than ravens."

Now everyone came eagerly to watch as Noah left and then returned with a snow-white dove. He held it in his big hands and then kissed it on the head. "Go and find your way," he whispered as he cast the dove into the air. He watched the white dove circle twice and then disappear.

It was later that afternoon when Roma called out, "Look, it's the dove! It's come back!"

Noah came at once, and when the dove descended, he put out his hand, and the snowy white bird descended and clasped his finger. He pulled it back in, stroking the soft feathers. "It's not time yet. I'll wait seven days, and then I'll send it out again."

The seven days passed, and all the inhabitants of the ark were impatient. This time they hoped fervently that the dove would not return, but return it did, this time with an olive branch in its mouth.

"Olive trees don't grow in the mountains!" Shem exclaimed.

"No they don't," Noah agreed. "That means the bird must have found the lowlands, and the olive trees are bearing there." His eyes glowed, and he said, "We will wait seven more days and try again."

The bow of the ark was tilted at such an angle that Noah had to walk uphill to get to the window. All around them now the land was dry, and it was indeed mountainous country. He scanned the horizon for any sign of the return of the dove, which he had put out for the third time, but he saw nothing. Noah felt a stirring deep within. He stood at the window and prayed, "O Holy One, what must we do?"

And then the voice of the Strong One whispered, *Go from the ark, you and your wife, and your sons and your sons' wives with you. Bring out with you every living thing that is on the ark, the birds, beasts, and every creeping thing, so that they may breed abundantly and be fruitful and multiply throughout the earth.*

Noah lifted his hands, tears streaming down his face. "I thank you, O Holy One. Forgive me for my doubts."

After this brief thanksgiving, Noah began to shout. Shem came running, followed by Ham and Japheth, and the women soon were there too.

"What is it, Father?" Shem asked, but he already sensed the answer.

"The Strong One has commanded us to leave the ark."

"And what about the animals?" Ham asked quickly.

"They are to be set free. We will have to build another ramp. Japheth, we will all help if you will tell us what to do." He looked up and expanded his chest. "I doubted the goodness of the Strong One, but I doubt no longer. He has brought us through the destruction of all things safely, and now we must serve Him with all of our being!"

The ramp took several days to complete. They tore timbers from the raised bow in order to build it. Finally Japheth sighed with satisfaction and wiped the sweat from his brow. "There, it's finished."

Noah nodded and smiled. "The animals will be glad to be free. It's been hard on them to be cooped up so long."

"They won't be any more glad than I am," Ham said, laughing. He had worked hard on the ramp, and there was a glow about him that the others had never seen before. The news that he was to have a son or a daughter had cheered him, and he went about his work whistling with his newfound joy.

"Can we release the animals now, Father?" Ham asked.

"Yes. All of them. It is time for them to multiply and fill the earth again."

None of them ever forgot the scene that followed. The birds went first, and the air was soon filled with fowl of every kind. Some of them sang, happy to be free of their cages, and as Noah and Adah released the pair of birds with brilliant blue feathers that had been among their special pets, she called out, "Have many young so that the earth will be filled with blue birds!"

The other animals were released quickly, and as soon as they touched dry ground, they shook off the somnambulism that had been their state during their captivity, particularly the lions. When the male lion reached the base of the ramp, he bounded across the rocky ground and jumped up to a small promontory, where he summoned his mate with a roar that shattered the air.

"I wouldn't want to put my hand on him now," Japheth uttered in awe.

Noah had been dreaming of lions lately, as he had when he was younger. Now as he watched the mighty beast bound away with his mate, he touched the circular medallion that hung on his breast. Almost every day he took it out and examined it, but he still did not know what it meant.

As the ark was emptied of its live cargo, a strange silence filled it. Noah stood beside Adah, looking down into the depths of the mighty craft that had saved them all.

"The only animals that are left," Adah said, "are those that came on by sevens, the clean beasts."

This had been one of the commandments—that seven each of the clean beasts, identified by the Strong One, still remain. Noah straightened up and said, "There is something I must do."

"What is that?" Adah asked.

"We must build an altar. We will not do anything on this dry earth until we acknowledge the Holy One."

The men gathered large stones together for an altar and built a fire; then, according to the Strong One's commands, Noah sacrificed the clean animals, shedding their blood as a covering for the sins of the eight who were now to populate the earth. It was a solemn moment, and even as they prayed, the voice of the Strong One spoke, and the burning light that Noah had seen before surrounded them. They all fell on their knees, and those who had never heard the voice of the Strong One were stricken with fear.

"Be fruitful and increase in number and fill the earth. The fear and dread of you will fall upon all the beasts of the earth and all the birds of the air, upon every creature that moves along the ground, and upon all the fish of the sea; they are given into your hands. Everything that lives and moves will be food for you. Just as I gave you the green plants, I now give you everything.

"But you must not eat meat that has its lifeblood still in it. And for your lifeblood I will surely demand an accounting. I will demand an accounting from every animal. And from each man too, I will demand an accounting for the life of his fellow man. Whoever sheds the blood of man, by man shall his blood be shed; for in the image of God has God made man.

"As for you, be fruitful and increase in number; multiply on the earth and increase upon it."

When the voice grew still, Noah could hear a man sobbing, but he knew they were tears of joy. He turned to see Ham staring in awe, and Noah understood. At last Ham too had heard the voice that the others had heard long before.

Then Noah asked God, "What will happen to men, O Holy One? Will you ever destroy the earth again?"

And then the Strong One spoke once more, and they all bowed to the ground.

"I now establish my covenant with you and with your descendants after you and with every living creature that was with you—the birds, the livestock, and all the wild animals, all those that came out of the ark with you—every living creature on earth. I establish my covenant with you: Never again will all life be cut off by the waters of a flood; never again will there be a flood to destroy the earth.

"This is the sign of the covenant I am making between me and you and every living creature with you, a covenant for all generations to come: I have set my rainbow in the clouds, and it will be the sign of the covenant between me and the earth. Whenever I bring clouds over the earth and the rainbow appears in the clouds, I will remember my covenant between me and you and all living creatures of every kind. Never again will the waters become a flood to destroy all life.

"This is the sign of the covenant I have established between me and all life on the earth."

Noah stood up, still bowing his head before the Strong One, tears streaming down his face. Even as the voice faded, Noah knew he had found his faith again in all of its fullness and even greater than it had ever been. Lifting his hands, he cried out, "Shout for the glory of the Holy One, for the Strong One, the Almighty, He is with us!"

And the sound of eight voices rose in the air, praising the God of all creation!

CHAPTER 37

A simple house sat in the middle of a clearing. Some of the reeds of which it was built were still green, although most had turned to a light brown, weathered by the sun and rain. The rough structure was pierced with windows on all four sides, and an animal skin covered the door. The two men who stood at some distance from the house were watching two others who were plowing. They were working in a distant field adjacent to a stream that caught the reflections of the sun above and glittered like a silver ribbon off in the distance. The land was flat and spread out in all directions until it reached a group of mountains over to the west, a day's journey away. On the other side of the plain, a bare, rocky ridge sheltered the area, and a new growth of emerald green grass covered the earth.

Shem was pacing nervously back and forth, and when one of the flock of bronze-colored chickens got in his way, he lifted it with the toe of his foot and sent it flying through the air squawking. It hit the ground, scrambled madly, and then rushed away, followed by the rest of the flock. The chickens stopped a short distance away and began pecking at the ground again.

Noah was sitting on a large rock and smiled briefly at his son. "The chicken didn't do anything, Shem."

Shem turned abruptly and started for the house. "I'm going to see what's taking so long."

"Don't bother the women," Noah commanded. "It takes time to bring a baby into the world."

"Why does it take so *long*?" Shem picked up a stick and snapped it in two. "How long will it take?"

"I don't know, but I know you're not going to do any good breaking sticks and kicking chickens around. Sit down and let's talk about something else other than babies being born."

Shem shook his head but moved grimly over near his father to sit down. Noah began speaking of a project he had in mind for building a common storage house, but Shem only half listened. The months that the family had spent working hard since leaving the ark had exhausted Shem as well as the others. At Noah's instructions they had built only one house for all of them to live in, for he had said, "We have to break the ground and plant the fields. We can build houses later."

The house they shared was little larger than one or two of the rooms in Noah's old house, but they had lived out of doors most of the time since leaving the ark.

Noah continued talking to take Shem's mind off of the cries of pain that were coming from the house. As he spoke his eyes lifted to the distant mountains where the ark had landed. There had been no question at all that they needed to leave that place. It was mountainous, rocky soil, impossible for growing crops, and besides, they were all used to flat country. Japheth had constructed a cart, and they had loaded it full, and the men had yoked the pair of wild donkeys they had saved from the flood and journeyed out of the mountains to this plain.

A warm feeling came to Noah as he looked over the land, pleased with the setting. They had plenty of fresh water, and the fields were already open for planting. New trees, which would provide both building materials and fuel in the future, sprouted in abundance.

An agonized scream from the house broke through Noah's thoughts, and Shem jumped again, his face rigid. "Why does it have to hurt so much to bring a human being into the world?"

"My grandfather, Methuselah, said his father, Enoch, told him that was part of the curse that has been handed down since our first father and mother disobeyed the Holy One. The curse on men was that they would be forced to do what Japheth and Ham are doing over there." He motioned to where the two figures, diminished by distance, were struggling to follow the plow pulled by the team of donkeys. "Men have to work and struggle to live by the sweat of their brow, and women have to bring forth children in pain. That's part of the fallen world we live in, son."

Shem shuddered and said, "I don't see how a woman stands it, all that pain."

"Women bear much pain in life, and they must be very patient. That is why you must never be unkind to them."

Shem sat down again heavily, tension rippling across his neck and shoulders. He looked around, and the immensity of the world compared to the small number of his family depressed him. "Things will never be like they were before," he said glumly.

"I hope not," Noah replied, shrugging his shoulders. "The world was terrible, and that's why the Strong One destroyed it."

"But there are only eight of us. Only three women at the age of childbearing. I don't see how we'll ever replenish the world, although I know that's what the Strong One has commanded."

"I'm surprised at you, Shem. Haven't you noticed how quickly the animals are multiplying? I expect we will multiply in a similar fashion. It will be hard on the women, but the Strong One will protect them—He has given us His promise."

"It'll take forever!"

"Not as long as you think."

Shem suddenly forgot his problems enough to smile. "You're sly, Father. I didn't know you thought about things like this."

"Of course I do. I think we all wonder what is going to happen to the family."

"I know one thing that will happen," Shem said. "Sooner or later we'll spread out instead of staying together."

Noah did not answer, for suddenly a different cry came from the house, followed by the shouts and laughter of the women, and both men turned quickly.

"Shem, come at once!"

Shem sprinted toward the house, followed closely by Noah. His mother was standing outside, and she smiled as he approached. "You're a father! Come and see the child your wife has given you."

Shem ducked inside and hurried through the large room to the smaller one used by his parents for a sleeping room. There on the bed lay Kefira, the sunlight coming through the spaces between the reeds to illuminate her face. Her head was dripping wet, and lines of strain etched her face. But she smiled as she saw him and turned to look at the bundle she held cradled in her left arm. "Come and see your son. A fine boy."

Shem moved slowly until he reached the low bed. He bent down on one knee and put his hand on Kefira's head, stroking her hair. "Are you all right?" he whispered.

"Of course! Look at the son the Strong One has given us."

Shem had handled babies before, since he came from a large family, but this was different. He took the bundle, cradling it in his arms and pulling back the coverlet. He studied the tiny face of his son, whose minute features were scrunched from the travails of birth. Then Shem turned toward his wife and smiled brilliantly. "He's beautiful, Kefira!"

"He looks like you."

"Do you really think so?"

Noah watched all this with a smile. Now he came over and said, "Here. Let me hold my grandson. I can see you're making a sorry business of it." He took the infant, and the two men stood looking down into the red, wrinkled face. Suddenly the infant opened his mouth and emitted a powerful cry.

"He has good lungs," Noah said. He held one of the tiny, perfectly shaped hands and stared at it. "It's always a miracle when a human being comes into the world."

Shem was entranced by the sight of the baby. He put his forefinger on the damp, light brown hair and said, "His hair is the same color as yours, Kefira. I'd hoped it would be."

Adah came and stood beside the two men. Her eyes took in the infant, and she had to speak loudly to make herself heard. "If he's as healthy as his crying, he'll be a fine one."

"What will you call him, Shem?"

Shem looked at Kefira and saw that she was waiting. "His name is Arphaxad."

"Arphaxad! Why would you call him that?" Kefira said. "I've never heard of that name!"

"I don't know what it means, but the Strong One gave me the name in a vision. Arphaxad is his name, and he will be in the line that will bring forth the one who will redeem the earth."

Noah held the fragment of humanity in his hands, tears coursing down his cheeks. He found himself moved to tears often these days, sometimes simply out of love for God, as was the case now. He stared into the face of the wailing baby and shook his head. "When we hold a child like this in our arms, he has his whole life before him. We never know what a baby will become."

"*This* baby will become a strong man," Shem asserted. He took the child from Noah and, moving back to the bed, deposited the screaming infant into Kefira's arms. He remained by her side and put his arm around her, whispering, "God is beginning all over, and this one will carry our blood down to times we cannot know."

Arphaxad proved to be a happy baby, feeding and demanding attention like any healthy newborn. It had become Noah's delight to sit beside Kefira as she nursed the boy and speculate on what kind of a world lay ahead of him. Noah prayed much now, both while he worked and while he lay in his bed. On cool mornings he walked outside, pleased with the increase that he saw. Every female animal was bearing as rapidly as could be expected, and he knew that soon the world would be filled again with birds and mammals and creeping things. Each day was a miracle to him now, and he loved to come out early in the morning before the hard work of the day started and spend his time meditating on the beauty of the Holy One.

He paused beside the stream that wound around the small settlement, and his quick eye caught the flash of a fish that darted away. He had always loved to fish, but now he had no wish to do anything but stand and soak in the cool breezes of the morning.

The brook made a pleasant sound, and the blue sky was scrolled out overhead, broken only by fluffy white clouds that moved along slowly. He heard the distant howling of a dog, but for the most part a profound silence rested over the scene.

He prayed for a long time, not kneeling, just standing, in his heart thanking the Holy One. As always, he felt a slight tinge of fear as the presence of the Holy One suddenly surrounded him. This time he saw no light, but he knew by the warmth in his heart that the Holy One was with him. He closed his eyes and sank down to his knees and bowed until his head touched the ground. His lips moved as he sang a hymn of praise he had learned from Shem.

When the song ceased, he simply rested in the presence of the Strong One. These were the best times of his life now, and as he grew older and more filled with faith, he noticed that it was becoming easier and easier to enter into the presence of God. It had occurred to him many times that his ancestor Enoch must have done this same thing in even a greater fashion.

Finally the Holy One spoke. *You have done well, my son. You have found grace in my sight, and you have not fainted.*

"But I have doubted at times, O Holy One."

Men and women will doubt. It is not the absence of doubt that marks a person as my joy but the overcoming of doubt.

"I always want to be obedient to you, O Strong One, but I cannot understand all that has happened. Nor do I know what will happen."

Ask of me, and I will show you what it is you wish to see.

"Will men go back to their old ways, to violence and sin?"

Some will love me and some will not. The voice seemed sad to Noah, and he could not keep the tears from his eyes.

I am glad, Noah, that you can weep for the pain of your God. But know that I will send one that will cleanse the earth. He will do my will, and he will save those who love me.

The words cheered Noah, but he hesitated before saying, "O Holy One, you have shown my son Shem a vision of the future of our family. I would love to see what he saw."

And so you shall. Behold your seed, Noah, man of grace.

Noah had listened carefully as Shem had attempted to describe the vision he had seen, but he had never been able to grasp it. Now Noah cried aloud as he saw his descendants stretching out in a long line. As Shem had seen, he saw individuals, men and women, those who loved God greatly and some, he suspected, who did not have such great love. He was thrilled when he saw godliness and honor etched on the faces of so many of them. Some grieved him because they were weak. There were kings and shepherds among them, some beautiful to look on and some not at all attractive, but he was waiting for the one that Shem could never describe.

Then finally he saw him! The earth seemed to move beneath him as he saw not one man but two. Shem had tried to tell him this, but Noah had failed to comprehend. Now he saw a man suffering, dying in terrible agony. Noah could hardly bear the vision and almost cried out for it to end, but then he saw another face, and he knew that it was the same as the one who was dying in such agony. This man, however, was so glorious that Noah could barely look at him. He was clothed in white robes that shone like the sun, and his face was different from any Noah had ever seen or even dreamed of. Noah cried out with rapture, "Which of these is your servant, O Strong One? The dying man or the glorious king?"

Noah waited and then the answer came very gently into his spirit. *They are the same, Noah. The suffering servant and the glorious king.*

"But . . . how can that be?"

The sins of all people must be paid for, and they can only be paid for by his suffering.

The one who comes will suffer for the sins of humankind, but he will also, after his suffering, be the mighty king who will rule with justice and righteousness, and to whom all will bow, great and small alike.

"When will he come, O Holy One?"

Then Noah heard the voice of the Holy One say, *You may not know when. I will only tell you that he will come from your line, my son.*

Noah could not take it all in. He felt weak, and he slumped to one side, weeping and calling out, "Oh, help me to love you, Strong One! O mighty, everlasting Holy One! Help me always to be obedient to you."

You will fail me, Noah, but I will keep you in the palm of my hand. For now, know that you are a new beginning of what I will do. Never forget that your seed has been chosen to bring peace to all people, to bring into the world the one who will bring peace and righteousness to the earth.

Noah wept, but there was joy in his heart, and he whispered, "At last I know that I love you, O Strong One, with all of my heart."

The family was gathered in the large room when Noah returned. He had been gone all day, but no one had gone to seek him. Now as he went over to Kefira and reached out his arms to receive the child, they all knew that he had been with the Strong One. His face was glowing, and his eyes were happy and joyous, so much so that everyone was afraid to speak.

"I must tell you what our gracious Holy One has said." He began to speak, telling them of his vision, but he had to pause more than once as tears overcame him. He told them the entire vision as best he could. He saw that Shem was staring at him with a knowing smile. He understood better than any of the others, for he had seen the same vision.

Noah looked at the child, stroked the silky hair, then returned him to his mother. "Come, wife, I will show you the spot where the Strong One spoke to me. Perhaps He will come again."

When the two left the room, the others were silent, but Shem said, "He has been in the presence of the Holy One."

Noah led Adah to the spot by the river where he saw the vision. "It was right here," he said.

"I knew something had happened the minute you came in," Adah said. "Your face was glowing."

"I've been thinking a lot about my ancestor Enoch. You remember

Grandfather said that God simply took him away. He never died. What a wonderful thing that must have been!"

"Do you fear death, husband?"

"I suppose we fear anything unknown, and no one can know death until he goes through its doors. But think of how it must be to live always in the presence of the Holy One!" There was a gentle light in his eyes and an eager expression on his face. "That's what I long for."

"But we may live many more years before we die."

"Then, Adah, we will serve the Strong One as long as he gives us breath. We will help with the children."

"Tell me again about the one who will come," Adah pleaded.

She listened as he struggled to explain the vision of the two men who were one. Finally he said, "I cannot put it into words, but we will see him one day."

"Yes, and if he does not come before we die, we will love him all of the days of our lives in our hearts."

The two stood there quietly, and Noah put his arm around Adah and drew her close. Noah was still filled with the glory that had touched him, and he was also filled with a certainty that both the present and the future belonged to the Holy One. He thought again of the face of the king and the glorious form that he had seen, and he whispered, "I love you, O Redeemer of all the earth!"

Adah stood in his embrace and also spoke the words on her heart. "Although I have not seen you, my eyes will look upon you one day, O Mighty One who comes to save."

The two stood beneath a crescent moon. The river spoke softly at their feet, making a gentle murmuring, and a peace filled them. They both knew at that moment that they were loved by the great creator of all things. And they also knew that they loved Him with all their hearts.

EPILOGUE

The warm rain had laid a glassy sheen on the tender green grass, and the sun illuminated each emerald blade. Evening had come, and the distant lowing of the cattle being driven to their pen made soft music on the air. Overhead, puffy white clouds rose in high pillars until they flattened out on top.

As he sat in the cool shade on the roof of his home, Shem took a deep breath, enjoying the smell of freshly turned earth. He smiled at the sight of his great-grandson, aged five, industriously digging a hole in the soft ground. With so many generations having been born since the flood, Shem found it impossible to keep his family separated in his mind—but not this one! The boy's grandfather, Arphaxad, had named the lad Gurion, which meant "lion cub," and truly the boy had showed signs of a bold nature almost from birth.

Leaning over the edge of the roof, Shem called to the boy, "Gurion—what are you doing?"

"Digging a hole in the ground."

"Why are you doing that?"

The youngster gave the man a bright smile. "To see what's down there, Great-grandfather."

"It might be a bad snake. What will you do then?"

Gurion snatched a small knife from his belt and brandished it. "I'll kill him and eat him!"

Shem laughed and shook his head. Straightening up, he let his gaze run over the village, and suddenly old memories flooded his mind. He remembered clearly the first time he'd come to this spot, after leaving his father's house. Both he and Kefira had fallen in love with the view. Arphaxad had been ten years old, and there were nine others younger than he.

They had built a tiny house and had reigned over the valley alone, just one family, but the children had grown up, and now there were many families in the valley. That first house was now a small back room of the one that stood in the center of the village. Shem had built it well of stout timbers and clay bricks, and now he liked the feel of the cool brick floor beneath his feet.

That was a fine time—I'd like to go back and live it again. The thought nudged at him, but Shem shook his head, rejecting it. *A man must move on in time—I wouldn't really want to go back.*

He thought of their second child, a beautiful daughter whom Kefira had named Shinar, which meant "beautiful." Other children had followed, one after another, and the Holy One had protected them. None had died, nor had any of the numerous children of Ham or Japheth died. Noah never failed to point out that they were all living under the shelter of the Strong One, for in the old world, many children died at childbirth or were killed by wild beasts or accidents.

Shem heard laughter and watched with pleasure as men and women and many young people moved among the houses that had grown up around his home. They were scattered with no pattern, as if they had been thrown about at random. A few were built of reeds, but they had eventually begun to make their homes of sun-cured bricks, so that many rose to a second story. The hustle of the men and women and the shrill cries of the children at play in the village pleased Shem, and he let his glance go from face to face.

A movement caught his eye, and he turned to see Kefira emerging onto the roof. She came to sit on the bench beside him, saying, "Aren't you getting hungry?"

Shem turned to her, put his arm around her waist, and drew her closer. "Just hungry for a good woman." He kissed her cheek and pulled her closer. "You're as beautiful as the first day I saw you," he said simply.

Even after so many years of marriage and the births of so many children, Shem still had the power to please her. She pretended to be annoyed and tried to push him away, saying, "Don't be foolish! I'm an old woman."

"Not to me. I see the same young girl I fell in love with." He touched her hair, which was no longer black but a beautiful silver. "I thought you had the most beautiful hair I'd ever seen—but now it's even more beautiful."

Kefira caught his hand and held it between her own. "I've always had a romantic husband." Her face, once as smooth as a face could be, was now lined, but the bone structure was the same and she smiled at him, adding, "Not many men your age tell their aging wives that they are beautiful."

"None of them have you."

They were quiet, and then Shem remarked, "I was just thinking of the day we came off the ark. How things have changed! The years have gone by so quickly. Look at our clan—how many there are!"

"And Ham and Japheth—they've prospered too."

Shem's eyes grew thoughtful and he said quietly, "I remember the day Arphaxad was born. There were only eight of us then, and I had doubts."

"You never spoke of them."

"I didn't want to tell you—but I had them. But now, look at what the Strong One has done—how He has made out of only eight people so many thousands!"

Kefira glanced down, and the sight of her family, now grown large, stirred her. She thought of the struggles they'd known and put her head against Shem's shoulder. "The Strong One has blessed us, husband."

Shem said with hesitation, "I still worry about Ham, though."

"I know you do. So do I." A silence fell upon them as they thought of Ham's stormy history. The big, rough man had never been truly happy, and both of them were thinking of the terrible episode that had almost destroyed Noah a few months after leaving the ark. No one ever knew exactly why, but Noah had drunk too much wine that day long ago. Ham had discovered his father in a degraded state and had told his brothers. Shem and Japheth had taken care of Noah privately, protecting his dignity and not divulging his disgrace. Later Noah had spoken to Ham in anger, placing a curse on him for his disrespect: *"Cursed be Canaan, the son of Ham! The lowest of slaves will he be to his brothers."*

After the terrible scene, Ham had left at once and taken his family and moved away far to the south. The rupture had made a painful division in the family, which had never healed.

"Japheth has grown strong," Shem said quietly. "He has prospered."

"He has prospered, but his clan doesn't love the Strong One as we do. He's accomplished so much—but somehow his clan has drifted away from the Holy One."

They grew silent, thinking of how the three brothers had fulfilled the prophecy given by the Strong One. Then, as if disturbed, Shem said, "Father is sinking fast, isn't he?"

"Yes. He misses your mother. After she died, he grew so lonely. They loved each other so much! I wish—" She broke off when a young woman emerged from the stairway to the roof and called out urgently, "Please—you must come at once!"

"What is it, Beeri?" Shem asked, getting to his feet.

"It is your father—he calls for you!"

Shem exchanged glances with Kefira, and the two hurried to Noah's room. Shem went to his bed, saying, "What's wrong, Father?"

Noah in his later years had grown thin, but his eyes were clear. He took Shem's embrace and then said, "The time has come for me to die."

"No, don't say that, Father."

"I am happy, son," Noah said quietly. "I will be with Him who loves me and has kept me all these years. And He has told me that I will see my Adah and all those I have loved."

"I have wondered about what will come after we leave this place," Shem said. "But it comforts me to know that you have faith."

"He made us for eternity, my son. This earth is only the beginning. He never dies, nor shall any really die who love Him." Noah closed his eyes, and a raspy breath escaped his half-closed lips. He was so still that Shem grew fearful, but then the old man opened his eyes and smiled. "Nothing good is ever lost, my son. I didn't always know this, but our God has shown me this truth. I have grieved many hundreds of years for my brother Jodak and for Tirzah, whom I loved. I thought I'd lost them forever, but it is not so! I will see them again soon and will love them more than ever I did on this earth."

Shem and Kefira listened as Noah spoke. At times his voice grew so faint they had to lean forward to catch his words, but then he would grow stronger and talk with ease about what would be when he entered the presence of the Strong One for eternity. To Shem, his father was like a man contemplating going home to rest after a long, tiring journey.

Finally Noah fell silent, and Shem said, "We have not seen the glorious Servant of God, the one He showed you so long ago."

"We have not seen him, but he will come! You must believe that, son! You must make it the center of your life. Wait for him, and if he does not come in your lifetime, give the hope that is in you to your sons and daughters!"

Noah reached inside his robe and drew the medallion from his breast. He ran his thumb over the engraving and whispered, "I have told you about this, how it came to me from my grandfather, Methuselah. He received it from his own father, Enoch. He told me to give it to one of my sons, the one I felt loved God the most. And so I give it to you, my boy."

Shem took the medallion, stared at the image of the lion, then asked, "What can it mean, Father? A lion?" He turned the medallion over. "A lamb? I don't understand."

"Some things are mysteries, Shem. I don't know what the lion means, or the lamb. But one day all will be clear to one of our family. Wear it, but do not speak of it. You must pray much, and the Strong One will guide you. Before you die, you must pass this to the one of your blood who loves the Strong One the most."

Shem slowly put the leather thong over his head and slipped the medallion inside his garment. He took his father's thin hand, then leaned forward and embraced him. Noah held him, then fell back and whispered, "Our line carries the hope of the world, my son. The Strong One has chosen us to bring His Servant into the world. He will bring peace to all who call upon him. Be faithful—never forget that God has chosen you for a holy task." His eyes closed and the thin body relaxed.

Shem rose and nodded to Kefira. "He's asleep." He led her out of the room to the stairs, and the two ascended to the roof. The twilight was blotting out the sun, and they stood quietly thinking of what had happened.

Kefira said, "I am glad that your father is so happy."

"He has wanted this for a long time." Shem shook his head and spoke with great sadness. "I will miss him. He's the greatest man I've ever known." He pulled the medallion from underneath his robe and held it up. Both of them studied the lion, wondering what it might mean.

Kefira whispered, "To think that the Servant of the Holy One will come from our blood! Are you afraid, husband?"

Shem thought for a moment, then said, "I feel unworthy—but my heart sings when I think of it! What will he be like, this mighty one who will deliver the whole earth from wrong? And how can he be so great a sufferer—and at the same time such a glorious redeemer?"

The two stood there quietly as he stroked the sign of the lion. He put his arm around Kefira, and she smiled up at him. "We will see him one day."

Shem kissed her cheek and then nodded. "Yes, dear one, we will. If not in this world, in the one to come!"

They stood together as a half moon rose into the black canopy of space, bathing the earth with silver. The stars did not seem cold but glowed with hidden fire against the velvet darkness of the sky.

Kefira stirred, then said quietly, "Yes, we will wait for him, my singer of songs—but while we wait, we must live. Come—I will feed you a fine supper."

Shem laughed and pulled her into his embrace. "You are a gem among women!"

He kissed her and hugged her so hard that she protested. "Don't treat an old woman so roughly!"

Shem took her hand and pulled her along toward the steps. He took one last look at the stars, then said with joy, "Thank you, O Strong One, for giving me this woman."

As they descended, the sound of their laughter echoed softly on the night air, and then all was still. Overhead the stars glittered, and a great peace descended on the house of Noah, the man of grace.

Letter to Readers

Dear reader,

Many years ago, someone suggested: "Gil, why don't you write a series of biblically based novels tracing one family from the Flood to the birth of Jesus?" At the time I was too busy to consider such a thing, but the seed fell into some fertile ground! Six years later, the LIONS OF JUDAH came to me in a rush, each story idea falling into place with seemingly little effort on my part. Naturally, each novel has to be hammered out with all the skill I possess, but the first novel, *Heart of a Lion,* felt like it wrote itself.

One goal of every good novelist is to give pleasure, to entertain. The other is to instruct, to give the reader more than an enjoyable diversion. The Scripture says, "Everyone who prophesies speaks to men for their strengthening, encouragement and comfort" (I Corinthians 14:3 NIV). I am certainly no prophet, but I want every novel I write to provide some level of those three elements to the reader.

Every story in the LIONS OF JUDAH series is intended to give pleasure, but I want readers to *learn* something too, to discover some truth that will strengthen them in their daily walk with God. I stick as closely as I can to history and try to paint a reasonable picture of how ancient people lived from day to day. I hope to offer readers an overview of the Old Testament, fixing in their minds the general history of the times and putting the heroes of the faith in the spotlight. Not as a *substitute* for the Scripture. Far from it! Indeed, my hope is that readers will turn to the Bible as a result of reading these books.

I want these novels to encourage as well, to somehow give the reader a desire to become a more faithful servant of God. Most modern fiction does exactly the *opposite* of this—it urges the reader to indulge in the false values that have come to dominate society. I spent many years teaching the so-called great novels at a Christian university. Many of these stress the values of this world, not those of God. But I believe fine novels *can* dramatize godly values—without being "preachy."

Finally, I want these novels to comfort. I don't know how it works, but some books give me assurance and build my faith that dark times are not forever. God, of course, is the source of all comfort, but I know He uses many means to comfort us, including poetry and fiction.

I pray that the LIONS OF JUDAH will give pleasure, enlightenment, motivation, and comfort to faithful readers.

I hope these books will help introduce readers to the most important history of all—how God brought a Savior into the world to deliver us from our sins. I trust that the men and women of the Old Testament will come alive for you through these pages, so they are not dim figures in a dusty history but dynamic bearers of the seed that would redeem the human race.

Sincerely,

Gilbert Morris

Excerpt from *No Woman So Fair* by Gilbert Morris
LIONS OF JUDAH, Book 2

Eliezer stood beside Lot, watching the men who were digging shallow depressions in the earth. They had reached what appeared to be a swamp. At least there were reeds, which always bespoke water. They were tall and topped with seeds. The herds had scented water and could not be held back; they stampeded wildly, but the water itself was too salty to drink. It had been Eliezer who had instructed the men to dig shallow depressions where the water was sweet. The two men watched as the animals drank greedily, shouting instructions to the herdsmen to be sure that all got a chance at the water.

Abram came up to stand beside them and said, "They call this marsh the Sea of Reeds. We have to go around it."

"This is the boundary of Egypt, then?" Lot asked, staring into the distance.

"We probably have been in Egypt for several days, but we've got to go farther before we get to the good grass."

Eliezer was not happy. He cast a cautious glance toward the way they had to travel and shook his head. "I'm not sure what kind of welcome we'll get. There are so many people coming into Egypt, they might try to keep us out."

"You might be right," Abram admitted. "But we're so worn down we look just like small travelers—easy to rob."

"I thought there was peace in Egypt," Lot said.

"There is . . . of a kind," Abram said slowly. "But Pharaoh is absolute ruler. He takes what he wants—or I might say his servants take what they want. That's what I hear."

The next day they moved the herds farther south, and at midday they saw two men who took one look at them and then dashed away madly.

"What are they running from?" Lot wondered.

"I don't think they're frightened of us. They're just scouts. I expect soon we'll be getting a visit from some official who wants to find out who we are and why we've come."

Abram was correct, for by the time the sun was high in the sky a party of men appeared. They were mounted on camels, but their appearance did not disturb Abram. He narrowed his eyes and watched as they approached, then said to Eliezer beside him, "Well, this is good news."

"What is, master?"

"They sent only a small group, enough to show respect, but more of a political move than a military one. Be careful what you say to them, Eliezer. These are strange people. Sarai was right about their morals. They don't have any that I've ever heard of."

The camels pulled up a short distance away from Abram and Eliezer. The men dismounted, six in all, and one of their number came forward, obviously their leader. He was a man of less than medium height and seemed even shorter because of his rotund body. He was, Abram saw, one of those corpulent men whose fat was at least underlain by muscle. His head was bald, his eyelids were painted green, and his brown body had been rubbed with oil so that Abram smelled him as he came to stand before him. "Greetings from Pharaoh, the god king. My name is Noestru. We welcome you as visitors to Egypt."

Abram bowed low and noted that Eliezer did the same. "Thank you, sir, for your kind welcome. My name is Abram. This is my steward, Eliezer."

"You have come a long distance?" Noestru asked.

"Yes. Our home originally was in the Chaldees."

"Ah, Babylonians, you are."

"No, we are called Hebrews."

"Hebrews? I'm not acquainted with that name," Noestru said, his eyes narrowing.

"We are indeed only a small body of people. We have come to Egypt seeking graze for our animals. The drought has driven us here, and we would ask for your hospitality."

"Pharaoh Mentuhotep is renowned for his hospitality. Perhaps you would show us your people and let us get to know one another."

Instantly both Abram and Eliezer understood this ploy. Noestru was obviously one who weighed the strength of those who came into Pharaoh's domain. Abram knew there was no avoiding this, but he bowed, saying, "It will be our honor to have you, sir. Perhaps you would refresh yourself, you and your men."

"Thank you." Noestru inclined his head slightly and followed Abram, who walked back toward the camp.

Eliezer ran ahead, and by the time the party had reached the camp, he had already started the women preparing food and drink for the Egyptians. He whispered to Sarai, "Don't spare anything, mistress. We must give them the best we have."

Sarai nodded. She quickly organized the women, and as Abram took the leader of the Egyptians through the camp, she saw that the Egyptian was looking carefully at everything.

"He's an ugly man," she whispered to Beoni.

"Yes. And look at what he's wearing."

"Not enough!" Sarai snapped. She had noted at once that all the Egyptian men in the party were wearing very thin linen skirts, and their upper bodies were bare. The linen was thinner than any cloth she had ever seen, and the outlines of their bodies were clear under it. "Shameless!" Sarai muttered. "I wish we had never come to this place."

When the meal had been prepared, Abram invited Noestru to sit down and gave orders that his men be fed. They served roasted kid with fresh bread, plums and raisins in copper cups, and Syrian wine of the finest quality.

Noestru was an astute interrogator, and soon Abram found himself speaking of his religion. "Which gods do your people worship?"

Abram hesitated. "We serve only one God."

"Only one?" Noestru raised his eyebrows in surprise, or where his eyebrows should have been, for they had been shaved. "I've never heard of such a thing. What is his name?"

"I call Him the Strong One, or sometimes the Creator of All Things."

Noestru chewed thoughtfully on a date. He ate daintily, taking very small bites, and his flesh quivered as he turned to study Abram. "I would love to see your idol."

"The Strong One does not embody himself in stone or wood. He is the God above all gods."

Noestru grinned suddenly. "That will not sound too pleasant to our pharaoh. He is a god himself, you know, and at times he likes to think he is the most important god of all!" A worried frown swept across Noestru's face, and he whispered, "I'd just as soon you wouldn't repeat that to my pharaoh."

"Certainly not."

"This God, the Strong One—tell me more about Him. If you can't see Him, how do you know He's there?"

"Because He's spoken to me."

"Oh, so you are a prophet? And do you make sacrifices as well?"

"Yes, I build an altar of stone from time to time."

"So, you are a priest as well as a prophet. Our pharaoh is very interested in this sort of thing. No doubt he will want to speak with you."

"I would be most happy to meet with the king."

Noestru continued to eat slowly but steadily, wading through the food that was before him, chewing constantly. His talking seemed to have no effect on his consumption, for he had learned, apparently, to eat, swallow, talk, and watch at the same time. He was, indeed, a clever man, and Abram was somehow uneasy about him.

Finally Noestru said, "The pharaoh is always interested in new wives. Perhaps some of your women would be chosen."

Abram could not speak for a moment. He did not know how to answer the man. He knew that Pharaoh's word was law, and if his eyes lit upon one of the women in his group, there would be no opposing him.

"That one over there, for example. Who is she?"

Abram glanced toward the direction of Noestru's gesture, and his heart sank. "Her name is Sarai."

"Ah, she is a beautiful woman indeed. Is she the wife of one of your people?"

Abram never knew afterward what prompted him to answer the way he did. There were so many factors in balance here! *If I say she is my wife, he would think nothing of poisoning me to get her if Pharaoh commanded it.* He heard himself speak, and it was as if he were listening to someone else. The words did not come out of his mind but simply flowed off his tongue.

"That, sir, is my sister."

"Your sister! I have rarely seen a more beautiful complexion."

"I do not think the pharaoh would be interested. She is not a young woman."

"The pharaoh has many young women. If she is your sister, I assume she is also a worshiper of the God you call the Strong One."

To Abram's horror, Noestru got up and said, "I would meet her. She is different from our women."

Abram had no choice whatsoever, for Noestru was walking toward Sarai. He fervently wished that Sarai had worn a veil. Though she was not young, her complexion was as beautiful as a young girl's, and her eyes were as large and lustrous as ever. Abram saw that Noestru was waiting for an introduction, and he caught Sarai's glance and held it, then said, "Sir, this is my sister. Her name is Sarai." He saw Sarai's startled look but shook his head in warning and was happy that she was a sharp woman. He said quickly, "This is Noestru, the servant of Pharaoh. He would speak with you."

Sarai bowed gracefully. "What could a simple woman have to say to the servant of Pharaoh?"

"Many things. Come. Walk around the camp with me. We can talk."

Abram watched as the two moved away, and Eliezer came over to whisper, "What is he doing with my mistress? Why is he talking to her?"

"It's not good news. The pharaohs have many wives, and this one, apparently, is looking for more."

Eliezer's face revealed his shock. "But ... but she's your wife!"

"I ... I told him she was my sister."

"Master, why did you do that?"

"Because they would kill me in a minute if they decided to. These are cruel people, Eliezer. I hated to lie, but it seemed to jump to my lips."

The two men watched as Sarai walked through the camp with Noestru. They finally returned, and Noestru said, "I must take leave of you." He smiled with an oily expression, saying to Sarai, "You are as beautiful as the moon, O woman of the desert."

Sarai did not answer but bowed, and the three watched as Noestru went back and mounted his camel. His men followed him, and as they turned, raising a cloud of dust, Sarai demanded sharply, "Why did you tell him I was your sister?" She listened as Abram explained and then frowned. "I wish you hadn't said that."

"I don't think you recognize how cruel these people are."

Sarai looked at Abram with something like scorn. "Isn't the Strong One able to deal with these people? Are they stronger than He?"

Abram knew there was no answer for that. Heavily, he said, "I think we will have to leave Egypt as soon as the cattle are rested. This place is too dangerous for us." He saw that Sarai was disturbed and followed her as she walked away. She said nothing, and he put his arm around her. "I've always said that there was no woman so fair as you, Sarai. I've never regretted it, but now your beauty has put us at risk."

"Let's go. Let's leave this place at once."

"As soon as the cattle are rested and fattened, we will go back to Canaan."